AN UKNOWN PARADISE

...but they found it. They knew they would.

A. K. ADAMS

Pen Press

© A.K. Adams 2013

All rights reserved

No part of this publication may be reproduced, stored in a retrieval system, or transmitted in any form or by any means, without the prior permission in writing of the publisher, nor be otherwise circulated in any form of binding or cover other than that in which it is published and without a similar condition including this condition being imposed on the subsequent purchaser.

First published in Great Britain

All paper used in the printing of this book has been made from wood grown in managed, sustainable forests.

ISBN13: 978-1-78003-573-4

Printed and bound in the UK
Pen Press is an imprint of
Indepenpress Publishing Limited
25 Eastern Place
Brighton
BN2 1GJ

A catalogue record of this book is available from the British Library

Cover design by Jacqueline Abromeit

Dedicated to my daughter-in-law, Christine Wheeler.
May she rest in peace.

Thanks go to those who encouraged and supported me during the writing of this novel, especially my wife, Nora. Also Teresa Robinson, Christopher Wheeler and Alan Rustage.

An acknowledgement is made to the Scottish singer/songwriter, Roddy Hart, for his words used in this story.

Prologue

The fast flowing waters ran down from the mountains as the snow gradually melted. Snowfields became drips and trickles of clear, cold liquid that turned from rivulets into cascading channels of water flowing with great tumultuous strength over solid rocks. The water brought life to the desert. Life that began as a seed and became a plant. The plants bore fruit and the fruit was eaten by those living in this arid region.

Some of the fruits were of the vine. The juices that came from the vine were greatly valued.

Over the years many came to drink of the fruit of the vines, including ancient civilisations. As time passed, improvements were made to the viniculture methods brought by the Spanish so that much later the heavenly liquid became a treasure. A treasure to own and a treasure to drink.

In this vast area lived many people, and some were descended from royal blood. Although this was the case, some of those were cast aside – left unwanted. A burden, in fact. If they did not fit into a plan they were given away. Given away to someone who would care for them.

The roaring rivers from the high altitudes that scythed through the country and brought life and hope to millions have a story to tell. Theirs is a tale of love, despair, hope and faith. Especially *faith*.

Yes, they have a story to share, but it only has meaning for those who want to believe. To believe that sometimes one's future is written in the stars.

A seed was planted a long time ago… and that seed grew. It grew into something special – very special. And the waters flowed. Over rocks, across deserts, through villages, towns and cities and ran all the way to the sea. All the way into the mighty, vast blue Pacific ocean.

In those waters there is the spirit of something special. Something so special that a price could not be put on it. If you listen carefully to the rivers as they flow by, you may hear the sound of laughter. And of tears…

PART ONE

Chapter 1

"When we get some of these things sorted out we must think about that holiday", said David scratching his head. He was relaxing in his favourite chair in the lounge, and wearing comfortable jeans and a sweatshirt.

Hazel nodded in agreement, her spectacles perched on the end of her nose, although she was concentrating on the supper plans for Godalming church later that week. A choir was booked and many of the regulars were looking forward to it. She'd been asked to bake some scones for the evening event, whilst other members had volunteered to bring sandwiches, cakes and 'little bits' to pick at – cheese straws, for example.

"Well I think it's down to either Canada or South America. I fancy heading south myself", David said as he looked through several brochures from the travel agent in the town.

"Whatever", Hazel sighed, "but I must get myself organised for the supper, you know what some of those church members are like when it comes to scones – they all think they're experts as they usually have one with coffee in several of the best cafes around here". David frowned to himself. Hazel was a regular churchgoer and felt she needed to make sure she did her best when it came to helping out. David didn't go to church, but helped out with moving chairs or putting up the marquee for the summer fete in July. They lived in a large semi detached property in Chalk Road, Godalming, four miles from Guildford. Hazel worked part time at a Godalming primary school, a fairly large school with over 250 pupils and where her administrative skills and financial acumen came in handy.

David was 42 and a Marketing Manager for the cardiovascular division with a Guildford-based pharmaceutical company where he'd worked for several years. Hazel was 40, enjoyed her work mixing with lots of children, especially as they were a childless couple. They had been trying for a baby for some time, but after several tests and checks at the Royal Surrey County Hospital they had been told that Hazel was unable to conceive.

David was born in Worcester where his father was a science teacher. He went to a good school in the city and left with three excellent A level grades before going to Birmingham university to study Physical Sciences. He had done well at school, had attended the Outward Bound School on Lake Ullswater, and played rugby for the county at under-18 level. During his time at university he captained the first team at rugby, taking them to the University finals at Twickenham. They lost to a strong Oxford side that contained three future England players. On leaving university David worked for a small manufacturing firm in the West Midlands that made medical equipment before joining Smith & Johnson, a pharmaceutical company in Guildford.

Hazel came from Suffolk where her parents were in farming. Their large four bedroomed house stood on the edge of two thousand acres of arable farmland. She had a lovely, carefree childhood, the type that only farm life can bring. Cleaning out the cow byres, feeding the sheep and pigs, and generally getting involved with all matters agricultural. She thrived on this outdoor existence, even getting up early in winter to help her father before she went to school. Her exam results at her Ipswich school got her into Birmingham university to read Sociology and that's where she met the love of her life. Hazel moved in with David after they graduated, much to her mother's disappointment. 'People shouldn't live together until they are married' she would often say, avoiding looking into Hazel's eyes when she said it.

The inability to have children had remained a big disappointment in their lives as both had come from large families. David had three brothers but he wasn't very close to any of them. Two, Peter and Allan, had emigrated to Canada several years ago and a Christmas card with a note inside was the only contact he had with them. Both were married with a family. Geoff, the third brother lived in Ireland and kept himself to himself. David hadn't seen Geoff for over seven years.

Hazel was one of three children, although her brother, Martin, had been killed in a boating accident in Florida four years previously. Her sister Maureen lived in the north of England and she would visit her occasionally. Most of their friends and relatives were either married or engaged, and the patter of tiny feet was often heard when they came to visit. Both had lost their parents. David's father had died from prostate cancer when he was 50, and his mother was tragically killed in a car accident on a railway crossing a year later. She was late for a lunch appointment and tried to get through the barrier as it descended. Her car was unrecognisable. Hazel's parents died in a hot air balloon accident whilst on holiday in Australia. The balloon had descended too quickly and caught high voltage electricity cables. Eight people, including the pilot, had lost their lives.

They had often sat down and discussed the whole issue of being without children but both were now resolved to the fact that they were not destined to have offspring. So that was that. David often privately wondered if Hazel's primary school job somehow substituted for her not being able to have children – if it did, so be it. He was a marketeer, not a psychologist. He knew she had wanted a child, preferably a boy, and although IVF treatment had been suggested, Hazel did not want to take that any further.

"What about Chile?" shouted David as he scrutinised a page from the South America brochure, "it seems good value for money".

"Cheese or sultana?" Hazel looked through Mrs. Beeton's recipe book and kicked off her slippers as she took another sip of her wine.

"I don't know. You know your church friends better than I do – a scone's a scone isn't it?"

Hazel decided on sultana since that way she wouldn't be criticised for too much or too little cheese. David always thought privately that they were a strange group at the parish church. Some of them liked to gossip, too, as well as being a little snobbish. When Hazel had a few church members round for tea she'd always put out the best biscuits since as far as Moya and Rosemary were concerned they only bought the most expensive of virtually everything. "I could write a book about the parish church and the goings-on", he said, "perhaps make it a thriller with the vicar running off with the organist after they'd poisoned her husband!"

"Don't be silly, they're a decent bunch. It's just that you don't know them very well. If you started going to church on a Sunday you might understand them better. They've all got their little foibles, but they're all right!" Hazel looked straight at him and smiled.

As far as church was concerned, David had grown up not being certain whether a God existed or not. He knew of Buddha and Hindu gods, and he knew Buddhism and Hinduism came third after Christianity in terms of numbers of people on the planet that followed these religions, so who did create the earth? Why should 'our God' have all the credit? If Professor Brian Cox was right, the earth and the other eight planets in our solar system were formed over 13 billion years ago out of spinning gaseous matter, along with the Milky Way and countless other suns and stars. So did God have a hand in all that? And when it came to earthquakes and other disasters, was God accountable? Or was it Buddha or the Hindu gods? Maybe it was His way of keeping the human population in check?

And when you die, is there life after death, or was it all made up to keep mankind thinking that if you have a poor life on earth then there's always something else to look forward to after you've gone? Or did everything just go black, like having a hospital operation when the anaesthetic kicks in, but never coming out of it in the resuscitation room?

"I'll need to buy the ingredients tomorrow after school and get the scones baked. I'll be home by four o'clock and I can always freeze them before the church supper".

"Don't forget we're going out tomorrow evening to see '*42nd Street*' at the theatre", David firmly said. "It's one of our favourite musicals and I've been looking forward to it for ages". They both enjoyed the theatre and went regularly. Hazel was a vice patron of the Guildford theatre where she'd acted in several of the local drama group productions. They were going with Edward and Dianah Butterscotch who lived in Guildford. Edward, or Ed to his friends, used to work with David until he was made redundant. He now did consultancy work and had just returned from a spell in India where he was based in Trivandrum in Kerala, a beautiful part of India on the south west coast. His wife Dianah also went to the local parish church and was involved with the harvest festival supper.

"Yes, yes, I'll get the baking sorted out before then, don't worry. I'll be spruced up by six thirty and that will give us time to get to the theatre and have a quick drink before the show starts. We should also remember to order our drinks for the interval – we forgot last time and spent the entire twenty minutes in a queue".

"I did you mean!" chipped in David, "while you caught up on the gossip with the parish church bunch!"

"Well I did have to hear about the verger who'd been caught chatting to Mrs. Jones long after the tea and coffee cups had been sided away last Sunday. Apparently he's good at D.I.Y. and she's got a dripping tap in her utility room. With her husband working away so much she has to rely on friends to help out. Allegedly he got the job sorted out for her, but some folk say two hours is a long time to spend with an adjustable spanner". Hazel blushed as she suddenly realised what she'd said. It was getting late. They had watched the BBC News at Ten, so after David took his capsules of saw palmetto for his prostate, they decided it was time to turn in. A recent blood sample had indicated an above average PSA level so the herbal remedy was taken daily although he wasn't sure if it was really doing anything. They were each reading a paperback book so it was always an incentive to get under the duvet for a chapter or two before lights out. Hazel put her book down as her eyes were tired. Thoughts of flour and butter and sultanas were drifting around in her head.

"Hmmm, I think I fancy South America, too. I think Chile is the long narrow country down the left hand side, isn't it?" She closed her heavy eyelids.

"Yes", David replied, "2460 miles long and about 150 miles wide with Santiago as the capital. They're four hours behind us and in January the average temperatures are just over 20 degrees C. There are some wonderful buildings in the capital including the Pre-Columbian art museum. North of Santiago is Valparaiso, the main port…"

Hazel was snoring ever so gently. He wasn't offended as he realised she was tired after working at the school all day and getting herself worried about scones for Godalming church. He decided on one more chapter of his book before setting the alarm for seven a.m. Just before he started to read again he realised he hadn't finished the report for his manager that needed to be handed in by noon tomorrow.

They both slept well, although David kept dreaming about being thrashed with birch twigs in the office.

Chapter 2

The morning dawned bright and sunny. David was in the kitchen first and put the kettle on. Two bowls of cereal were soon dished up, with a carton of soya milk ready to pour onto them. David and Hazel tried to stay healthy, ate little red meat and preferred fish and chicken to steaks and chops. News and music came out of the Roberts radio speakers in the kitchen as the disc jockey tried to wake up the British population. The travel news indicated slow traffic on the A3100.

"I don't want to be late this morning, Nutty", said David starting to spoon his cornflakes into his mouth, taking a gulp of coffee in between. 'Nutty' was his pet name for Hazel that he'd used since they met at university fourteen years ago. With a name like Hazel it suited his dry sense of humour.

"I need to finish a report for Trevor before noon otherwise he may thrash me with twigs". Hazel looked at David enquiringly.

"Just ignore me. I dreamt that I was being punished with a flogging if I didn't get that report on his desk by a quarter to twelve".

"You'll be OK. From that last dinner party we gave I got the impression that your name is on the Marketing Director's door already". David and Hazel had invited a few friends to their home last month, and that included the Managing Director, John Stephenson, and his wife Carol. Over coffee John had made positive vibes to Hazel about David's progress in improving profits for the cardiovascular business and increasing brand awareness through solid marketing strategies. Some of this went over Hazel's head, but the message was clear. David was in line for promotion in due course – as long as he didn't 'blot his copybook'. In business nothing was ever guaranteed. He knew that after seeing the previous MD sacked by the chairman of the business in unusual circumstances.

After brushing his teeth and rinsing with anti-plaque mouthwash, David grabbed his briefcase and gave Hazel a kiss. "Bye, Nutty" he shouted as he shut the front door, the lock clicking firmly as it closed. He got into his company car, a silver BMW, turned the key and the two litre engine burst into life. He carefully reversed off the drive and dove-tailed into the slow traffic towards Guildford. He didn't need to set the satnav, the car virtually knew its way. Classic FM soothed him as he drove the familiar route to the office.

There was a noise from the boot of the car. The only slight problem was that he hadn't put the bowls bag back as he normally did and a couple of bowls rattled slightly as he drove on. It reminded him that he'd lost last Saturday at Milford Bowls Club to Ray Kingsbridge, one of their neighbours. Ray was a retired draughtsman, had worked in York for five years, and who had been a club member for over 25 years. He popped in to see David from time to time, particularly around teatime when he assumed the kettle was on. He was interested in gardening and horse racing and helped a few older folk with their gardens along Chalk Road, trimming lawns and tidying garden edges.

David made a mental note to try to remember to adjust the bowls bag when he got to work. Right now he was focused on getting to his desk to put the latest marketing statistics and cardiovascular share data in the report, double check any other numerical data, and get Denise his secretary to type it up for him. He knew he could email the document to Trevor, but this was an important piece of work and David wanted it to look right – good spacing, clear headings, pages numbered, and nicely bound. Denise would do a good job.

"Coffee?" asked Adam, one of David's colleagues. David glanced at his radio controlled desk clock, it was 0845. His brain told his body an intake of caffeine was just what was needed. "Yes, please, but then leave me alone for an hour. I must finish this document by ten so that Denise has time to get it pulled together. I don't want a repeat of last month when it was late and Trevor was unhappy". Annual appraisals were coming up in two months time and every little positive item of accuracy, promptness, performance, efficiency and behaviour were all taken into account. David sipped the coffee, feeling the caffeine and sugar spurring him on to get the report completed. The slightly rough rim of the brown plastic cup left a little to be desired, and the coffee machine was over two years old, but what the heck – it was hot and wet.

By twenty past ten Denise began work on the document and David knew she'd have it finished within thirty minutes. He could now spend some time with one of his Product Managers who had come back from a field visit with one of the company representatives and was clearly concerned.

"He ignored the questions of the Consultant and kept rabbiting on about the features and benefits of the product!", said Mark, clearly embarrassed that he'd used up a whole day with Clint Jones, the Bristol hospital rep.

"We were in Southmead Hospital for three hours during the morning, wandered the corridors until he eventually found the Cardiovascular Department, and saw three people – one Consultant who'd forgotten Clint had an appointment – and two nursing staff. The coffee in the hospital dining room was like dishwater, and Clint simply had to tell me about his new pet hamster! And if that wasn't enough, after we had a sandwich around one o'clock, he popped out to his car for more brochures and the new pens we're giving away, only to come back to the dining room to tell me he'd locked his car keys in the boot!" Mark's blood pressure was up and his face was beginning to resemble a beetroot.

"Calm down, Mark, you'll burst a blood vessel in a minute. Talk about working with cardiovascular products, you'll need some yourself very soon!" Mark crossed his legs and tried to relax, looking at the ceiling as they do in films. The double neon light strip glared back at him. He ran his fingers through his thick, black hair and let out a long sigh. David waited for a few more seconds.

"So what happened then?"

"We spent all afternoon waiting for a blinking car repair unit who had an emergency call out facility to get to the hospital car park, locate us, and find ways of getting into the car! What a bloody waste of a day!" Mark was obviously exasperated. David decided to leave it there. Mark wasn't in the right frame of mind for a discussion, and certainly not to begin to think about the forthcoming sales conference scheduled for six weeks time. Later in the afternoon Trevor asked David to pop into his office to discuss the report. Everything went well but Trevor wanted more detail on competitive activity in the market place. Mark needed to make a few phone calls and check out some details, but it wouldn't be a problem. He knew some other people in the industry from time spent at exhibitions and industry meetings so these would be helpful, he was sure. He needed to talk to Roy Whitehead, the Sales Director, about Clint Jones.

On the way home David was looking forward to the theatre – at least for respite from his daily grind. He and Hazel loved musicals, 'Les Miserables' being their favourite. They had the

CD and DVD at home. He drove away from his regular parking spot and got back on the A3100 to Godalming. The traffic wasn't too heavy but the skies were dark grey and the automatic car headlights came on. David reflected on his day and knew Trevor could wait until the morning for the updates, so he hadn't rushed back to his office with the additional information. There was something powerful about keeping the boss waiting – sometimes...

'Knowledge is power' he mused to himself as he drove away from a zebra crossing where an old lady with a labrador Guide Dog had just crossed. The Belisha beacons shone brightly against the grey, leaden sky, and the Guide Dog's yellow harness was easy to see.

On the way home David could hear a gentle clunk from the boot, and thought about playing bowls this coming Saturday.

Chapter 3

"Hi, Nutty, I'm home", said David as he entered the house after having adjusted the bowls bag in the boot and locking the car. The smell of fresh baking gently wafted past his nose as he entered the kitchen. They had ordered a taxi for seven o'clock so David had just over an hour to get himself ready. That was never an issue as he was quick in the shower, knew exactly what he wanted to wear, and would inevitably be waiting for Hazel to put finishing touches to her face when the taxi arrived. He would make time for a gin and tonic and pour Hazel a glass of her favourite red wine while she got ready. The taxi journey to the theatre would take about twenty minutes depending on road conditions and residual rush-hour traffic. David had phoned Ed during the day to say they'd meet them in the theatre bar just before half past seven.

"I've finished baking the scones, with lovely juicy sultanas, but not too many, just as they should be", replied Hazel giving her husband a gentle kiss on the lips and a cuddle. "Have you had a good day and were you thrashed with birch twigs?" she teased.

"It was fine, no thrashing, just a few PR matters to be sorted out, but Trevor got his report and I think he's happy with it. I rang Ed and we'll see them as usual before the show starts. Do you want a glass now, I'm having a gin and tonic?" David reached for the gin bottle in the lower kitchen cupboard and a small can of tonic water from the fridge. "Yes, might as well.

There's a new bottle of shiraz in the wine rack that I bought this afternoon when I did the shopping. It was on special offer so I got two". Hazel was often on the look out for special offers and usually had a few vouchers in her handbag to redeem against various products, sometimes those containing alcohol. David poured the drinks and asked Hazel how her day had been, and especially the baking. She'd got home at just after four pm, changed into her old, comfortable clothes, and got on with sifting and mixing the scone ingredients while the oven warmed up and got hot enough to put the twenty four neatly cut round pieces of pastry onto the metal tray.

While they were baking she had looked at the local newspaper and finished the sudoku, and the other foodstuffs were put away into cupboards or the fridge in no time. She'd forgotten to put the extractor fan on in the kitchen and soon the lovely smell of the scones began to meander through the house. After her shower she'd rushed downstairs to remedy that – she didn't want the smoke alarms going off!

"I wonder what Di will be wearing tonight?" Hazel pondered loudly so that David could hear.

"It's not a fashion show", he replied, "you'll be fine whatever you wear!" Hazel didn't think Di would be dressed to the nines and her 'little black number' stayed in the wardrobe. She reserved that for special occasions. Hazel decided on a blue silk blouse and black trousers with a leather belt, a light suede jacket and her most comfortable black shoes. The matching necklace and earrings she wore had been an anniversary present from David. He gave her an approving look. He was wearing a smart pair of light denim jeans, black leather belt and a grey long sleeved cotton shirt under a thin sweater. He wore his most comfortable casual shoes, but gave them a quick polish before shoehorning each foot into them. David's father had taught him that 'if a man's finger nails are clean and short, and his shoes were well polished, he'd always make his way through the world'. He'd loved his father. Job done.

"Taxi will be here in five minutes, Nutty!" David drank the last of his gin and tonic. Hazel put the finishing touches to her hair and applied her lipstick perfectly. She'd enjoyed her wine and thought to herself that she may just have another in the theatre bar? The theatre often had a decent Chilean merlot. How apt, she thought to herself. Let's get used to wine from Chile before we book our holiday!

The taxi was on time and they got into the back seat. The driver, Mike, had picked them up before and he knew the destination. After a few pleasantries with Mike on the journey they were pulling up near the theatre. David slipped Mike the fare plus tip and they got out. The dark grey clouds had eased and it was a pleasant evening. "Give me a call if you need me later on", said Mike.

They made their way upstairs to the bar to be greeted by Ed and Dianah. The interval drinks had already been ordered by Ed, and David added their requirements. "Don't forget mine's a Chilean merlot". Hazel had briefly mentioned merlot wine to David in the taxi as she had quietly nibbled his ear lobe hoping that Mike hadn't used the rear view mirror during their short taxi ride other than for looking at traffic behind them! The four of them swapped stories about their week so far, Ed had been offered another project abroad, China or somewhere, and he'd turned it down. They weren't short of money and Ed was able to pick and choose jobs as he wanted. Hazel and Di discussed various aspects of the church supper and the choir that was taking place next Tuesday evening in the parish church.

"I hear that Shelagh has been spreading gossip about the verger", said Di. "Apparently fixing taps isn't all he's good at!"

"Go on, what have you heard?"

"Well, last week someone, Tracey I think it was, had seen him helping Jean Anderson with her supermarket shopping and he carried it into her house. She watched from behind her blinds and he was in there for over an hour. An hour! I know Christians are supposed to be helpful people, but it makes you wonder, doesn't it? Maybe it was tea and sympathy."

"Oh, there can't be anything to it", replied Hazel. He's harmless enough, although thinking about it, sometimes he has a shifty look in his eyes as though he's looking at you and wondering what colour pants you've got on". The overture to *42nd. Street* started up, they finished their drinks, and the two couples made their way to their seats in the balcony. David bought a programme before they got to the aisle from Julie, one of their friends who was a volunteer at the theatre. "Enjoy the show", she said quietly as they moved down to row D, disrupting a few others who were already sat reading the list of performers and musical scores. The orchestra gaily played 'Young and Healthy' followed by 'Lullaby of Broadway' as the final three minute bell rang. It was almost a full house, and then the lights began to dim. Just before it got dark, Dianah whispered to Hazel, "I don't believe it. I've just seen the verger and Sarah Jones down in the stalls! I wonder if her utility water tap is OK?" Hazel giggled, and the man in front turned round to give her one of those looks you get in theatres, as when you carelessly unwrap a toffee.

Chapter 4

After the wonderful performance at the theatre, concluding with three curtain calls, Ed and Dianah offered David and Hazel a lift home. David had initially refused but Ed had insisted and so they accepted. They could drop David and Hazel off first and then take a slight detour to a local fuel station. Ed had calculated that by filling up the Mondeo there he would save about £2.20 compared to another local garage nearer to where they lived. It was well worth doing as Ed liked to get discounts off almost everything and save a few 'bob'. It was a game with him – always trying to beat the system. He'd given David a few web site addresses to search for reduced prices on televisions, laptop computers, cameras and much, much more.

"Good night", shouted Ed and Di in unison as they drove away from Chalk Road, "see you soon!" Hazel would see Di at Godalming church on Sunday when plans for the supper on the following Tuesday would be finalised by Gertrude Smithson. Gertrude was the senior matriarch of the ladies of the church, a retired headmistress, and few dared argue with her. She was married to Harry, a man of small stature and receding hairline. He wore his spectacles on the end of his round nose and looked a bit like Mr. Magoo. Some time ago one of the group had suggested they ask for volunteers from within the church to pose nude for a calendar to raise funds for a new church organ. The current one was over sixty years old and the bellows often stuck, especially in damp weather. "Heavens to

Murgatroyd. Over my dead body!" screamed Gertrude, leaving everyone in no doubt at all that she was not bearing her 48 DD bosom for anyone. Especially not for Clive Simpkins, the local photographer, who often took photos for the parish magazine. He often seemed to have a lecherous sneer.

"We shall find other ways to raise money, ladies. I do not think it appropriate that the fairer sex of this church should bare all with our organ in mind!" A loud snigger from Moya began a rapid ripple of laughter that was difficult to control. Gertrude reflected on her statement and began turning a deep crimson – she couldn't believe that she had used the word 'sex' and 'organ' in the same sentence. She had made a quick excuse about checking the central heating settings and departed quicker than her sixteen stone bulk should have physically allowed. The ladies erupted with gales of laughter once Gertrude was out of earshot. Rosemary ran to the toilet as her recently diagnosed overactive bladder and stress incontinence was about to get the better, or worse, of her. She made it in time. The calendar never happened, but Hazel, Di and a retired teacher called Margaret were co-opted to form a committee to consider future fund raising activity.

At the office, the rest of the week went OK for David. He'd met with Roy Whitehead and told him about Clint from Bristol. Roy said he'd have a word with Clint's Area Manager and make it very clear that he'd better pull his socks up or else he would be on his way. A decent rep was hard to find, and if word got around that you had a poor reputation in medical sales there was little future for you. He could always try 'medical disposables' – it was generally said that this area was not as tough as pharmaceutical selling. Trevor was pleased with the report and he told David so. It wasn't just a case of keeping the boss happy, David enjoyed his job, the cut and thrust of pharma marketing, the camaraderie within the industry, and most of all the group of people he worked with in Guildford. He had three Product Managers reporting in to him, Mark was the senior of the trio, and Doug and Ken were the other two. Mark was four years younger than David and had worked hard to get an MBA from the University of Surrey. His first degree was in biology, and he was making a good contribution to growing market share for the company. He wasn't married, didn't seem to bother with women and lived in a small flat in Merrow. David sometimes wondered if Mark was gay, but he'd never bring it up in conversation.

David thought that women were usually good at detecting if men were gay and one day he might broach it with Hazel. For now, the key issue was that Mark was good at his job and could replace David himself as Marketing Manager if he got promoted. The two others, Doug and Ken were fairly sound. Doug was the oldest and had a beard that he kept trimmed – he didn't want to look old even if he was the senior of the department by a decade. He had been married for fifteen years to Virginia and they had twin daughters. Whenever Doug talked of the girls David would listen, but also think to himself of his own situation with Hazel. He was still coming to terms with being childless and often wished he could reply to Doug with stories about birthday parties, or Father Christmas, with his own children.

Ken had come into the Marketing Department straight from the sales force where he'd been a senior sales representative for three years. Nobody took advantage of his good nature although it would have been easy to do so. He had a girlfriend, but nothing seemed to last long with Ken. Was it Ken or was it the girl? A young lady called Rebecca went out with him for nearly a year. She'd borrowed three thousand pounds from Ken with some story about her grandmother who had pressure sores and needed a posture bed with an inflatable mattress. As he trusted her he gave her a Lloyds cheque that she banked quickly. One Monday evening he went to pick her up to go to the cinema after she'd had a weekend away visiting her sick grandma but he found her flat was empty. He'd called her office on the Tuesday morning where she had a temporary job in finance to be told she'd handed her notice in on the previous Friday. They had no forwarding address for her. Her mobile phone went unanswered. Ken never really got over that.

At the end of the day, David finished off a few things, logged out of the in-house computer system and put his jacket on. He grabbed his briefcase, picked up the car keys and headed home. Classic FM had the same calming effect as he drove away from Guildford in the pouring rain. That helped, especially when idiotic drivers had omitted to put headlights on, or cars made turns without the use of their indicators. 'You bloody fool', he screamed at a white van man as the van pulled across in front of him just a few hundred yards before he turned into Chalk Road. 'It's true what they say about those bloody van drivers!' he said to himself, 'and it's always the ones with no signage on the side of the van – no address and no phone number so you can't ring them to give them a bollocking or report them!' He listened to a few more minutes of Claudio Abbado on the radio conducting his symphony orchestra when he'd parked up, trying to stay as calm as he could.

"It's only me," shouted David upstairs as he heard the bedroom radio.

OK, I'm coming down now". Hazel skipped down the last two steps of the stairs and hugged her husband.

"You'll never believe what I've discovered", she said with a mischievous look in her eyes.

"What?"

"The verger, Thomas Pilkington-Smythe, has a prison record!"

Chapter 5

The day of the harvest festival supper dawned bright and clear. David had left for the office and Hazel resolved to get on with defrosting the scones and generally getting things ready for the supper that began at 6. 30 p.m. She telephoned Sheila and invited her round for coffee at eleven o'clock. Sheila was a good and trusted friend whom she's known since school days. During her brief conversation Hazel mentioned the information she had gathered on Tom Smythe, as he was commonly known. "Never!" screamed Sheila "that can't be true! He was interviewed three times to my knowledge before the post was offered to him. The Reverend Keith Blandford couldn't speak highly enough of him!"

"I'll tell you more when you arrive, don't be late, you can be a guinea pig and try a sultana scone!" Hazel put the phone down and reflected on what he she found out the previous day from browsing a few web sites. She had typed 'Tom Smythe' into a search engine and it brought up three names in the county. She'd looked at each one, the first two being fairly innocuous, but the third showed up as 'Thomas Pilkington-Smythe' with some biographical details. Hazel had been unaware of his full name. She knew Tom lived in Bramley on the outskirts of Godalming and it gave his address from the electoral register. He had often used 'Major' as his name prefix. Therefore many assumed he'd had an army career as an officer. He lived alone.

Hazel used another search engine and entered 'Major Thomas Pilkington-Smythe'. This allowed her to enter a list of military personnel. Eventually she was able to discover that Tom had been discharged form the army seven years ago on February 29th. His rank was second lieutenant. No reason was given, but something in her memory bank came to her. The fact that it was a leap year made researching the matter easier. She recalled a news item in 'The Northern Echo' newspaper when she had visited her sister, Maureen, in Durham. It had been discussed between them as Maureen had just had Pilkington double-glazing installed by Smythe & Sons. She remembered talking about the co-incidence of the names! Hazel went onto 'The Northern Echo' website and entered Tom's details. It brought up an archived news report entitled 'Army officer disgraced'. It went on to state how he had raped a woman in Stockton-on-Tees after a night out, been found guilty and discharged without a pension from 'The Royal Engineers' where he'd served for twenty years. He was given eight years in Durham jail. Further 'detective work' by Hazel revealed that Tom served seven years of his sentence. She surmised that he'd wanted to leave the north east and moving south suited his need for future anonymity. So he'd arrived in Surrey.

"Well, well!" said Sheila, "that is just unbelievable" as she took a bite of her scone, her expression showing approval of Hazel's baking.

"How do we handle this, and what do we do with this information?" They discussed the issue over coffee and eventually agreed that they had to tell the Reverend Blandford. Was the timing right? The harvest supper was to be held that evening and Tom Smythe would certainly be there. Hazel and Sheila were aware of his 'friendliness' with three ladies from the church group – taps, shopping and the theatre came to mind! But how safe were any of them?

"Hello, is that Keith?" asked Hazel. "I've got some news for you that can only be discussed face-to-face. Can we meet soonest?"

"I'm having lunch with the padre at Charterhouse School but should be finished by 2.30 p.m."

"That'll be fine, do you want to come to Chalk Road? I'll have the kettle on". Keith Blandford turned up just after the suggested time. Hazel told him all she knew about 'The Major'. Keith asked some searching questions of Hazel as he needed to be absolutely certain that she had her facts correct. She quickly showed him some evidence on her laptop. He was convinced. The Reverend Blandford left Hazel's house after a cup of tea and phoned the Chair of the District, The Very Reverend James Miles, from his mobile. They met at the vicarage as soon as possible that afternoon. As the Reverend motored up the tree-lined drive to the front door he decided in his own mind that something needed to done about Tom Smythe – and quickly.

When David got home from Guildford, Hazel brought him right up to date. He expressed some surprise, but then he didn't. The church supper went off as well as possible and the choir were wonderful. Godalming church was almost full. The funds would help towards the organ. Many tucked into the good spread, and compliments were paid to Hazel as regards her sultana scones. Not one was left! There was little food left on the tables as appetites had been totally satisfied, only the odd curled- up egg sandwich, half a plate of 'Twiglets' and a few halves of Scotch eggs remained. Partners of members of the ladies group had turned up, and even David had enjoyed the whole event. Gertrude had 'been in control' and all went swimmingly well. However, one person was absent – the verger.

"I have an announcement to make", said Keith Blandford, above the buzz of conversation as things began to slow down.

All went quiet within a few seconds. "I want you all to know that Tom Smythe has resigned from his position of verger here at the church. I accepted his termination of tenure letter this evening and we wish Tom well in the future and would like to thank him for all he has done here in Godalming. I'd also like to thank all of those who have made this evening a success, especially Gertrude and her team. Good night and God bless you all". Gertrude's 48 DD heaved with pride as a ripple of applause spread throughout this ancient church. These walls had vibrated to over a thousand years of 'heaving' and 'appreciation' since it had been built with its great, square Norman tower.

A few whispers spread, and the eyes of Hazel and Sheila met across the room. The glance said it all. Soon people began to leave as hats and coats were put on, and 'goodnights' were said. Some chattering went on as they went down the steps and out into the cool night. Another regular couple, Doreen and Peter, shouted goodnight to those still leaving the church.

No doubt some were wondering about 'The Major'? Hazel noticed that Mrs. Jones, whose tap Smythe has mended, seemed to have a tear in her eye – or was it the reflection of a low, church light glinting off her spectacles?

Chapter 6

Saturday had started a bit dull with a hint of drizzle but the weather forecast had promised that it would brighten up later in the day.

David had finished playing bowls at the club by noon. He hadn't seen Ray Kingsbridge but had enjoyed a couple of games against two other club members. Some of David's friends had teased him, saying that bowls was an old man's game. David had ignored that comment totally. His Uncle Harold had taught him to play bowls when David was six years old and he'd kept it up since then. Before he'd left home that morning he'd suggested to Hazel that they go to the travel agent after lunch and talk to someone about the planned trip to Chile. Hazel prepared a salad lunch. Two wholemeal bread rolls and low fat spread were alongside the 'green mountain' and two glasses of cloudy apple juice sat next to the plates. David never tired of salads, and they helped keep both of them healthy. They sat down at the kitchen table and David reached for the pepper mill.

"One of the bowls club members was at the harvest festival supper this week. Apparently it's now common news that Tom Smythe 'left under a cloud'. I don't think anyone has betrayed any confidences, but the rumour-mongers have been at work. You can't stop people gossiping, but I didn't get involved apart from the odd nod and grunt when he made comments".

"It's done now", replied Hazel. She felt she had done the right thing after her fact finding on Pilkington-Smythe. She wasn't sure where he'd gone but another friend from church had seen a 'For Sale' notice outside of his place and the house looked empty. Maybe she had prevented another woman getting hurt or worse. A number of church members didn't trust Smythe although they never made their thoughts known publicly. Keith Blandford had considered the whole matter carefully, too, as he had been one of the church board to have interviewed Smythe. He had come over in a very professional manner, answered questions succinctly and his military background gained him the post of verger of Godalming church. Smythe had clearly lied about his rank in the army, and on reflection Keith Blandford recalled that he gave 'heads or tails' answers to a few questions. He must have made up some parts of his CV as regards previous jobs, but then one didn't always check these things.

After putting the crockery into the dishwasher, David and Hazel left for Guildford town centre. They parked in the multi-storey car park near the theatre and walked to the travel agent. The large front window of the agent advertised a dozen holidays. There was also a good offer on euros against sterling. David and Hazel surveyed the window and chatted about a few Christmas deals to Spain and Tenerife. "Wow, look at that deal there", said David as he saw a holiday advertised for the Costa Blanca for ten days at £399 full board. "Oh, no thanks," replied Hazel, "imagine being with all those Brits wearing Union Flag shorts near Benidorm. I can't think of anything worse!"

"Can I help you?" asked a young blonde girl as David and Hazel walked in. Her lapel badge showed her name was Sarah.

"Yes", said Hazel taking command of the situation, "we're interested in a holiday to South America, possibly Chile". David sat back and listened – he was happy for Hazel to get involved with the details.

"Let's see what we've got available". Within minutes Sarah was able to give them a number of possibilities that they eventually narrowed down to two. Both involved direct flights from Heathrow to Santiago with British Airways, but one included four excursions and the full time services of a tour manager. The hotel also seemed to be of a better quality. The king size double bed, drinks cabinet, large screen TV and laptop Wi-Fi connection seemed perfect.

"I think that's the one for us", said Hazel enthusiastically. David mulled over the details on screen whilst Sarah went to the catalogue-laden shelves and picked up a brochure that included this holiday. Santiago sounded like a lovely city. It had museums, theatres, an old historic quarter, universities, and a cathedral founded in 1558 and was situated on the river Mapocho. The country itself stretched from the dry Atacama desert in the north to the wet and cold Tierra del Fuego at its southern tip. The brochure quoted its length as 2,860 miles. The Andes mountains stretched for a total of 5,000 miles alongside and beyond the eastern boundary of Chile. The world's highest active volcano, Guallatiri, rose over 19,000 feet up into the Chilean skies. It seemed a wonderful country! Both David and Hazel had a digital camera and enjoyed photography. They would make the most of their two week holiday, and chose a departure date of 20 January. Santiago boasted daytime temperatures of 22 C on average at that time of year so there would be the added bonus of the possibility of escaping another harsh winter in Surrey!

"I'll need to take a deposit from you", said Sarah, almost apologetically. David reached for his wallet and removed his VISA card, being careful to select his own and not the company credit card from Smith & Johnson! Trevor wouldn't be very pleased with that! Hazel and David's eyes met. They didn't speak but knew that this was the holiday they both wanted.

It was something to look forward to in the dark winter months and they knew they were able to take time off work. David got 25 days annual holiday, plus the statutory eight days, and Hazel's primary school was very good at giving her time off when required. After the 10% deposit was paid, they left the travel agent with the brochure and thanked Sarah for her help. They made their way to a small cafe and Hazel found two comfortable leather seats near the window. David went to the service counter and ordered one café latte and one Americano, both regular. He picked up a blueberry muffin, two serviettes and a knife. They were going to share this, although he'd make sure Hazel got the biggest half.

When he got to the table he sat down and gave Hazel a quick kiss on the cheek. "I'm going to cut this muffin into two equal parts" he said, "but your part will be more equal than mine". Hazel forced a smile as she knew David had a string of quips that he came out with from time to time, and this one she'd heard many times before. "Well, the deposit is paid, so we can now relax and look forward to Chile in January", David remarked reassuringly. "Yes, it will be chilly in January!" Hazel replied, playing him at his own game. They picked at their muffin whilst browsing the brochure, and eventually finished their coffees. They had read lots of facts and information on the hotel and the excursions, as well as the area around Santiago. They were quietly excited. "I see the flight from Heathrow departs at ten o'clock on a Sunday in January so we'd better be sure we get our lift sorted out. And by the way, I don't want you taking your laptop. You can leave your office work in Guildford!" From the look in Hazel's eyes, David knew it would be a waste of time to argue with her, but she was right. This was going to be a holiday they'd enjoy, but at this stage they were unaware of the impact it was going to have on their lives. Totally unaware.

PART TWO

Chapter 1

On the other side of the world in South America life went on for millions of people in its thirteen countries. Industries manufactured, services served, jobs and tasks were carried out and children – where possible – were educated. Slums and the wealthy lived side by side. Starving infants rummaged for scraps of food within sight of a Rolls Royce. Old men dressed in rags walked or staggered past up-market stores with suits in their windows priced at over one thousand US dollars. In less savoury circumstances, youths stole what they could to fuel their drug and alcohol habits. Hub caps and unlocked bicycles were easy pickings for those with no conscience, and worse were those who killed or maimed the elderly or infirm to grab handbag or pocket contents as though they were picking apples. This continent, the fourth largest in the world, occupied almost one seventh of the surface of the planet. It was, in some ways, no worse nor better than some other continents on the planet and in many respects maybe it was similar?

Colonised largely by the Spanish in the 16th century, much of this land remained part of Spain's overseas empire for almost three hundred years. They had brought viniculture and their language, as well as other contributions to the 'civilisations' of the Aztecs, Inca's and Mayans.

Brazil with the mighty Amazon is by far the largest South American country, and British, Dutch and Portuguese influence was noticeable, particularly in the northeast part of the continent. This continent is so large, especially north to south, with mountains and deserts that climate and the surrounding oceans have a strong influence on agriculture, and therefore the types of food and drink found across the landmass.

The wine industry in Chile had developed significantly since the Spanish conquistadors arrived. New grape varieties had gradually been introduced, initially from Spain and later from France. An area almost 800 miles in length on the west coast from Atacama to Bio Bio is where the grapes are grown – fed by rain and melt waters from the Andes, and enjoying an ideal temperate climate. Methods of production had changed over time, with oak barrels replacing other types of wooden vats to mature the wines. Bouquets improved. So much so, that Chilean wines had won gold awards at international festivals. The country had become the world's fifth largest wine exporter.

"They must produce 'happy' grapes in Chile", someone once said. It was for a variety of such interesting reasons that David and Hazel had chosen this part of the world. It was unlikely that they would ever go back. They intended to maximize their time there and soak up as much of the Latin atmosphere as possible. Chile was waiting to welcome them, and the holidaymakers from Surrey couldn't wait to get there. There were just a few last minute things to do. Central heating had been left on low, lights set to come on at dusk, and a key left with their trusty neighbour Gladys. A tick list had been printed off Hazel's laptop. This was used to ensure they did not forget anything. Clothes had been sorted, along with a wide range of bits and pieces they needed to take – passports, cameras, binoculars, mobile phone, medication, guide books and so on. The ticks on the list grew and grew until finally they had finished. All ticked off!

"Our lift has arrived", shouted Hazel from upstairs. David carried the two suitcases and hand luggage to the front door. Ray

Kingsbrdge was waiting to take them to Heathrow in his estate car. The adventure was about to begin. A real adventure.

It would turn out to be more than that, but little did they know that at the time.

Chapter 2

The BA flight to Santiago was fairly uneventful. The plane took off on time and once in the air drinks and snacks were served followed a little later by lunch. The cabin crew were up to their usual efficient levels, with attention to passenger comfort being top priority. Everything spoke 'quality' from the small branded packets of peanuts to the etched stainless steel cutlery. The motto 'We serve to fly' appeared almost everywhere you looked.

"Which film are you going to watch after lunch?" Hazel asked David, browsing the entertainment brochure. "Probably 'Contagion'. You know I like Brad Pitt."

"Boring"

"Well what about you?"

"It's got to be *Mama Mia* ", replied Hazel.

"You've seen that a hundred times".

"So?" She looked over her glasses at him.

David didn't bother to respond. He knew Hazel had made her mind up that she wanted to see the film, and David knew she liked Dominic Cooper. In any case, *Mama Mia* was a film to give you that happy and contented feeling with a good story to it. "Any more drinks?" the steward asked David sitting nearest to the aisle.

"I'll have a gin and tonic. What about you, Nutty?" he turned to his wife.

"Do you have any carmenere?" she enquired.

"Of course", said the steward, "we are flying to Chile after all!"

Hazel had done some detective work on the internet before leaving home. She had discovered that carmenere was a red wine from Chile, and with a better nose and body than some of the other reds like merlot. David was impressed. "I may as well get a bit more practice in", she said. "The glass of merlot in the theatre was hardly a tasting session!" The drinks were duly served, the gin and tonic was a double with ice and lemon, and the red wine was in a 250 ml glass, just at the right temperature. Hazel closed her eyes as she sipped the wine. She visualized the rows of red grapes growing in the vineyards with the Andes towering in the distance, the warm sun beating down. She imagined herself looking out over the Pacific ocean from the verandah of a small blue wooden hut on a wide, white sandy beach, sitting in a rocking chair with her white loose cotton dress gently blowing in the breeze. A small wooden table to her left held her bottle of carmenere and half-full glass of 'blackberries, old leather and cherries'.

Two people were lazily walking along the seashore, hand in hand. Hazel guessed they were honeymooners but couldn't be certain. The sun was bright and she had to put her hand above her eyes for shade. They talked and laughed as they frequently stopped to gather seashells and put them into a small, jute sack. She wore pale lemon Bermuda shorts and an open light green blouse while he was dressed in faded denim shorts. They both had wide-brimmed straw hats and carried their sandals in their hands.

Hazel imagined that she would have a name like *'Juanita'*, while he was a *'Pedro'*. Yes, he was definitely Pedro. She liked that name. She liked it a lot. Suddenly Hazel fell off her rocking chair, almost knocking over her bottle of wine. She woke up with a start.

"Goodness me! Had I drifted off?"

"You were almost snoring!" joked David. He realised that Hazel was tired after the last few days of planning and packing. The drone of the aircraft engines, coupled with half the glass of carmenere had sent her into a kind of reverie. "Hmmm", she sighed as she stretched her arms above her head.

"When's lunch?"

"It should be served soon, I guess" answered David finishing off his drink and folding the complimentary '*Daily Telegraph*'. He'd almost finished the cryptic crossword and had a go at the sudoku but had made a mistake on it. He was annoyed with that. Hazel bent over towards David and kissed him on the cheek.

"I do love you, you know", she purred. "Are you sure?" He looked her directly in the eyes with his. "Well, maybe", she teased.

"Ladies and gentlemen, this is your captain, Christopher Myers", oozed a dark brown voice from the aircraft tannoy system "and we're flying at thirty five thousand feet at a speed of five hundred miles per hour. The outside air temperature is minus forty degrees Celsius. If you wish to alter your watches I can tell you that Santiago time is four hours behind GMT. Our scheduled time of arrival into Arturo Merino Benito airport is nine thirty five tomorrow morning. I'll get back to you later with an update on progress. Sit back, relax, and enjoy your flight with British Airways".

"With a voice like that I bet he's a smoker", suggested David.

"It sounded sexy to me", Hazel's eyes lit up. "I can't wait for his next announcement!" Lunch was served with charm and efficiency. The chicken was cooked to perfection. The tiramisu for dessert and post lunch drinks admirably set the scene for an afternoon of watching films, or maybe just dozing? They both put their headphones on and settled back to watch their films. Soon Hazel's eyes closed as the golden sound of ABBA's music sent her into a deep sleep within minutes of the start. She hadn't even seen Colin Firth yet and she adored him – as well as Dominic Cooper. Not long afterwards David began to lose the plot of 'Contagion' as he slowly drifted off to the gentle drone of the four powerful engines powering them towards their destination.

They dozed and dreamt...and in Hazel's dream Pedro appeared again.

Chapter 3

"David, wake up!" said Hazel, pulling at his sleeve.

"What is it?" he replied, rubbing his eyes with both hands.

"Look at that gorgeous sunrise!" The sun was like a golden crescent peeping over the horizon, casting long rays through a few banks of white cloud. David reached for his camera and took half a dozen shots. He reviewed them within seconds and thought how good they looked. He showed Hazel the best one.

"Hmmm, worth framing, don't you think?"

"Not bad," replied Hazel, "but wait until I get my camera out in Chile – I'll show you a trick or two!" The loving competitiveness showed through as David gave her a cheeky grin. She ignored him in her usual manner. They always liked looking at all of their pictures on the laptop, Hazel's first and then David's second. Once seen like that, David would click 'View' and 'Arrange in date order'. Within a few seconds all of the photos would then be in sequence by time and date. There was a waft of bacon gently coming through the cabin as Captain Myers announced that their landing time was to be thirty minutes ahead of schedule.

"I wonder what the Captain has for breakfast?" enquired David.

"With a voice like that, a big Havana cigar and a large black coffee!" joked Hazel in reply. Breakfast was served on board just after half past seven local time. It was a good selection of scrambled eggs, bacon, sausage and tomato, with toast and marmalade to finish. The freshly squeezed orange or pineapple juice was excellent, as was the freshly percolated coffee. Within an hour breakfast was eaten and trays tidied away. Passengers began to get themselves organized for the landing in Santiago. Blankets were handed back to the cabin crew and old newspapers were collected along with empty cans and plastic bottles.

"That was great", said David patting his firm stomach. "I'm looking forward to tasting the local food, especially the steaks that are supposed to be juicy and tender".

"We won't overdo it on the red meat front. We'll have one or two but we'll eat plenty of salads as we do at home. Let's just hope the restaurants wash the greens well! We don't want to experience Montezuma's revenge! Fish should be plentiful, after all". Hazel had packed sufficient tablets and capsules to last them through their holiday. The screens in front of them were now showing a map of the southern part of South America with the red-coloured aircraft icon making its way toward Santiago. The distance was shown as four hundred and fifty miles and arrival in just over an hour. The Boeing was over the eastern border of Chile as the Captain made his final comments, wishing that everyone had enjoyed their flight, would have a safe onward journey, and looked forward to welcoming passengers back again in the near future. It was the normal PR stuff that for which BA were well known. Myers also sounded as though he actually enjoyed going through it!

Hazel wondered to herself if he was single, and what he'd be up to in Santiago before he flew back to Heathrow? Was he tanned with a moustache? Just a woman's thought – as quickly dismissed as it had come into her head. Finally, Brooklyn, the senior cabin crew member who had floated down the aisles during the whole journey, or so it seemed, asked everyone to fasten their seat belts and place the small tables in front of them into the upright position. Hazel and David heard the giant wheels drop into place and a little later the lightest of tyre skims on the tarmac as the aircraft decelerated to a sensible one hundred miles an hour with engines in full reverse within less than a minute. The aircraft slowed right down to walking pace as it turned through ninety degrees and came to a complete stop at holding bay 32.

"We're here at last!" Hazel let out a sigh as she looked out at the white terminal building, shimmering in the sunshine. David gently squeezed her knee reassuringly. As soon as the seat belt sign went off, David was up and getting the two pieces of hand luggage from the overhead locker. Very soon all passengers were going through passport control. Only the occasional passenger seemed to be scrutinized carefully and most were checked through in a matter of seconds. Once at the BA carousel they waited for a little while as a multitude of shapes and sizes of luggage came around. It always amused David when people watching as he'd see an individual pick up a suitcase, examine it thoroughly for what seemed an age, and then put it back on the moving belt! When their own came round it was a different colour and often with a bright ribbon on the handle! David lifted both of their cases off the carousel and turned them upwards and extended the handles. The plastic castors touched Chilean 'soil' and off they marched towards customs control. Both smiled slightly as they walked straight past four customs officers in their splendid uniforms. As Hazel went past the last officer she noticed the name badge on his left lapel. It read 'Pedro Gonzalez'. She wasn't particularly looking at names, but for some reason she particularly noticed this one.

A comfortable coach ride took them to the Santiago Plaza Hotel in the Providencia district in under an hour. Once in their plush room Hazel couldn't wait to get her shoes off. She laid on the bed, closed her eyes for few minutes and ran her fingers through her hair. As Hazel drank a cup of coffee that David had made she scanned a number of brochures on a side table. She picked up a brochure on a charitable group called 'Christian Foundation for Children and Aging' that had been founded in 1981 and existed in twenty two countries. This group was mainly run by lay Catholics and the nearest one was in Valparaiso – the Refugio de Cristo.

Hazel had an overwhelming sense of wanting to visit this refuge. Somehow she knew that she had to go and see it. She just knew.

Chapter 4

Their first day was described in the brochure as 'at leisure', so after breakfast David and Hazel decided to venture out and get their bearings around the beautiful city. Dinner in the hotel was included in their holiday apart from when they were away on two excursions, so a hearty but healthy breakfast would usually last them through the day with a small snack around noon. The hotel had its own minibus that departed from the large tarmac area in front of the hotel and stopped in the Plaza de Armas, the historic centre of the city surrounded by colonial buildings and the cathedral. David suggested they catch the ten o'clock bus into the Plaza to give them time to look around, so after filling their stomachs to a sensible extent at the breakfast buffet table they got themselves organized. Cameras, some money – but not too much, one credit card, and a choice of sensible clothing and footwear saw them making their way down from the fourth floor to the foyer in the lift.

Outside the temperature was 21 C with slight humidity and no cloud, so basically it was a very pleasant change from Surrey where the temperatures were around 1 C and snow was due. Hazel had received a text message from Rosemary saying that she hoped they had both arrived safely and were enjoying what Chile had to offer. Rosemary also gave Hazel a brief update about the church as Hazel had missed the Sunday service, as well as the local weather conditions. David hoped that Hazel wasn't going to be trying to use up her one hundred free Orange texts per month while she was away! He need not have worried as Hazel had already decided that this was time for her and David and she was determined not to be contacting friends back home on a regular basis. 'They can wait until I get back' she mused to herself.

The minibus stopped in the Plaza de Armas, and fourteen hotel passengers alighted. They blinked as the bright sunshine assaulted their eyes. The high-rise buildings rose into the azure blue sky, making you feel almost giddy as you looked up at the tops of them. Traffic seemed heavy, with a host of old taxis driving madly up and down the streets radiating off the Plaza. You took your life into your own hands when crossing the street, and only did it where it was safe to do so! Using the brochure from the hotel room, they made their way to a museum – the Pre-Columbian Art Museum. This wonderful building contained a range of cultural relics and ancient textiles. David and Hazel were keen to understand what Chile, and this part of South America, was all about. They marvelled at the displays and began to feel humbled at the history unfolding before their eyes. The colours of the textiles and the array of old antiquities, as well as the art and architecture of the native inhabitants were amazing.

Thousands of years before the Spaniards had arrived the civilizations in this part of the world had developed their own amazing methods of metalwork techniques, particularly in gold. The Andean civilization is associated above all with the Incas who had developed a far-flung empire linked by a road system superior to that of the Romans. The earliest distinct Andean culture was called Chavin and flourished from about 900 BC until about 200 BC. The Chavin peoples produced pottery, goldwork and textiles. Other cultures included the Mochica and Chimu that showed skills in ceramics, especially jugs in the form of realistic portraits of heads. The Incas have much in common with the Aztecs of Mexico, but were great builders, all the more remarkable for having been achieved without knowledge of the wheel.

"I'm feeling a little hungry", said Hazel after they had spent a couple of hours in the museum.

"Me, too", replied David, patting his stomach in his characteristic way. "I spotted a little restaurant over the way before we came in here. Let's give it a try." The restaurant was called *Las Olas* and although it was just after one o'clock, it was becoming busy. Diners were sitting at the pavement tables outside but David spotted an empty table with two chairs. His beginner's Spanish course, completed six months previously at the local college, might pay off! He was reluctant to try too hard as they'd had an experience once before in France when the local waiter fires off words at you like a Gatling machine gun because you've taken the initiative to speak their lingo! Or do they just try it on, knowing you're British? They searched the menu for something a bit different. After all they had promised themselves to get immersed in Chilean life, hadn't they? Hazel noticed a dish called palta reina. This was an avocado filled with tuna fish or ham. David fancied carbonada, a meat soup that consisted of diced beef and different vegetables. One item on the menu they wished to avoid was congrio frito – deep fried conger eel! The waiter came to their table and, poised with pencil and small note pad, took their order. David managed to ask for most of it in Spanish, and added "y dos vasos de carmenere, por favor – two glasses of carmenere, please."

"Bravo!" clapped Hazel as the waiter walked away.

"Don't get too excited" replied David, "let's see what appears from the kitchen.I might have mispronounced something!" Over lunch they reflected on the museum and all they had seen.

The South American Indians had truly been a great civilization. One could argue that the colonization by the Spanish in the 16th. century had added something to their culture, or had it? Where would these cultures be without the influence of the Spaniards? Would they be good at football? It didn't really matter, did it? They decided they would like to take a souvenir home but weren't sure what? A jug shaped like a head? Some silver or gold metalwork? Neither realized over their glass of red wine just what they would be taking back home to England at the end of their holiday. It would be something unexpected. After finishing their lovely meal and wiping their mouths on paper napkins they paid the bill and left. Another couple, probably locals, was anxiously waiting to grab their table. They both smiled at David and Hazel, showing their lovely white teeth against mahogany coloured faces.

"Muchas gracias!" said the man to Hazel giving her a slight wink that David didn't notice as the Chilean pulled back the wooden chair for his partner. "De nada", replied David, 'don't mention it', showing off his limited Spanish. Time was getting on a bit, they were both a little tired and still jet lagged so they decided a visit to the cathedral for a couple of hours, plus some photography around the Plaza would be enough for them. The cathedral was a magnificent building, with a large ornate wooden door. Inside were tombs and inscriptions going back over four hundred years. The stained glass window was immense, and there were many others along the knave. Several small candles were lit in the corner and the couple added another two. They sat on a long, oak pew in the centre of the cathedral, looked around them, and marveled at the inside of this building. They tried to imagine what it would be like on a Sunday, with people bustling about, and the senior padre getting up the steps to the pulpit to deliver the sermon.

"Come on, Nutty", said David quietly after looking at his watch, "let's make our way back to catch the hotel bus, I'm wacked!" They got back to their hotel room not long afterwards, made a cup of tea, and just relaxed on the large bed after kicking off their shoes. The first full day had gone well, and they were just easing their way into their holiday. Tomorrow they had an organized trip to Valparaiso, north of Santiago.

They were looking forward to that. Very much so.

Chapter 5

Feeling refreshed after a good night's sleep and a healthy breakfast with plenty of fruit and some cereals, David and Hazel walked outside as the coach arrived outside the Santiago Park Plaza hotel at just after half past eight to take a group of thirty six tourists to Valparaiso, a city situated on forty two hills and a main Pacific coast port for South America as well as Chile itself. It's historic quarter is a UNESCO World Heritage site. The city was founded by the Spanish in 1536 and is now a terminus of the trans-Andean railway. It was known to many as the 'Jewel of the Pacific', and not without reason. The day was bright, with a clear blue sky. 'Perfect for photography' David thought to himself. They'd got one small ruc-sack between them to carry their cameras, sun cream, a bottle of water and a few other bits and pieces.

Hazel got onto the large air-conditioned coach first and found a window seat in between two pillars so that they could get a good view. David climbed in beside her and got his digital camera out of the ruc-sack in case there were any good views or wildlife – he was always on the look-out for opportunities to get a good camera shot. Within a few minutes all passengers were on board and settled down. All that is apart from a large lady on her own that both David and Hazel had spotted at breakfast. She was sat three rows in front on the opposite side. Her frame occupied two thirds of the double seat. David thought she resembled a Yorkshire pudding in shape!

"There's the one who helped herself to three fried eggs, sausages and all that bacon", whispered Hazel, nudging David gently in the ribs. "I'm glad she's not sitting too close to us."

"Hmmm", David responded somewhat unconcerned. He was busy looking at some photos he'd taken the day before in down town Santiago on his camera screen. 'Ha, typical', thought Hazel to herself, 'men!'

"Good morning, ladies and gentlemen, my name is Estrella", said the tour manager over the microphone. A broken English accent suggested that she was local, but unfortunately had a slight lisp. "Our journey today takes uth to the wethst of Thantiago towards the mighty Pathific ocean. We shall stop once on the way to Valparaiso at a thmall thervice area where you can freshen up and take a coffee and pathstry. Pleathe remember which seats you are in as you need to thit in these on your return journey". When she had uttered these words, she commenced walking along the aisle of the coach to do a head count.

"Do you think she'll count thirty thix?" asked David. Hazel chuckled, knowing full well that he was taking the mickey! They were sat in seats 6A and 6B, whilst *'Miss Pudding'* was sat in 3C, or was that 3C *and* 3D? Once Estrella had done her addition she nodded to the coach driver, whose name was Paco, and the old Mercedes Benz coach slowly eased forward and onto the main road. Once beyond the Santiago city boundary the countryside opened out and the views towards the Andes in the north east were magnificent. They crossed a river whose waters were crashing over the rocks on either side, and gradually descending towards the Pacific. The distance to their coastal destination was about 120 km along a modern toll highway.

With one short stop en-route to their destination, the journey took two hours. The stop at the service area was uneventful, although Hazel had wished the ladies toilets were cleaner. There always seemed to be something about the 'ladies' that affected women. Rarely did you hear the men complain about odours coming from the urinals. Was it a 'man thing?' As the coach came into the city, the sparkling blue ocean was clearly visible. There was the usual hustle and bustle associated with a port with many large lorries approaching and leaving the docks but this did not detract from the central part of Valparaiso as a ring road had been built to take commercial traffic away from the centre. The port was visited for about four months every year by large cruise liners bringing thousands of visitors to this area. The buildings were excellent examples of late nineteenth century urban and architectural development in Latin America. Estrella pointed out some landmarks to the passengers as the coach began to park up in a large area on the southern edge of the city. She reminded them that they now had five hours to explore this lovely, historical city, and the coach would be waiting for them at the exact point where they were about to be dropped off. Each was given a brochure to the area that contained a detailed map of the city. Estrella was also careful to point out how careful they all needed to be with their personal possessions. 'No looth necklaces or jewellery, keep wallets and purthes clothe to you, and camera thtraps should be used' was the gist of her message.

Miss Pudding was last off the coach and linked up with another couple that she seemed to know. He looked like an undertaker whilst his wife was taller than him with red hair. The trio wandered off in one direction and Miss Pudding was bringing up the rear with her waddle. David was tempted to take a picture with his camera, but one look from Hazel said 'Don't you dare!' He put his digital camera in his ruc-sack and they both walked off holding hands towards a large building that looked like a university. The temperature was a pleasant 20 C and the colours of some of the stonework were a gorgeous shade of autumnal bronze. David and Hazel ambled along looking at everything this city had to offer and tried to imagine how it may have looked three or four hundred years ago? They used the city map in their brochure to find their way to the key tourist areas, taking many photos from all angles.

The *Severino* public library, Chile's first public library, and the *El Mercurio de Valparaiso* buildings looked resplendent against the clear blue sky behind. The 'Mercurio' is the oldest Spanish language newspaper in the world and they were proud of it. David and Hazel wandered towards the port and saw the *Iglesia de la Matriz,* a wonderful Roman Catholic church, situated in the heart of this district. To get down to the port itself meant using one of twelve funicular railways. Because Valparaiso resembled an amphitheatre everything falling under gravity headed downhill towards the blue Pacific ocean, including the mighty rivers that scythed through the land. The major buildings and commercial centre were downhill whilst houses and apartment blocks were above. They were amused to see old trolley buses that were over seventy years of age, and these trundled around the city carrying their human cargo, stopping every few minutes to let people on and off. The tourist couple decided it was time for coffee and were told a number of bars and cafes were situated at the port. They took one funicular descent and noticed a sign that said that this particular wagon had been in existence since 1883! 'How many million metres had that travelled?', David asked himself.

Down near the port they found the Plaza Sotomayor and saw a couple of bars – the Bar Playa and El Bar Ingles. They decided on the latter, especially as the word Ingles meant English in Spanish. This part of the city was a labyrinth of alleyways and cobbled streets and was very quaint. David ordered *dos cafe con leche* – two milky coffees, and they sat back and relaxed, absorbing the sunshine and thinking briefly of the snow in Godalming. David and Hazel chatted about the city and its spectacular setting and historical buildings. Hazel took a few more photos, and then suddnely noticed a small sign across the street. The sign was for the *Refugio de Cristo* that she had read about in the leaflet in the hotel room. The sign indicated that the refuge had been founded by Padre Rene Pienovi in 1952. It's objective was to care for children whose rights had been damaged by poor parental care. They were provided with food, drink and shelter and were given specialised professional care. As they relied largely on charitable donations, they obviously publicised the refuge in and around the city.

"Oh, David, do you think we could visit the Refugio de Cristo today? We've had a look around, and we've time to spare." David looked at his watch, aware they had to be back for the coach at half past three.

"Do you really want to, Nutty?"

"Yes, I would – very much".

David noticed that the waiter who had served them spoke good English. He went inside to pay the bill and asked him about the refuge. It was on the outskirts of Valparaiso and they'd need a taxi. A taxi rank was close to the bar, and within two minutes they were on their way. The waiter watched them depart – a holiday visit to a refuge?

English tourists seemed so strange at times.

Chapter 6

Their taxi driver knew very little English, but enough to know exactly where they were going. Within forty minutes they arrived outside of the refuge. The road was dusty, and the local area was sparsely populated. David expected to see Clint Eastwood walk down the road smoking a cheroot. David paid the taxi driver and added a ten per cent tip. The driver returned a toothless grin as he pocketed the paper money. The day seemed to be getting hotter as the sun beat down. They'd be pleased to get into the shade. 'What if we can't go in?' Hazel suddenly thought to herself! She recalled what David sometimes said – "Never assume, it makes an ass of you and me". David strode up to the big wooden double door that was in shadow. The large, brass door-knocker in the shape of a crucifix felt easy to lift, and he brought it down heavily three times. They waited for what seemed ages before a small wooden panel on the left door slowly creaked open a few centimetres. She needn't have worried as a small, wizened face appeared at the square hole.

"Si?"

"We read about your refugio in Valparaiso and would like to understand more about what you do here?" Hazel said clearly and slowly.

"Uno momento!" The wooden panel slammed shut. David and Hazel looked at each other for a few moments.

The panel opened again. "Yes, can I help you?

Hazel repeated her first enquiry made to the wizened face man. This other person, with friendly, large brown eyes, nodded once slowly. "Come in, please". He was Father Rodriguez. The right hand door creaked open, revealing a small inner courtyard with a fountain surrounded by potted cactus plants. The brown eyed man gestured for them to enter. They walked in together. On the wall in front of them a purple bouganvillea cascaded across a white wall, almost hiding three windows with light green shutters. In the right hand corner of the courtyard was a bronze statue of Christ on the cross. At the feet of the statue a cat stretched its legs as it lay full length next to the base of the cross. It seemed very content. Over to the left were three terracotta pots containing red geraniums, matched by three other pots with the white variety to the right. Hazel thought of the words of a hymn – 'be still for the presence of the Lord is moving in this place'.

"You are both welcome here. How can we help you?" asked Father Rodriguez. Hazel introduced David and herself. "We read about your refuge and we felt we'd like to know more of your charitable work with children", replied Hazel, who briefly explained that she worked in a school in England and was a regular churchgoer. "We're on a day trip from Santiago where we're staying in a hotel for two weeks, and we wanted to make time to visit you".

"Thank you. Do you have children of your own?"

"No, we're a childless couple, Father" said Hazel. He looked deep into her eyes. Hazel wasn't sure if she sensed something, but it passed in a moment.

Father Rodriguez began to explain the work of the refuge, but then suddenly asked if they would like to have some refreshment. "You are welcome to come this way", he pointed to a light blue door to his left, "and join me for bread and soup with a glass of water. The soup and bread were freshly made here this morning". They couldn't resist, and followed Father Rodriguez into a room with a plain tiled floor and two windows. A rustic table approximately one metre square was laid with an embroidered cloth. A large, handmade broom with long bristles stood in one corner. They sat at the table on three-legged stools and after a brief prayer, Father Rodriguez passed the bread around. They were soon joined by another of the lay Catholics, Juan, who served the soup and poured out a glass of water each. Juan sat at the table next to Hazel, and crossed himself before starting to eat. Juan had been at the refuge the longest of any, and was there when it opened in 1952. He must have been in his mid seventies. Because of his length of service, Juan was seen as the most senior member of lay staff. He had a lined face, teak brown in colour, and a large droopy moustache. His eye were small, but twinkled as bright as stars.

Father Rodriguez explained to Juan that their visitors had become aware of the refuge through information in their hotel room in Santiago, and again in Valparaiso. He continued to talk about the work of the refuge, satisfied that David and Hazel were genuine in their interest. Father Rodriguez had dealt with hundreds of human beings over the years, both within and outside the church and refuge, and knew honesty when he saw it. He could read it in their eyes. He went on to summarise the founding of the refuge for children who needed protection and care. The emphasis was on the latter. He described the basic work they did, how many children were there and the way that the refuge was run. Juan chipped in from time to time with additional comments, which Father Rodriguez accepted. It was almost as though they had done this many times before. They also mentioned that they were a charity and relied heavily on donations. However, David noticed that this was not over-emphasised. In other words, not a 'sales pitch' for more cash! Father Rodriguez excused himself for a few minutes.

David and Hazel had listened intently and were fascinated by the unfolding story. 'What wonderful work they do here' she thought to herself.

They had finished their basic meal and felt satisfied and refreshed. Juan offered to show them one of the classrooms where teaching was in progress, and also a clinic where two small boys were having cuts and grazes cleaned and dressed. The whole ethos of this place was about caring for the children. Every child they saw had a smile on their face, their grins revealing gleaming, white teeth. The children looked clean and healthy, and the classroom seemed to be a place of enthusiasm to learn, with hands shooting up whenever the teacher asked a question. David glanced at his watch. Goodness, it was getting late and they needed to get back to the city to catch the coach by half past three! Hazel also realised that fact, too. They explained to Father Rodriguez that they needed to leave and asked if there was a possibility that he could arrange a taxi to take them back? Juan heard their plea.

"No problema", said Juan and offered them a lift in his car. "I need some shopping from the town so I can take you!" David and Hazel were relieved at the offer. They shook hands with Father Rodriguez and thanked him profusely for his kindness. He took Hazel's hand and gently squeezed it. "Thank you very much for taking the trouble to come", he said. He discreetly placed a small envelope into the palm of her hand.

"Come quickly", shouted Juan, "we must go". Within seconds he had pulled up in front of the big wooden doors in the oldest car they had ever seen. It was a blue 1950 Chevrolet, with four doors and a boot that would carry a snooker table. Big chrome fins adorned the two corners at the rear of the car, whilst large headlights either side of a shark-like chrome radiator grill that screamed 'get out of my way' glared from the front. Not a speck of rust was to be seen. When they set off David sensed that their return journey was going to be quicker than their trip to the refuge. They both looked out of the back wrap around window and waved farewell to Father Rodriguez through the rising dust clouds.

On the way back, David explained to Juan as best he could where the coach had dropped them off earlier in the day. He described the nearby buildings. Juan knew where the coach park was and said he would take them right there. The skill of Juan's driving was hair raising! He cut most corners, overtook on blind bends and bridges, and narrowly missed three hens on the road! The use of the car horn was second nature to him.

"The Lord Jesus Christ, he look after me!" he said with a grin, his wrinkled brow getting more deeply furrowed. In just under thirty minutes the Chevvy came to a stop at the edge of the coach park, dust swirling up and around the car. David and Hazel got out, thankful to be in one piece. They thanked Juan as they got out.

"You know Juan Fangio, racing driver?" he shouted at David as he slammed the door. "He my uncle! God bless you both", and with that he sped off coating the tarmac with streaks of jet black rubber. The coach was parked up with its diesel engine gently throbbing. It was exactly half past three! Everyone else was on board.

"It's nithe to thee you got here OK", said the Tour Manager waiting at the coach door. "I haven't theen a taxi like that before in Valparaitho". The last two holidaymakers on this tour climbed the four steps and took their seats. David and Hazel sat back and laughed. And they laughed again. What a wonderful experience they'd had! It had certainly been better than looking around the shops or drinking in the bars. They felt they'd seen just enough of the city itself, with its old age charm and special character. They'd taken loads of photos. It had been good, really good. After a few minutes of the return journey, both David and Hazel realised that they had not taken any photos at the refuge! More importantly, Hazel remembered the envelope that Father Rodriguez had put into her hand that was now in her handbag.

She took it out and opened it. She wan't sure what to make of it and read it three times. Slowly. Very slowly.

Chapter 7

'Dear Hazel, thank you for coming to see our work here in Valparaiso at Refugio de Cristo. We all hope your visit was not only enjoyable but also that you were inspired. Christ works in many wonderful ways, with and through people. His methods are not always known to mortals like us, but rest assured the Christ Jesus never stops sharing His word around the world. I felt today after we met that you were destined to visit our refuge. Before you return to your home, may I suggest, if you have the time, to visit another place not far from Santiago. I feel this place may give you some inner peace. God bless you, Father Hernando Rodriguez.'

At the bottom of the page was a 'please turn over'. Over the page were the details of a nunnery and the name 'Mother Caterina'.

Hazel took in words like 'inspired', 'never stops sharing', and 'some inner peace'. She had never felt like this before. It was as though some inner calm had enveloped her, as though angels were with her – right there and then! Had Father Rodriguez seen something in her eyes? Did he have a sixth sense? Why had an inner voice told Hazel to visit the refuge?

"Are you all right, Nutty?", asked David back in their hotel room as they relaxed before dinner."You seem to be away with the fairies?"

"I've just read a note given to me by Father Rodriguez. I think you should read it".

"A note, what note? I didn't see him hand you anything".

"He gently pressed it into my hand as we were leaving. I didn't want to say anything at the time and slipped it into my handbag as Juan brought the car to the door".

David read the note and confessed he did not know what to make of it. It had been written with deep feeling and understanding.

"What do you think we should do?" he asked Hazel. "We need to go", she replied instantly. "I've never felt like this about any other situation in my life – ever. Only my wedding day came close to this in terms of a sense of joy and peace. We have to go to the nunnery. Look there's a map over there. Can you find where the town is? We have a free day tomorrow. If we act quick we can plan it all and go!"

David could see that she had made her mind up, and until they had made a visit to the nunnery, she would not be happy. David scanned a map found amongst the other brochures on the side table in their hotel room. His index finger moved over the large page for several seconds until he spotted the place – San Felipe – just over seventy miles north of Santiago. 'It's less than two hours in a taxi', David thought to himself. They could do that in a day. If they booked a taxi now to depart the hotel at nine o'clock they'd be there late morning, take some lunch and water with them, and be back at the hotel by tea time at the latest. They continued to discuss it while they got ready to go down to the restaurant and agreed on their plan. In the foyer they asked the receptionist if she could book a taxi for the following morning. They handed her the note with the address on. She gave them both a quizzical look and then smiled. She said nothing and made the telephone call.

After a few minutes she looked up at them and said, "That's done. Your taxi, driven by Miguel, will pick you up at nine o'clock sharp. The fair will be twenty five thousand pesos and he takes credit cards".

"Thank you very much", said Hazel as they walked into the restaurant. They both felt hungry after their lunch of bread and soup, and looked forward to dinner. The full board included a three course dinner each night that they were in the hotel, but they had to pay for their own wine. They perused the menu, deciding on breaded mushrooms and prawn cocktail to start, to be followed by tuna for Hazel and sea bass for David. Desserts, if they could manage one, would probably be fresh fruit salad or pistachio ice cream. Hazel's stomach rumbled slightly as they ordered, and they chose a Chilean white wine to accompany the fish course.

Over dinner they talked about their day. It still seemed like a dream. Things had worked out well. The fact that they had seen parts of Valparaiso, spotted the sign for *Refugio de Cristo*, got there and been welcomed, had a look around, and even a free lift back to the coach by Juan Fangio's nephew! They felt blessed. Maybe they both had been *truly* blessed? They talked about the Christian work of the refuge and how well everything seemed to be. How kind Father Rodriguez and Juan had been during their visit, including the lunch invitation. The Roman Catholic father was clearly in charge of the refuge, but Juan was his 'right hand man', there was no doubt about it. David could see what an influence this place had been on her. He understood Hazel quite well, and she was obviously taken with what she had seen. 'Almost smitten', he thought to himself.

After dinner they had coffee in the large lounge, seated in deep brown leather chairs. Diners were milling around looking for seats as waiters weaved in and out of guests carrying trays of after-dinner liqueurs. David and Hazel, although not always wanting a liqueur, decided to have one. They were on their holidays, after all. They chose a brandy and a Cointreau. Orange was one of Hazel's favourite flavours so she chose the liqueur from the large brown, square bottle.

"Is anyone sitting here? Do you mind if I join you?" asked Miss Pudding. Hazel was taken by surprise as the plump lady approached from behind. Hazel gave a David a quick glance as if to say 'what do you think?' Before she could interpret the look in David's eyes, Miss Pudding had plonked herself down next to Hazel, amply filling a tan leather chair. She placed a large glass filled with clear, sparkling liquid and a piece of lemon on the small table in front of her.

"I noticed you on the coach today. You were the last ones to get on in Valparaiso. Another two minutes and you might have missed it!" Hazel didn't feel the need to explain themselves, but simply said that they'd been looking around and lost track of the time. When they realised they needed to be back at the coach park for half past three they'd managed to get a lift. Miss Pudding introduced herself as Amelia Harcourt which sounded much nicer than the nickname she's been given by David and Hazel! They introduced themselves to Amelia. She had no wedding ring on, and was dressed in a loose cotton dress that seemed to hide her large figure as well as it could. She wore a big dark necklace made of a material that looked like burnt amber, and a silver bracelet with lots of charms on it. Hazel wasn't certain about Amelia, but she was only stopping by for a chat, wasn't she?

"I had a lovely time," began Amelia, "I used three of the funicular railways to go up and down to the port and harbour, and visited the cathedral and museum. I took lots of photos and that clear blue sky was wonderful. I think my camera memory card will hold up to one thousand pictures so that should last until I get home! I had lunch in a lovely tapas bar and asked for extra patatas fritas." David knew that these were potato chips and imagined Miss Pudding stuffing them into her mouth! Over the next ten minutes both parties exchanged pleasantries, Hazel telling Amelia where they were from and what they did in Surrey. Amelia sipped her drink, trying not to swallow either the ice cubes or the lemon slice. Hazel realised that she was doing most of the talking, and then excused herself. "I must go to the loo", she said, "be back in a minute". Hazel made her way to the ladies toilets in the far corner of the lounge. Amelia asked David about the pharmaceutical industry and what he did as a Marketing Manager. She was a good listener and leaned forward intently as David explained the ins and outs of his role within the company. Within no time Hazel had returned. David wondered if she was jealous of leaving her loving husband alone with this lady? Surely not!

When Hazel got back to the table she stayed standing upright and slowly sipped her Cointreau until the glass was empty.

"David, I'm tired, don't you think it's time we went to our room? We've got a full day tomorrow". David drank the remains of his brandy and stood up.

"Good night," said Amelia, "and enjoy the nunnery tomorrow".

"By the way, Amelia, what do you do?" asked Hazel. "I'm a psychic", she replied nonchalantly and walked off. As they went back to their hotel room Hazel looked at her husband and said "Why did you tell her we were going to San Felipe tomorrow, David?"

"I didn't", said David looking into her eyes, and the hairs on the back of his neck tingled a little. Hazel shivered slightly as though someone had walked over her grave.

Chapter 8

The nunnery was attached to the church and convent of St. Francis of Curimon. Franciscans had arrived in the late seventeenth century and began building soon after. The earthquake of 1730 had ruined much of the church itself and it was rebuilt into a house of prayer measuring forty eight by nine meters. At the front was a large square tower with three arches supported by four columns. It was a wonderful structure and marvellous to behold. Against the clear blue sky it was a picture.

The nunnery lay behind the church, slightly hidden by some trees and a few kilometres off the beaten track The sun was getting higher in the sky as David and Hazel got out of the black and white taxi. The air was full of the scent of flowers and it smelt clean and wholesome. There was no industry in this area, and it was so clear you could see for great distances towards the mighty Andes, with its highest mountain, Aconcagua, rising majestically somewhere to the north east.

David paid the taxi driver with his credit card. The fare was about thirty pounds in sterling. He grabbed the ruc-sack containing a sandwich and some fruit and water. He took hold of Hazel's hand, firmly but softly, just to let her know that he was there for her. They walked towards the wide wooden door of the nunnery and Hazel thought she could hear the voices of children. The sounds were happy ones. Was her mind playing tricks? There was a slight breeze blowing so perhaps the noise came from the wind rustling the leaves. Maybe invisible cicadas were making their presence felt? They did not have a telephone number for this place so they were unable to ring to ask if they could actually visit, but Hazel had an intuitive feeling that all would be fine. In fact she sensed that today was going to be a special day, a very special day. She reached into her handbag for the note that Father Rodriguez had given her. It would act as her 'passport' when she met Mother Caterina.

A heavy metal knocker hung on the door. It looked like solid copper with a layer of vedigris. David used it to signal their arrival by banging it three times on the round metal stud underneath. Again, the day was warm. It felt hotter than yesterday when they were in Valparaiso, but here they were inland with no sea breeze to cool things down. They were dressed for the climate, with cotton shorts and shirts and both wearing a good pair of walking sandals. They each had a hat. Within a minute or so the wide door swung open, creaking on its hinges. A nun, dressed from head to foot in black and wearing a white wimple stood before them. High overhead David noticed a vapour trail left by a jet on its way to some far off destination.

"Hello, buenas dias", said Hazel quietly. "Our names are David and Hazel and we are on holiday in Santiago. We come from England. I have a letter". She handed the nun a sheet of paper. The nun read it carefully and then gestured for them to come in. "Entrada, por favor – come in please". They walked in slowly, and almost felt as if they were intruding into someones personal home and life. They were asked to sit down on a double, rustic wooden bench. The seat was in the shade so it gave them some relief from the morning sun. David glanced at his watch. It was approaching eleven o'clock. They looked around the open area of the nunnery. It had a quadrangle, with a grass lawned area in the centre. Along each of three sides were rooms with windows looking onto the quadrangle, but not to the outside. A terracotta, pantile roof covered the tops of each side. There were several small chimneys on each roof, the white edges blackened by smoke over time. Each chimney pot had a curved terracotta covering to prevent rain getting in. Hazel listened carefully. She could hear voices...children's voices.

"Welcome to our orphanage. I'm Mother Caterina". Hazel turned round to see where the voice had come from and they both stood up. In front of the visitors stood a woman with the most beautiful face Hazel had ever seen. Her eyes were ice blue and her features were perfect. She can't have been more than thirty years of age. Only her hands and face were exposed for she also wore a black habit and white wimple.

"Sister Fatima told me about your note from the Refuge of Christ" she said turning to the other nun. "I know Father Rodriguez very well. In fact, he called me late yesterday so I knew you were coming. We have prepared some iced lemonade for you. Please, come this way". They went into a sparsely furnished room with white walls. A metal crucifix was in the middle of one wall at head height.

Had Hazel heard her welcoming words correctly? 'Welcome to our orphanage' – is that what she had really said? Mother Caterina pointed to two bamboo chairs and asked them to sit down. She handed David and Hazel a glass of the cool lemonade made in the nunnery. Ice clinked against the side of the glass and the freshly cut lemon bobbed on the surface. They thought it may be inappropriate to say 'cheers' so they sipped the refreshing, cloudy liquid once Mother Caterina had taken a sip of hers. Mother Caterina sat opposite them on a wooden stool, whilst Sister Fatima stood in a corner like a statue – observing but not interfering.

"We have taken children into our orphanage for over forty years", began Mother Caterina. "I have been here for quite some time, and Sister Fatima is my senior assistant". She nodded towards the corner. "We have twelve other nuns here, most of them have been with us for over ten years. Four of them are qualified nurses who left their profession to take the oath here. The children come from broken homes all over Chile, and some of them have been completely abandoned by their parents. Their age range is from a few weeks up to about ten years. Currently we have fifty six children here, but the number is growing".

Hazel was trying to take it all in. David had listened intently to Mother Caterina and was overawed at the committment shown by her and the staff. It was clearly a 'labour of love'. No it was more than that. 'These nuns have dedicated their whole lives to the service of God', he thought. 'They own virtually nothing, live in this nunnery which is their world, and care for poor kids who have no mum or dad. How great is that?' He felt humbled. No, he felt almost ashamed! His thoughts went back to Godalming. A large house, lots of clothes, a big car, a good salary with Smith & Johnson. He looked at the stone floor with his elbows on his knees for a few seconds, hung his head and closed his eyes.

"Are you all right, David?" asked Hazel as she took his hand. She noticed a tear in his eyes. "I'm fine", he replied manfully, not wanting anyone to notice his feelings at that moment in time. He wiped away a few tears, pretending that he was mopping his brow with his shirt sleeve. "Come", said Mother Caterina, "let us show you what we do here." The four of them went out into the sunlight. The air was fresh and the sky was cloudless. They were shown into one of the corridors of the part of the nunnery on the left side as they had come through the main door. As they slowly walked along they were able to glance into small rooms where groups of ten or so children were being taught. In others much younger ones were in a creche, playing happily under the supervision of the nuns, whilst the very young were in cots or sitting up in play-pens. Every child looked content and well nourished, most with a lovely smile. 'Their big, round dark eyes are gorgeous', Hazel thought to herself. Hazel obtained permission to take a few digital photos, but decided to be discreet.

Every room that they saw had a crucifix on a wall, was simply decorated, and oozed love and care. The dedication of the nuns was clearly evident everywhere one looked. The two visitors were introduced to several of the older children. Almost none of the children had seen a 'white' person before. They looked at the long blonde hair of Hazel and giggled, their white teeth gleaming. Some pointed at her but the nuns quickly curbed their enthusiasm so that they didn't go too far. Hazel spotted one boy aged about six. He stood out because of his facial features – almost Aztec in nature. He had looked at Hazel for some time, which she had noticed, and his dark eyes were smiling at her. His olive skin was smooth and his hair black as jet. 'He almost has a look of royalty', Hazel reflected to herself.

"What's his name?", Hazel whispered to Sister Fatima. "He is called Pedro", replied the Sister quietly. Hazel felt a tingle go through her as though she had touched a live electrical wire. *Pedro!* She somehow knew he'd have that name! But how did she know? How was it that she had seen several 'Pedros' since their arrival in South America. Was it an omen? Hazel dismissed the thought immediately. She quickly decided that she'd been reading too many paperbacks lately and had got some strange ideas into her head.

"Do you want to stay for some lunch?" enquired Mother Caterina. "We have brought our own and we're happy to eat that", replied David.

"If you wish. Let us go to the cantina where I can introduce you to some of the other nuns who will be taking a break". With that they all wandered back across the lawn, made up of a tough, drought-resistant grass. Hazel turned around briefly and saw Pedro still watching her. He smiled and she responded. Mother Caterina noticed that out of the corner of her eye. Mother Caterina said 'Grace' and during a lunch of bread, cheese and a green salad they sat at a large round table with a few of the other nuns. The visitors ate their sandwiches and fruit and they chatted amicably about the orphanage and the children. They talked about how they had different personalities and characterisitcs. The staff were careful to be diplomatic and not give anything away about the children themselves. However, Hazel asked one of the nuns, Sister Carmelita, about Pedro.

"Where did he come from, Sister?"

"We do not know. He was left at our front gates one night when he was only a few days old. We found him the next morning when we heard his cries. He has been here all his life."

"What will happen to these children?" asked Hazel. Sister Carmelita replied. "Oh, eventually we find homes for them via contacts we have thoughout the country, or people approach us and make enquiries about the children. We have to inform the Ministry in Santiago of any interest expressed, and then there's lots of paperwork to complete". Sister Carmelita suddenly stopped talking as though she had said enough, or even too much.

"That's very interesting, thank you very much" said Hazel appeciatively. When they had all finished eating and drinking, Mother Caterina said a prayer. She thanked God for the fellowship that they had enjoyed together, for the safe return to England of their visitors, and for the future of their orphanage in San Felipe. She offered to arrange a lift for them to the local railway station, explaining that trains went to the main railway station in Santiago from the small station less than three kilometres from the nunnery.

"The train fare will be much less than for a taxi", she smiled, "and much more interesting! You'll have wonderful views of our mountains, and you can see the Pacific ocean at times." Mother Caterina asked Sister Fatima to see if the gardener could get the minibus to take David and Hazel to *estacion ferro-cerril de San Felipe* – the local railway station. They said farewell to the nuns at the front door, shaking their hands and thanking them for their kindness. Mother Caterina gave their guests, for that's what they had been, a small embroidered cloth edged in white lace. It read *'May the Lord always keep you'*. Nothing more, nothing less. The letters were royal blue in colour, and a crucifix was neatly stitched in the middle at the top. The gardener appeared with the minibus and David and Hazel got in the back seat. They were praying that he was not related to any South American racing drivers as they set off along the dusty road. David and Hazel looked out of the back window of the vehicle expecting to see the nuns, but there was no one there.

Within five minutes the gardener was helping them out of the side door of the minibus, parked within a few metres of the south-side platform. He pointed to the ticket office and then at his watch. He held up three fingers to indicate that the train was due to leave at three o'clock. He had said very little on their journey, perhaps out of respect. David went to purchase two tickets to Santiago and Hazel had a quick word with the gardener to thank him for the lift.

"Mother Caterina is a wonderful person", said Hazel, "and so young to be in charge".

"She do very well for woman of seventy two years of age", he replied in broken English. He turned away, and with that he was gone.

"Come on, Nutty", shouted David from the platform, "I can hear the train coming". They sat down on slatted bench seats in the second carriage. "How old do you think Mother Caterina is?", asked Hazel.

"Oh, she'll be almost thirty years old, I would think", he responded looking out of the window at the snows on the Andes resembling a giant knickerbocker glory ice cream. "Yes, she must be about that," Hazel lied. What an incredible lady. What a privilege to be in her presence, albeit only for a short time. The engine driver sounded a shrill whistle as the train slowly chugged away, and Hazel looked down at the embroidery she was holding.

She didn't want to talk for a while. She just wanted to absorb what the day had given to them. It had given them such a lot.

PART THREE

Chapter 1

The rest of the holiday went by in somewhat of a blur. David and Hazel enjoyed several excursions that were part of the package deal, and particularly liked the Lake District part of Chile. Her hills, lakes and beautiful views over wide vistas were made for photography. Clear blue skies were sometimes dotted with a few cumulus clouds and generally the weather was excellent. They decided they loved this country but weren't sure if they'd ever return. One evening they saw Amelia Harcourt in the hotel lounge with another couple. The three of them seemed to be chatting amicably. David and Hazel had discussed her comment regarding 'enjoy the nunnery tomorrow' and Hazel decided she would broach this matter with Amelia. Although she had said that she was a psychic, Hazel was intrigued to understand how Amelia actually knew where they were going. Hazel waited until Amelia went to the bar for a drink and then took the opportunity to talk to her. She glided across the lounge floor as though on castors and slightly surprised Amelia who was about to order a drink.

"Hello, Amelia, how are you?"

"I'm fine, thanks, and you?

"Yes, things are going well and we're enjoying Chile. Pardon me for asking, but how did you know we were going to San Felipe?"

"Where? I didn't know exactly *where* you were going. All I sensed when we were talking to each other the other evening, and after I'd touched you by shaking your hand, was that you were going to visit a place associated with 'holy orders'. Either a nunnery or an abbey. I'd read that there are several Roman Catholic places in Chile, and I virtually guessed it was going to be a nunnery. I had no idea where it was. I've always had an ability to pre-guess some situations. When I was young and our home telephone rang, I almost always knew who it was. Once I anticipated a fire breaking out in a neighbours house, and alerted the fire brigade. They told me not to waste their time, but ten minutes later two fire tenders arrived to contain the flames that had enveloped a bedroom. When I took a flight last year I decided to put some important items in my hand luggage for a conference. My suitcase that I'd checked in was misdirected to another destination."

Hazel knew that she was talking to someone who was 'gifted'. Clearly Amelia had this ability to 'sense' things. Perhaps touching Hazel's hand on their first meeting was all that was needed to gain her innate sense of where they were going the following day? Maybe having looked into Hazel's eyes, Amelia was able to read something? "Thank you, Amelia, for being so frank with me. We'll probably see you before we get back on the flight to Heathrow. Bye for now."

Hazel went back over to David who was chatting to a fellow hotel guest about bowls. She sat next to David and put her hand on his knee. The guest, whose name was Tom, was from north London and played bowls for a club in Tottenham. Tom, who was in his fifties, was on his own. He'd lost his wife five years ago to breast cancer but declared he was just getting over it. He loved to travel and was the kind of person who could strike up a conversation with anybody. He had been explaining the origin of the modern day game of bowls, a game invented by the Greeks over two thousand years ago. Although David and

Hazel were sociable and could hold their own in most company, they were not the types to get too close to others on holiday. They had spent most of their time in each others company and they preferred to eat on their own, too. What they hated was getting a full medical history from a stranger when you casually asked them 'how they were'.

David concluded his chat with Tom who decided it was time for bed. "I'm usually tucked up by ten" he said sipping the last of his whiskey and ginger ale. As he walked away he winked at Hazel. "Dont' be late yourselves" he remarked in a cheeky manner and walked off.

"Nice guy," observed David, "and knowledgeable about the history of bowls, too".

"Yes, he seems OK", agreed Hazel, who then went on to share her encounter at the bar with Amelia.

"Blimey, what a person! Do you think she could pick six lottery numbers out for us before we leave?"

"Don't be silly, David!" Hazel was a little annoyed with him and he sensed it.

They had two days before they returned to the UK, and tomorrow there was a trip to a vineyard organised. They hoped that would be a chance to try some carmenere wine.

Chapter 2

The holidaymakers had travelled just over one hundred kilometres west of Santiago during the morning. They arrived at an old building looking as though it had been in the film 'The Magnificent Seven'. All got off the coach and went inside out of the warm sun. It took several seconds for eyes to become accustomed to the dimness of the internal wooden surroundings. They were treated to a visit of the original winery and walked past hundreds of old oak barrels and more up-to-date stainless steel vats Their tour ended up in the sales room. Here a short wine tasting session was going to take place. The master winery owner asked them all to smell the bouquet of the red liquid in their glasses. They did so. He asked for a shout of any aromas anyone had sensed. There were a handful of comments with words such as 'blackberry', 'cherry', 'old leather', 'oak' and 'sherry'.

Thirty visitors to *'Vinos y Licores'* were tasting the hosts' red wines sat on rustic stools on a stone floor. They were surrounded by large dark oak barrels that would hold up to three thousand litres of wine. The host, Senor Antonio Fernandez, nodded in agreement and added a few more such as 'currants', 'plums', and 'cowboy's saddles'! The last raised a chuckle from most of the crowd sipping their drink with a knowledgeable pensive look.

Antonio Fernandez, a short stocky man, was the third generation of his family to run this winery in Chile, and three of his wines had won gold medals at international wine fairs. These clearly showed the small gold medal in the bottom right hand corner of the decorative label and the year it had been awarded. The grapes were grown on ten thousand hectares of prime Chilean soil fed by pure waters from the Andes. He explained how the grapes were cared for and eventually harvested.

"Also, it eez important to look at the inside of ze glass as you swirl the wine gently around ze glass. See 'ow the 'tears' of ze wine slowly fall down the glass wall. If they go slow it eez a good sign that it eez a quality wine." The tears were often referred to as 'lachryma Christi', the tears of Christ. Everyone had a go at swirling – some were better than others! One elderly man spilt his wine onto the stone floor and cursed.

"Do not worry" said Senor Fernandez looking at him, "it is eezy to do unless you practice. The more you practice, the more drunk you get and sometimes the more you spill". Another round of chuckles ensued. The old man blushed and lowered his head. In doing so he noticed that the stone floor appeared to have the consistency of hard blotting paper with deep red blotches. No, he wasn't the first to spill a drop of the *vino tinto* onto this old floor.

"Now we taste the red wine. Slowly sip ze wine, only a little at a time, and let it run around ze inside of your mouth for several seconds. Then swallow and wait to see what you can taste." Again, everyone followed his guidelines. There were gulps, glugs and even gargles for a while. After less than a minute Fernandez smiled and looked around. "Well, what 'ave we found?"

"More blackberries," said one, whilst a wag at the back shouted that he thought he'd maybe chewed on a cowboy's saddle! Fernandez politely agreed with a look that spoke volumes – probably thinking to himself 'what a load of ignorant Eenglish peegs!'

Fernandez went on to explain how the taste of the elements of the wine could vary over time – from the first mouthful to the swallowing of the liquid, and the second glass would taste slightly differently from the first. The peppery aspect of some wines may not be experienced for a few seconds after the initial sip, and the hint of sherry flavours from the aged oak barrels would magically appear even later! The group began to agree, and took the hints and tips of the wine master to heart as they sipped and concentrated on the tastes – some even closing their eyes as if in prayer. A lot of positive, gentle grunts indicated that most were getting a better understanding of what wine tasting could really mean. Once in the blood stream, the 12% or 13% alcohol content made its way slowly to the brain via the cranial arteries and had a pleasing, calming, almost nostalgic effect on one's personality. At least for moderate wine drinkers. David and Hazel exchanged approving glances as they put their glasses to their lips every few seconds.

"This makes a lot of sense now", observed David. "No more glugging mouthfuls of merlot or cabernet sauvignon for me!" Fernandez went on to get the visitors to try three more red wines from his estate, one of which was a carmenere that had won gold at the San Francisco wine festival several years before. Of course, one objective in all this was for the thirty visitors to be persuaded to buy a few bottles each. Most took the opportunity to select a couple of bottles at a 'discounted' price. The old man who'd helped to improve the intensity of the blotchy stone floor bought four bottles of merlot, whilst several others tried a variety of other types. David and Hazel bought one gold label carmenere that they were going to savour in their hotel room when they got back.

"You can keep ze glasses", shouted Fernandez to his guests, "and remember to enjoy Chilean wines when you get 'ome!"

With that the group made for the door. Unexpectedly, it was raining quite heavily outside. Some ran for the coach but others waited inside the winery. The ground was almost a quagmire and it needed careful steps on the raised paving stones to ensure shoes weren't to become full of dirty water. Those that remained inside were treated to a small glass of port that *'Vinos y Licores'* also sold. However, a honk on the coach horn meant that it was time to leave. The rest ran to the waiting vehicle as quickly as possible, one poor lady tripping over a stone and falling flat on her face! One or two who saw it happen had a little laugh, wondering if she had drunk too much wine? Thankfully two men went to her assistance and carefully lifted her up. One of those was Tom.

"At least there are some gentlemen still around!", she said starchily, but thanking the two who had helped her. She swept as much water off her dress as she could, even wringing out the hem. She got onto the coach and sat down as quickly as possible, feeling suitably embarrased. Tom spotted David and gave him a 'look' with a little hand gesture that mimicked drinking with fingers and thumb slightly opposed. David nodded briefly, hoping the 'wet lady' would not see them.

"You men!" whispered Hazel, "you can be so cruel sometimes". With that the coach pulled away with Senor Fernandez waving at them from his large door, almost seeming to be slapping his wallet in his back pocket and thinking 'thank you for your contribution to my wine funds!' They had enjoyed it, though, and it was well worth the visit.

On the way back they stopped for lunch at an 'up-market cantina' come bistro. A large rectangular table had been reserved for the tourists and once everyone was seated and the simple menu consulted, the waiter came round taking orders for lunch. The wine was complimentary – red or white – and everyone had the red! Before the food came, each and every individual smelt the bouquet, looked at the 'lachryma Christi' and gently sipped the wine. The waiter looked on from a distance, speechless! How had thirty experts suddenly arrived at his cantina? When the second lot of bottles were placed on the tables about twenty minutes later Hazel noticed that they were a different wine. Needless to say the tears of Christ ran down the inside of the glass much more slowly. After a selection of fish, salami and chicken dishes, accompanied by bread and salads, everyone was adequately refreshed. Toilets were visited, and hands washed by most, prior to getting onto the coach for the return journey to the hotel. On the way back Hazel could not help but think about Pedro at the nunnery. She and David travelled in silence. He sensed she was thinking about their visit to San Felipe.

Although interesting, their trip to the winery paled into insignificance when she thought about the work of Mother Caterina and the nuns. She dozed a bit on the way back and thought she heard voices in her head... a sudden jolt brought her back from her semi-conscious state.

"We're back," David said gently as he squeezed her hand. He noticed Hazel had tears in her eyes. Neither of them felt like opening the carmenere wine, and as they had not reached their maximum baggage allowance they felt it may as well go into one of the suitcases and back to Godalming.

It wouldn't taste as nice in Chalk Road, though.

Chapter 3

Their last day was spent visiting a part of Chile just south of Santiago. The hills were not so high, and were lush and green. Several small lakes were dotted around and one or two were quite close to the road. Some had a small bar and restaurant by the roadside with parking spaces for cars and buses. As several coaches stopped at these places there were also souvenir cabins that sold both cheap and tatty items such as chalk fridge magnets, as well as more decent souvenirs like wooden carvings and hand made woollens. David and Hazel decided they would like to take something home to remind them of their holiday, but would select carefully. It certainly was not going to be a chalk fridge magnet

It was nearing eleven o'clock as the coach pulled off the road. The tour manager was not with them today, she had been feeling unwell, so it was left to the coach driver to issue basic instructions with regard to how long they had at each stop. This one was going to be for thirty minutes which gave everyone time to use the toilet, get a coffee and browse the souvenir cabin just a few yards away from the cafe. Hazel looked around at her fellow passengers. She could not see Amelia or Tom, and at this late stage of their trip she decided that it was a bit late for making friends. She certainly did not want to add to this year's Christmas card list.

The toilets left a little to be desired, but the water was hot and the liquid soap ample. The hot air hand drier also worked!

David ordered two milky coffees at the counter as Hazel found a table with two chairs. As they hadn't had much breakfast that morning, David took a risk and picked up two sweetmeats, a sort of croissant made with sultanas and custard inside and a chocolate glaze at one end. When he got to the table Hazel gazed at the 'treats', felt a guilty pang for a few milliseconds, and then grabbed the nearest one to her. She bit into it holding a napkin under her chin as the thick, sweet yellow custard oozed out and gave her a temporary moustache. David laughed and got his camera out quickly but Hazel wiped her mouth before he could take the 'shot of the holiday'!

"You swine!", she said affectionately. She knew he would often try to get a picture of her in a compromising position.

"Too late", he grinned, as he too picked the pastry up with one hand and bit off the chocolate end. His plan was simple, suck out the custard slowly and then finish eating the whole thing without wasting a crumb. He didn't manage it. Half of the pastry fell on the floor and a dog had the remains in its mouth before you could say 'cabernet sauvignon'! Hazel yelled with delight as others looked around at the slight commotion they had caused. Most saw the funny side of the whole event but the waiter didn't seem too chuffed. He'd have to mop the floor where the dog had missed some of the croissant contents!

They finished their coffee, and although Hazel had offered David a small bite of her pastry he did the gentlemanly thing and declined.

There were ten minutes before departure so they both had a walk outside. An old rustic cart passed by on the road, pulled by a donkey that looked ready for the knackers yard. It was being driven by an old man who had a long grey beard and a large black hat. The speed was no more than walking pace and it gave David an opportunity to take three photos as it went by.

A few minutes later the old man stopped the cart, put the reins around a handle and alighted. He walked back towards David who was reviewing the pictures on his camera screen.

"Senor, donde es denero para mi?" (Sir, where is my money?") His black hat was held in both hands as he looked up at David with big dark, pleading eyes. Hazel quickly explained that nothing comes free, even on a quiet road in Chile. David reached into his pocket and gave the old man 500 pesos. His dark eyes smiled as he winked at David. He bit on the coin to check it was genuine and put it into his waistcoat pocket. 'Blimey', thought David to himself, 'I've never seen anyone do that before'.

The old man got back onto his cart and within minutes was pulling around a corner down the road. A good bargain had been struck – three decent photos for little money – and both parties were happy at that moment in time. Maybe they were good enough to exhibit back home? David's reminiscing was halted when the coach driver shouted to the group that it was time to get on board for the next stage of the excursion. It was very likely going to be a lunch stop, and then back to the hotel by mid afternoon for everyone to start, or finish, their packing. The diesel engine gently burst into life as everyone settled back in their seats. It didn't seem that anyone had bought a souvenir, although one man in front of them was wearing a felt hat with a feather in it!

David and Hazel wondered if he'd looked in a mirror before buying it?

Chapter 4

At just before one o'clock the coach came to a halt outside a hotel in a small town called *Gata de Gargas*. Everyone got off within five minutes and the loos were visited yet again for a wash and brush up before a light lunch. The restaurant were clearly expecting the group and a long table was set out for the party. The manager of the restaurant soon got round asking for orders from the *menu del dia* (menu of the day). There was a good selection of starters and the main course was either lamb or pork. David chose sardines to begin, followed by the lamb. Hazel had the same meat but ordered ham and melon to start. Others soon placed their orders and the table quickly filled with red and white wine bottles and everyone was expected to pour their own. The hotel was a little rough and ready but Hazel noticed the napkins were made of yellow cotton and not paper. After picking up a leg of lamb, which they sometimes did, you were better off with a substantial napkin rather than getting hundreds of tiny bits of tissue paper stuck all over your fingers!

As everbody was sat on either side of a long table it was inevitable that you'd be sat next to someone else, unless you were right at the end. David had a pleasant retired man next to him. His name was Bob and he had been an RAF pilot – his large moustache giving the game away before they had exchanged pleasantries. They chatted together for most of the meal and got on well together, with Bob originating from Margate. Hazel was sat next to a middle aged lady called Dorothy who seemed to do most of the talking. Dorothy came from Yorkshire and was rather brusque. Almost from the start of the conversation she told Hazel that she was an atheist – not only that, but she never stopped talking, only drawing breath every few minutes. Hazel bit her tongue and felt she didn't want to get into a long, drawn discussion about Christianity.

"It's all made up, you know. Jesus may have existed, but those parts of the Bible where he performs miracles are not true. He was probably a magician of sorts and created illusions. And as far as the Christmas story goes, well, he wasn't born in a stable at all, there's no mention of a donkey in the Bible and goodness knows how many wise men there were!" said Dorothy. At that point Hazel didn't want to hear anymore and excused herself to go to the toilet. David looked across at Dorothy, aware that Hazel had got up and left somewhat flustered. With lunch finished, it was a relief that the coach driver herded the diners back onto the coach. Although the food was adequate, Hazel left the restaurant feeling a little upset over her conversation with the Yorkshire woman. When David asked if she was OK, she simply replied 'yes' and left it at that. David decided not to pursue matters.

The rest of the journey took them over two mountain passes and back down to the green pastures and towards Santiago. The driver told them that they could expect to be back at their hotel by mid afternoon. Gentle South American pipes of pan music drifted out of the speakers of the sound system and quite a number of passengers closed their eyed and drifted off to sleep. 'Often the sign of a good lunch', thought David to himself. They arrived back at their hotel just after four o'clock and David shouted 'cheerio' to Bob as they alighted from the coach. As they had not bought any souvenirs so far, they decided to visit the shop in their hotel. The quality of the merchandise was above average – no chalk fridge magnets – and they spent some time searching for that one item that would remind them of their lovely holiday. Suddenly Hazel shouted "David, look!" An original oil painting of the nunnery at San Felipe was right there! It was about thirty centimetres wide and twenty centimetres deep and in a beautiful frame.

"We must have it!", Hazel exclaimed, picking the painting up and taking a long look at it. "I agree!", replied David.

The painting was by a little known Chilean artist called Fernando Larca. It showed the nunnery as they had remembered it, with its white stone walls and large wooden door – all under an azure blue sky. It was perfect. David got his wallet out, chose the correct credit card and bought it there and then. Hazel purred like a kitten as the assistant carefully wrapped it, first in bubble wrap and then in a simple patterned blue and white paper. She even tied it with a thin ribbon and curled the ends with a small knife. Spot on!

"Come on, Hazel, we need to finish the packing and get that painting into the luggage between some clothes to protect it!" With that they went up to their room in the lift to complete filling the two suitcases. A bus was taking them to the airport at eight o'clock in the morning and they decided on an early night as they both felt weary. After a light dinner they made their way back to their room, watched some TV for a short while and were soon in the 'land of nod'. David dreamt of cardiovascular product market shares and Hazel found herself back at the front door of the nunnery…

Chapter 5

The transfer bus was on time and eleven tourists got on for the short trip to the airport. Hazel noticed Amelia was sat near the front and Tom was also a passenger. The other seven were an assortment of fellow holiday makers that David and Hazel had seen coming and going during the fortnight that they were in Chile. The driver ensured all suitcases were loaded into the luggage compartment underneath the bus as some passengers, who still seemed tired, laid their heads back. Soon the bus pulled into the appropriate parking slot at the airport on the outskirts of Santiago.

"Aqui esta el aeropuerto AMB" ('here we are at the AMB airport') announced the driver through the microphone. The front passenger door opened with a gentle hiss that sounded like a tyre deflating. The driver jumped out and opened the hatch to expose the luggage – an assortment of expensive and cheaper looking cases. David and Hazel recognised their mid green coloured suitcases with luminous address tags. David had put their home address on the labels the previous evening, along with the flight details. They had never lost any luggage and clearly were hoping this wasn't going to be a first. As the driver pulled the luggage out David got a one thousand peso note from his wallet ready to tip him.

"Let's hope the flight's on time, David" said Tom coming up behind them. "I'm ready for off and getting back into my routine. If I don't see you again on the flight, enjoy the trip and easy on the vino!" David and Hazel reciprocated, and Tom made off with his small suitcase towards the large departures sign. The couple soon followed as they got their cases and David slipped the paper money into the driver's hand.

"Muchas gracias, senor", the driver acknowleged the tip and winked at Hazel. She smiled at him, more out of courtesy than any sense of fancying the driver. His toothless grin and early morning stubble didn't do much for Hazel at that time of day. In fact it wouldn't have done much for her at any time of day. They found check in desk 23 for the British Airways flight to London Heathrow. It was just two hours before take off so that gave them time to get rid of the suitcases and find a cafe for a hot drink. They passed a newsagents in the shopping mall of the airport and David perused the newspapers. He fancied *'The Daily Telegraph'* to look at the latest British news and have a go at the crossword but when he saw the price he decided against it. He hoped that BA would do the decent thing and provide newspapers on board. They had a coffee at a Starbucks coffee house. Hazel indicated to David that Starbucks probably had a cafe on the moon somewhere, they seemed to be so ubiquitous. In another five years the brand would very likely join Marlborough, Coca Cola and Budweiser as the best known brands on the planet.

David could see the departures monitor from their table. The Heathrow flight came up and showed gate 5 as their next destination in the airport building. They finished their *cafe con leche* and wheeled their hand luggage along a wide walkway towards the gate. Passengers gathered and sat where they could. It seemed busy and David estimated this flight would be at least two thirds full. With passports and boarding cards at the ready they then joined the queue as the announcement came up regarding boarding by seat numbers. David and Hazel were in row 12 on the starboard side with a window seat. Hazel always liked to look out of the window on take-off to see what landmarks she might spot. The usual pre take-off routine was performed by the cabin crew, with most passengers paying attention. As often happens there was a continual hum of discussion coming from a few seats behind them as those who obviously knew the complete evacuation procedure in the event of landing in the sea fiddled with their Walkman sets. David was tempted to shout out 'shut up' but resisted.

For fun, they guessed the first name of the pilot. They remembered that on a flight to Barbados three years previously they were both wrong when they thought it would be 'Tobias Wilcock' made famous in the song "We're going to Barbados."

"I think he'll be a Martin" said Hazel. "Never", replied David, "more likely to be a Roger". The cabin crew dispensed with their life jackets and models of seat belts and buckles and began busying themselves in preparation for serving drinks and nibbles before the meal. Within a few minutes of take off, the captain's smooth voice filled the aircraft.

"Ladies and gentlemen, welcome on board this British Airways flight to London Heathrow. My name is Captain Miguel Sanchez. We shall be flying at a ground speed of just over five hundred miles per hour, or if you prefer, eight hundred kilometres per hour. The flight data will be shown on the screens in front of you throughout the flight. Now sit back, relax and enjoy the comfort of British Airways. Thank you".

"Well, blow me", said David, "he's a local lad!"

"Doesn't sound like it", replied Hazel, "he could be from Surrey!"

The Boeing aircraft banked left and increased in height. Hazel looked down at the ever smaller buildings and natural features. Suddenly, she grabbed David's sleeve. "Look down there! Look,

look!" Hazel's eyes were wide open as she thought she saw the nunnery. "That white building there!", she pointed with her left index finger to a building in the distance. David leaned over to see what the excitement was about, but by the time he'd leant across Hazel's lap, the wing of the aircraft obscured his view.

"It was, it was!", she blurted out excitedly. "Yes, you could be right, Nutty", David gently answered. He honestly didn't know from his knowledge of the geography of the land and the direction of the Boeing whether it was a possibility, but he kindly replied, "Yes, I'm sure you were right" and sipped his gin and tonic that had just been served. Hazel looked out of the window at infinity. David said nothing. He sensed that being silent at that time was what was needed. He glanced at Hazel. Her glass of red wine remained untouched as a tear slipped down her cheek.

"Are you OK, Nutty?" David whispered into her ear. She did not reply. She was deep in thought – very deep in thought. David left it at that. He knew when she wanted some peace, and it was right now. The rest of the flight was pretty much as the outbound journey – drinks, peanuts, the main meal with wine and coffee, followed by sleep if possible. The choice of DVD was limited. David chose 'The Iron Lady' with Meryl Streep, while Hazel opted for a Miss Marple 'whodunnit' film. She wasn't really in the mood for watching much as her thoughts once again turned to Mother Caterina and San Felipe. Those coal black eyes of Pedro were looking at her yet again. When the cabin lights were eventually dimmed the general noise and hubbub died down as passengers made themselves as comfortable as possible. Thin woven blankets were used by some to cover themselves, but others just reclined their seats and dozed off. The two passengers in row 12, starboard side, dropped off to sleep minutes after their DVD's had come to an end. Their trays had been cleared of cutlery and glasses so they stowed them in the upright position. The drone of the jet engines behind them helped them to drift away into dreamland.

Hours later David woke up first. He looked at the large screen on the division wall a few rows in front of them. The outside temperature was minus 40 C. David saw that they were only two hours and eight minutes to landing. Other passengers began to move and stretch. The trip to the toilets began and David decided he needed to freshen up. He joined a short queue at the nearest facility and had soon washed his hands and face. He felt better for that, although his electric razor would have been his best friend at that moment in time. The toothbrush and minute tube of toothpaste provided by BA helped freshen his mouth, whilst a dab of cologne, also courtesy of the airline, made him feel 'manly'. He gently woke Hazel by tugging on her sleeve. She was fast asleep, but David knew she'd appreciate it. He kissed her on the cheek.

Captain Sanchez announced the details of the landing in London. The aircraft speed decreased and the outside temperature began to rise as the Boeing flew over southern Ireland to approach Heathrow from the west. Soon the gentle clunk of the wheels was heard as they dropped into their landing position. The engine tone changed slightly as Captain Sanchez, or his on-board computer, put the finishing touches to a perfect landing on a dull, grey day in the capital. As the Boeing came to a stop at the terminal, drizzle swept across the windows. The air temperature was 6 C.

Soon David and Hazel had collected their two suitcases from the second carousel and were walking out towards Customs and Passport Control. David excused himself as he popped into the gents toilet. Suddenly, Hazel felt a hand on her left shoulder. It was Amelia Harcourt. Hazel had not seen her since she'd got off the bus at the airport in Santiago.

"Hello, Hazel. I hope you've had a lovely holiday, I certainly have. Do take care on the way home, and by the way, you realise that this was not meant to be your only visit to Chile? You will love it the next time you go". She turned and walked away.

David came out of the gents and walked over to Hazel. "Nutty, whatever's the matter? You look like you've seen a ghost!" David gripped her arm as she suddenly felt dizzy.

PART FOUR

Chapter 1

Monday morning dawned cold and foggy. 'What a contrast to Santiago', thought David as he got down to the kitchen and put the kettle on.

Hazel wasn't working today and she was still in bed. David took her a cup of coffee.

"You get up when you're ready, Nutty," David said thoughtfully as he placed the mug next to her on the bedside table. "I want to get into the office and see what's been happening, check out how the market shares are doing and I hope all the folks are happy!"

"I've got lots of washing and ironing to do," replied Hazel sleepily. "What do you want for dinner?"

"Oh, a dish from Chile would be fine, with a glass of carmenere."

He was just out of the door, having kissed her lightly on the lips, as a small paperback book hit the door. Hazel's aim wasn't very good as she shouted "You'll be lucky!" They both smiled to themselves as Hazel turned over and David descended the stairs two at a time. He knew she'd work like a Trojan during the day and get all the holiday washing finished and put away. 'Thank goodness for the hot air spindrier' she mused to herself as she got up and put on her dressing gown. She walked to the window and looked out over houses in Chalk Road, shrouded in thick mist, as she stood with her legs against the warm radiator. She finished drinking her coffee that had warmed her up, and got into the shower. She turned the mixer tap on and switched it to hot. Within seconds a cascade of water covered her body. It was beautiful! Hazel thought, 'there is always a sense of relief when you come home – especially when you get into your own shower and use your own shampoo and body wash. The hotel stuff is OK, but it's not the same'. She spent a full ten minutes washing her hair and her whole body. It really felt good! She stepped out of the cubicle and reached for the fluffy white towel. As she was drying her hair the telephone rang. She walked over to the bedside and picked it up. She noticed it was Rosemary's home number on the display.

"Hi, Rosemary! How are you?"

"Hazel, I've got some bad news. Tom Smythe committed suicide while you were away. I didn't want to spoil your holiday by texting you." Hazel sat on the bed. She was stunned. Was she to blame for having told Keith Blandford about Smythe?

"Oh, no! What happened?"

"He hung himself using a long piece of car tow rope. He'd rented a place away from Godalming. We saw it in the local paper. The funeral was private and donations could be sent to the Army Benevolent Fund."

"Why don't you come round for coffee later," suggested Hazel. "We can talk more easily then. Make it around eleven."

Rosemary agreed and hung up. Hazel was still trying to understand why Tom Smythe had taken his own life? She got dressed, made the bed, and got herself downstairs to a pile of washing in the corner of the utility room. This was sorted into lighter items and heavier clothes. She'd have to put the washer on at least twice. This was always the worst part of coming back from holiday – unpacking and doing the laundry followed by the ironing. Hazel closed her mind to everything around her and got on with things. Ken Bruce on Radio 2 helped with the chores as she scuttled around the utility room and the kitchen. She kept thinking about what Rosemary had told her. By the time Ken Bruce had finished his usual 'popmaster' phone-in competition, she had finished the washing and the spindrier was whirring like a jumbo jet engine, only quieter. Hazel put the kettle on as it neared eleven o'clock. She kepy busy until she heard the front doorbell and then went to answer it. Rosemary stood there in a heavy outdoor jacket, her small car parked on the drive. Hazel noticed the vapour of her breath that drifted lazily into the air.

"Hi, come in Rosemary." Hazel shut the front door quietly and ushered Rosemary into the lounge where a gas fire with coal effect gave off a satisfying glow. "Here, give me your jacket and take a seat, I'll make the coffee and be back in a jiffy". Rosemary sat down as Hazel walked into the kitchen and poured the coffee. Cups, saucers and the sugar and cream jug were already on a painted wooden tray with a handle at each end. Within less than one minute Hazel was back carrying the tray. Rosemary sniffled slightly and wiped her nose gently. "I'm sorry, Hazel, I forgot to ask about your holiday. How did it go?"

"Don't worry about that just now, but, yes thanks it was fine. I'll show you the pictures on the laptop when I've had a chance to download them. Now, do you want to tell me more about Tom Smythe?"

"It all came as a shock. Harry was reading our local newspaper just after you had left to go to South America, and he spotted a small article headed 'Local man found dead in garage'. He read it first and then read it out to me. Basically, Tom had thrown the rope over a rafter in a rented garage near where he was paying rent on a two-up, two down. A neighbour hadn't seen him for a couple of days and noticed the garage door was slightly open. He looked in and saw Tom hanging there, his eyes bulging and his tongue sticking out. A stool was laid on its side below his dangling feet."

"How awful! Did he have any family around here?"

"We heard someone had contacted the funeral directors to ask about burial service details but were politely told it was to be a family affair. If you wanted to, a donation could be made to the benevolent fund I mentioned before, cheques to be sent to the undertakers. It sounds a bit mysterious, somehow. Next Sunday at church Keith is going to say a few words about him. I know a few people are upset at the whole affair, including Jean and Mrs. Jones." Hazel remembered that Smythe had been 'helpful' to both of these ladies in the past. "I expect that Keith will be looking for a new verger, then?" suggested Hazel.

"I've heard that James Miles wants to make the appointment himself. The Circuit Minister feels he wants to be directly involved. Maybe he doesn't want a re-occurence, or doesn't fully trust Keith to do it?" Rosemary had finished her coffee, refused a refill, and stood up. "I really must be going, Hazel. I've some shopping to do for Harry's tea. I hope you didn't mind me telling you about Tom like this, but you may not have heard the true news from somebody else. He had his good points and it was a shame when he resigned." Hazel realised at that moment that Rosemary probably didn't know the whole truth about Tom Smythe, or Major Thomas Pilkington-Smythe as he was preferred to be known. Sheila had been the person Hazel had confided in, and Sheila could be discreet when she wanted to be.

"Yes, I'm sure. Let's hope and pray that Godalming church finds someone suitable sooner rather than later."

Rosemary put her jacket on and headed for the front door. "Thanks for the coffee, and the company. See you on Sunday, God willing!" Rosemary got into her car and carefully reversed off the drive. It was still foggy so she put her lights on. In seconds her rear red lights disappeared around the corner. Hazel cleared up and quickly washed the crockery, put the cream jug in the fridge, and listened to the twelve o'clock news on the radio. She emptied the spindrier and put another load in. By the time David was home she'd have got most things sorted out.

'I wonder who we'll get to replace Tom Smythe,' wondered Hazel to herself. To be honest, she didn't really care. She had other things on her mind right now.

Chapter 2

David made his way along the corridor to his office. It was just after half past twelve and he'd bought a sandwich in the company restaurant rather than sit down in the dining room. He closed his door and sat down, unwrapping the cheese and tomato sandwich as he did so. He already had a cup of coffee on his desk that Denise had brought in. The company did not encourage staff to eat at their desks, but it was allowed, especially for senior employees like David. He'd been in two planning meetings regarding the upcoming sales conference, met with his Product Managers for short discussions, and been debriefed by Trevor on some matters concerning loss of market share following a poor quarter's performance in the cardiovascular market for the company.

One problem David now reflected on was that his meetings did not include his senior Product Manager, Mark. He recalled the discussion after Mark's field visit with Clint Jones in Bristol. Somehow Jones had heard that Mark was complaining about the trip to Southmead Hospital and brought the subject up with Roy Whitehead. Jones claimed he was victimised and wanted to take the matter further, after all it wasn't his fault that he'd had problems with locking his car keys in the boot that day. Whitehead, not liked by many in the Marketing department, took the whole affair up with Jenny Bear who was the Human Resources Manager. David had heard from Trevor that Mark had flown off the handle during a three way meeting between himself, Whitehead and Jenny Bear. It hadn't been fully resolved, but Mark resigned on the spot. He was told to clear his desk the same day. That was it, he was gone. David ate his lunch and thought it over. 'Why did he do such an impulsive thing? He was a good Product Manager, going places in the company'. David had Mark's home telephone number and he resolved to call him to see how he was and to offer him a reference if he needed one.

As if that wasn't enough, the meeting with Trevor revealed that their main heart drug had fallen from a 22% market share down to 15%. The Managing Director was very unhappy and had made Trevor aware of just what he thought. He'd suggested that the strategy was wrong, that there was insufficient clinical evidence being used to promote it, and the literature was too comic book style. Trevor had passed all of this onto David. A new competitor in this field, with strong clinical support from the USA and the UK, had grown several percentage points and taken share from. 'Bloody hell', thought David to himself as he finished his coffee. He threw a crust and the wrapping from his sandwich into his waste paper bin, wiped his mouth with a napkin, and got back to his computer screen. He couldn't believe he'd only been away a fortnight. Two key issues were needed to be considered urgently and the sales conference was looming.

David wanted this meeting to start on a positive note and met with Trevor later in the afternoon to suggest how he would tell the sales force about Mark's departure. "We need to replace Mark as soon as possible, Trevor". "Well, I was coming to that", replied Trevor, swivelling his chair and looking out of the window behind him. "The MD has put a hold on recruitment for the time being".

"Your having a joke, aren't you? Turn round and tell me that's not true!" David was annoyed. He knew he was raising his voice. "I'm responsible for a three million pound product with a promotion budget of six hundred thousand pounds and you're telling me I can't recruit another PM for a forty thousand pound salary?"

"OK, OK, calm down!" Trevor turned his black leather chair round to face David and leaned forward on his elbows. "It's a fact – no hiring for at least six months! It's the current financial climate we're in". David stood up. He leant over Trevor's desk, palms firmly down on the polished wooden top. "For goodness sake, Trevor, how are we supposed to keep things going? I've been away two weeks and I come back to this!"

Trevor looked at his computer screen. "I've got things to do, David. See you tomorrow." David bit his tongue. He knew his fuse was getting short at that instant, and he may regret something he might say. He turned to the door and walked towards it thinking 'shall I bang it on the way out?' His brain shouted 'slam it hard', but his heart said 'stay calm and in control'. He went out of Trevor's office fuming. His heart won. In his office, David reflected on the day. He sat down in his chair and laid back. Had he really been in Chile only a few days before, enjoying the climate and the food? It seemed a distant memory now that he was back to reality. Mark's departure, no recruitment, market share down, criticism from the Managing Director, bloody hell – what a day! He looked at the clock on his desk. It was almost five o'clock. 'Sod it', he mused to himself. He grabbed his jacket, put on his overcoat, and went out with his car keys in his hand.

"Denise, I've got an awful headache and I'm going home, I'll see you tomorrow".

"OK, David take care. I'll get that stuff typed for you by ten in the morning."

David left the building. He didn't give a toss about anything being typed. After all, tomorrow would be another day.

Chapter 3

David called into the bowls club on the way home. It was something he rarely did, but he felt like going somewhere to relax for half an hour before getting home. If he got in too early Hazel would ask questions.He wanted time to think about the day and be calm before pulling up on the drive. He parked his car close to the front door of the clubhouse, locked it, and walked into the bar.

"Welcome back, David", said Ted, the barman. Ted had been at the club since Adam was a boy, and if pushed could tell some very interesting stories. He had served behind the bar at many club functions including the annual dinner dances. He was a tee-totaller. Many would say that was unusual in a barman, but Ted only touched soft drinks. His current favourite was lemonade and blackcurrant juice. He said he'd read somewhere that blackcurrant juice was good for the memory, but he couldn't recall where he'd seen it. David smiled when he first heard that tale. He'd told David, in confidence, a few stories of misdemeanours at a dinner dance some ten years previously when one member had turned up with his wife, only to be asked by another members' wife if she was his sister? 'Sister?' said the first wife, 'why do you ask that?'

'Sorry, but another lady in the club had seen your husband having coffee with someone matching your description. When asked who it was he replied that it was his sister as he wasn't married!' The ensuing kerfuffle had delighted some members, with lots of chortles and gentle coughing, but the club chairman was not amused. The couple were asked to leave. David seemed to recall that the gentleman had resigned shortly after. Nobody heard of them again. David ordered an apple drink with ice. He didn't want to risk being stopped for drink-driving, although right then he could have enjoyed a double gin and tonic. He walked over to the corner of the clubhouse and sat down in a red leather wing chair. The club was over one hundred years old and had its standards – including comfortable chairs! He sipped his drink and sank back into the chair. He looked out over two greens, one of which was bathed in floodlights. A few members were just finishing a game that had obviously overrun. The lighting had been installed three years ago following some fund raising that had resulted in securing sufficient funds to pay for them.

'Hell, what a day', David said to himself again. He started to get philosophical, and it wasn't the alcohol. 'Do I really need this? All the hassle, back stabbing and politics? Shit!' He took a gulp of his soft drink. But what would he do if he decided he'd had enough? Right at that moment he didn't know. David finished up and went out into the cold evening air after having said goodnight to Ted. He reminded himself that he really ought to make more time to chat with the barman – there'd be lots more stories to hear from him!

"Hi, Nutty, it's me", he shouted as he entered the hallway. Hazel was upstairs tidyng up a few things and putting some clothes into the airing cupboard.

"Down in a second", she replied. David picked up the daily newspaper and scanned the first few pages. There was little that caught his eye so he folded the paper to take a peek at the sudoku puzzle. Before he could fill in any numbers, Hazel was next to him looking radiant. "Hey, you look good!", exclaimed

David as he took Hazel in his arms and gave her an extra big hug. She kissed him on the lips and then on the forehead. She didn't do that very often so he wondered if everything was OK?

"How has your day been?" he asked. "Well not too bad at all in terms of getting the laundry done as well as a few other jobs, including grocery shopping. But there was something..." she trailed off. "What was that?" enquired David.

"Well, Rosemary came round with some bad news this morning. Tom Smythe committed suicide while we were away on holiday. He was found hanging from a rafter in a garage. Apparently he'd left a note for the vicar which was found in his trouser pocket. It's all so sad."

"That sounds awful. I suppose the church will be looking for a replacement, then?"

"Yes, they will. Do you fancy the job?" Hazel said teasingly. Just for a split second David was tempted to say 'yes'.

"Who me – I don't even attend church!"

"You could start! Anyway, what about your first day back in the office?"

"Lousy, absolutely lousy. I've come home without my briefcase since I don't intend doing any work tonight." Hazel knew that was not like David. Often when they returned from a trip away he'd be catching up with reports and reading medical or marketing journals. She'd noticed he hadn't even opened his Institute of Marketing magazine. This was the catalyst for both of them to have a quiet relaxing evening at home and maybe watch a DVD together with a glass of Chilean red.

"Do you want to talk about it? If not I'll understand."

"Oh, it was just that Mark has left, I can't recruit a replacement, the market shares are down and the MD doesn't think I've got the strategy right for our main brand – we need more clinical evidence. Apart from that, it was a damned good day!" Hazel took him in her arms and kissed him again. Her hug lasted for almost a minute. She didn't speak. Eventually she said, "You should do what you think is right. Sod the lot of them! Let me get you a drink". With that Hazel poured a large gin and tonic for David and a glass of merlot for herself. A delicious smell came from the kitchen where Hazel, despite her hectic schedule, had found time to put some steak, beef stock, potatoes and winter vegetables into the slow cooker. It was cooked to perfection. She knew that it was sometimes better to let David have his thoughts to himself for a while, but she would give him that look that said 'I'm right here if you want to talk to me'. They both had that sense of knowing when it was best to keep quiet. After watching some news and weather on early evening television they sat down to eat. Hazel lit a small, vanilla scented candle and placed it in the centre of the table. She asked David to open a bottle of red wine that was in the rack beneath one of the cupboards in the kitchen. He saw it was the bottle of carmenere from Chile! That would do nicely. He also spotted three other reds.

"Where did you get this from?"

"I did my shopping this afternoon and couldn't believe my eyes when I saw the main wine offer this week was three reds from South America!" David and Hazel chatted over dinner about a range of items, from their holiday to friends to going to the theatre again. Hazel mentioned church a couple of times, and an upcoming coffee morning with sale of bric a brac to raise some funds for the church. A drainpipe had come away in high winds and some guttering needed repair. By the time they'd had a small tiramisu for dessert and finished the bottle of wine, neither of them felt like watching television or a DVD. Hazel put the plates and cutlery in the dishwasher. They decided on an early night.

"Why don't you come to church on Sunday with me?" David was taken slightly by surprise at the question. "You never know, you might even enjoy it?" He finished brushing his teeth in the bathroom and dried his face. He walked into the bedroom where Hazel was already under the covers holding her paperback book, still closed. He'd been reflecting on Hazel's question of four minutes ago. "You know, Nutty, I think I will!" He smiled at her. "I love you so much".

"I love you, too", replied Hazel. They kissed once more before the lights were put out. Touching each others bare flesh hadn't felt so good in a long time.

Before he fell asleep, David remembered he hadn't phoned Mark. He would do it from the office tomorrow.

Chapter 4

The next few weeks went by quickly for both of them. Hazel got back into the routine of working part time at the local junior school and her church work while David spent time re-thinking the cardiovascular business. He had proposed to Trevor that he would prepare a revised marketing plan. Although the sales conference was rapidly approaching, David was able to work on his report and get prepared for the sales meeting to be held at the Marriott hotel just a few miles from Guildford. Good, clear delivery was important for the presentations, as well as dress code. A dark suit, white shirt and sensible tie, along with black socks and shoes, were considered to be the right thing to wear. As it turned out, the sales conference went well. Some aspects of David's revised plan were included, and the decibel level of the applause from the sales force was a good indicator that it had been well received.

Meanwhile, Hazel was busy in Godalming. She'd met with Gertrude, Margaret and Di over coffee to discuss some fund raising initiatives for the church. They had plans to collect items for the bric a brac sale and for the raffle. The event was to be held in the church and permission had been sought to have the central heating and lights on for four hours, Keith Blandford had been invited, helpers for serving tea and coffee were picked, and volunteers came forward to help with baking. The community spirit in Godalming church was excellent, and despite some politics, all seemed to go well from week to week. The main topic of conversation was the new verger, but no one seemed to want to talk too loudly about the matter. It seemed best to wait until Keith and the Chair of the District, James Miles, had interviewed the final three applicants. An announcement would be made in due course, they were sure.

At the following Sunday service, which David attended, the Reverend Keith Blandford told the congregation that a woman called Elaine Spriggs had been appointed to the post of verger. Elaine was a slight woman weighing no more than about six stones, with spectacles and hair neatly tied back in a bun. She was in her mid fifties and a spinster. She'd got an MA from Cambridge in Divinity and had taught at Ladies Cheltenham College, amongst other things. She seemed the ideal person or the job. She looked tough and tenacious and seemed like an achiever. Time would tell. Hazel managed to have a chat with her at the end of the service. "How did you hear of the job here?" "Well, my dear," replied Elaine, pushing her spectacles further up her little sharp nose, "I was online looking at some religious material when I saw a link to church matters in Surrey. I clicked on the link and it took me to your church web site, where the post was advertised. I applied and hey, presto, I'm here!" Her little blue eyes lit up. Hazel liked the sound of Elaine, and saw the keeness in her eyes as she explained how she saw the job going. Hazel assumed that she had interviewed well.

David was talking to a number of people after the service, including Keith Blandford, and explaining why he hadn't been a regular churchgoer before. "I've never been totally certain of the existence of God, but I'm coming round to thinking that there must be a God, otherwise everything we see and feel wouldn't be here. I'm quite prepared to give it a go over the coming weeks and months." Perhaps this wasn't quite the answer that Keith wanted or expected. 'But we all have to start somewhere with religion' Keith thought to himself. For some it's the flash of lightning and vision of a bearded figure in white robes. For others it slowly creeps up on them over time and eventually they're happy to go along with the Bible. The Bible is a sort of history book. It contains a chronological listing in the 66 books of what happened both before and after the birth of a man called Jesus Christ. God's message is covered in the Old Testament, with people like Moses sharing the word of God. Jesus Christ was born in Bethlehem, performed some miracles and died around the age of 33, crucified on a wooden tree or cross by the Romans.

David could go along with this. After all there were millions of Christians on the planet – they couldn't all be wrong, could they? David struggled a bit with his concept of heaven. Did all Christians go to heaven when they died? Would you see all of those who you had known on earth? How busy was it? What did you do all the time? Nobody had come back from death to reveal just what heaven was like. He'd read somewhere that the image of walking towards a bright light and feeling as though you were floating was nonsense – it was all connected to some neurological activity in the brain with cells firing off all over the place? And what was hell? Fire and damnation down below?

Somebody had mentioned the 'power of prayer' to David, and given examples of how prayer had worked for them. He decided on that Sunday morning that he would give church a chance, to see if it 'would rub off on him' as he put it to himself. Although he and Hazel had an old Bible at home, he was going to buy the new international version that he had heard about. Yes, he was going to give it a go.

"Time to go, David", Hazel said as she came up to him having helped with the washing up of cups and saucers. "OK, ready when you are," he replied. They gathered their coats from the coatpegs at the back of the church and wandered outside. They had booked a table at a nearby restaurant for their Sunday carvery. It was a monthly treat for both of them. Although they were careful about calorie consumption, they had decided that an occasional roast potato and piece of beef or pork wasn't going to hurt them. They took twenty minutes to get to their destination after first calling at an ATM to withdraw some cash. The staff knew David and Hazel, and they were ushered to a table near the front window. After sitting down and ordering drinks, Hazel noticed that Keith Blandford was sitting at the back of the dining room.

He was sitting with Elaine Spriggs. She was crying.

Chapter 5

Hazel's return to school during the week went reasonably well except that there had been a problem with one of the teachers. Harry Manning had taught the six year olds at the school for three years. He got on well with the other staff members, although a few thought him a bit odd. He was married, but he and his wife took seperate holidays, and were rarely seen out together. He had slicked black hair, parted in the middle, just perfect for a hair gel advert. One of the girls had told her mother that Mr. Manning had touched her on her legs and tugged at her knickers. Mr. Manning had told the girl, whose name was Lucy Watts, that it was their secret and she was not to tell anyone. Lucy had gone home one day and became upset about not doing well in an arithmetic test. She burst into tears and blurted out that if she had let Mr. Manning touch her a bit more she might have got better marks in the test. Her mother, Ann, questioned her before her father came home and managed to get the full story out of Lucy. All this, of course, was the talk of the administration office at Godalming junior school. "I never liked that man", said Jennifer, one of the assistants, "he always had a strange look in his shifty eyes".

Ann Watts had telephoned the school to make an appointment to see the headmaster. The head, William Craddock, had made himself available immediately and met with Ann Watts the same day. Craddock invited his secretary to join them in the meeting in his office. Lucy was still being taught during the discussion about Manning, but when Craddock heard what Ann Watts had to say, Lucy was removed straightaway. She had gone home with her mother within one hour of the meeting.

Craddock briefly discussed the whole issue with his secretary and decided to contact the police. It was then mid afternoon and school would be finishing in half an hour. Craddock telephoned Guildford Central police station himself and spoke with the duty Sergeant. The police duly arrived in an unmarked car and were ushered into Craddock's office by his secretary. The two police officers sat down, refusing coffee that had been offered. "Start at the beginning", said one, "take your time and let us have the facts about the situation." Craddock related to them what Lucy's mum had said, keeping the details factual. Craddock said that Manning was well qualified and always punctual and reliable. "You can never tell about things like this. Some of the most notorious criminals wouldn't let butter melt!" observed the senior officer. "We'll need his home address. We need to pay him a visit this evening. Please keep this under wraps for now Mr. Craddock. We'll be in touch tomorow. Thank you." With that the two policemen left the school.

"Let's hope they can sort this out quickly. Tomorrow should prove interesting". With that, Craddock picked up his briefcase and lifted his overcoat from the coatstand in the corner. "I'll lock up", said Mary, "and I'll see you in the morning. Don't take it personally, Bill." Craddock had gone out with the worries of the world on his shoulders. The police had paid a visit to Priory Gardens in Godalming the same evening and found Manning alone. His wife was out with friends. After questioning for some time, Manning eventually confessed to 'interfering' with three or four little girls at the school on a regular basis, saying that he couldn't help himself. His laptop computer was taken away by the two officers and found to contain over one thousand images of young girls. So that was that, Manning was tried and sentenced to four years in prison. Lucy had received counselling and seemed to be getting over it, if a little girl like Lucy ever could? Hazel reflected on the incident which made the local papers. 'Why can't life just be normal, why can't people just get along, have a routine?' She thought about Tom Smythe, and of David's problems at work, and Manning resident at Her Majesty's pleasure. Since coming back from Chile a few things had changed in their lives, and not for the better.

She continued at Godalming junior school but somehow became less enthusiastic in her job there. The incident had troubled her and she disliked being drawn into 'tittle tattle' with other staff in the school. When she got home one evening she took the Bible down from the bookcase and began reading some chapters from Mark's gospel. Normally she never did this, but gained some solace beginning from chapter one – 'This is the beginning of the Good News about Jesus Christ, the son of God, as the prophet Isaiah wrote...' She read for half an hour and gently closed the book and then her tired eyes.

The next day David had an appointment in Outpatients at the Royal Surrey County Hospital to see the Urologist about his prostate. His latest blood sample had shown a PSA level slightly above normal. Although he was only 42, David recalled that his father had died from prostate cancer. It eventually turned out that his PSA level had stayed a little above normal, and although the Urologist was somewhat concerned with that, it was suggested that a biopsy should be carried out. The biopsy results showed no evidence of cancerous cells, so David and Hazel could at least get on with their lives for another twelve months before the next check up.

'It never rains but it pours' Hazel mumbled to herself as she busied herself in the kitchen at home and looked heavenwards. 'It seems to be one thing after the other. Please, oh, please look after us. Where is our path in life leading us?' As Hazel was asking the Lord for guidance, the telephone rang. It was Rosemary. "Hi, Hazel. I've just heard that Elaine Spriggs was insulted last Sunday morning, apparently. Someone had suggested that the verger's job should always go to a man. She had got very upset. Keith took her out for lunch to that posh restaurant in town to console her."

"Oh, really? Well let's hope she's OK now, Rosemary. Sorry, but I must fly. Got to phone my sister as she's going away for a month tomorrow. Talk soon. Bye". Hazel just didn't want to talk about Elaine Spriggs right at that moment, nor tell her that she and David had seen the two of them in the restaurant.

Her thoughts were elsewhere. Far, far away in fact.

PART FIVE

Chapter 1

The postman was early for a change. Hazel had seen his red jacket from a distance as she tidied away the breakfast dishes. She and David had enjoyed porridge for breakfast as it had been a cold start to the day. David had wanted to get into the office early, and having forgotten again to phone Mark, thought he'd do it before the business of the day took over. The letter box made its usual metallic snapping sound as John the regular Royal Mail postman dropped a few envelopes through the wide slit. Hazel put the coffee mugs in the cupboard and went to the front door. On the mat lay four items. Two of them were junk mail for car insurance and double glazing. The other two were a telephone bill from BT, and the other one, a brown envelope with Sellotape on the back, had two stamps from Chile in the top right hand corner. It was addressed to Hazel in clear, neat handwriting. She looked at the address for several seconds, trying to work out who may have sent it. Perhaps the hotel had found something they had left in the room? Maybe the Tour Manager in Chile had got some news or information for them – perhaps a refund from a trip? 'Why am I trying to work out who it's from', thought Hazel. 'Just open it for goodness sake'. She pushed a knife under the slit at the top of the envelope and opened it. Inside was a one page letter from Mother Caterina at the San Felipe nunnery. Hazel took the mail and sat down in the lounge. She began to read.

'Dear Hazel,

I hope you do not mind me writing to you. I got your address in England from the hotel where you were staying. I remember you mentioned a nice hotel in Santiago. I asked one of the Sisters here to make some enquiries and she tried three hotels. The hotel where you stayed did not want to give us your full name and address but we persisted and with the help of Father Rodriguez they gave it to us.

The reason for writing is to let you know that since your visit here Pedro has been very unsettled. He talks about you almost all the time. Sometimes I have seen his big dark eyes full of tears. We thought it would pass, but it has not. I have discussed the matter with Father Rodriguez and he suggested I send this letter. I hope you don't mind this.

In the past some of the orphans here have been adopted. It can be a lengthy procedure to make certain everything is OK before any of the children are allowed to leave. They must be checked medically, and the Chilean government will ensure the correct paperwork is in place. I am not stating that Pedro must or should be adopted, that is for you to consider, along with your husband, David. But I do recall you said that you did not have children. I could tell from your eyes that there was a longing in your heart and soul for a child.

I have been praying to God for guidance on the matter but He has not made it clear what should happen. Sometimes we need to seek the deepest part of our hearts, and listen carefully to it.

If you want to have any more information, please write to me at the nunnery. Any correspondence will be treated in the strictest confidence.

Yours in Christ,
Mother Caterina.'

Hazel put the letter down. She lay back in the chair and began to sob. Her sobbing turned to floods of tears as she thought of Pedro. She could picture his little round, smiling face and his black hair, and those dark eyes looking at her! She vividly recalled the visit to the nunnery on that warm day, and how they were both made so welcome. She recounted how the visit had come about – almost as if by fate, she thought to herself. Hazel sat in the lounge for almost an hour, weighing things up in her mind. She asked questions of herself. She went through the current situation in which they found themselves in Godalming. Her situation at school, David and his company problems, their friends. She knew that they both wanted a child. Her sister Maureen had a gorgeous daughter, and they had many friends who spoke of their 'little ones' with much love.

'What am I to do?' Hazel stood up after wiping her eyes. She looked out on Chalk Road, the raindrops running down outside on the double glazing. It may have been impulse, but Hazel decided there and then that she would go to their local church and pray. She tidied her face and put on her make-up. Her large double-layer outdoor jacket would keep her warm. Hazel looked in the hall mirror before going out, pushed her hair up with her fingers, and felt she was presentable. She took three or four deep breaths, opened the front door and put her umbrella up as she set off for church. The large wooden door opened creakily as she turned the iron handle and walked in. A slightly musty smell greeted her nostrils as she made her way down to the front. 'Perhaps the guttering really needs doing soon?' she mused to herself. She went to the front pew of the church on the left hand side near the tea lights and candles. In fact, she decided to light a candle in memory of her parents before sitting down.

'This is for you both. I love and miss you more than words can say'. A lump came to her throat. She had never got over the hot air balloon accident in Australia. The agony of receiving the news, and then the repatriation of their bodies and the funeral service would for ever be on her mind. Hazel sat and looked up at the large wooden crucifix. She was silent for some time. She looked around at the church and its contents, the names of the dead from two world wars on one wall, and the names of those who were interred in the church. She felt safe and secure here. No worries bothered her right now. She felt at peace with herself, as if she could just drift off to sleep...

"Good morning, Hazel!" boomed a voice from the door. She was startled, and turned to see Keith Blandford walking towards her. "What are you doing here?" Hazel had a split second to decide whether to tell Keith the truth, or make something up. She opted for the truth. After all, she knew him and felt she could trust him. She also needed someone to talk to. Hazel spent the next hour telling Keith about their visit to the nunnery. He listened intently as she went into details about the orphanage and their experience there, and also how she felt drawn toward the place. She told him about Pedro and her feelings about adoption. In fact, Hazel surprised herself at how many words flowed out from her mouth. Eventually she finished and felt mentally exhausted. As she sat there looking up at the stained glass window, Keith went and put the kettle on. Tea bags were in a jar and some milk was in the small fridge.

He brought her a mug of tea. "Here", he said, "drink this." Keith Blandford sat down next to her. "You must talk to David, discuss the matter, and follow your instincts. I shall pray for both of you". Sometimes he had a 'matter-of-fact' style about him, but Hazel knew Keith meant well, and he was a good listener. She had certainly needed to talk with someone today.

Hazel finished her drink, got up and rinsed the mug in the small sink. "Thanks for being here for me today, Keith"

"No problems. I felt that I needed to walk through this door this morning." He nodded to the north end of the church. "Jesus works in marvellous and wonderful ways sometimes." He walked away from Hazel and turned to look at her before going out. He patted his heart with an open hand, and was gone.

The rest of the day was a kind of dream for Hazel. She went through a routine of housework, washing and cooking. The evening meal was prepared, and she watched some news on television. David let himself in with his latch key and put his briefcase down in the hall. "Hi, Nutty, it's only me. Any news on anything?" Hazel walked from the kitchen into the hall.

"There is something we should talk about", she replied, kissing him on the lips.

Chapter 2

David couldn't take it all in. Hazel showed him the letter and he read it several times. He stood up and switched the TV off and said to Hazel "What do you think we should do?"

"I've been thinking about the whole situation all day. I went to church to pray for some guidance, and spoke with Keith Blandford about it. He said we should search for the way forward by looking deep into our hearts."

"Let's sleep on it", suggested David. "They say you wake up with a clearer outlook on things if you go to bed with something to think about."

Hazel sat looking at the picture of the nunnery that they had brought back with them. It was hanging on a wall in the lounge. After several minutes of silence between them, David suggested that they could look into the whole matter of adoption and do their homework first. Perhaps see what it entailed, especially as Pedro was in a different country, no, a different continent! How complex might it be? Maybe they could write back to Mother Caterina and ask some pertinent questions. How much did they know of Pedro, for instance? What of his parents? Were they known to the nunnery? Was there a fee involved, or costs associated with taking him out of the country?

David was wearing his Marketing Manager's hat. His logical mind and systematic way of approaching issues meant he was looking at this as a project. Hazel wasn't. She wanted something inside her to shout out! Something to say 'blow all the potential problems, let's do it!' She decided not to share her feelings with David at that moment.

They had dinner and chatted about a few things other than the letter. David had telephoned Mark for a catch up. Mark explained how things happened and felt he'd been made a scapegoat in the situation with the Bristol sales rep. Roy Whitehead didn't like Mark and Mark felt he had it in for him. Human Resources weren't much help and Jenny Bear seemed to take the side of the Sales Department. The bottom line was that the whole affair had soured Mark's taste of the pharma industry and he wasn't going to rush into anything just yet. He was taking a couple of months out to travel around Europe. David had wished him well and offered to provide a reference anytime.

Hazel served out a salmon meal. Two glasses of Chardonnay went well with the fish, and David added a little 'lower your cholesterol' spread to his new potatoes. Hazel told David that she'd telephoned a couple of the girls from the church group and confirmed more aspects of the forthcoming coffee morning. They had agreed on who was going to collect bric a brac, serve the teas and coffees and do some baking. Gertrude would organise some raffle tickets and Rosemary had offered to get a few bags of copper and silver coins from the bank to help with giving change. Margaret also said that she would pitch in and help out, too.

David and Hazel finished their meal with a yoghurt and a cup of coffee. They then sat on the large comfortable sofa in the lounge and put on a classical CD. Hazel curled up at one end, put her feet up and scanned the latest edition of *'Hello'* magazine. She had changed into a burgundy, velour jogging top with matching bottoms. She felt relaxed. David was scanning *'The British Medical Journal'* and catching up on some of the latest medical matters in the NHS. He was also searching for the latest papers on cardiovascular research. After about twenty minutes he dropped it on the floor in favour of the his daily newspaper. It was almost ten o'clock and Hazel had yawned twice in the past ten minutes. The day had taken its toll in terms of stress and her body was showing it. David suggested an early night would do them good. They both had their paperback books waiting on the bedside tables if they could keep their eyes open, or had the inclination to read.

Suddenly the telephone rang. "Who on earth can that be at this time?" said Hazel. "It could be anybody, Nutty, pick it up!"

"Hello?" Hazel tentatively said.

"Sorry to bother you, Hazel, it's Keith Blandford here. I know it's a little late, but after our chat this morning I remembered that a good friend of mine is employed with a child adoption group. I haven't seen him for some years but I have his contact details. Would you be interested in meeting with him – off the record, of course." Hazel looked surprised as she glanced at David. "Yes, that would be useful, Keith. Could you email me his telephone number and address?" Keith confirmed that he would do so immediately and hung up.

"What was that about, Nutty?" Hazel explained the essence of the discussion. "How do you feel about that?" asked David.

"Why not? We have nothing to lose. If you can take a day off work we could suggest a lunch meeting. Let's wait for Keith's email, after all we don't know where he works, do we?" True to his word, Keith had sent the details on Terence Williams within minutes of the call. Hazel was quite excited about the prospect and, although it was getting late, logged onto her emails. She saw the email from Keith. Terence worked in the High Street in Chobham, near Woking. His office number was shown and Hazel wrote it down. She checked on eating places in Chobham and spotted 'The Four Seasons Restaurant'. She would propose that both her and David would meet with Terence at the restaurant, if he was agreeable to the idea. David would take the day off rather than pretend he had a business meeting. In that way he could focus on the meeting and drive both of them there and back. It would also make a change for him to have a weekday with his wife.

The following morning David left for the office as usual. Hazel telephoned the Chobham number just after nine o'clock.

"Hello, Terry Williams speaking." He sounded professional.

"Good morning, Mr. Williams. My name is Hazel Tate and I got your information from the Reverend Keith Blandford who I believe you know?"

"Oh, hello. Yes, Keith contacted me first thing this morning and briefly explained the situation. What would you like to do?"

Hazel kept it brief and then suggested a meeting at lunchtime at 'The Four Seasons' to discuss things. Terry sounded an amenable type, and David and Hazel would pay for his lunch by way of thanks. The following Tuesday was agreed on, and Terry offered to book a table for half past twelve as it was close to his office.

"By the way, do call me Terry. Mr. Williams sounds too formal. Can I call you Hazel?" She agreed.

Hazel marked the calendar on the kitchen wall with the date and time. She was looking forward to it. All she had to do now was do some thinking, and make a list of questions. She made sure she kept a notebook handy at all times.

She thought about her first question...'will my heart speak to me?'

Chapter 3

David and Hazel parked up in the multistorey car park just off the High Street in Chobham. It was nearly a quarter past twelve and they had timed things right. Once they had put the BMW between two white lines on the third floor of the parking block and walked out of the grey concrete pile it was a short walk along to the restaurant. They walked in and indicated to the manager that a table had been booked by a Mr. Williams. "This way," said the small Italian waiter with a large black moustache, "he is waiting in the back of the restaurant for you." They were led to a table set for three people where Terry Williams was sat sipping a tonic water. He stood up as the couple approached.

"You must be Hazel and David?" said Terry, "do sit down. Can I get you a drink?" He pointed to the chair next to him as he looked at Hazel, placing a business card on the table in front of her. They both sat down and ordered a large bottle of Evian water and two glasses. Terry Williams was well dressed, wearing a dark suit, with a light blue shirt and matching tie. His cufflinks caught the sun, as did his Rolex watch. He was aged about fifty and was not wearing a wedding ring. Hazel quickly decided that he seemed a trustworthy type.

"Let's browse the menu, order, and then we can chat," he suggested, taking matters in hand. Hazel liked his air of authority. The waiter jotted down their requirements. All ordered a small starter followed by a simple main course. Both came with a side salad. When the waiter went away Terry Williams kicked off the conversation. He looked first at David and then at Hazel. "Hazel, why don't you start. Tell me about your situation and your trip to Chile." His eyes were firmly focused on Hazel and showed compassion.

Hazel began with a short explanation of their inability to have children. She told him of their trip to South America, the visit to the nunnery and what had happened. She brought out the letter and showed it to Terry. He read it carefully. During their starters he talked about the basics of adoption, referring to UK law and the situation in England. Fundamentally, any governing authority would need to be convinced that prospective parents were suitable for adopting a child. Dependant on the age of the child, they would also need to ensure that the child was suited to the couple who had filed for adoption. In other words, complete compatibilty was sought.

Terry explained that a medical examination may be needed for both the child and the parents. All avenues would be explored with regard to any diseases or hidden blood dyscrasias, and most importantly, the parents would need to be deemed mentally and psychologically fit for being parents to an adopted child. Hazel and David listened to every word, interrupting ocassionally to ask questions or make a point. They talked as they ate, and David noted down a few points on a note pad he carried in his jacket pocket. Terry was careful to point out that some aspects of adoption may be quite different in Chile. The government there might have a different viewpoint on their own children being taken out of the country.

Once the mains plates were sided away, coffee was ordered. "If I was you I'd think this through and write to the nunnery with some key questions. There may be some information you could get from the internet?" After another twenty minutes of discussion, David asked for the bill. When it came he told Terry to put his wallet away – the lunch was on them. "Thanks very much, I hope I've been of some help. Don't hesitate to contact me if you think I can be of any more assistance. Give Keith my best wishes when you see him." Terry glanced at his watch. "Must be off, I've got a meeting in half an hour. Good luck!" With that he was striding out of the restaurant and then gone. David and Hazel walked out of the restaurant, each sucking a complimentary mint.

The couple walked back to the car park, hand in hand, thinking but not speaking. They got into the car. It was a few seconds before David brought the engine to life, they fastened their seat belts, and the car smoothly pulled away from the parking bay. "How do you feel, Nutty?"

"Numb", she responded. "There seems to be so much to consider."

"I know", he acknowledged. They slowly drove back to Godalming. They said very little. It was mid afternoon but beginning to get dusk as light rain began to fall. The leaden skies resulted in the auto car lights coming on. Hazel didn't feel like cooking and she thought about making a telephone call to their favourite pizza house. "Do you fancy an Hawaiian special tonight?"

"Sounds good to me!" Hazel didn't feel hungry but she knew he liked a pizza now and again so it would be a treat in a way. They pulled up on the drive in Chalk Road. The drizzle was getting heavier but they managed to get inside the front door fairly quickly, mopping rain drops off their coats as they firmly closed the door. David switched on a couple of small lamps in the lounge and the place seemed homely as the central heating clicked on. A red light was flashing on the telephone hub on the sideboard. "There's a message on the 'phone, Nutty. I'll get it".

David put the 'listen' control to the 'on' position. "Hello, Hazel, this is Bill Craddock. I'm sorry to have to tell you like this but the school governors have been reviewing staff and costing levels here at the school. We're having to let you go, I'm afraid. When you come in tomorrow, can you clear your desk as soon as possible. Give me a call before you leave school. Bye."

Hazel was dumbfounded. Dismissed with a telephone message! She sank down on the sofa. She was speechless. How could the headmaster, who she respected and worked for, given her such news over the 'phone? She thought about anything that was personal to her that may be in, or on, her desk? A letter opener from Spain and a paperweight from Canada – both gifts from friends. Nothing else. So, no point in going in then, was there? She'd given years of loyalty to the school. And that was it? Hazel felt empty – very empty.

David poured them both a glass of red wine in the kitchen and walked into the lounge with them. Hazel took one sip and stood up.

"Blow it. Blow the lot of them!", she said suddenly. "Let's do it, David. Let's adopt Pedro!"

Chapter 4

For the forseeable future Hazel was thinking and planning the next steps. The meeting with Terry Williams had been very useful. It gave them an insight into what was required as prospective parents. The key difference, however, was that Pedro was thousands of miles away. They were unsure of what the first big step would be, but a reply to the letter from Mother Caterina seemed a sensible first move. Hazel also used the internet to glean more information on what may be legally necessary. It appeared that there was a UK Social Services desire that a couple wishing to adopt abroad and to bring a child into the UK needed to complete appropriate documentation. The relevant UK department would then need to liaise with their counterparts in Chile to approve and verify all the aspects of the adoption process. It had been suggested to David and Hazel by Terry that together they write down a few paragraphs on their background, the medical checks they'd had, why they wanted to adopt, and why they thought they would make good parents.

The two of them had sat down at the kitchen table that morning before David left the house, chatted things over, and Hazel had made some notes. Before David left they agreed not to talk to any of their friends or colleagues about the matter. Keith Blandford had already indicated that the matter would not go any further. They were also assured of confidentiality with Terry Williams. After David had kissed Hazel and closed the front door, she sat down with a large pad and jotted down some thoughts. She wrote out a short biographical CV for each of them. She wrote down the dates and checks that Hazel had undergone at the Royal Surrey County Hospital in Guildford, as well as the names of the senior hopital staff. Noting down why they wanted to adopt wasn't difficult. Both David and Hazel believed their lives could be more complete with a child in the family and would give extra meaning to periods like Christmas. Making good parents demanded some reserve, but Hazel honestly felt that they both had it in them to be a caring father and mother. Their relationship had not really suffered because they did not have any children, but sometimes Hazel would go into what David called 'her dark box'. She would become introverted for a few days, lose her sense of humour, and sit around the house doing very little.

When she felt happy with the notes, she began to draft a reply to the nunnery. Part of her said 'wait a little longer and think things over more', whilst another part said 'just get on with it! Do it!' Hazel had decided she'd spent too much of her life 'thinking things over'. She was not an impulsive person by nature, but she really considered that the time had come to take action. She put the kettle on to make some coffee and as she waited for it to boil she really felt pleased with herself. It was as though some shackled, pent up feelings had been unlocked and she was beginning to feel a different woman! She smiled inwardly as she made the coffee and then added a little milk.

She took the pad and began to write a letter to Mother Caterina that she would type on her laptop. Hazel wanted to get it right. She began with thanking her for taking the trouble to find their address and the consideration given to Pedro. She didn't want to jump straight in and reply saying that they definitely wanted to adopt Pedro, but she also wanted to indicate that that they were taking steps to find out what they needed to do in England regarding adoption. They would need to know what was required in Chile, for if they were able to adopt Pedro it would all have to be done in one visit, if possible. She asked Mother Caterina what others had done when adopting any of the orphans? What steps had been necessary? She also asked about a medical check up for Pedro. It was clear that if David and Hazel were to bring Pedro back to the UK, he would have to be in basic good health. She concluded by thanking Mother Caterina and asked her to pass on their kindest regards to Father Rodriguez.

Hazel finished the draft and read it to herself three or four times. She wouldn't type it out until David had seen it and added his own comments. She put the pad down, finished her coffee and gazed out of the kitchen window onto the back garden. Two blue tits were squabbling on the seed feeder and a house sparrow was pecking at the peanuts. Hazel felt a strange contentment spread over her. It seemed as if she was in a dream. Her thoughts drifted from one subject to another. Her work at school began to seem so insignificant, so petty. All the tittle tattle by members of staff, miniscule matters of no significance, unruly children without parental control – it was so unimportant somehow. Perhaps her dismissal from the school – 'thanks Mr. Craddock, for nothing' – was meant to be? 'God moves in mysterious ways' she thought to herself. Having no current job allowed Hazel to spend her physical and emotional energy on reaching her goal of getting Pedro adopted. But wait, what if there were insuperable barriers that couldn't be ovecome? If the Chilean authorities declined an application, if David and Hazel were considered unsuitable…what if, what if...

"Stop it! she shouted out loud, frightening herself as she did so. She dropped the coffee mug as she abruptly stood up, the handle breaking off as it hit the floor. Then she began to cry again and the tears flowed. After a short while she reached for a piece of kitchen roll, wiped her eyes and blew her nose. It was such a good blow, in fact, that she had to unwind another piece. She looked at the images of small elephants printed on the paper before lifting the kitchen waste bin and dropping both bits inside.

Hazel resolved to be strong and to try hard not to have any negative feelings about the whole situation. She would carry on being a good wife to David, doing her household and domestic tasks, and being fully involved with the church. She would adopt a 'positive mental attitude' to Pedro and everything concerned with him. Hazel would look forwards, and give her committment to this 'project'.

'That's a good way to consider this', she mused. It was to become Project Pedro or PP for short. In this way, she and David could converse discreetly about the matter in public, or among friends, by referring to PP. Perfect!

Hazel picked up the coffee mug and the handle, and swept up a few very small fragments of china afterwards. She had some washing to do and the bedsheets needed changing. More sparrows gathered at the bird table as the skies darkened. It looked like rain again.

The telephone rang as Hazel was about to go upstairs and change the bed. The phone display showed it was Gertrude. "Hello Gertrude", said Hazel, trying to sound as bright as she could. "Have you collected any items for the bric-a-brac sale at church next week?"

"Only four so far", replied Hazel, fibbing slightly. She knew she had a few things that she herself could donate for the church coffee morning.

"Well don't leave it too late! We need at least twenty items and Rosemary has only got three!" Gertrude was in 'she who must be obeyed' mode.

"Don't worry, Gertrude, I'll make a few phone calls this afternoon and do some collecting in the next few days. You'll have twenty items by next Wednesday in time for the event."

"Bless you, Hazel, you're a darling. Must dash – lots to do. Bye."

Hazel put the phone down. Raindrops were gently hitting the window. She went upstairs wondering if she'd get any washing hung out today?

Chapter 5

David and Hazel checked and re-read their letter to the nunnery. They felt it was the right balance – firstly, indicating that they were very interested in adopting Pedro, yet needed to check out every avenue prior to their total committment. If they could sort out as much as possible before returning to Santiago things would be made easier all round. David suggested telephoning Terry Williams again with a few specific questions that had cropped up. For example, if the couple were ever asked to give up the adoption of David for any reason, would they be able to say no? How thorough would they need to be with a medical history for Pedro? How long would it take for Pedro to become a British citizen? What forms did they need to complete in the UK, if any, before they travelled to South America?

Hazel jotted their queries down and then took the letter and typed it using *Word* on her laptop. She felt that the letter would be the first of several that would pass between Santiago and Godalming in the coming weeks and months. She knew all of this would not happen overnight and resigned herself to not flying back to Chile until the summer months. Hazel made sure that their home telephone number and email address were included – just in case the nunnery or Father Rodriguez wanted to contact them quickly. The letter was posted the following day.

Meanwhile Hazel went onto the internet and found a few sites that were useful. She spoke with Terry over the telephone and he suggested they meet for coffee later in the week. She agreed, thinking that a face-to-face conversation with him was preferable to trying to get some more answers courtesy of BT. She began to see Project Pedro as a full time activity – a hobby almost – in a respectful way. Most of her waking, and sometimes her sleeping, time was pre-occupied with the task. She wondered if there was anyone she could talk to in confidence, apart from Keith Blandford? Yes, that might be a good idea. It would help clear her mind and maybe make her feel as though a burden was lifted off her shoulders? Her sister Maureen in Durham city seemed a good bet. She was close to Maureen and hadn't seen her for a while. She emailed her sister that morning and asked if she could spend a couple of days with her 'for a break'. Hazel suggested the week after the church fund raising morning, by which time she would probably be clearer on the way ahead.

Hazel met with Terry in a small bistro in Guildford since he had some business in the area. They sat near a window at the side of the open room. The bistro was smart, with blue and white tabelcloths and real cotton napkins. Each table had a vase containing two or three fresh flowers. The tables were far enough apart to make a conversation private. After they'd ordered coffee and a sultana scone each they chatted away for over an hour. Hazel took out her check list and made notes as they talked. Terry was very helpful, and started several sentences with "in confidence". She liked him and trusted him and said how they'd listed some facts about themselves as well as why they wanted to adopt. She felt he was open with her and trying to be as helpful as possible. His key piece of advice was that David and Hazel should get in touch with the relevant authorities in Santiago as soon as they'd had a reply from Mother Caterina. She might be well placed to offer Pedro for adoption, but if he wasn't allowed to leave the country for any reason, everything they hoped for would come crashing down like the proverbial 'house of cards'. At the end of their discussion Terry insisted on picking up the tab. He helped Hazel to put her coat on and they walked out to a chilly, damp day.

"Hello Hazel, how are you? Fallen out with David?" Maureen was on the telephone not long after Hazel got home. "No, silly, I want to see you that's all!"

"I thought I'd phone you instead of emailing. John is away on business soon so your timing is perfect. What about next Tuesday? You could arrive here at teatime and go home on Friday morning."

"OK, let's agree on that. I'll talk with David when he gets in and confirm details. Perhaps you could pick me up at Durham railway station?"

"Of course! No problem, sis! We'll talk again soon! Love to David." With that Maureen rang off. The timing of Hazel's visit to the north meant that she would miss the church fund raiser, but she had promised Gertrude that she'd collect things for the bric-a-brac stall and would keep her word. They would manage without her and Hazel decided she needed to come up with an excuse for not being at church. She asked the Lord for foregiveness, but she decided she would tell the ladies at church that her sister in Durham was unwell, and a family visit was called for. Yes, that sounded plausible. David had given his blessing to Hazel's plan to visit Maureen. She knew he would, of course.

The church event came and went. It was a success according to Rosemary and others, and it raised over £125. Keith had called in and won a teddy bear in the raffle, Elaine bought a book called *'Christianity in Far Off Lands'* by the Rev. Chaddington Smallpiece D.D., and Di had raised over twenty pounds selling her home made chutneys. All in all it had gone well. Hazel wished she had been there, but right now it seemed more important that she opened up her heart to Maureen in her quest to make Project Pedro a success!

The train pulled to a smooth stop at Durham station. Hazel got out and was greeted with wonderful views over the city. Durham Cathedral looked stunning in the evening light. Maureen rushed towards her and gave Hazel a big hug. She took her case and they walked off the northbound platform arm in arm. Maureen had parked her Ford StreetKa in the station car park around the corner. Her husband John was a Senior Lecturer in Zoology at the local university. His main interest was in marine invertebrates, especially cephalopods. He was in South Africa working on a project with the University of Cape Town and looking at declining numbers of octopus in the waters just off the Cape and how that could be halted.

Within ten minutes Maureen and Hazel arrived at the large semi-detached house near the Botanical Gardens, and pulled the car onto the front drive. Maureen's neighbour, Harriet, was looking after Jessie, their eight year old daughter. Jessie jumped up as Hazel walked into the lounge. "Auntie Hazel!" screamed Jessie, "how lovely to see you again!" They hugged for what seemed ages. Hazel often remarked what a loving nature Jessie had. Jessie opted to go up to her bedroom to finish some homework. She was actually working on a project on South America and Hazel thought she might be able to help her on parts of it, but later. Harriet shouted her farewell as she closed the front door on her way out.

"OK, come on, tell me why you're here?" Maureen asked Hazel as she poured the tea. "Where do I begin?" replied Hazel.

"At the beginning, of course, it's a very good place to start". Maureen partly sang it as though she were in a local amateur dramatic production. Hazel began her story. She told Maureen of their holiday, the best parts of it, and the visits to Father Rodriguez and then to the nunnery. When she spoke of Pedro she began to fill up and her eyes moistened. Maureen passed her a tissue from a box on the side table. After a while, and a refill of her teacup, Hazel came to the end of her account of the trip to South America. Not only that, but she also mentioned losing her job at school and David's relative unhappiness at work.

"It's as though it's written in the stars" said Hazel wiping her eyes again. "As though there is a major plan – a theatrical production and we're just playing our part. Everything seems to be heading towards us actually adopting Pedro – things seem too organised somehow." Maureen sat looking at her sister. She was not religious but she believed in fate. The way she had met her husband John was fate. How she missed a flight because her car got a puncture and the aircraft crashed, killing everyone on board, was fate. How she managed to get a job by accidentally clicking on the wrong web site was fate. Life was fate! Maureen explained how she felt about Hazel's situation. "Maybe it was meant to happen, it's as simple as that", concluded Maureen. "It's fate, F-A-T-E", she spelt out the word. It made Hazel feel better.

They continued chatting for some time and then Maureen started to prepare the evening meal. She was happy to do that on her own – it was pasta with sun-dried tomatoes and garlic bread – so Hazel went upstairs to talk with Jessie. Jessie chatted about her school and her favourite subjects, and least favourite! She really enjoyed English but hated Maths. Drama was good, especially when she got a good part, but often forgot her lines! Hazel encouraged her to talk about her South America project. "It's something we have to do for geography during this term.

We're studying the continent but everyone has to write a report on a country. I chose Chile, but I don't know why? I looked at a map of South America and Chile just seemed to jump off the page at me! It was the strange shape of it, perhaps?"

"Yes, it's a long narrow country, with the Pacific ocean to the west and the Andes mountains to the east. The climate is very good for growing grapes in some parts of the country," said Hazel. "The capital, Santiago, is a beautiful city." Jessie opened her eyes wide and her jaw dropped!

"Auntie Hazel, you're an expert!" Hazel went on to explain that she and David had enjoyed a two week holiday there recently, and Jessie begged her to tell her more about it. As Hazel spoke about the country, Jessie listened carefully, asked questions, and made notes. The odour of garlic wafted up the stairs and soon Maureen shouted that 'dinner is ready!' Jessie put her notepad away, they both washed their hands, and went down stairs to eat at the large pine kitchen table.

"Wine?" Maureen asked Hazel. "Oh, please." Maureen poured two glasses of wine and a glass of fresh orange juice for Jessie. The meal smelt delicious and Maureen put out generous portions on large oval plates. Jessie quickly told her mother about Hazel's knowledge of Chile and 'volunteered' Hazel to help her with her project. Hazel smiled. She was more than happy to help. Over dinner the three of them chatted about all sorts of things – local events, family matters, the weather, future holiday plans. When they had finished Hazel offered to wash up and Jessie wanted to dry the plates and cutlery.

"You've had an affect on her!" said Maureen. "She doesn't do that when we're on our own!" As they washed and dried the telephone rang. Maureen walked into the lounge and picked the phone up. It was John in Cape Town. "Hi, honey, are you OK?"

"Yes, we're all fine", replied Maureen, "Hazel's here and she and Jessie are tidying up in the kitchen. How's your day been?"

John phoned home as often as he could, but his kind of work – often offshore on small boats – meant he couldn't always guarantee when he was able to call. John and Maureen talked for ten minutes, and then he spoke with Jessie. Jessie again told her dad how clever Auntie Hazel was, and she was going to help with her geography project! The telephone conversation over, the three of them sat and watched some TV. Jessie yawned twice and that was her cue to go to bed. She was a good girl, no fuss about going upstairs, and she had a busy day tomorrow. It was double English first thing and drama in the afternoon. However, maths was before lunch just to spoil things! Jessie said 'goodnight' and went to her room, eager to re-read her notes on Chile.

Maureen and Hazel sat with a glass of cabernet sauvignon until after eleven o'clock, talking about the adoption matter. Maureen gave Hazel her opinions on some aspects of the whole affair, and asked the question 'why adopt abroad when you could adopt in England?' Hazel had explained her deep inner feelings and the simple answer to that question was that she felt in her heart that Pedro was the one that she wanted to adopt. The chemistry between them was palpable, he was the one she wanted. Maureen asked if Hazel had any photos of Pedro? She hadn't. Although they were allowed to take pictures, Hazel took only a few when they got to the orphanage. Maureen asked if Hazel had brought her camera with her? She had. Hazel usually took it with her wherever she went – just in case. Hazel got her digital camera out, switched it on and reviewed the pictures taken during their holiday. "Hmmm", Hazel hummed to herself. She got to the photos of the orphanage and went through them. Thankfully they had not been deleted since she had downloaded them onto her laptop computer. She scrolled through the images. She gasped. "What's wrong, sis?" said Maureen. "He's here, he's here!"

Hazel found one picture taken in the courtyard of the orphanage! There in the lower, left hand corner was Pedro! His little face beamed as he had been looking at the camera. Why hadn't Hazel noticed that before? After all she had put them onto her computer, and David had looked at them, too. Never mind, here he was! Maureen suggested that they could go into town in the morning and get a print, straight off the memory card. Great – in that way Hazel would have something to look at during the coming months to remind her of Pedro. As Hazel was about to turn the camera off, Maureen suddenly jumped up and screamed as she saw a large, black spider on the carpet. "Ahhhhh!", she shouted loudly. At that instant Hazel's index finger accidentally pushed the 'delete' button on the back of the camera and Pedro's image was gone.

Hazel looked at Maureen as it slowly sank in. She looked forlornly at her camera. Was it an omen, she wondered?

Chapter 6

Hazel's stay in Durham came to an end. She had thoroughly enjoyed the break and caught up on most of the news with her sister. She felt relieved that she was able to off-load her concerns and innermost thoughts with her big sister. Jessie was a little gem, and Hazel had loved talking with her. Before she left she suggested to Jessie that they stay in touch. Jessie gave Hazel a big hug and a kiss before going off to school. Maureen helped Hazel with her case, putting it into the back of the car. The train was due to arrive at the station at 09.50. They made time to have a coffee in a small cafe near the station.

"You need to do what you think is best, Hazel. But then I know you will!"

"Yes, David and I have more to think about. When we get a reply from Chile, assuming we do, we should have more to go on. I'm not expecting all this to be quick. If I assume it'll take until the early autumn, I won't be disappointed if nothing really happens until then. I don't know whether to try to get a job?"

"Be positive, of course you'll get a reply! As to a job, you could do some volunteer work in Godalming. The community volunteer service are always looking for helpers – either as drivers or for home visiting. I know they are around here. A friend of mine places and empties collecting boxes for Guide Dogs." Hazel smiled. They finished their coffee and Maureen walked Hazel up to the south-bound platform. The train arrived on time and Maureen gave Hazel a sisterly hug. She got into the carriage and found a seat. Maureen waved her off and blew her a kiss. She put her hand on her heart as she waved the train away. It reminded Hazel of Keith Blandford – he had done the same when he walked out of the church. The journey back to King's Cross enabled Hazel to sit back and reflect on her stay and also on what needed to be done in Chile. Had they done enough homework? They'd listed all the things they thought they had to do. Neither of them feared a CRB check – no prison sentences, no debts incurred, no court appearances. Their home and environmental situation was good. David had a good job with a decent income. Hazel loved children. It all seemed fine.

Hazel had taken a short nap on the way but was wide awake as the engine pulled into platform three on schedule. Hazel had phoned David at work to let him know where she was. She'd be home by mid aftenoon and he promised to leave the office at five o'clock. She planned to prepare a nice evening meal, have a bottle of wine between them, and cuddle up on the sofa. She'd tell him all about the visit to Durham and about Jessie's project, of course.

David was working quite hard at the company. His new marketing plan was kicking in, some new clinical evidence was likely to be available in six months, and the unexpected appointment of a new Sales Manager to replace Roy Whitehead was welcome. He was beginning to feel more positive about his work but knew that Hazel had her mind fully occupied with Pedro and the likely outcome of the letters between them and the orphanage. She'd had a setback when she lost her job, but after the incident at school with the teacher Mr. Manning interfering with little Lucy, she knew she was pleased to be away from there.

David thought he might try to persuade Hazel to find another job, possibly part-time. Being in the house almost all day would mean she'd probably be thinking about Pedro whereas if she had something to occupy her things may be better. Neither of them were able to state how long this would go on and David didn't want Hazel to get stressed about it all. He decided to scan the local newspapers to see if there was anything suitable in the area and then 'gently' suggest the idea to Hazel.

Hazel was turning the front door key at just after three o'clock. She let herself in and dropped her small leather bag on the floor in the hall. She hung her coat up and put the kettle on to make a mug of coffee. She glanced around. The house was as tidy as when she went away. David was quite good when it came to keeping the place looking respectable, but the odd sign like a badly folded dog-eared newspaper and an unwashed tea cup indicated he wasn't up to Hazel's standard on the domestic front – 'but not too bad', she thought to herself. She took her bag upstairs and quickly unpacked her bits and pieces from the Durham trip. Back in the kitchen she trawled through the freezer and found two nice tuna steaks that she could defrost. These she'd serve with vegetarian stuffed peppers and some new potatoes. Hazel defrosted the tuna and picked six small potatoes from the vegetable basket. Two large peppers were 'decapitated' and de-seeded, whilst she cooked some rice to make the stuffing along with finely chopped mixed vegetables and oregano. She enjoyed cooking and saw it as a science, although she didn't much care for Heston Blumenthal.

Hazel hadn't checked the phone for messages. She went over to the telephone and saw a small red light on. At least one message had been left. "Hello, Hazel and David. This is Amelia Harcourt. You may remember we met on the holiday to Chile. Sorry to bother you but it might be a good idea to meet up, Hazel. I think there's something you might like to know. You can reach me on the following number..." Hazel scribbled it down on the pad next to the phone.

Her blood ran cold. How did she get their home telephone number? What did Amelia know? Was she being helpful, or interfering? Hazel sat down in the lounge and took several deep breaths. This was Miss Pudding, *the* Miss Pudding from the holiday! What on earth could it be? Hazel recalled that Amelia said that she was a medium or had psychic powers, or something like that? Her pulse raced. She stood up and went back into the kitchen. This was awful...how was Hazel supposed to concentrate on anything now? David would be home before six o'clock and she'd promised him an early dinner so that they could relax together.

There was nothing for it but to contact Amelia. She looked at the number she'd written down. It began with 0207 so Hazel knew it was an inner London listing. She punched the 0207 followed by the next seven numbers into the phone. After two seconds it started ringing. It continued for about ten seconds before it went into voicemail. It was Amelia's own voice..."I'm sorry I can't take your call right now but if you leave your name, number and a short message, I'll get back to you as soon as I can." Hazel didn't know what to do – it was that awful moment when you have a chance to leave a message on someone else's phone and you just can't think of the right words. Her hesitation meant that she had to put the phone down. She did.

'You damned fool!', Hazel chastised herself. 'Why didn't I leave a message? Look where it's got me now!' She was very annoyed with herself. If she'd anticipated a voicemail message from Amelia she could have given a message some consideration. Something! But her mind had gone blank – like being on a quiz show when the clock is ticking – you know the answer but it just won't come! Hazel sat down. Her mind was racing now but she poured herself a glass of filtered water and swallowed it in one. So many questions, too few answers. She didn't want her thoughts to spoil her evening with David and she considered not telling him. Why not keep it to herself, meet with Amelia, and then tell David afterwards? No, she couldn't do that. David was involved in all of this and she ought to share this with him. Maybe she should toss a coin? Heads she tells all, tails she doesn't. She felt like a schoolgirl again. Almost like tossing a coin to see who gets first strike with the conker in the school playground...

'Oh, blow this', Hazel said to herself. She reached for a twopence piece in her purse. She flipped it up in the air with a deft flick of her thumb. She caught the bronze coin as it fell under gravity onto the palm of her hand and turned it over onto the back of her other hand, just like tossing a pancake. It came down tails. When David arrived home there was a good smell in the kitchen. He walked across to Hazel and gave her a long hug and a kiss. "I've missed you and I'm glad you're back", he said looking into Hazel's eyes, "what news from today, then?"

"Let me get this meal served out, you go and wash your hands, and I'll tell you all about Maureen and Jessie."

Hazel put two warm plates on raffia mats and began to put the food out. She would need all of her amateur dramatic skills to get through the evening and the night. She looked at the ceiling for a second. 'Forgive me', she said quietly to herself as she took a sip of her wine.

Chapter 7

As soon as David had left for the office a little after eight o'clock, Hazel looked at Amelia's phone number again. She decided that it was impolite to call someone at home before nine o'clock in the morning, but then again, if Amelia worked she might be faced with another message option? She waited until just after a quarter to nine and then began to enter the number. This time Hazel was prepared to leave a message – if required.

"Hello?" Amelia spoke authoritatively. "Hi, Amelia, it's Hazel here. I got your message yesterday."

"I hope you didn't think I was interfering, but I think it may be useful if we meet up. I'm in Guildford this afternoon. There's a nice tea room near the Yvonne Arnaud theatre if I remember rightly. Shall we say three o'clock?" Amelia said little else, but Hazel had agreed. The call lasted less than one minute. Hazel knew of the tea room, she'd used it before. Hazel had some domestic jobs to do, and some shopping, so filling in time before mid afternoon wasn't an issue. She decided that by keeping busy, her mind wouldn't be on Chilean matters.

"Hello, Amelia", Hazel greeted her 'friend'. "Nice to see you again. Tell me how did you get our home phone number?"

"When we arrived back at Heathrow David was chatting to Tom, the chap he'd struck up with from North London who plays bowls. David gave Tom your home phone number – it was on a scrap of paper but I happened to see it briefly. I can recall things like that. It stuck in my mind so I knew your home number and gave you a call."

Hazel asked Amelia why she had left the message. What did she want to talk about? Amelia saw the enquiring look on Hazel's face.

"I sometimes have premonitions. Recently I've had visions of you and your husband with a little boy. You are all together for a while but then things change. I can't quite visualise what occurs, it gets blurred, but it's not right – there's a problem of some sort..." Amelia trailed off as the waitress took their order.

"Can you be more specific?" asked Hazel, her eyebrows knitting. "Not really, but all I can say is that there may be some kind of issues with you and this child. You need to check out every aspect of the whole matter. I'd be careful if I was you."

Hazel and Amelia talked for another fifty minutes. The conversation was like ping pong – it went backwards and forwards. Hazel's queries on some aspects went unanswered. Although Amelia was a psychic she didn't know all the answers. What she had done was to highlight some elements of the planned *adoption*, although Amelia never actually used that word 'adoption'. Was Hazel was getting cold feet? Wouldn't it be better to forget the whole matter? Just stay childless. Don't complicate their lives with all this. Maureen had asked why they didn't consider adopting in the UK? Well?

The tea room meeting came to an end. Hazel paid the bill and they got up to leave. As they walked to the door of the tea room Amelia took Hazel's arm and they looked at each other. "Hazel, it's up to you, but I can see there is a wonderful opportunity for you and your husband here. Ultimately you must decide. I can foresee that you will be happy and content. There are a few things in your way, that's all." Amelia either couldn't, or wouldn't, expand on the 'few things in your way' comment. Hazel didn't want to push her.

Hazel had Amelia's phone number. Amelia offered her time to Hazel if she needed to talk. Hazel thanked her and they exchanged a brief kiss on the cheek and went their seperate ways. Hazel never thought that she'd be having such a conversation with *Miss Pudding* when they first met in Santiago! Amelia didn't have to contact Hazel. However, she felt that because she had a special gift she somehow owed it to her. Was this all part of some big 'overall' plan written in the stars? Was it fate? Why had Hazel got a negative feeling in the pit of her stomach when only a few days ago she'd almost vowed to be positive? She was walking back to her car parked in the multistorey car park, her mind all over the place, when she bumped into Keith Blandford. "Hello, Hazel. What are you doing here?"

"I've just had afternoon tea with an old friend. We've caught up on some newsy things."

"I'm glad I bumped into you, Hazel. It's not public news yet, but Elaine Spriggs has resigned. I'm somewhat disappointed, but she has a sister in New Zealand who is a pastor of a large church and she's asked Elaine to join her. She had tendered her resignation and leaves at the end of the month. I was wondering, now that you're not working, whether you might be interested in helping out more formally at the church?"

"Helping out?" said Hazel, her eyebrows raising.

"Well, it may take time to get a suitable replacement for Elaine, and the post of verger is quite key to church life. You know everyone, and how the church operates. It could even be temporary if you preferred – dependant on your plans to adopt Pedro."

"Can you leave it with me, Keith. I need a little time to think it over. I'll phone you before seven o'clock this evening with an answer."

"That's fine. And, Hazel, let's keep this between ourselves for the moment." He touched her arm gently and gave her a knowing look.

"Of course. Bye for now, Keith." And with that they parted, Keith striding off in a manner suggesting he had something else to attend to.

Hazel walked back to the car park and found her car. She got in and started the engine. Before setting off she spent a few minutes thinking about what Amelia had said. Just when she thought she might be able to clear her mind following her meeting in the tea room, Keith had come up with this offer to help in the church. She hadn't even told David about the plan to see Amelia. She decided that she needed to offload all of this onto David – but gently. To keep life simple, the best option for dinner was to order home delivery, maybe an Indian. They liked spicey food from time to time, and her current curry blood level reading was near zero. There were some bottles of Tiger beer in the garage. Hazel would put four in the fridge. She'd check out the 'India Gateway' restaurant menu pinned to the corkboard in the kitchen and place an order for delivery at half past seven.

Hazel didn't remember her journey home. She'd heard some friends once say that a person can drive along a familiar route, arrive at their destination, and not be able to recall the trip! Now she believed it! She pulled onto the drive and used the garage door zapper to open the white up and over door. Within seconds she had driven into the garage and turned the engine off. She put her forehead on the top of the steering wheel, gripping the black leather rim on either side tightly with her fingers. Her eyes were closed.

At church the previous Sunday, a visiting preacher had talked of being in the 'wilderness' like Jesus was for forty days and nights. The message in the sermon was that we all have our own 'time in the wilderness'. Hazel felt exactly like that right now. She was in her own wilderness. She had to be strong. She had to handle it. She wasn't going to let herself down. She wasn't going to let anyone down. The big imponderable question was 'how long will it be before we can adopt Pedro?'

She went inside. The beers were placed in the fridge and the takeaway menu placed on the kitchen table. Keith's request kept coming into her head. Was she cut out for being a verger, or acting verger? Did that complicate matters right now? Did she need that additional responsibility? The answer was simple really. Hazel rang Keith's number.

"Hello Keith. It's Hazel. I've given your proposal a lot of thought and I won't be taking up your offer."

"That's OK, Hazel. I rather thought you'd say that. Thanks for giving it some consideration. Good luck and God bless. See you on Sunday. Bye." Keith put the phone down. Hazel wasn't totally sure if he was disappointed with her reply. Right there and then she wasn't bothered. She felt her head had been cleared.

'Now it's time to move forward', she said to herself, and browsed the Indian menu.

Chapter 8

David finished eating his king prawn byriani and mopped up the juices with the last of the garlic naan bread. The sag aloo and okra bowls were almost empty. He'd enjoyed it. Hazel had done all the talking, narrating the events with Amelia in Guildford.

"I wish you'd told me you were going to see Amelia, Nutty, I would have taken the afternoon off and come with you." He took a gulp of Tiger beer from the bottle. Hazel had not said anything about seeing Keith Blandford. She thought that was best – female intuition.

"No, it was best for just the two of us to meet I'm sure. Amelia may not have been as open as she was if you'd been a gooseberry on the side."

"So where do we go from here?" David swallowed the last of the naan. "I mean it seems we're playing a waiting game. You've written to the orphanage and we may or may not get a response?"

"David, we will get a reply!" Hazel was adamant. She willed herself to be positive, to make it a habit. "Stop putting things in the way. We both want to adopt Pedro and that's what we'll do!" Hazel surprised herself at her full on frankness and guts. She hadn't eaten much and maybe her blood sugar was low, or some hormone was kicking in.

"OK,OK. Take it easy. I was thinking that maybe if you got another part time job it would keep you occupied. I saw in the local newspaper that the community services group are looking for volunteer drivers. You pick up and take people from home to wherever and get reimbursed at forty five pence per mile."

Hazel glared at him. "Is that what you think I am? Is that all I'm worth? A blinking chauffeur!" She was annoyed. David saw the look in her eyes and he knew.

"No, of course not, but it's something for you to do while we wait for the next step..."

Hazel cleared the dishes and her left over food. Her chicken rogan josh had hardly been touched. Her best defence at that moment was to be silent. Not to say anything she'd regret in the morning. David sensed that she was upset, but he honestly felt he was trying to help. Was she going into her 'black box'? After ten minutes or so, he went up behind her and put his arms around her waist, gently at first, then more firmly. He expected her to pull away, but she turned to look at him. She looked sad. Her face was drawn and her cheeks lacked colour.

"I'm sorry, David. Everything is getting me down just now. I'll be OK when things become clearer. Why can't life be simple?"

"It will all work out, I'm sure," replied David. He had a few work items to attend to and told Hazel he was going upstairs to the study. She was fine with that. She could wash up and dry the dishes whilst she worked things out in her mind. "OK, I'll sort these out and we can relax on the settee later."

David went upstairs and turned on his computer. He had a revised strategy to write up on the cardiovascular business using some additional clinical evidence that he'd received from the US only a few days ago. He revised his three year forecast slightly downwards. Roy Whitehead's replacement, Jim Smithers, had just started and David had already met with him. Smithers was a bright sales professional with good interpersonal skills and a sense of diplomacy. David liked him. Things were looking reasonably good at the moment for David and his team.

He'd heard that his old colleague Mark was happy – he was a survivor.

The computer screen lit up the room. He clicked on the internet logo on the screen and went onto the Smith & Johnson site. He put in his user name password and got into his emails. There was nothing that needed his attention at that moment. He then spent some time on his proposal to win back market share in this busy and valuable sector of the healthcare industry – drugs to help those with heart problems. Hazel came up with a cup of cafe latte and kissed him gently on the right cheek. She placed the cup on a small, round bamboo coaster.

She then went into the bedroom and began to get undressed. It was just after nine o'clock but she felt tired and needed an early night. David wasn't sure if they'd make love that night. Sometimes her body language suggested she wanted to be loved all night long, and at other times she was genuinely weary. The giveaway was whether David could detect a hint of Chanel No. 5? If so, he'd approach carefully to check out Hazel's response!

After writing for some time, he reached a good point to stop and closed the tab after saving his work. He decided to check emails on their own BT site before retiring to bed. He logged on and saw that there were six new emails in the inbox. There seemed nothing special. One from Ed and Di suggesting a night out at the theatre soon to see *'South Pacific'*, a couple from Amazon and Tesco with special offers, and one where the subject box was showing 'Child adoption'. Child adoption! David clicked on this one immediately. It read:

'Dear Mr. & Mrs. Tate,
This email is from the Child Agency, Chile Government Office. Your information was passed to us by Mother Caterina and

Father Rodriguez with regard to the possible adoption of a child called Pedro Caterinos.

We have examined the possibilty of this, but we have to be sure that this arrangement is suitable for both parties. You need to complete the attached form and return it to us as soon as possible via email.

You will need to finance the medical examination of Pedro, at a hospital fee of possibly no more that 50 GB pounds. There will be a sum payable to the nunnery. This has been agreed internally at 100 GBP.

The formality needs to be approved at a monthly meeting here in Santiago. Our next meeting is in six days time. Once, and if approved, extradition proceedings will commence and can be quite quick – less than four days. Pedro will need to be provided with a provisional passport that will be acceptable to your immigration authorities. We can arrange this.

For him to travel to the UK he will need some basic clothing and you must forward a sum of 75 GBP to cover this.

Once we have received your completed form as attached we shall be in touch with you again.

Thank you.
Senor Jose Luis Henrejos
Chief Adoption Executive – Government of Chile'

David gasped! He re-read the information and carefully digested it. This is exactly what they, and Hazel in particular, had been waiting for! He clicked on 'Attached Form' and saved it to Documents. He got up and went to the bedroom. He knew Hazel would be very excited to hear about this wonderful news! He slipped open the bedroom door. The room was dimly lit by a small bedside lamp. He tiptoed across to Hazel's side of the bed. She was fast asleep. Her face looked tranquil. She had rosy cheeks. The news from Chile would have to wait until morning.

David returned to the study and turned off the computer. He checked that doors were locked downstairs and nothing had been left switched on. He went back upstairs and got ready for bed. He slipped in beside Hazel. He quietly said 'good night, Nutty, I love you' but got no reply.

He slowly drifted off to sleep. He could smell Chanel No. 5.

PART SIX

Chapter 1

David and Hazel had completed the emailed form and returned it the next day. They'd included all of the requested information, including personal details, two references, and a testimony. Hazel wrote a short thank you letter to Mother Caterina. They'd had a positive response from the Chile Government two days after the monthly meeting. Hazel and David had paid the three amounts of money, two via credit card and the one to the orphanage was by money transfer. It had all happened so fast! The few days between receiving the first email and getting the reply was a blur. David and Hazel had restless nights and ate sparingly as their metabolism quickened up.

Hazel had told her friends and her sister. Everybody was delighted, especially Maureen to whom she was close. Her friends at church were clearly overjoyed, some mentioning the 'power of prayer'. David had mentioned the sequence of events to his friends and colleagues. He told Trevor first, asking if he could take one week off work. Trevor had agreed once David promised to have his strategy proposal on Trevor's desk before departing Heathrow airport. That was fair bribery, David thought to himself. They booked the same flight on a Sunday from Heathrow that they had caught when they departed on their holiday – a ten o'clock take off. The return flight was booked for Wednesday. It had been suggested by the Chilean authorities that two working days would be enough to make all the arrangements for the three of them to return to the UK.

Hazel said that to herself…"the three of them"…she said it out loud four times! There would be *three* of them!

Ed and Di offered to take them to the airport. They chatted on the way and exchanged lots of information about their holiday and how things had come to pass. Di asked about Pedro – how old he was? What did he look like? How would he settle in England? These and many other queries were made, but obviously Hazel couldn't answer them all. They would wait and see the outcome, but were positive in their own minds that things would work out. She recalled that Amelia had said it would be OK. But wait, hadn't she also said there "may be some kind of issues?" Hazel cleared her head. She was not going to have any negative feelings. Ed's Mondeo pulled up at the departures sign near 'Drop Off point only' just before eight o'clock. Ed and Di jumped out and Ed helped with the suitcase. They made the usual friends hugs and kisses farewells and David confirmed with Ed their return date and time. He'd written it on the back of one of his business cards. David and Hazel made their way to check in desk 37, got rid of their suitcase, and headed to a cafe for refreshments. A nearby screen showed boarding time as 0920 so there was time for coffee and a look at a newspaper. Hazel had bought *'Hello'* magazine as a treat for herself.

The flight to Santiago almost mirrored their departure some weeks before. The BA staff were there 'to serve' and they were well looked after. Pre-lunch drinks were offered and accepted whilst they flicked through the BA in flight magazine. The captain's announcement came over the speakers – estimated arrival time, weather conditions, co-pilot's name and so forth. It seemed to go over their heads. They didn't even bother trying to guess his name. Was it Tobias Wilcock? Myers or Sanchez? It didn't matter. Both of their minds were focused on one thing, and one thing only. David got out a small notebook from his inside pocket. Before lunch they begun to make a list of things to do and ask when they arrived in Santiago.

They had been told they would be met at the airport by a government offical who could be indentified by his ID badge. He'd also be wearing a white stetson hat and carrying a red leather briefcase to make identification easier. His name was Miguel Lugendo. Miguel would take them to their hotel in central Santiago, allow them a few hours rest, and then collect them just after lunch to take them to the offices of the Child Agency. All documentation would be completed in the afternoon, and then Miguel would drive them out to the nunnery, complete the final administrative requirements and to collect Pedro the following day, Tuesday. Pedro had already been booked into the small hotel where David and Hazel were staying. The next day, Wednesday, Pedro and his 'parents' would be flying back to England. Mother Caterina had organised some basic, suitable clothes for Pedro. Hazel had brought an overcoat for Pedro to wear on arrival in London.

David and Hazel began their list. Lots of who, when, where and how? Terry Williams had been extremely helpful before they left and had given guidance on a number of matters. He'd also been in touch with the county adoption agency to smooth the path for Pedro's arrival in Godalming. He had to have a medical examination, but they hoped it was just a formality. A school had been earmarked for him, as well as a private tutor to teach him English. The tutor would be part financed by the county council social services, but the new 'parents' would have to make a contribution. So, Pedro's arrival seemed to be well planned. Or did it? Something was nagging at the back of David's logical mind.

He didn't want to discuss it with Hazel – he'd let it pass for now.

165

Chapter 2

The man with the white hat and red leather briefcase and wearing an ID tag showing the name *Senor M. Lugendo* was waiting for them once they had collected their suitcase and cleared customs.

"Good morning", he said politely and in perfect English, raising his hat. He introduced himself, clarified his role, and asked them to call him by his first name. "Please come this way." He walked out of the airport and David and Hazel followed.Fifty metres outside along the arrivals pavement a white Mercedes Benz waited for them. Lugendo opened the nearside back door and Hazel got in, closey followed by David. The chauffeur in the car put their luggage into the cavernous boot and returned to the driving seat. Lugendo got in alongside the driver, a young man with a smartly trimmed black beard and ivory linen suit.

Lugendo said very little apart from pointing out a few buildings of interest on the trip into Santiago. He told them that their first destination was the hotel that had been booked for them. He also went on to inform them of their itinerary for the next few days. When he had finished he handed David a sheet of paper showing all of the details for their visit, as well as contact telephone numbers including Lugendo's mobile phone number. The car pulled into the small car parking area in front of the hotel. David saw the sign *'Hotel Rocinante'* and noticed it had three stars so assumed it would be satisfactory. They were only there for two nights so it wouldn't be an issue, he was sure.

Hazel looked up at the front of the hotel and wondered what Pedro would make of it? She wasn't absolutely certain of his domestic situation at the orphanage, but she assumed it would be different for him here at the Rocinante. They would cope, she knew they would.

Severiano, the chauffeur, lifted the suitcase out of the boot and carried it into the hotel foyer. Miguel Lugendo, minus the stetson and briefcase, walked into the hotel with David and Hazel close behind. He spoke in Spanish as he informed the receptionist of the arrival of 'Senor and Senora Tate', although he pronounced their surname as 'tartay'. David and Hazel filled in the registration form and entered their passport numbers. The receptionist, with the widest smile Hazel had ever seen, handed them their room key. Room 35, the same as their house number in Chalk Road. Hazel picked up the key and large fob attached to it. She thought that this was a positive omen for them.

Lugendo bade his farewell and said he'd be back to collect them in the same car in exactly three hours time. A porter took the suitcase and ushered David and Hazel into a lift to go up to the third floor. The room was comfortable, simply furnished, and with a large double bed. Pedro would use a single room next to room 35. There was a connecting door between the rooms. David and Hazel unpacked the few items they had brought from Surrey. The overcoat for Pedro was hung on a hanger in the wide wardrobe. David filled the kettle on the side table and switched it on. "Fancy a cuppa?" he asked Hazel. "Yes, please. I'm gasping for a drink." David opened the door of a small fridge and removed a bottle of *'agua sin gas'* – still water. He unscrewed the blue plastic cap and passed it to Hazel. She drank from the bottle. She also took two paracetamol tablets to help soothe a headache she'd had since they'd landed.

They'd said little to each other after their arrival at the airport. David poured the tea out and placed the two cups on the bedside table. "Come and sit over here, Nutty," he patted the top of the bedspread. Hazel joined him on the bed. "What are you thinking? You've been quiet."

"I'm thinking about Pedro, of course. How he'll feel. What he's been told so far. How I'll feel when I see him?" David took her hand in a reassuring manner.

"You'll be fine. When I think about everything, we know so little about him, don't we?"

"Oh, David, don't say that! We have discussed this for some time now and I believe we both agreed on the adoption!"

"Yes, yes, I know, Nutty. I'm not getting cold feet. It's just..."

"It's just what?" Hazel stood up and went to the window. David took her hand again and turned her around. He looked intensely into her eyes.

"Listen. I'm OK with this, honestly I am. It's just that we are going to be on a steep learning curve for the next few weeks, months and even years. Nothing has really prepared us for this experience. We shall 'learn-by-doing' and do the very best for Pedro." David decided this wasn't the time for a mini lecture. Hazel needed all the love he could give her right now. He hugged her closely for a while. She went back to get her tea and sat on the bed again.

"David, I'm going to be on edge for a while. Until we see how Pedro takes to us, and we get him back to the UK, I'll be anxious. I want you to be there for me. Do you understand?" She looked at him, her eyes focused on his. David nodded and confirmed his willingness to be there. He'd be her guardsman – red jacket, bearskin and rifle – keeping watch over her night and day. Yes, he felt he liked the sound of that as he spoke to himself. Her guardsman! He would be her guardsman until the day he died.

David and Hazel had time for a stroll and some lunch before Severiano and Miguel returned. There was a small cafe close to the hotel and they took a table outside. Neither felt really hungry and decided the tapas menu would suit them both. They chose a few small dishes – tortilla, sardines and onion and pepper salad – and a large bottle of still water. David ordered the food and felt pleased with himself as he practised his Spanish again. They ate leisurely, chatting about their recent holiday. David avoided more conversation about Pedro as he felt it would be good to take Hazel's mind off things for a while. It didn't seem five minutes since they'd left Chile! Here they were again, sitting in the shade, eating and watching the world go by. David checked his watch. They had twenty minutes before the car was due to collect them so they finished up and asked for the bill – *'la cuenta'*. David picked up his shoulder bag, paid the waitress and they left.

As they wandered back towards the hotel the Mercedes headed towards them. They recognised Lugendo, although he was becoming a 'Miguel' to them by now. The car stopped and Miguel got out. "I hope you are both suitably refreshed?" he asked. David and Hazel were ushered into the back seat of the car and fastened their seat belts. As the car drove away, Miguel turned to them and reconfirmed their intinerary. " We are now going to our offices to go over some details. That should not take long. Then we are going to the orphanage where Mother Caterina is expecting us. You and Pedro should be back here by early evening if all goes according to plan. Do you have any questions?"

At that moment they did not have any questions. Hazel's mind was working at fifty to the dozen.

Their adventure was about to begin.

Chapter 3

"We need to review the document before you" said Senor Valasquez who was leading the discussion regarding the adoption. Valasquez was a swarthy man with jet black hair and a small scar above his right eye. He could have been off the set of a spaghetti western, although he was smartly dressed in a pinstripe suit. Next to him was a woman who David and Hazel assumed was his secretary. She had a pad and pen and would probably take notes during the meeting. His office was tastefully furnished. He'd given David and Hazel a copy of the *'escritura de adoptione'* which covered all the details regarding Pedro. Pedro had never been given a proper surname, nor was anyone sure of his date of birth. A space had been left for the insertion of a second name for Pedro. His date of birth was listed as 29 June. He was assessed by the Paediatricians at the local hospital as being six years of age. Measurements of the length of his leg bones and the size of his rib cage had put him between five and seven years old.

"How do you know his date of birth if he was abandoned at the orphanage as a very young infant?" asked Hazel.

"We don't", replied Valasquez, "but the 29 June is St. Pedro's day in our calendar, so we give him that as his birthday!" He raised his eyebrows and smiled, showing a gold tooth. "Also, we want you to be happy with the second name we give him. We suggest 'Caterinos' after the Mother Superior at the nunnery. Do you agree?"

"Perfect!", replied Hazel instantly. She had thought about that very point several times. Pedro would need a name on his temporary passport, and at the airport for check in. His surname would not be changed to Tate until they were back in Surrey. The Chilean authorities had gone through the whole procedure with a fine tooth comb. They had booked the additional room at the hotel and a seat on the return flight to Heathrow the day after tomorrow. Valasquez wrote Caterinos in the space on the *escritura*. Further information was discussed, including his medical examination and the results.

"He is a very healthy boy!", Valasquez beamed at David as though auditioning for a toothpaste advertisement. "His blood levels are good with no problems shown. There are no signs of disease nor blood dyscrasias. Dental hygiene has been excellent. His blood pressure is fine and his body mass index sits in the middle of the graph. He has a birthmark on his back in the shape of an eagle. This could be useful for indentification at some time in the future. Mother Caterina has been informed of everything and given her blessing to this adoption procedure. The relevant Chilean ministries are aware of this and clearance has been given for Pedro Caterinos to leave the country with you two as his legal guardians once you have signed here." His thick left index finger pointed to the bottom of page three. "We have contacted your government and have been assured that Pedro's entry to the United Kingdom will raise no issues. We shall give you a copy of this document and a seperate letter to this effect."

Within twenty minutes they had gone over the aspects regarding Pedro. David and Hazel had checked their own notes made on the flight to Santiago and felt they had covered everything. Valasquez gave them his business card as they stood up and told them to call him if they needed to. When the final items were concluded, including the confirmation of the payment for the adoption which Valasquez called an administration fee, they moved towards the door. His secretary called Miguel who was drinking coffee at a machine at the end of the corridor. He came to meet the 'new parents' and lead them down stairs to the waiting car.

"Goodbye and good luck!" said Valasquez as they walked along the corridor on a thick, blue carpet.

"Thank you very much, Senor Valasquez", Hazel replied, clutching the A4 manilla envelope containing the folder, receipt for the fee and the letter. He beamed at them again, turned on his heels and walked away. His secretary followed him as though tied to him by a piece of string.

Miguel went in front and took them downstairs. Severiano, or Sevvy as he liked to be known, sunglasses perched on his forehead, waited in the drivers seat of the car, the engine purring gently. The automatic gearbox went into 'drive' and they slowly edged away from the large car park. David and Hazel looked at each other, almost unable to believe what they had just gone through. Somehow it seemed all too easy. A short meeting, a few questions, pay the fee and leave. Job done. However, they were aware of what they had gone through to get to this point. They held hands as the chauffeur got up to speed once they had left the city. It was mid afternoon and still warm but the aircon was doing its work. The light tan leather seats were comfortable and the tinted windows kept out some of the bright sun.

"I have some cold, bottled water if you need a drink" said Miguel. He pointed to the cooled glove locker at the front.

"Oh, yes please", gasped Hazel, her throat feeling like fine sandpaper. She took the bottle from Miguel and put it to her lips. It tasted good. When she'd finished drinking she passed the remainder of the bottle to David. He was less polite and gulped the remainder of the clear, cold contents. They both thanked Miguel, who was continuing to look after them very well. The car cruised along at just over 80 kph and David and Hazel looked out at the dry countryside, each deep in their own thoughts. Hazel was trying to imagine what the meeting with Pedro would be like? How would he look and behave? Would that gleam in his dark eyes still be there? Should she hug him, hold him, even touch him? Obviously she had no experience of such a thing – ever! Maybe she should 'play it by ear'? Just let things take their course? There was nothing for it but to wait and see. Mother Caterina would take charge up to the moment that they departed. Yes, let the Mother Superior be in control. That would be easiest.

Soon the car was pulling up in front of the large wooden doors of the nunnery. David and Hazel had chatted in the back of the car on the journey about a few things. David had tried to reassure Hazel that all would be well and suggested she take deep breaths before getting out of the car. He squeezed her hand lightly as she got out, Severiano holding the rear door open. The warm air hit them like a blast from a hair drier. One of the gates swung open, creaking on its hinges. The four arrivals waited in the sun, that was relentlessly beating down. One of the Sisters came out. David and Hazel didn't remember seeing her before, but then some of them had been busy at the time. They all looked similar, too, with their black full length habit and white headwear.

"Welcome, I'm Sister Bertomeu. Do come inside." She led the way through the oak gate and into the courtyard. It seemed only like yesterday that they were stood in the same spot. The paving and the red geraniums were the same as Hazel had remembered it. It felt cooler here, though, than before. Miguel and Sevvy discreetly walked a few paces to the side to be out of the way. Hazel's eyes were darting around, looking for Mother Caterina, but more importantly, Pedro.

"Hello, Hazel and David. Welcome." It was Mother Caterina who stood behind them. She looked serene. "Pedro is waiting for you. Follow me."

Chapter 4

He stood there, a small figure with jet black hair. His hair had been washed and combed and he was wearing shoes. A clean shirt and shorts completed his almost perfect look. His eyes were as big as saucers. He smiled enigmatically, somewhat like the Mona Lisa. Hazel and David looked at him for a few seconds. Hazel had told herself not to cry but her emotions began to get the better of her. She held back the tears as she looked at Pedro. He was everything she had remembered. Their eyes locked for what seemed an age.

"Hello, Pedro. How are you?" Hazel opened the conversation.

"His English is poor but he is a willing learner", interrupted Mother Caterina. Hazel hadn't really thought about any language difficulties, but of course he had been left at the orphanage door as a baby and had spent virtually all of his life there.

"Me like you, me want go home with you". When Hazel heard those words she could not help herself. Tears welled up in her eyes and she sobbed into David's chest. He held her very closely and whispered "it will be all right, Nutty." Hazel got out her hankie and wiped away the salty tears. 'I must be strong for his sake', she thought to herself. She blew into the hankie and wiped her eyes.

"You no cry. Me help you." Pedro walked across to Hazel and David and despite his small stature seemed able to put his little arms around both of them. Hazel broke down. She couldn't handle this. This little boy that they had come to take back to Surrey and care for and bring up was in charge of this emotional situation!

"Come, let us go into the nunnery and get some refreshment" suggested Mother Caterina diplomatically. She pointed to a door to their right as she held out her arm. Hazel and David were able to relax for a few moments as they began to follow her in. Pedro took Hazel's hand as he looked up at her as they walked into the cool room. He smiled and Hazel smiled back. Drinks and fruit had been placed on a long table. They were offered a small plate and a glass and told to help themselves. A large glass jug held lemonade made at the nunnery whilst another contained water with lemon wedges in. The fruit consisted of oranges, bananas and apples. Hazel poured out three glasses of the lemonade for Pedro, David and herself. Mother Caterina had invited two of her senior Sisters to join them, as well as Miguel and Sevvy. The conversation was light and they spoke of the warm weather, as well as their journey to the nunnery. Oranges and bananas were peeled and apples chomped as they chatted. Within twenty minutes everyone was satisfied. Mother Caterina stood up and indicated to David that she wanted him to join her. David nodded at Hazel and then followed Mother Caterina into her office. Sister Bertomeu was already sat there.

David put his small backpack on the floor and wiped his brow. He felt warm despite the cool glass of lemonade. Mother Caterina asked him if Hazel was all right and if she would be able to cope.

"She'll be fine, thank you. It's been a traumatic experience for her. We've been looking forward to this for a long time and finally we're here. It's caught up with her, that's all." David realised how perceptive the Mother Superior was. She could read body language and was fully aware of the situation around her all the time. Sister Bertomeu opened a folder and took out a form. David assumed it was the agreement for the adoption of Pedro. He was right. In Chilean law it was the male of the couple who needed to be the sole signatory for adoption. He read the agreement carefully. It contained nothing surprising except that he and Hazel were to send a report, verified by a UK court, on the progress of Pedro in England after one year, and again at three years. A copy of the document on the table was to be kept by the nunnery and a copy would go to Senor Valasquez in Santiago. David and Hazel, of course, would also have one.

At the bottom of the form was a space for two signatures, the date, and the adoption fee amount. David signed on the appropriate line and passed the form back to Sister Bertomeu. He reached for his backpack and said that he wished to make a further small payment to help with the running of the orphanage. A jiffy-bag contained some pesos. He had counted out the amount in notes earlier and he placed the jiffy-bag on the table. Mother Caterina and Sister Bertomeu thanked him very much, and then both signed the document and the date was entered.

"Do I need to do anything else?" David enquired.

"We trust you. Otherwise you wouldn't have got this far." David felt immensely reassured at those words.

"I now declare that you are formally the parents of Pedro Caterinos." stated Mother Caterina sounding like a vicar at a wedding. David couldn't really take it in for a moment. He looked at both nuns and smiled. "We should ask Hazel and Pedro to come in now."

Sister Bertomeu brought the two of them in. Pedro was all smiles as he held onto Hazel's hand. All five of them stood in silence. Mother Caterina began. "The Lord God is present among us. Let us pray. Heavenly Father, we ask you to bless

David, Hazel and Pedro as they enter a new chapter of their life together. We ask you to care for them and to lay your hands upon them. We know you will always be present. Please grant them a safe journey to England. We ask all this in the name of our Saviour, Jesus Christ. Amen." They all opened their eyes together. Nobody said anything for a few moments as the reality of the situation slowly dawned.

"Great!" exclaimed Pedro. He looked around for what would be the last time for him. This place, this *'special place'* that had been his home for about six years, was about to become a place of the past. He was sad to go, but Hazel sensed that he was pleased, very pleased. 'If he smiled much more his little face would split', she thought to herself. Mother Bertomeu excused herself to go and get Pedro's belongings.

Mother Caterina shook the hand of both new parents, and gave Pedro a gentle but firm hug. "We will miss you. Never forget us", she said to him in Spanish. "I won't, I promise. Thank you for my life here," he replied in his native tongue.

Within minutes Sister Bertomeu was back with a small bag little larger than a case for a laptop computer. "Here are his things", she said holding the black bag aloft. Hazel was taken aback – so little for six years of life in an orphanage! Children of Pedro's age in England would have at least two large suitcases full of clothes, toys, comic books and bric-a-brac.

"Time to go", said Hazel, sensing that there was nothing left to do. Miguel and Sevvy had re-appeared and began to move outside. "Thank you so much, Mother Caterina, we will never forget what you have done for us." David had picked up Pedro's bag.

"It's what you have done for yourselves," replied the Mother Superior. "With God's help. Good bye, and God bless you." She turned and walked back through the large oak gates. Sister

Bertomeu waved them off as Pedro nestled between his parents on the back seat. Hazel looked back out of the rear window but in seconds the gate had closed. David and Hazel looked at each other and held hands for a moment as if to say 'we've achieved what we came to do'. Pedro had never been in a car before, let alone a Mercedes Benz! He perched on the leather seat and looked at the dials and knobs on the dashboard and then out of the windscreen.

"How we move when no horse at front?" With that all four adults in the car burst into laughter that lasted for several minutes.

Pedro beamed at his mum and dad, his large beautiful eyes filling Hazel's soul with a pleasure she'd never experienced before. It wasn't to be the last time.

Chapter 5

Within no time Sevvy had got them safely back to the hotel. Tomorrow they would have to themselves, and on the day after which would be Wednesday, Miguel agreed a pick up time to take them to the airport. Sevvy had got out of the car and along with Miguel bade them good afternoon. Pedro and his new parents went into the hotel and Pedro was checked in. Hazel sensed a new feeling for her – here she was standing in a hotel foyer and getting a room allocated for her son! Her son!

"Yes, we already have the room next to yours Mrs. Tate. You have a connecting door. His room has it's own shower and toilet."

"Toy-let" Pedro said slowly and loudly. He repeated it three times. "Toy-let, toy-let, toy-let!"

Hazel smoothed his black hair and smiled reassuringly at him. "OK, Pedro" she said and put her index finger to her pouted lips. He stopped immediately. He knew what that sign meant! David and Hazel gazed at each other. In an instant they realised that there may be other signals that Pedro would understand. It was clearly going to be a learning and teaching period for all three of them. Here they were, a newly formed family partly seperated by a language, that was going to have to almost begin again. They walked to the lift door with Pedro's bag. As the door opened Pedro looked inside. He was confused and scared. He did not want to go into that small room! David sensed his anxiety.

"It's OK, Pedro, look!" David went into the lift first and turned and smiled broadly. He curled his finger and gestured to Pedro as if to say 'it's not a problem.' Pedro looked up at Hazel. She smiled at him. Pedro took a few steps forward and very carefully went next to David's side. He was not happy. Hazel held his hand as she got in and smiled at him. Eventually the lift button was pressed and the lift went up. Pedro still appeared concerned but Hazel kept hold of his hand. Within seconds the lift door opened and they got out. They walked to the double room and David unlocked the door. They walked in together. Pedro wandered around the big room looking at the TV set and the mini-bar as well as other items he had never seen before. He was clearly amazed!

David and Hazel allowed Pedro to explore things, for that was what it was. Exploration! He was in unfamiliar territory and needed time to adjust. Hazel had bought some soft drinks earlier and poured a *Fanta Lemon* for Pedro. They had one each, too. Hazel had decided that if she and David were to do what they wanted Pedro to be reassured about, they would need to do the same. At least for a while. Pedro sat on the floor, crossed his legs, and sipped his drink. Little was said between them for a while and then Pedro yawned. He stretched his arms up and crossed them behind his head, gripping his fingers together. Hazel made a sign as though to say 'do you want to go to sleep?' He nodded. She pointed at the connecting door and Pedro went over to it. He opened the door and went into his own room. Hazel followed but David remained sitting on the double bed. With no hesitation Pedro went to the single bed, pulled down the covers and kicked his shoes off. He smiled up at Hazel as he lay down. He closed his eyes and Hazel thought about kissing his forehead. She decided not to, but smoothed his ruffled hair instead. How soon could she begin to show her love towards him? She knew she would have to be careful. Within less than a minute Pedro was asleep. He lay on his back with his hands clasped together as though he were praying. Maybe he was?

Hazel crept out of the room and closed the door to within a few centimetres of shutting it. She went over to David and sat next to him.

"We've got a big job on our hands here, Nutty."

"Yes, but it will all be worth it in the end, just you see!"

David and Hazel spent the next hour discussing what they needed to do with Pedro. David made notes as usual. They had a shopping list of over twenty items such as 'language', 'signs', eye contact', 'travel', 'toilet', and so forth. They would have to implement corrective behaviour at some stage, but would go very careful on that. It was best, they decided, to go easy to start with until they got to know each other better. David and Hazel would have to teach Pedro about all sorts of new things, but first they had to see how much he knew or did. His six years in the orphanage meant his experience of the outside world was limited, but then he'd lived a normal life in a community that ate, drank, slept and worked together. Where they needed to raise their awareness level for Pedro would be with things of which he had no experience. The lift in the hotel was such an example. How would Pedro cope with the airport and the aircraft on Wednesday?

They decided that the following day would be used to familiarise Pedro with as much as possible. They'd take a walk around Santiago, point things out, and try out some words on him. An English-Spanish dictionary would be a good idea! Tonight they would eat in the hotel, be together and just relax. Little did they realise that all would not be that simple!

Chapter 6

"Get that child out of the kitchen!" screamed the sous chef in Spanish just after seven o'clock. Pedro had woken up early and, as was normal for him on a Tuesday morning, he worked in the kitchen. He walked downstairs and found his way by following his nose as the coffee aroma began to waft through the dining room. The sous chef walked over to Pedro and asked where his parents were? He told them they were upstairs, probably asleep. Sure enough, David and Hazel had slept well after a tiring day on the Monday. They'd eaten in the hotel as planned and then watched some TV in their room with Pedro before they all went to bed around nine o'clock. Pedro did not have jet lag to cope with and he normally woke early. He had got up, washed and dressed himself. As far as he was concerned it was just another Tuesday for him – so get down to the kitchen to help prepare food!

The hotel duty manager woke the new parents and explained what had happened. David and Hazel got dressed in double quick time and raced down stairs. Pedro was sat looking dejected on a small stool in the corner of the kitchen. Hazel went over to him.

"Hi, Pedro, are you OK?" she asked taking his hand. He understood the question. "Me OK", he replied. "Me think I help with breakfast but man no want me here!" Hazel led him out of the kitchen and into the hotel foyer. They sat down on a large brown leather sofa and Hazel tried to reassure Pedro that he was not in the wrong. She explained that here in a hotel others got breakfast ready, unlike at the orphanage. Hazel thought he understood but wasn't sure. They went back upstairs using the lift and Pedro went into his room. David sat with him for a few minutes and realised that their new committment was going to be hard work.

"Do not worry, Pedro. Everything will be OK." David stroked his black hair as he looked at Pedro. Pedro seemed a little confused but David felt that as time went on, Pedro would get used to a different way of life. He hoped it would be sooner rather than later. "Today we are going to look around the city and we shall walk," said David as he made his left hand index and middle fingers into legs and twiddled them. Pedro smiled. David knew they would need to be careful as Santiago was going to be a new experience for Pedro. Every sight, sound and smell would fill his head with new sensations. After breakfast they all got ready to leave the hotel for a wander around the city. To begin with, both David and Hazel held Pedro's hands, his black hair bobbing up and down in the gentle breeze. Their plan was to share experiences with Pedro, let him fill his heart and soul with life outside of the orphanage. They would carefully watch his face for changes of expression, whether quizzical or otherwise.

They had all day to fill so there was no rush. A long tree-lined avenue some two kilometres from the hotel led them toward the city centre. David had brought his trusty ruc-sack that contained a few items including his digital camera. Pedro looked around at everything, his eyes darting from passing cars to people walking by to tall buildings coming into view. David let go of his hand and allowed Hazel to walk in front with him. He pointed to a silver-grey Mercedes Benz passing by and said 'no horses!' They all laughed as they remembered the trip back to Santiago from the orphanage. Within half an hour Hazel suggested a drink in a cafe. This would test Pedro a little, although he was used to eating and drinking in the canteen during the past few years it was going to be a bit different; small tables, a waiter or waitress, paying for what they ordered. David checked with Pedro before they entered – "zumo de naranja o Coca Cola?" Orange juice or Coke? It was the orange juice that Pedro seemed to prefer. They weren't even sure if Pedro had ever had a coke? They went in and David chose a table near the door. The waiter came over and asked what they wanted. David again tried his limited Spanish.

"Dos cafe con leche y uno zumo de naranja, por favor." The waiter scribbled the order down on a small notepad and went to get their two milky coffees and orange juice. Within a few minutes they were served. David was getting the hang of this lingo! Once all three had finished David paid the waiter and left a small tip. Pedro sipped his juice and kicked his little legs under the table. He seemed content to wait, looking around at the paintings on the walls and a small dog asleep under a ladies chair. 'How calm he seems' Hazel thought to herself. Will he always be like this, or will he change when he gets to England? They would have to see, but for now they seemed blessed with a gentle boy with the looks of an angel.

The rest of the day passed quickly. They went into an art gallery and a museum, walked past the fountains and stopped to look at trams in the busy main street. David had got out his camera and taken almost eighty photos during the day. Some were posed, others natural. Everything they did Pedro seemed to enjoy, his face going from mild amusement to wide grins. He did lots of pointing and between the three of them they managed very well with the language. Pedro would ocassionally come out with shouts of 'look there' or 'great'. At other times he spoke in his native tongue and both of his new parents were able to understand him. 'What joy' Hazel mused. She had thought that language would be an issue but it was not. She decided there and then that once back in Godalming she would seek a place where she could learn Spanish – a local college, perhaps.

At the end of the day, all of them feeling weary, they found their way back to their hotel. Pedro ran to the lift, his fear of going into a very small room had disappeared! David got the room keys from reception and joined the other two. Pedro was holding the lift door open for him.

"Muchas gracias, Pedro".

"De nada, papa". Oh, my God! Did David and Hazel hear that correctly? Pedro called David 'papa'. Hazel gently bit her bottom lip to stop herself letting go emotionally. *'Our adopted son just called David dad'.* The lift took six seconds to reach their floor. In that time David and Hazel exchanged a look between them, a look that Hazel couldn't remember ever seeing in his eyes before. She saw a tear in David's eyes, but as usual he did the manly British thing and quickly brushed it away. Once in their room Hazel put the kettle on to make a pot of tea.

"Me help, me help" shouted Pedro. Hazel looked at him and said that he could go and wash his hands first, then he could put the tea into the tea pot. Pedro was back from his room in under a minute. Hazel indicated what he had to do. He put two scoops of tea into the pot and watched the kettle boil. If she had let him, Pedro would have poured the boiling water into the pot. Common sense prevailed and Hazel did her best to make Pedro understand the danger of that. He understood, but looked a bit disappointed. She asked him to put milk into three cups from small, sealed containers. He had never seen these before so Hazel showed him what to do. Eventually, the tea was poured and they each sat on a chair sipping their tea. When they had finished, David got a children's Spanish / English book from his ruc-sack that he had bought downtown. He sat on the bed and Pedro joined him. The book was a simple illustrated dictionary and it proved to be invaluable in the coming months.

Chapter 7

They had another early night since the three of them were tired after walking around Santiago. David was awake first and checked that Pedro wasn't downstairs or anywhere he shouldn't be. He peeped into Pedro's room and he was still fast asleep. Hazel was slowly wakening and rubbing her eyes.

"What time is it?" she asked. "Just after seven. We need to pack and get some breakfast. Miguel will be here at nine. I'll wake Pedro."

David went into Pedro's room and gently shook his shoulder. "Muchos suenos!" said Pedro, waking abruptly. "OK, OK," said David quietly. David didn't understand the word 'sueno' but would find out by checking the children's dictionary or asking Miguel.

"Buenas dias, Pedro,"

"Hola, papa," replied Pedro, his dark eyes now fully open and his face smiling broadly.

"OK, Pedro, you get up and have shower," David pointed towards the en-suite bathroom. As he did so, Hazel came in and opened the little bag that Pedro had brought from the orphanage. She found one clean shirt and a pair of underpants that she placed on the bed. Pedro popped into the bathroom and the sound of splashing water was soon cascading off the walls of the shower. David and Hazel both got showered and dressed quickly. A knock on the adjoining door came from Pedro who asked if he could enter. 'What good manners', Hazel decided. "Come in", she shouted. Pedro entered looking very presentable in his clean, white shirt, albeit slightly creased.

After coffee, croissants and fruit, Pedro and his parents finished packing and waited in the hotel foyer for Miguel and Sevvy. David had paid the hotel bill with his credit card and they were all ready to depart. Right on time Miguel walked into the foyer smiling.

"Everyone OK and ready to go?" Pedro jumped up and ran to Miguel. "Buenas dias, Miguel, mi amigo!" he said. Miguel helped with the luggage and the four of them went out into bright sunshine on their last day in Chile. David had double-checked the passports, papers and flight tickets. Everything was in order. They just needed to get to the airport and check in for the Heathrow flight and a new chapter in their lives would begin. David reflected on their trip as they got into the car, Pedro in the middle of the back seat. He recalled how it had all began, so simple somehow, with the nunnery visit. One thing led to another, as though it was meant to happen or had been ordained? Almost everything they did had worked out easily, too easily somehow. What did the future hold? What would become of Pedro as he grew up? What kind of job would he get – university, perhaps? His head was full of questions as Miguel announced their arrival at Departures.

Miguel and Sevvy jumped out. Both helped with the large suitcase that contained Pedro's little bag and made sure they were heading for the correct check-in desks before wishing them good luck and shaking their hands in a formal manner. Both made much of Pedro as he was about to leave the country of his birth for a new life in England. Hazel had remembered to get out a coat for Pedro – he'd need it in England.

"By the way, Miguel, what does the word 'sueno' mean in English?"

"Sueno is a dream, senor David. They can be good or bad." Sueno? Had Pedro woken up to a bad dream this morning? David didn't want to make an issue of it. Hazel asked him what Miguel had said. David replied that it was just a general enquiry and changed the subject. Had Pedro had a nightmare? There was no point in bringing it up. David decided to leave it.

They headed to check-in desk 82 where the illuminated sign for London Heathrow was glowing red above the head of the attractive female desk clerk. David passed their three passports and flight tickets over to her. The desk clerk, Esmerelda, looked carefully at the documents. After what seemed an eternity she picked up an internal phone and David thought he heard the words 'security' and 'extradition'. Within minutes two airport security guards arrived at the desk. Poor Pedro was confused – such a large building, lots of people and now two men in uniform with guns!

"He cannot travel with you," said the taller of the two guards, pointing at Pedro. David and Hazel gasped. They'd come this far! It sunk in slowly. Would they travel without Pedro? Would they have to go back into Santiago? What was to happen? They looked at each other blankly. "The passport number does not appear to be correct."

"Please," said David, pleading with both guards. "We have adopted this boy, Pedro Caterinos. All of the administration has been done and we have a letter from the government to that effect." David got the letter out and showed it to the tall guard. The security man dismissed the letter. "He cannot go with you!"

David reached into his wallet and found the business card of Senor Valesquez. He asked Esmerelda if he could use a telephone? The queue behind them was growing and some passengers were becoming agitated. "You must be quick," she said passing David the phone. David dialled the office number. In seconds the secretary of Valesquez answered. David explained the situation to her at the check-in desk. Valesquez came on the line and asked to speak to the guard who had done all the talking. As the guard spoke to the government minister his face reddened until he looked like a lobster. "Si, si, si," he answered. Clearly, Valesquez was tearing a strip off him for daring to refuse the three passengers to go to the boarding gates. After less than one minute the guard handed the phone back to the desk clerk and waved the three of them through. The suitcase was rapidly checked in, the LHR flight label attached, and they were on their way. There were no further problems as they passed through airport security.

David and Hazel took stock of the situation as they found three seats in the lounge near gate 37. They bought some water and a ham and cheese *bocadillo* to share, and it wasn't long before the flight was called. Pedro's new parents took his hand and gave him a reassuring look as if to say 'everything will be all right'. The three found their seats on the Boeing and settled down. Pedro was excited as was to be expected, trying to make out what was happening around him. Soon all quietened down, the hostesses went through the safety procedure, and the calm voice of the captain gave the passengers the usual details of aircraft speed, height and arrival time in London. Hazel looked out on blue, cloudless skies as the giant plane took off. She wondered what awaited them in Godalming? She looked across at David, Pedro between them. He smiled at her as if to say 'soon be home, Nutty'.

They looked down at their new son. His cherub face was serene. He was fast asleep. As they sped through fluffy white clouds gaining height, Hazel turned to David, held his hand and said "There must be a God. He's been with us for a long time now."

PART SEVEN

Chapter 1

There was a lot to sort out now that Pedro and his parents were back in Godalming. Ed and Di had collected them at the airport and Hazel had given them all the news on their trip. Hazel would contact Social Services who had helped arrange schooling for Pedro. She'd phone Terry Williams to give him an update on the adoption process. He'd been so helpful. She wanted to phone her sister Maureen and give her the all the news. The local college may have Spanish lessons that Hazel decided she would try to attend so she needed to book that. Keith Blandford ought to know what had happened, followed by the ladies in the church group, especially Gertrude and Rosemary. The other person that Hazel would consider would be Amelia. Should she call Amelia to give her the news? But, wait a minute. Why should she contact Miss Pudding? Hadn't she been a prophet of doom for Hazel and David? What help had Amelia been, casting doubt on the whole adoption process and suggesting 'that there may be a problem with the boy' or words to that effect? No, blow her, Hazel said to herself. It had all gone very well. She decided there was enough to consider without worrying about Amelia what's her name!

Before they left Chalk Road, Hazel and David had redecorated the single room for Pedro. They had agreed that it was to be kept fairly simple so that he didn't see a great contrast between the orphanage and his new room in Godalming. There were colourful curtains and a bright red, blue and white rug – the colours of the Chilean flag. They had enough furniture for Pedro's clothes but they needed to buy quite a few more things now that he was in England where it was some twenty degrees Centigrade cooler! On Saturday they would go to town and look around for shirts, trousers, underpants, socks, jumpers – in fact almost every article of clothing they could think of! And especially a decent outer jacket and woollen hat to keep the cold at bay.

The first afternoon back home they allowed Pedro to slowly get used to the house. He was not used to stairs so going up and down the flight was a novelty to him. Hazel explained a number of things to him – how to use the shower, where towels were kept, items in the kitchen and in the fridge, where the cutlery draw was and so on. She was also careful to tell Pedro about other potentially dangerous areas – the electrical products that had a plug fitted – like the kettle, television, and radio. Hazel took care to emphasise the danger of the sockets and as she pointed things out she would shake her finger to indicate that they presented a hazard. From Pedro's body language he did understand, Hazel decided. David was helpful, too, and went over some of the points that Hazel had made. Pedro liked that. It made him feel important.

Hazel showed Pedro his bedroom just before their evening meal. She had indicated that food would be served at the large kitchen table (she had managed 'mesa de cocina') as she patted her tummy. Pedro did the same and laughed. She couldn't help but smile herself when she saw his eyes open wide. David had bought a couple of simple Spanish books from W.H.Smith before they had gone to Chile. They were from Dorling Kindersley and were amply illustrated with pictures of animals, common everyday objects, maps, modes of transport and lots more. In addition, he had the book David had bought in Chile. As soon as

Pedro opened these he was entranced. He went from page to page seemingly absorbing all that the DK books had to offer!

David had stayed with Pedro while Hazel put the finishing touches to a meal of lasagne, crusty bread and ice cream. She thought that orange juice all round would be the best. They'd all have a clear head in the morning. David was going into the office to catch up on various projects before the week-end and to see how his staff were doing. They all knew where he'd been so he felt they'd want an update on the trip. Hazel had phone calls to make and would write out a list first, beginning with the most important.

They sat down as a family at home for the first time. It was almost impossible for Hazel at that instant to put her feelings into words. In fact she closed her eyes for a second in case she was dreaming. No, they were all sat there! Pedro was seated on one side of the table, with Hazel and David at each end. Hazel dished out the lasagne onto their three plates and placed each one on the table – Pedro's first. David picked up his knife and fork and was about to put a portion of the pasta dish into his mouth when Pedro shouted out.

"We pray, we pray! Always pray before eat!" Of course, here was his new mother, a churchgoer, not about to give thanks for their food!

"Yes, you are correct, Pedro. We had forgotten." She clasped her hands together and gave David a look that signalled 'do the same'. They closed their eyes and Hazel began "Dear Heavenly Father, we thank you for the food on this table, for the family love that we share, and for everything that you provide. Amen." Pedro and David said 'Amen' in unison and Pedro laughed. Clearly, Pedro had been brought up to say prayers before each meal and also at bedtime, no doubt. David and Hazel would need to remember that. As they ate they chatted in 'broken English and broken Spanish'. Pedro enquired about lots of things and between them they were able to hold a sensible conversation, apart from a few Spanish words that neither Hazel or David could comprehend. David had placed a small notebook and pencil on the table and jotted down a word or two, or at least how it sounded, from time to time.

When they had finished eating and drinking, Hazel began to clear the dishes away. Pedro asked if he could leave the table and Hazel said 'yes'. Goodness! She couldn't recall when she had last heard a child ask if they could get down from the table? As she placed dishes in the washer, Pedro gazed in amazement at the large white cube with a big glass eye at the front. 'Absolutely amazing!' his eyes said. He smiled again. He wanted to help tidy up, and Hazel realised that the institutional life he'd led for the last six years must have involved all, or most, of the children helping out. She let him assist, of course. He needed to find his way in their domestic routine. David and Hazel agreed that he should be allowed to help – no point in not letting him be a part of the family. After all, that's what all this was about. Pedro had to feel a part of things and become integrated.

They all sat in the lounge and watched some television. An hour at the most Hazel decided, and something Pedro could easily watch. David put on a DVD about wild life in the sea. David Attenborough had been at his best for a series on the oceans and Pedro was captivated watching whales and dolphins glide effortlessly through the blue waters. It wasn't late but after a short while the three of them felt tired. Jet lag had caught up with them and Pedro's eyelids were droopy.

"Me sleep," he said, pointing upstairs. "OK, Pedro, time to climb the stairs", Hazel suggested. He walked over to her and took her hand as though to say 'take me up'. David would check his emails before going to bed and put the alarm on for 0700.

Hazel took Pedro up to his room, showed him where some of his clothes were for the next day, and went into the bathroom with him. She put some toothpaste onto a toothbrush and made an up and down movement to indicate how to brush his teeth.

"Me know, me do many times before," he came back. No worries there for Hazel then, but she hadn't remembered to do this at the hotel two nights before! 'Oh, well, his teeth are healthy and strong' Hazel reflected, recalling the medical report read out by Velasquez.

Hazel popped back into Pedro's room a few minutes later. He was in bed wearing a borrowed pair of striped pyjamas that were a little too big. She had borrowed them from one of her church friends before they left. He was almost asleep and Hazel bent down over him. She felt that she could kiss him on the forehead now. The time was right. He was here, spending his very first night in his new home. Hazel leaned down towards him. As she did he looked up at her. His dark eyes seemed bigger than ever.

"Buenas noches, mama. Love you." Hazel kissed him, switched on the nightlight, and went across the landing into the bathroom.

She sat on the edge of the bath and sobbed her heart out. She just sat there and listened to the words of Pedro – 'good night, mama, I love you' was what he had said. He called me mama! He said he loved me! She couldn't take it all in. Hazel knew that she had a romantic and emotional nature, but this was too much right now. She cried into a hand towel, her tears cascading down her cheeks.

"Thank you God," she whispered when she was able to speak. She stood up and looked in the mirror. He eyes were red and slightly puffy. She wondered what David would say when she went into the bedroom. She needn't have worried. He was fast asleep.

Chapter 2

During the coming days and weeks, and after Hazel had told all of her family and friends about Pedro, things began to get into a routine. Hazel and Pedro had met with Terry who was surprised and delighted at Pedro's good manners and splendid looks. She was able to thank Terry personally for all of his help before they flew back to Santiago, and for putting them in touch with the right people to arrange schooling for Pedro. Hazel and David had also been to Godalming church each Sunday since they'd returned and their friends there were pleased to meet the 'little chappy' as someone had called him.

"What is chappy?" Pedro had asked after they left church and were walking home. "Oh, it's just a friendly name – they like you, that's why!" replied David. The ladies at church were quite enamoured with Pedro. Rosemary exclaimed that he would grow up to be a handsome man one day whilst Gertrude actually gave him a hug, Pedro almost disappeared into her ample cleavage! It was clear that the 'little chappy' was going to be a firm favourite with them all. Keith liked him, and asked Hazel in a quiet moment whether she and David would like Pedro to be baptised? They did not commit to that at the time and decided to discuss it with Pedro. After all he was now six years of age and would be seven on 29 June which was only a few of months away.

Hazel had partly prepared Sunday lunch before they went to church and so it took only a little time to get things onto the table. Pedro helped, of course. After eating and clearing away, Pedro and his parents sat down in the lounge together to talk a few things over. On their list was the baptism, schooling and a holiday later in the year. When Pedro understood what a baptism was – and it took all of David and Hazel's skills in explanation – he agreed saying he wanted to be baptised if it brought him closer to Jesus. That was the clincher.

As regards school, he had spent one week at his new place of learning in Godalming. The three of them had been to see the headmaster and met several other members of staff. The school and teachers seemed very good. Pedro had been registered with the Social Services at Terry's suggestion, and with the Local Education Authority. One of the teachers at the school was fluent in Spanish which would inevitably prove to be a great help. Pedro had confirmed that he was enjoying school and had found three new 'chappies' that he played with during break times. Hazel smiled. Pedro had picked up on the word 'chappy' and decided it meant a 'friend'.

David explained to Pedro that it was common for many people to go away for *'vacaciones'* during the year and that during the month after his birthday they could travel somewhere for a vacation. David showed Pedro a map of Europe and pointed to some places. However, it soon became apparent that the map meant nothing to Pedro. How could it? For a boy who had spent all his life in an orphanage, at best he might have seen a map of the world pinned on a wall? Maybe not. David suddenly decided that the best solution was to send away for a couple of DVD's on different destinations that travel companies now seemed to do. Then they could put them on the TV and watch them. He told Pedro what he intended to do and Pedro understood, after Hazel pointed at the TV set and pretended to use the zapper as though changing channels or the volume.

They went out for a walk mid afternoon but came back after an hour as it had started to rain. Before they'd got home, puddles had formed on the pavements and Pedro took great delight in splashing in every one that he could. He was wearing his new wellingtons from the local garden centre. Hazel smiled as she thought of her own childhood, her parents holding her hands as she did the same in her little pink wellies. 'They didn't deserve to die in such a horrible way', she briefly told herself. She missed her parents dreadfully. They had done everything for her. Given her good schooling, a lovely upbringing, always been kind, and she loved and missed them very much.

"Nutty, we're home!" Hazel came out of her daydreaming as they reached their house. "Sorry, I was miles away." They went in and quickly got out of their wet clothes. Pedro seemed to see rain as a novelty which David could understand. After living under relentless sunny, blue skies in Chile for most of the time, grey clouds and drizzle was a definite change for him! As he grew older that opinion might change, David mused. They were still feeling tired from their Chile visit so they opted for an early night. It was no problem for Pedro to go upstairs to bed. He loved running up two steps at a time and his own room was his palace – no more sharing with others anymore! He had soon got used to living with his parents. He could boil a kettle, make a pot of tea, fill the dishwasher, turn the TV on and off and had got used to using the bathroom. That included the shower, too.

As well as his new 'gumboots', David and Hazel had bought Pedro lots of clothes that would be suitable for school and for home. A lilac and maroon North Face anorak, with detachable lining, was his favourite. He's also been treated to a seven inch DVD player that he could use in his room. David had ordered a few 'spaghetti westerns' from the Amazon website and

Pedro loved them! The sight of cowboys riding across desert interspersed with cacti made Pedro grin from ear to ear. Did it remind him of 'home'?

Hazel looked into Pedro's room just after nine o'clock and he was fast asleep. Lee van Cleef was about to hit a guy in a saloon bar as Clint Eastwood walked in chewing a cigar. "Leave him alone, punk," said Eastwood as he raised his poncho to reveal a Colt 45 revolver.

Hazel switched the DVD player off and kissed Pedro on the forehead. "Goodnight my little cowboy," she whispered.

Chapter 3

David was becoming increasingly frustrated at Smith & Johnson, although he didn't let it show at home. The senior management team were cutting back on expenditure and asking questions about the value of brand advertising. He was under pressure to perform as Marketing Manager and he knew that cash had to be invested in promotional tactics to reinforce product awareness. The additional clinical evidence that was available from the US was not having the desired effect with the sceptical GP's in the UK. David was convinced that his strategy was the right one and he was determined to fight his corner. However, he was not going to give up and would continue to motivate his small marketing team.

David looked at a small photograph of Pedro that he had on his desk. Hazel had taken it a fortnight ago when they were out in a park. He was wearing a dark green fleece jacket and sitting on a swing. Those who came into his office would comment on it and ask after Pedro. David wondered about the little boy – his 'little cowboy' – his Pedro. Where did he come from? Why was it that he was left abandoned outside the big gates of the nunnery? Was it coincidence that he and Hazel visited the nunnery after seeing Father Rodriguez at the *Refugio de Cristo* in Valparaiso? What powers had been at work when Father Rodriguez pressed that note into Hazel's hand? Was it serendipity? What of Pedro's parents, or at least his mother? Maybe he was left because his mother couldn't afford to keep him? Many different scenarios went through David's mind as he gazed at the picture.

"Penny for your thoughts!" said Doug as he knocked and entered. Doug was the father of two lovely girls and showed a lot of interest in Pedro. David sensed that Doug wished that he had a son but he and his wife Virginia had decided against any more.

"How's the young man?"

"He's great and doing well at school. His English lessons are proving worthwhile – we can hold a two way conversation with him now without me having to use sign language!"

"Have you seen the latest IMS stats?" asked Doug. Doug showed David the *Intercontinental Medical Statistics* tome that came out monthly. In the Cardiovascular drugs section David looked down the page and found the company products. Market shares had dropped by several percentage points. "Blast!" David exclaimed. "We need to do something about this and quick." He told Doug about a plan to carry out market research. After further discussion Doug asked David to pass on his best wishes to Pedro and then he was gone, carrying the large black IMS with him. David was about to check his emails when John Stephenson the MD came into his office. "Hello, David, how's the little fellow?"

"Fine thanks, John," replied David standing up and holding his right hand out. John shook David's hand and they both sat down. John had closed the office door which was always an ominous sign, especially when the company had an 'open door policy'.

"David, I've been thinking about the structure of your department. I feel we need to trim it in terms of staffing." David swallowed hard. "I've been talking to Trevor and we think it's a good idea to transfer Doug to the Sales Management team.

He'll be able to use his marketing skills in a selling situation as a Regional Manager and help build a bridge between your department and the sales force. A vacancy has just come up for Scotland as Jim McTavish has resigned with immediate effect. Trevor will be having another word with you later but I felt you should hear it from me first. Keep it to yourself for now, won't you?" Stephenson stood up and walked out leaving the door open.

David sat there for a few minutes, trying to digest what he been told. John Stephenson was not one to waste a thousand words when a hundred would do. No discussion, no pre-amble, just the bare facts. 'Bloody hell' David said to himself. His secretary, Denise, came in. "Are you OK, you look as white as a sheet?"

"Yes, nothing that a couple of paracetamol can't handle." David smiled, often the actor in the office under circumstances like these. "I've finished that report for you and can I remind you about tomorrow's meeting at ten o'clock. By the way, Trevor wants to see you before you leave today. Any time in his office, he said." She turned in her efficient, secretarial – like manner and went out. David took in a deep breath and slowly breathed out. He decided that he'd wait a while before heading to see Trevor. He gazed out of his office window and tried to relax. Eventually he went to see Trevor. "Trevor has left for the day" said his secretary. He apologises but it was an emergency. He'll be in at half past eight tomorrow and he'll see you then."

David wasn't hanging about today. He didn't want to see Doug until after he'd met Trevor. On the way home David stopped off at the Bowls Club. He thought about an apple juice but then decided on a gin and tonic, or 'gin and sonic' as BA had called it! Always careful with drink-driving he made one drink last for half an hour before going home. With his car parked on the drive and an extra strong mint in his mouth, David walked through the front door in Chalk Road.

"Hi, Nutty, I'm home."

Pedro ran to greet him, arms outstretched. "Daddy, daddy" he shouted. David hugged him tightly, then kissed Hazel. "How's your day been?" she asked him.

"Fine, just fine!"

Chapter 4

Pedro continued to do well at his school. His first report contained phrases such as 'bears himself well', 'is a good example to others in the class', and 'is often the first to offer to do tasks in the classroom'. His English had certainly improved, and he showed interest in history and geography. The headmaster, Mr. Reynolds, remarked that 'Pedro could have blue blood in his veins, such is his manner and bearing in school'.

David and Hazel were pleased with his progress. He was making friends and asked if he could bring one home the day after tomorrow. His friend was called Clarence. Pedro pronounced it as 'Clarensay'. Hazel thought it was best to leave it at that rather than correct him. If Clarence didn't like it, he would be best placed to tell Pedro. He had brought some homework back and was keen to do it. 'What a change from other children!' Hazel said to herself. Her friends would often say that the TV or an X-box game was all that interested their children when they got home after school. Pedro went up to his room where David had fitted a small drop-down table against a wall that acted like a desk. It was perfect for Pedro. A three-legged padded stool provided his seating and a bookcase held his bits and pieces such as pens, pencils, notepads and rulers as well as a few books. A map of the world covered most of another wall and Pedro would often stare at that. David was certain that Pedro was getting an idea of distance, and he certainly knew where South America and Europe were!

As requested, Pedro brought Clarence Bosanquet home after school later that week. Hazel checked with Clarence that his mother knew where he was. She did. Clarence showed Hazel a piece of paper from his mother on which she had written that she was pleased that Pedro and him were becoming good friends. A home telephone number was shown in case Hazel needed to call. Hazel provided a drink and one wrapped wafer biscuit for each of them. Pedro asked if he could show Clarence his bedroom.

"Of course you can, but be careful with your drinks, we don't want any stains on the carpet."

The two boys went upstairs. Hazel heard them chattering about football and Chile. Pedro was probably telling Clarence how much better Chile were than England? Hazel listened again. She was wrong! Pedro was saying the opposite! He was actually using the phrase 'my country' to describe English soccer! Hazel was stunned. He'd only been in the country a short time but was becoming so integrated that he called England his team! They played and talked together for almost an hour before Hazel called time on their activities. They came downstairs together, taking the steps in unison as though tied at the ankles. Clarence thanked Hazel – "Thank you very much, Mrs. Tate," he chirped, putting his cap on his head. "I've really enjoyed it." He waved as he went out of the front door. Hazel forgot to ask but she assumed Clarence was all right for getting home? She hadn't asked him where he lived. She had to assume that he was quite capable to find his way home. Pedro went back upstairs and sat at his desk and began looking through a history book. If he was going to be a good pupil he thought he'd better know something about the Kings and Queens of England. He seemed to have an appetite for knowledge. Hazel recalled that Mother Caterina had remarked how studious Pedro had become during his time at the orphanage. He was developing rapidly.

While Pedro was busy, Hazel made another list of "must-do's". There was the baptism to consider. Keith Blandford had proposed a date but Hazel hadn't yet confirmed it with him. A passport was needed for Pedro. No European holiday without that! She planned to visit her sister in Durham at half term and take Pedro to meet Maureen and Jessie. She'd phone Maureen later and suggest a couple of dates that suited them all. She thought about her friends and worked out who she hadn't yet told about Pedro. She didn't feel inclined to get in touch with those at the junior school where she'd worked – not after the way she was dismissed. All the girls at church had been told. Best to do that before the baptism to prevent surprises or heart attacks! Hazel finished her scribbling on the notepad. She put it down and rested in the lounge for a few minutes. Pedro was quiet in his room and she wanted a little time to herself. To reflect on things – a lot of things.

She checked the diary and phoned Keith. David was happy for Hazel to decide on the baptism Sunday. He'd go along with whatever she decided. Keith and Hazel agreed on the last Sunday in the month. He said he'd pop round soon to go through it with her, and she could tell Pedro so that he was informed. Keith sounded a little uneasy on the phone but Hazel didn't enquire as to why? Maybe he had a good reason. Did he need another new verger?

Hazel was about to go into the kitchen to do some preparation for the evening meal when the phone rang. 'It's probably Keith suggesting a date to come round', she thought.

"Hello, Mrs. Tate?" a strange voice said. "It's Mrs. Julia Bosanquet here. Is Clarence with you?" Hazel's heart missed a beat.

"No, he left here over half an hour ago. Where do you live, Julia?"

"In the next road to you."
'Oh, my God', Hazel said to herself.

Chapter 5

Hazel needn't have concerned herself. Within a few minutes of the first call from Julia, Clarence had arrived home and Julia immediately phoned Hazel to let her know. He had called into a friend's house on the way home because he had left one of his favourite pens there two days previously. Hazel hoped Pedro wasn't going to be doing things like that – she'd be out of her mind with worry!

The baptism came and went without any fuss. Everyone thought what a nice young man Pedro was and many spoke to him in church after the ceremony. David and Hazel gave thanks to Keith Blandford whilst they were having a cup of tea and folks were tucking into a nice spread that the ladies of the church had put on. Pedro was talking to some of the younger members of the congregation and seemed to be getting on very well with them. Hazel knew that meeting people and making friends was paramount for Pedro to feel a part of the community. One of the people that Pedro was chatting to was a girl called Elizabeth. It turned out that Elizabeth was half Spanish. Her mother, Maria, had come to England as a student some years ago from Spain to study at London University. There she met a man called Bob Menzies and they married soon after. Maria was teaching in Godalming whilst Bob was an accountant with a well known firm in the city. Bob and Maria had been attending the church for just under two years. Hazel went over to talk with them.

"Hello, Maria, I'm Hazel Tate. If I remember correctly, you helped out with the church fete some little time back, so thank you for that."

"I didn't mind at all – it went very well. This is my husband Bob." Hazel and Bob shook hands. David was still chatting to the vicar.

"Your son, Pedro, seems to be keeping Lizzie amused!" Maria flicked back her jet black hair with a deft movement of her right hand.

"Yes, he's a chatterbox now that his English is improving. He loves telling stories!"

"Well, Lizzie is fluent in English and Spanish so who knows, maybe they're talking in both languages!" Maria's spoken English was near perfect.

David joined them and he was introduced to Lizzie's parents. The four of them got on well after the service, but close to one o'clock the Menzies bade their farewell as they left the church.

"Hmm, nice people," said David. "Can't say I've really noticed them before. It takes children to make friends, though, they do it so naturally."

"Lizabet so very nice," exclaimed Pedro as they walked out into the sunlight. "Yes, she is," replied Hazel taking his hand. They talked about the baptism and those who they'd met at church as they went home. It had all gone off well and Pedro's parents were happy. During the coming week they posted the passport application, with enclosed fee, to the London passport office. Pedro Tate was going to have his very own British passport!

Hazel had made arrangements to go to see Maureen and Jessie at half term. Pedro would probably enjoy the train journey – what an adventure for him. So much was unfolding for this little boy from Chile. He was settling in at school, he was virtually the perfect child, and his school reports so far had been positive. David and Hazel counted their blessings. In the space of a few months they had gone from a childless couple to a family of three. Pedro had come 'ready made'. Like a McCain's easy to cook dish, from frozen to piping hot within minutes! Not that she was comparing him to lasagne or over ready chips, but there did seem to be a parallel.

Before they went up to Durham, Pedro's parents had received his half term report which was excellent. He gained top marks in History and Geography, came second in Maths. and his overall behaviour was described as 'excellent' by Mr. Reynolds. David was incredibly pleased and told Pedro so.

"You've done really well, Pedro! We are both very pleased with your progress."

"I can do even better than theez! You wait and see!" His big eyes widened and his thick black hair flopped over to the left.

David had met with Trevor to thrash things out at the office. Trevor made it clear to David that he felt he was doing a good job for the company but couldn't change the plans of John Stephenson. Trevor had a neighbour whose daughter was studying for a Master of Business Administration degree at Surrey University and who needed to get some industrial marketing experience.

"As part of Mandy's MBA, a three month spell with us is an option for you to keep your numbers up. What do you think? She graduated in Physiology at Edinburgh with a first class honours. It won't cost us a penny." David had little option but to agree. Trevor told David he'd already broached Stephenson who'd approved of the idea in principle. That meant he had to get his boss to OK it and it would happen. Two weeks later Mandy Trueman joined the Marketing Department. She made an immediate impact and she also had market research experience. Jane Jones, who had joined the department after getting her degree in Business Studies, was continuing to do a good job for David. 'Strange how things work out', thought David.

Doug had agreed to become Regional Manager for Scotland and been offered a good relocation package. His wife, Virginia, was originally from Stirling and had always had strong ties to 'bonnie Scotland'. By the end of the month they had found a nice property just outside Stirling with views of the Wallace monument from the bedroom window. They all settled in quickly and Doug got to grips with sales north of the border. Market shares grew by 10% within no time at all. It was all going well…

That was until one of his daughters was killed in a car accident on the M8 motorway outside of Glasgow…

Chapter 6

Doug and his wife never got over that. Life had everything going for it for his family. A new start, a new adventure, a new challenge. Shortly after the funeral, Doug resigned from the company and took a job with a market gardener. His passion had always been vegetable growing and he just needed to downscale in terms of mental effort and responsibility. David wasn't sure if John Stephenson ever felt any regrets. He doubted it. One of the most unsettling parts was that the cause of the accident was never made fully clear by Strathclyde police. The whole company was subdued for weeks after that.

Hazel and Pedro had been and come back from Durham. Pedro really hit it off with Jessie, especially when she told him about her South American project for school. Pedro helped her with it and she squealed with delight as Pedro came up with lots of suggestions on what she could do to make it interesting. He looked at a large map of the continent with her and pointed to all thirteen countries one by one, adding his own comments as he did so. "This is the biggest country, it is called Brazil…" Maureen and Hazel watched in amazement. Pedro was only six, yet here he was sounding like a mature geography teacher with his pupil!

Maureen took several photos of Jessie and Pedro together, as well as the four of them on the ten second delay setting on her digital camera. She promised to email them to Hazel as soon as they'd left Durham. They'd all had a good time, and the highlight seemed to be the visit to Durham cathedral. Pedro stood in awe as he looked up at the high vaulted ceiling and stained glass windows.

"Eez very big and good", he remarked, "bigger than Santiago altogether!" They laughed at that. They departed with hugs and kisses before catching the train back south. Jessie promised to keep in touch with Pedro. "I'll miss you, Pedro, see you soon, I hope". She blew him a kiss as the train left Durham station.

"Why eez she puffing on her hand?"

"She's blowing you a kiss, Pedro. I think she likes you!"

"I love her already!" His face beamed. "I want to see her again – soon?"

Hazel wondered if this was young love? No, *younger* love! Pedro was six, Jessie was eight.

"We'll have to see. Maybe in a few months?" There was little conversation on the train journey as Pedro was fully occupied looking at the rapidly passing countryside. He was intrigued with seeing cows, lots of grass in fields, and the exciting sudden whoosh of a train on the other track going in the opposite direction. His senses were being overloaded, he looked fit to burst. Maureen had made them a snack for the return journey which they ate as they passed Peterborough. Tuna sandwiches, small cakes and several cans of lemonade helped the trip go well. Pedro ate as though he hadn't been fed for a week!

When they got back to Chalk Road mid afternoon, Pedro's passport in a brown envelope was on the door mat along with some other mail. Hazel opened it and showed it to Pedro. The photo, which had been taken at the local post office, made him look regal. A crown would have befitted his appearance in the passport. He was impressed! He'd seen images of himself on David's laptop computer but this was a real photo! Hazel let him hold the burgundy coloured document, and he held it close to his chest.

When David came home, Pedro ran to him waving his passport shouting "Daddy, daddy, me Pedro Tate! I go anywhere now!"

"You sure can, Pedro!" David kissed Hazel and hugged them both. Hazel told David about the northern trip and they caught up on bits of news. David had received two travel DVD's at his office as his secretary Denise had telephoned a couple of travel agents in London.

"We'll watch these later," he said holding up the discs. "They cover parts of Europe including islands like Cyprus and Malta." After their evening meal, and Pedro's assistance with putting things away, they settled down in the lounge to see where they may go for a holiday in Europe during July. That is, when Pedro would actually be seven years of age.

David had just inserted the first DVD when the phone rang. "Hello, Hazel, it's Amelia here. I hope you are OK and sorry to bother you at this time but are you free tomorrow? I think we need to talk. Something is disturbing me about your adopted son. Best done face to face. Let's leave it at that for now. Same place as before. Say eleven o'clock for coffee? Bye."

David, Hazel and Pedro watched the two DVD's but Hazel wasn't concentrating. She had a restless night. A very restless night.

Chapter 7

Amelia was already sitting near the back of the cafe. She had taken a table away from a few other couples who were sat chatting. One pair looked as though they were trying to patch up an argument over an old feud. Two old spinsters in Harris Tweed jackets looked as though they were about to gossip about someone, whilst two smartly dressed young men on another table were discussing business matters, mobile phones at the ready.

Hazel had taken Pedro around the corner to the house of Julia Bosanquet at just after ten o'clock and promised to pick him up around noon. Pedro was looking forward to seeing Clarence's bedroom and his books. These two young boys were forming a strong friendship – Pedro often talking of Clarence when he came in from school. She knew she could leave Pedro there, and Julia seemed a pleasant person. The house was a large detached property with a double garage and wide drive. The flowerbeds looked perfect and the grass seemed manicured. They probably had a gardener? Did Ray Kingsbridge help out? Hazel didn't like to ask what Mr. Bosanquet did, but maybe she'd broach the subject soon?

"I'm sorry to bother you, Hazel, but something has been praying on my mind for the last day or two," Amelia opened up the conversation after they'd ordered coffee. "When I've been in one of my deep thinking sessions, a bit like a seance, I've seen some problems with your son."

"What sort of problems? Is he in trouble at school?"

"No, nothing like that. It's his background – where he came from."

"Where he came from? I can tell you that he was abandoned at a nunnery a long time ago and the nuns brought him up. Some of the children there have been adopted over the years and we've done that with Pedro. All the documentation is in order and he's now got a British passport."

"I'm sure you're right." Amelia was beginning to sound a little patronising. "I can see that he will be returning to South America before the year is out. There's something not quite right here."

"I'm sorry, Amelia, but have I wasted my time coming here this morning? He's our adopted son and he'll be brought up in England. He's made some good friends and everyone likes him, so I can't see what the problem is?" Hazel was firm and stared right into Miss Pudding's big brown eyes.

"You're going to get a letter or some form of communication soon. Whoever sends that will want Pedro to go home."

"This is his home! He belongs here!" Tears began to form in Hazel's eyes. She wiped them away with her hankie. One of the Harris Tweed spinsters looked round. Hazel sipped her cafe latte and looked at Amelia. "Go on, you may as well finish."

"There seems to be an issue with his parentage. Whoever left him, or a close relation, wants him back. That's all I can see right now – it's a very strong feeling. I felt it best that you know."

Hazel did not want to continue the conversation. "Thank you, Amelia, but I need to go now." Hazel stood up and put two pound coins on the table as she threw her handbag strap over her shoulder.

"If you need to talk, you've got my number." Amelia's voice trailed off as Hazel strode out of the cafe door. Well, there it was.

A trip into town for Hazel seemed wasted. She had jobs around the house that she could have been doing. Hazel hurried to the car park, paid at the exit and drove home. She stopped on the drive and cried. 'My God, what's happening to us? We've been through all this and now that woman is warning us that there's a problem. I won't let it happen. She's wrong, she's wrong!'

Hazel walked round to Julia's house after she'd checked her face in the car rearview mirror. Her mascara hadn't run, thanks to the new brand she'd started using. She composed herself as she rang the bell.

"You're early," said Julia, looking smart in a white blouse and light blue skirt. Her long hair was tied back. "Yes, I got sorted out quicker than I'd thought," replied Hazel beginning to feel a little better. "Come in, Hazel."

Hazel walked into a large open area and noticed the sweeping stairway leading upstairs. An expensive looking vase stood on each of two semi-circular tables whilst a large oil painting of a tea clipper adorned one of the walls. The carpet was thick, and probably Wilton or Axminster. A crystal chandelier hung above their heads.

"Would you like coffee or some other refreshment?"

"No thank you, Julia, we'd better get off." Julia called upstairs for the two boys. They came down the staircase holding hands and smiling. Pedro's teeth seemed to gleam whiter than those of Clarence, Hazel noticed. What a handsome boy he was!

"Mummy, mummy," Pedro ran to her and held her around the waist. At that moment she felt complete union with her new son. It would have been easy to have cried right there and then, but she had to hold it in.

"Come on, it's time to get you home. Say thank you to Clarence and Mrs. Bosanquet."

Pedro thanked them, shaking Julia's hand as he did so. They walked to the large front door and Julia showed them out.

"Thanks again, Julia," said Hazel as they walked down the wide drive and back to Chalk Road. On the way back home Pedro never stopped telling his mum about Clarence's room and all that was in there. Toys, books, maps, play games. Everything. 'He's made a new friend there, for sure', she said to herself as they went through their front door.

Pedro ran straight upstairs. Hazel knew he would be happy going through his books or watching a DVD on wildlife or nature. "I'll get some lunch ready" she shouted up the stairs. "OK, salad will be fine", came the reply. Hazel enjoyed salads, too, so she began to get a number of items out of the fridge and two medium sized plates. Within ten minutes all was prepared and the table set. Pedro came down and sat at his usual place. They began eating, and Pedro chomped on his radishes and lettuce. Hazel didn't feel too hungry after her meeting with Amelia but decided to make an effort.

"I love you, mummy." Pedro looked at his mum. "I never want to leave here." Hazel was somehow able to clear her mind of Amelia's haunting words.

"We love you, too. You're not leaving here, silly. This is your home now. You belong here." Hazel smiled the best smile she could as she looked at her little cowboy. "Eat up, there's some ice cream for dessert." Hazel had to decide whether to tell David when he came home. Would it be a problem halved if she shared the details of her meeting with Amelia? Why should she burden her husband with this when he might be having problems at work? Maybe best to leave it. After all, Amelia was probably mistaken. Nothing was going to come from South America. What nonsense that 'some form of communication was coming soon'! Hazel could hear Amelia's voice in her head...

Little did she know that something was already happening.

Chapter 8

In Peru eight hundred years ago Manco Capac became the first emperor of the South American Quecha-speaking Incas who established a growing and sophisticated empire centred on the Andean city of Cuzco. Some considered that king Atahuala of the Incas was decended from Capac. Atahuala was killed by the Spanish conquistadores in the 1530's and his family fled the country. Over 250 years later Tupac Amaru led a failed revolt against the Spanish in the 1780's. Amaru claimed to have descended from the last Inca chieftain.

The Inca civilisation, which stretched from Quito in the north to south of Santiago, eventually died out but they had brought many civilised ideas to the world. Medicine and surgical techniques, as well as advanced agricultural methods, were developed. Descendents of the chieftain Amaru moved south to Chile, and many related facts were discovered in a chronicle found in 1987 that dated back nearly five hundred years. The chronicle showed family histories of the chiefs of the Incas.

Pedro Tate was descended from a chieftain. The main library in Santiago housed family histories going back several hundred years, and anyone who wished to research the subject had full access to these documents. A girl called Marie Amaras had given birth to a boy whose birth name was Cesar. He was born illegitimately in a clinic on the outskirts of Santiago. Marie was a direct descendent of Amaru, but she was in disgrace as she, a Catholic, was not married. Her wealthy family would disown her if she had not got rid of the boy. She was told to leave home and not to return unless she came back alone. She opted to take Cesar to the nunnery and leave him there in a small basket. He was found the next morning crying loudly. He was taken in by the nuns and named Pedro.

The Amaras family were landowners and had farmed thousands of acres in Chile for three generations. They had made many investments in industrial projects, and had shares in the copper mining industry. Marie had begun to think a lot about Cesar, wondering what had happened to him? She had recently got married and confessed to her new husband that she gave away a baby boy nearly seven years ago. Her husband suggested she should not try to discover his whereabouts and forget him, but she was adamant in her own mind that she would. Her heart had been heavy as her baby was a beautiful little boy, and she cried when she placed that basket at the front gates of the nunnery. It had taken two or three years to get over the heartache. She thought she'd never completely recover from it.

Marie and her husband lived on the opposite side of Santiago in a palatial, five bedroomed house. He was a managing director of an engineering company and drove a silver grey Bentley Turbo. She had a bright red Mazda MX5. Their marriage was more a political union than one of true love. Their families had known each other for a long time and their parents had put pressure on them to marry. Marie went along with it, after all, her new husband was a millionaire and very handsome. Three months after their wedding, Maria's parents were killed on a flight from Brasilia to Santiago. Their small plane had crashed into the Andes during a storm and all on board had died. Maria was the only child and she inherited the family fortune.

She disregarded her husband's advice about Pedro and one day she drove to the nunnery. She parked near the big wooden gates and got out of her car. She banged the knocker three times and the door was soon opened. It was Sister Bertomeu. Maria explained her presence and reminded the Sister that she had left a handwritten note with the boy. Sister Bertomeu recalled the scribbled note and invited her inside. A short meeting was held with Mother Caterina. She told Maria about the boy they had named Pedro, and why he was no longer at the nunnery. The note that had been left had not given Cesar as his name, but they were talking of the same child. Pedro had inherited his mother's dark eyes and black hair. Maria was shocked. Quite simply she still expected him to be there, and had prepared herself for the reunion. Maria asked for details of his new home in England, but the Mother Superior refused. She told Maria it was confidential information. Maria's attitude changed immediately. She demanded the information from the nunnery. She stormed out of the building, and turned to Mother Caterina saying "you'll be hearing from my lawyer about this!"

During the coming days Maria employed a lawyer with specialist skills in adoption, and connections with the government, who would be paid handsomely for his work. Very soon his enquiries with the minister superior to Senor Velasquez paid dividends. Velasquez was ordered to give the lawyer a copy of all the documentation provided for David and Hazel earlier. A DNA check was requested to prove that Maria was his real mother, and this proved to be positive. There was no doubt – Pedro Tate's biological mother was living in Santiago and was wanting to know more about him. In fact, she wanted more than that. She wanted him back in Chile, irrespective of what her husband wanted.

Maria told her lawyer to write a letter and send it via the most secure route to Chalk Road in a place called Godalming. Maria approved the letter in a private meeting with her lawyer and was given a copy. She never told her husband what she had done. He was busy with business meetings and travel, often staying away for several days at a time.

Maria had changed over the last few years. She had become harder. Her parents death had made her take stock of her life and her forceful husband had made her more self reliant. There was little love between them. She attended ladies' lunch meetings and played bridge three times a week. Her wardrobe left nothing to be desired, only the best would do. In fact she was thinking of getting rid of her small sports car. A Mazda MX5 was all right, but she'd passed the BMW dealership recently and seen a blue M3 convertible. That was next on her shopping list!

The letter from her lawyer was on its way as Hazel took Pedro to school after half term. A copy was sent to Mother Caterina as a matter of courtesy.

Soon Hazel's life would be turned upside down. No, it was to be worse than that. Much worse...

# PART EIGHT

Chapter 1

Pedro's first day back at school went well. He and Clarence compared their half term break. Pedro got to know three other boys by the names of Eric Karper, David Vasage and Clive Gannin. His English language was improving and his pronunciation got better. Words ending in 'ice' became less 'eez' and more acceptable to the ear. All in all, Pedro Tate was becoming a good all-round pupil at the school. His physical education was also good and he enjoyed playing soccer, showing deft skills with the football.

The lawyer's letter had just landed at Heathrow. It would soon be in the Royal Mail sorting system in London and then sent out to the provinces by county and post code.

David was having a meeting with his Product Managers, Mandy and Jane. A sales conference was coming up soon and a preliminary planning meeting had been called to draft out the key aspects of the marketing presentations.

Hazel had gone to the supermarket to do the grocery shopping. She walked up and down the aisles with her trolley and list, picking up items as needed.

Keith Blandford was at the vicarage preparing his sermon for Sunday. It usually took him a couple of hours – give or take ten minutes.

Gertrude, Rosemary, Doreen and a few others from church were discussing a new banner for church at Gertrude's house. It would be embroidered by four of the group and put on the west wall in church. It was to feature the 'Hands', a painting made famous by Albrecht Durer who lived in the fifteenth century.

The letter was loaded onto a large Royal Mail van.

Maureen had gone to visit friends near Lumley Castle, just past the golf course that overlooked the ground of Durham County Cricket Club. A game of cricket was going on at the Emirates ICG.

Jessie was at school, not liking the biology lesson she was taking. Words like 'chlorophyll' and 'photosynthesis' were challenging her memory banks. She thought of Pedro from time to time and decided to write to him soon.

The weather in Godalming and much of England was settled with temperatures around 15 C. It was dry but rain was forecast later in the week for the south of England..

The letter was unloaded and soon began to get sorted by Royal Mail employees.

Ed and Dianah were taking a holiday in the Cayman Islands with their friends Pam and Tony Garret.

Some members of the Bowls Club were playing crown green bowls and looking forward to lunch in the clubhouse when they'd finished.

In fact life was going on pretty normally for a lot of people. But that was about to change for Hazel and David Tate.

The next morning, after David and Pedro had left the house, the postman knocked on the front door of Hazel's home – the home of David and Pedro, too. The house and home of the Tate family. Hazel opened the door and the postman asked Hazel to sign for an airmail letter with foreign stamps on it. She did so and closed the door. It was addressed to both of them. The address was typed. It looked official. Hazel was about to put some washing into the washing machine but decided to open the letter. She sat down in the lounge and reached for the letter opener in the shape of a small sword.

Who could it be from?

She saw the Chile postmark. Father Rodriguez? Senor Velasquez? Mother Caterina?

Rip! The envelope was scythed open and the letter taken out.

Hazel slowly unfolded it. For a reason she could not explain she had a sense of foreboding. Amelia's words came into her head – "whoever sends that will want Pedro to go home." She laid the letter, now flattened out, on her lap. She began to read …

"Dear Mr. and Mrs. Tate,

I am a lawyer acting on behalf of the biological mother of Cesar Amaras. He is known to you as Pedro Tate. You have adopted him, or at least you believe you have adopted him.

His mother Marie Amaras, now wants to have him returned to her care. I have carefully gone through all of the legal aspects of this case and I'm afraid to inform you that she has the right in Chilean law to reclaim her son. What you now need to do is…"

Hazel never got to the end of the single sheet of paper. The room began to spin, slowly a first, then more quickly. In an instant everything went black. She went downwards in a spiral towards the blackest void imaginable. Down and down into an abyss that had no ending. It was the end of the universe with no stars, no planets, no lights. Nothing. There was nothing.

'Welcome to nothingness, Hazel'.

Nothingness. Nothingness. Nothingness

Chapter 2

David had not seen the juggernaut coming. He simply had not seen it. Over fifty tons of steel with white, red and green *Eddie Stobart* written all over it had flattened the BMW. His body was a crumpled mass. For some unknown reason only his face had survived damage. His arms and legs were crushed. His body cavity had been rolled flat. Ribs had looked like pins sticking out of a pin cushion. His wedding ring was never found.

In the coffin the day before the funeral Hazel looked down at his serene face, knowing all too well that beneath the white lace that covered him were crushed bones and ripped skin that had been stitched together. His face looked demure, with the hint of a smile. He had been washed and shaved, and his dark hair was neatly combed.

Hazel felt oddly untouched by this. Behind the coffin stood a thin man dressed in a white suit. His longish hair was white, as was his beard. She glanced at him. His sky blue eyes didn't move. It was as if he was standing guard over David. Hazel decided he was a member of staff at the undertakers. In the background Hazel could just hear some classical music – Brahms perhaps, or Tchaikovsky. The feeling was one of total serenity and peace. Total tranquility.

"He's at peace now, you have nothing to worry about," said the man in white.

Hazel opened her mouth to speak but no words came out. She concentrated and tried again. Nothing. No sound, no utterance. She looked at David's face almost believing that he would open his eyes. He had not said 'good bye' to her. How could he leave her without saying farewell? She looked at that nose, those eyebrows, the shape of his chin. She recalled many happy days that she had spent with him. Days at the seaside sharing an ice cream, trying to eat a large candy floss at the fairground, the bungee jump for charity.

As memories entered her head, David seemed to smile as though he could see what she was thinking. How absurd. Totally absurd.

Behind her she heard a door slowly open. She turned to see her mother walk into the parlour. She looked younger than when Hazel last saw her. The day before her funeral.

"Hello, Hazel, I'm sorry to see David like this. All is well. Do not be afraid. He has gone to a better place."

Hazel opened her mouth to speak. No words came out. Her mother held her hands out with palms facing upwards. Hazel reached to take her mother's left hand but there was nothing there. Just nothing. She turned to ask the man in white what was happening. She looked over the coffin. He was gone. Nobody stood there now – where had he gone to? Hazel looked back towards the door. Her mother had gone, too.

She closed her eyes for what seemed only a few seconds. When she opened them, the coffin was empty. A tiny spot of blood was on the small white, lace edged pillow that showed a depression where his head had lain. She thought she saw a thorn, but could not be certain.

Hazel couldn't understand what was going on. She had to get out of this place. It was growing dark. The music had stopped. She began to scream. She wanted to scream, she tried to scream, she just had to scream...but nothing came out of her mouth. She saw the man in white in her head again. She tried to recall what was odd about him? Was it the colour of his eyes? His white beard, perhaps? No, that wasn't it at all. She could see in her mind that his hands were unusual. She tried hard to remember his hands. She closed her eyes tight. Then she knew. His hands had a hole through the palm of each one. His wrists had rope burns.

The man in white appeared to her again – he was just there, right in front of her! He knew her name and began to call loudly.

"Hazel. Hazel! Can you hear me? Hazel what happened?"

She slowly opened her eyes. Where was she? Looking down at her was Keith Blandford, his crucifix dangling from his neck.

"Hazel, are you all right? I was passing by and decided to call on you. I rang the bell but you didn't answer. When I looked through the window I saw you laid out on the lounge floor. Thankfully, the front door was unlocked. Here, let me help you up."

Keith helped Hazel into the chair. She felt groggy.

"I'll get you a glass of water and then you can tell me what happened."

She wanted to thank him, but no words came out.

Chapter 3

Hazel realised that it had all been a dream. A dream? She was unsure as to how long she had been laid on the floor. She trusted Keith and told him about the situation and what had happened. She showed him the letter from Chile. They read the whole of the letter together. Hazel began to feel better after sipping the water and sitting upright in the chair. Keith seemed to have a calming effect on her.

"What are we going to do?" asked Hazel. She was clearly depressed. Her eyes were dark rimmed.

"Seems you need some expert advice here. You and David have been through a lot and done it all by the book. It's difficult to believe that the authorities can allow his biological mother to have him back. After all, she abandoned him at the nunnery. You've got all the paperwork."

"I wish I could get some advice from somewhere," Hazel sighed. "Maybe I'll get in touch with Terry Williams. He must know about such matters, or know someone who does?"

Keith stood up after half an hour's discussion. "If you're feeling OK now I'll leave you to it. I've a meeting with the District Superintendent and can't be late. God bless you." Hazel got up, too, and saw Keith to the door, thanking him kindly for his concern and words of advice. The front door closed. Hazel went back into the lounge and read the letter again. It was now late morning and she had some jobs to do. Her head was still spinning so she decided to take two paracetamol tablets and have a cup of coffee. So many questions were going through her mind – the why's and what's and wherefore's of the whole matter.

Pedro had arranged to go to Clarence Bosanquet's house after school for an hour. Hazel had asked Julia to phone her so that she could walk round and collect Pedro once the boys were finished – just to be on the safe side. Hazel decided to phone David at the office to check if he was all right? Why had she had such an unpleasant dream? Was it an omen? She firmly decided that she wasn't going to tell him about the letter until he got back that evening. She'd pick the moment after dinner when Pedro was in bed.

She called David, told herself to be calm, and spoke with him for a few minutes. He was fine but his journey into work was a bit scary, he'd said. Just before getting into Guildford a large red, white and green truck had just missed his car at a nasty junction. The driver was on his mobile phone and was not concentrating on his driving. He said he loved her and had to attend an important meeting with Trevor. He rang off.

Hazel closed her eyes, thought for a while, and then finished her coffee. Would she tell David of her dream? Probably.

Did she want to discuss the letter with anyone else other than her husband and the vicar? Possibly.

Could Terry Williams advise her? Maybe.

Would Amelia be able to help? Perhaps.

Hazel went through the day in robot style. She knew what needed to be done physically, but mentally she was elsewhere. Washing, dusting, cleaning...but then some woman in Chile was actually claiming that her son, Pedro, belonged to her? What if they ignored the letter? Sod them all. Let's not do anything. What can they do to us? Would someone actually come and take Pedro away? Hazel didn't think so.

What would she feel like if Pedro was taken from her now? Pedro – who had told her he loved her? Hazel was his mother! Impasse?

The phone rang. It was Julia. "Hello, Hazel. Pedro has just finished going over the geography of South America with Clarence. They've really enjoyed themselves. Do you want to come round now?" Hazel confirmed the request and put her jacket on and walked the three hundred metres to Julia's home. Julia was waiting at the door and invited Hazel in. The boys were still chatting excitedly as Hazel walked into the entrance hall.

"Hi, mum!" said Pedro as he clutched her around the waist. She held him closer than normal, and tighter. This was her little cowboy. Nobody was going to take him away – nobody. She had made up her mind that if there was going to be a fight, she was going to put the gloves on!

"The boys have been good," said Julia. "They seem to teach each other all sorts!" Clarence was a great little guy – bouncy, witty and polite.

"We need to go before Pedro's dad gets home," said Hazel, emphasising the word 'dad'. "Of course," replied Julia.

"By the way," asked Hazel asked as she moved towards the door, "you didn't tell me what your husband did for a living?"

"Oh, Jeremy. He's a senior partner in a solicitor's firm that specialise in family law. He spends most of his time on international matters."

International family law? Hazel couldn't believe her ears. Could Jeremy be the answer to her prayers?

"Come on Pedro, let's head home."

"OK, mum, I'm ready. Thank you Mrs. B. and you, too, Clarence." Pedro took Hazel's hand and walked out the front door. They didn't speak on the way home. Hazel kept thinking about the letter, her conversation with David, and the future of her 'new' son. She also wondered if Jeremy Bosanquet would be able to assist them? She was seeking divine intervention.

Wait a minute. After all, hadn't she met Jesus that morning? He with the holes in his palms and the rope burns on his wrists? But that wasn't real – it was only a dream. Or was it?

On entering their front hall in Chalk Road, Hazel looked down and thought she saw a thorn on the front door mat. A thorn... was He here?

Chapter 4

After dinner Hazel confided in David. Pedro was fast asleep upstairs so they could talk. She told him about the dream and that Julia's husband was into family law. They discussed the in's and out's of the whole affair. David confessed that he wasn't sure what to make of things? What was certain was that they had to take some action. The ending of the letter from Chile strongly suggested a response was required within two weeks.

If Pedro had to go back to Chile, would they go with him? David would have to take time off work. Hazel hadn't taken up any volunteer work, and other than her church duties she had no real commitments. David could not make any sense of her dream, but agreed that if 'push came to shove' they would return to Chile with Pedro and damn well sort things out! He had been having thoughts about the work at Smith & Johnson... was it really what he wanted? The cut and thrust of business, worrying about market shares? For 'almost the toss of a coin' he might give it all up?

Hazel had told David about Jeremy and they wondered if they could approach him informally or if there would be a hefty fee involed if they became formal clients? The only way forward was for them to meet Jeremy, possibly at home, and take it from there. Hazel agreed to phone Julia the next day and tell her about the situation with Pedro. Julia seemed to be a discreet person so they did not have any issues with that.

The next morning the post was delivered, and only one

letter arrived on the door mat. It was from Jessie in Durham and addressed to Pedro Tate. Pedro had left for school before the postman arrived. Hazel looked at the Durham City postmark and the junior handwriting on the envelope. It could wait until Pedro came home...or should it? Hazel was not one for prying into affairs of others, but she felt it prudent to open the letter. She would explain to Pedro that she had mistaken the addressee to be her. Hazel took the sharp letter opener and slit the top seam of the white envelope.

'My dearest Pedro,

I have missed you so much since we last met. I've been busy with my South American project and got top marks at school. Thank you so much for helping me. The weather here is quite miserable, and I feel miserable without you.

When will you come and see me again? Can you try to persuade Hazel, your mum, to travel north and we can meet up again?

I have a small photo of you on my dressing table so that every night when I go to bed I can look at you and your dark eyes.

I hope all is well with you.
Love,
Jessie xxx'

My, my! A love letter from an eight year old! Hazel had flashes back to when she wrote letters like this, but not as 'flirty'. Jessie really did feel something for Pedro – that was clear. Hazel decided to put the letter back in the envelope. She would play the innocent role when Pedro opened it, apologise to him, and wait for his response. Oh, how young love could run so smooth.

Hazel had a lunch meeting with some of the girls from church regarding a future fund-raising event as money was needed for more church repairs. Gertrude, Rosemary and Margaret were instrumental in getting volunteers to bake cakes, bring bric-a-brac, and sell raffle tickets. Another church newcomer, Norah, was helping out, too. Hazel behaved as if nothing was troubling her, but deep down she was churning inside. Any acting skills she had came to the fore – 'pretend, pretend', she thought to herself. Let's practice amateur dramatics again.

Pedro came home from school on cue and Hazel gave him his letter with her explanation of how she had mistakenly opened it but not read it. He went upstairs. She wanted him to be able to be on his own. Pedro took out the letter and opened it up as he sat on the edge of his bed. He read it, and read it again. Pedro was growing up, but this touched his heart. He was only six years of age, but if there were any male hormones in his blood system, they were beginning to surge now. He had never felt like this before about anything. Unknown to Pedro or his new parents, this was the start of a love affair. Jane Austen, the Brontes and many other authors had written classical stories about love. Was this a new one?

When Pedro came downstairs he looked lovely. His usual smile was there. His ebony eyes were bright. Should Hazel make a comment? She didn't need to. Pedro looked up at her and said "Mum, I'm in love with Jessie." Hazel's eyes slowly began to fill with tears but she didn't let Pedro see.

"Ah, well, let's see what happens, Pedro." She carefully wiped away her tears. If Pedro was to be taken from them now, what would become of Jessie? Of their contact and friendship?

What would become of any of them? World's would collide – and everything come to an end? Totally.

Chapter 5

"I think you may have a good case here, to keep Pedro in England," said Jeremy in the lounge of his own home. "However, I'll need to make some enquiries – strictly between us, of course – to double check on the matter." Hazel and David listened intently. Jeremy was a man of standing. He wore a bow tie and had the persona of a physician or a politician He probably wore a bowler hat in the City.

"In my experience many of these cases can take years to reach a conclusion. On the other hand, an international court could decide within a few weeks. I'll do my best to get some sort of a decision for you by the end of tomorrow." Jeremy was doing his best for Pedro's parents without any suggestion of a fee. Hazel and David had already decided that if Jeremy, or his associates, were to request a financial contribution, they were willing to make one.

"We can't thank you enough," Hazel stated. "This whole matter is so important to us, as you can imagine. We've been through so much over the past few months."

David added his comments to the discussion, affirming that this was a key moment in their lives. Not wanting to take up any more time with Jeremy or Julia they bade their goodbye. Julia saw them to the front door and Hazel and David went out into the evening air. They had left Pedro in his room looking at a new school project on his laptop, knowing he was safe and having told him that they were just having a quick glass of wine with Clarence's parents. On getting home, Hazel and David were met with Pedro coming down the stairs looking satisfied.

"I've finished my homework! Another project on geography – I really enjoyed it!"

The parents wanted to have a relaxing evening with Pedro. It had been a stressful day all round so Hazel prepared a chili con carne and jacket potatoes with a side salad. Pedro, as normal, wanted to help. He laid the table and placed serviettes next to the plates. Hazel dished out the hot, red savoury mincemeat, spreading it out over the split potatoes. The aroma of chili, with a hint of garlic, filled the air. Pedro was smelling the scent of memorable flavours from his sub continent, stirring memories of his childhood. He smiled broadly. He sipped on his fruit juice while David poured some Chilean merlot into two glasses. The meal was a sort of 'coming together' after the meeting with Jeremy. Hazel wondered how much longer they would be sat as a family of three? There wasn't much conversation, although Pedro seemed to keep it going with quips about school, Clarence, the teachers and his other friends. The meal passed amicably and then Pedro, typically, offered to clear up.

Hazel looked at her son and thought how kind, how unselfishly, he wanted to help. She couldn't but think about his pedigree, for that was that it was – a pedigree. Descended from an Inca chieftain, his veins flowed with blood that had been shed for freedom and right over hundreds of years. His parents, grandparents and beyond had been a proud race. A race that knew how to fight. Proudness was their inheritance. It was genetic...it had to be. Here, in the dining kitchen of a simple house in Chalk Road, Godalming, Surrey, was a boy – no, a man – who probably deserved better? He wasn't destined to be here, was he? In the midst of normal folk from England, descended from Anglo Saxons? It didn't make sense, somehow. Was Pedro really meant to be here, in Godalming, right now? Was it providence?

'God works in weird and wonderful ways', Hazel reflected. Her thinking was interrupted. "Why don't you and dad go and sit down and I'll finish with the pots and crockery." Pedro was almost forceful in his suggestion. He was only six years old, for goodness sake! He was taking over!

"OK, cowboy," replied David. "There's a DVD I got today that we can watch together. I know you'll like it." David and Hazel settled down in the lounge and five minutes later Pedro came in. He brought the half bottle of merlot in and topped up their glasses. He actually poured wine into their glasses! Hazel was impressed. But then he had a pedigree . . .she looked at him and in that instant, that very *'life changing instant'*, she knew beyond all shadow of a doubt that she would never leave him – never. Never. What Hazel didn't know was that Pedro had already thought the very same. His young mind had gone through the thought processes associated with someone ten years older. He was aware of the circumstances that had brought him to his new home. He knew of his orphanage heritage. He knew how he felt when he first saw Hazel on that fateful day. He knew...

They watched the DVD that finished at just before ten o'clock. "OK, I'm away to my bed," Pedro jumped up. "Thanks, dad, it was great. Night, mum. See you both in the morning. Love you lots." With that he was up the stairs as though taking part in an Olympic hurdle event.

David was checking the locks on the outside doors as usual before going up to bed when the phone rang.

"Hello, David, it's Jeremy here. Sorry to bother you at this time of night but I've been in touch with a colleague who's an expert in the area that we have discussed with regard to Pedro.

I thought you might want to know. I gave him all of the details. I'm afraid to say that Pedro is going to have to return to Chile."

"Thank you, Jeremy, thanks for your help. I'll let Hazel know. Goodnight."

"Who was that, David?"

"It was BT with some message about a new deal on broadband and TV."

David heard Hazel getting ready for bed.How could he tell her this news?

How the hell could he tell her that the most important thing in her life was about to be taken away? She would be torn apart.

Unable to have her own baby – unable to have Pedro.

Chapter 6

David slept fitfully that night. His mind was working overtime. Firstly, what a cruel blow this was! Secondly, how would Hazel take the news from Jeremy? In the morning he would stay home until Pedro had left for school on some pretext of a business meeting before he needed to be in the office. He'd then sit down with Hazel and discuss the whole matter and try to reach some sensible conclusion as to what they would do next. David had looked at the bright green numbers on the radio alarm clock throughout the night and had probably seen most 'top of the hour' times. The alarm went off at 0659. The whole house was fast asleep, including David who'd nodded off around five o'clock in the morning.

    He opened his eyes and switched the alarm off. He felt awful, almost as though he'd drunk two bottles of wine himself. Hazel looked calm and serene as she slowly came round, stretching her arms high above her head and yawning. "Morning, Nutty, I'll grab a shower while you get yourself wakened." He went into the bathroom and stepped into the shower cubicle. He kept the water on lukewarm in an effort to get his muscles toned up and blood flowing through his arteries and veins. He turned it colder. That certainly woke him fully! After a few minutes, and thoroughly cleansed, he stepped out and dried himself off. His dark hair didn't take too much grooming, and the electric shaver soon got rid of overnight stubble. He splashed some aftershave over his face, got dressed, and was ready to face the day. Or was he? He had a job to do. He had to share a secret with his wife.

Downstairs Hazel had made coffee and put cereal into three bowls. The toaster was humming as four slices of bread were being given the treatment, set to medium. David poured out three glasses of orange juice, the type with bits in that they all preferred. After they had eaten, Pedro left the house at twenty past eight as normal. He kissed his parents goodbye, said he'd see them later, and picked up his small ruc-sack. He skipped to the door, it closed with a thud, and he was gone.

From the utility room David had phoned his secretary on her mobile to say he had a meeting with a Senior Nurse Manager at the Royal Surrey County Hospital and would be in the office around half past ten. Hazel had got showered and dressed and came downstairs.

"Shouldn't you have left for work?"

"No, I've got a business meeting at the local hospital at nine thirty." He hesitated..."actually, I haven't. I need to talk to you. Sit down." He pulled a kitchen chair from under the large wooden table and gestured for her to take a seat.

"The telephone call last night was from Jeremy, not BT. I'm sorry for lying but it was not a good time to share his news with you."

Hazel looked into David's eyes without saying a word. Her face looked pale. She had bags under her eyes and David couldn't help but think how all this was taking its toll on Hazel – no, on them both.

"What did he say?" Hazel almost asked the question as though she didn't want to get an answer. Her mind drifted. She looked out of the kitchen window at a sparrow on the bird nuts. The dream was becoming a nightmare. How things were changing. They'd gone from being a childless couple to a happy family in an instant – or so it had seemed. Life could be cruel, but how cruel? Surely they would all stay together? Pedro was growng into a fine young man, his English was improving, making friends, becoming a part of the community...

"Nutty, can you hear me? Have you heard a word I've just said?" Hazel seemed to come out of her reverie with a start.

"What. No? What did you say?"

"I said that Jeremy believes that Pedro will have to return to Chile. Legally, his biological mother has the right to claim him back."

Hazel stared straight ahead. A sparrow was struggling to get at the bird nuts. Two starlings came down to the bird seed, while a blackbird was drinking from the bird bath. Hazel felt as though all of her strength, her willpower, her all, was ebbing away. Just flowing out of her leaving nothing but emptiness. She was becoming a shell, an empy shell. What did life have left for her? If Pedro went out of her life, she didn't want to live.

The tick tock of the kitchen clock seemed to have grown louder. She hadn't heard it before. Now it was as though someone was tapping on her skull with a hammer. Tick tock, tick tock, tick tock. She stood up, but felt unsteady. She sat down again. David didn't know what to do. He had never seen Hazel like this before.

"Nutty, are you all right? Do you want a glass of water?"

Hazel started tugging at her loose belt, playing with the ends as if to keep her occupied. She toyed with the charm bracelet on her wrist – the one David had bought her as an anniversary gift five years ago. Hazel felt each of the twelve charms in turn. She stared at the back garden. The birds were still busy feeding. The sun was trying to shine. Tick tock, tick tock, tick tock.

After a period of silence Hazel stood up. "How much do you love me, David?"

"Very much, you know that."

"How much do you love Pedro?"

"You don't have to ask that. He's our everything, our world."

"In that case we know what we have to do, don't we?", she said firmly. She stood up and went over to the bookcase and pulled out the Holy Bible. Her demeanour had changed instantly. She looked calm and her face was its normal colour. David felt more at ease now. She placed the Bible on the kitchen table.

"You'd better get going – you'll be late for your meeting!" She smiled and winked at him, took his hand and kissed him. "Will you be OK?" David asked.

"Of course. I've got some reading to do," she replied as she touched the black leather cover of the 'good book'. She saw David to the front door and kissed him again. "And I love you two more than anything else in the world. Simple isn't it?"

David reversed the car off the drive and headed to Guildford. He had been worried about his wife, but now felt she would cope and wanted to be on her own.

Hazel sat at the kitchen table, opened the Bible and began to read. Faith, she began to read about faith. Whatever she had left, she knew she had faith.

She looked out of the window. The birds had flown.

Chapter 7

With the help of Jeremy Bosanquet, David and Hazel compiled a reply to the lawyer acting on behalf of Marie Amaras in Santiago. In it they indicated that they were willing to return to Chile with Pedro. They used his adopted name rather than Cesar, more as a gesture of defiance than anything else. Jeremy suggested an e-mail resonse as it was both quicker and more reliable than posting a letter. In law, an e-mail was as acceptable as a written letter. Once David and Hazel and Jeremy were happy with the content of the letter, David e-mailed it to the lawyer, to Senor Fernando de Gama. They gave a two week time period when they would be able to travel to Santiago with Pedro.

David checked the home files and found the letter from Velasquez that had apparently given all the rights they required to ensure Pedro was able to be adopted by David and Hazel. He even had a new UK passport for goodness sake! David had suggested sending de Gama a copy of the letter from Velasquez and Jeremy agreed.

By way of thanks, Hazel proposed that she and David take Julia and Jeremy out for dinner which they duly did. Pedro had been taken round to spend the evening with Clarence and both Julia and Hazel felt that they would be safe. Clarence had Julia's mobile phone number to ring just in case. The two couples visited a newly opened Italian restaurant in Godalming within walking distance of Chalk Road. Over their delicious meal of lasagne and tagliatelle followed by creme brulee and Italian cheeses, and all washed down with a litre of chianti and sparkling water, they chatted for ages. All four of them got on very well and the evening seemed to pass quickly. It had been good for Hazel as she seemed, for a while, to have taken her mind off more serious matters. As they finished, David specifically thanked Jeremy for all that he had done.

"It was nothing. I made a couple of phone calls to friends and *voila*, we seem to have been able to get things sorted out as far as possible and be on the right side of the law. Do keep us informed of progress. I'd be interested to hear how it all goes for you."

The e-mail was sent to de Gama who replied within a few hours. His response read:

'Dear Mr. & Mrs. Tate,

Thank you for your email and for agreeing to bring 'Pedro' back to Santiago. I have been in touch with his mother, Senora Amaras who has retained her maiden name, and she wants to see Cesar as soon as possible. She and her husband have plans to move away from Chile to another country in South America and Cesar will be going with them.

We are looking at next Wednesday, the 17th. If possible, we would ask that the three of you be at my office at 1400 hrs. local time.

Please confirm, or otherwise, that you will be able to keep this appointment.

Thank you for sending a copy of the letter from Senor Velasquez. You should know that he was not in a position to have given permission for Cesar Amaras to have been adopted and taken out of the country. Senor Velasquez has now been moved to another government department.

I await your reply which should be sent within 24 hours.

Your obedient servant,
Fernando de Gama.
de Gama, de Gama & Torres – Lawyers.'

"Next Wednesday!" exclaimed Hazel. "How on earth can we be there next Wednesday?"

"We either refuse, or we go with their request", replied David. "If we co-operate we'll stand a better chance of coming through this with a positive outcome than if we don't go back." Hazel sat down on a chair in the lounge. She sighed and lay back, closing her eyes. She'd found faith in the Bible. She'd read chapters from Matthew and Romans on faith. Jesus had preached that faith was important – that it could move mountains. She told herself that the time had come for her to be strong, stronger than ever before.

"What about your job? The office, your staff? Will you be able to get time off work?

"I'll tell them I'm taking time off. If they don't like it, I'll resign." David felt good as he said that. In fact, he couldn't believe that he'd been so positive in his slight outburst. Hazel smiled a reassuring smile at him. It was a positive gesture on his part that he was prepared to give up a good job with excellent prospects to go back to Chile. "I love you", Hazel smiled at him as she said it.

"What about costs? Our bank account is a little low after recent expenditure, things for Pedro, and we've just paid out for house and car insurance", David uttered.

"It's my turn to be honest with you," Hazel responded. "When my parents were killed in Australia they left a large sum of money to me. You never asked me how much I got, and I told you that I'd put it into a bond with Legal & Generality. Well, I took some private financial advice and placed half of it –

£75,000 – into an Emerging Markets fund. I got an update from the EM fund last week through the post. I was going to tell you about it then. Several markets, including China, India and Brazil have done very well over the past twelve months. The holding is now valued at just over one million pounds."

David's knees felt like jelly. He was speechless. One million pounds! He sat down next to Hazel and stared at her. "Oh, my giddy aunt" was all he could think to say.

"But it's your money, Nutty! Your inheritance".

"It's our money, ours, not mine. I know that I can withdraw an amount, any amount, in one immediate transaction. They need 48 hours clearance. We can have some cash in the bank account by Monday, book the flights for Tuesday and be in Santiago for the meeting with de Gama on Wednesday." Hazel made it sound so easy. So simple. Had she found faith? David was amazed at how positive Hazel had become over the past few days. He liked it. She had appeared to bloom – like an English rose.

"How much should we draw out, David? Ten thousand, twenty thousand, more?"

"Well, to be safe, and to cover any unexpected costs while we're away, what about twenty thousand?"

"I'll make it thirty." She stood up. "I'll phone the fundholders office now and give them the bank details, sort code and account number."

Hazel went upstairs and retrieved the notification of the holding – £1,124,097. She showed it to David to prove she wasn't joking – as if she would! She picked up the phone and began to dial. Within one minute and twenty seconds, and after a few checks on birth date and her mothers maiden name £30,000 would be on its' way to a bank account in Godalming.

Hazel put the phone down. Her hands were trembling slightly. She took in a deep breath. For a moment she stood still and looked around her. The house, the furniture, the pictures hanging up – including the one of the nunnery, the fitted carpets, the china cabinet with her collection of glass elephants, the love inside its four walls. She played gently with her charm bracelet. She touched one of the charms. It was a teddy bear.

Was all of this going to change for her, for David, for Pedro? What was *really important* in life, she wondered? It wasn't the material things, the items you could see and touch around you. Oh, no. It was the things you couldn't see! Love, trust, emotions, feelings – matters of the heart...

"Nutty. Haven't we forgotten something in all of this?" David looked serious.

"What's that?"

"How are we going to tell Pedro? Tell him that he may be going away. That his real mother wants him back!"

Hazel looked at her husband and smiled an enigmatic smile. Almost *Mona Lisa-esque.*

"Oh, David. Have faith! Faith will conquer everything."

Just then, Pedro walked through the front door and smiled broadly at his mum and dad, his socks down and his ruc-sack hanging off one shoulder. He looked as though he was meant to be one of the *'Bash Street Kids'* from the *'Beano'*. Right at that instant, the sun came out and shone brightly through dark, charcoal-grey forbidding clouds overhead. A sunbeam shone onto the nunnery painting on the lounge wall.

David realised Hazel was absolutely correct. One must have faith. Without it, you had nothing. Nothing at all.

Chapter 8

David and Hazel took their time explaining things to Pedro. He asked many sensible questions, and they were open and honest with him. This was no time to be telling him fairy stories. Hazel told Pedro that she would contact the headmaster to say that they were all going back to Chile to sort a few things out. Nothing more than that. Pedro understood. Hazel would tell Julia the truth, but Clarence wouldn't know the real reason. Maureen and Jessie would be told, as well as Keith Blandford and a few close friends from church. David emphasised that they would do everything they could to bring Pedro back to England and that it would be sorted out – somehow. He should try not to worry.

When they had finished, Pedro had tears in his large, dark eyes. Hazel felt herself beginning to go, to break down. No, she had to be strong! Now was not the moment to be weak in front of her son. Just as she was about to give Pedro a hug, he dashed upstairs and banged his bedroom door shut. David and Hazel looked at each other. What had they done? In less than ten minutes they had brought his world crashing down. Pedro wept on his pillow. His mind was confused. How and why was all this happening to him now? He didn't want to go back to Chile. Who was his real mother? Why had she given him away – no, not even given him away. Left him abandoned at a nunnery! She didn't love him – how could she? His home was in England. This was where he wanted to be – forever.

David and Hazel did not turn the TV on. They played a classical music CD quietly and read, or tried to. David skipped through the paper and attempted the sudoku and cryptic crossword. Hazel tried to read another chapter of her latest novel. They both failed. They couldn't concentrate. Their minds were on other matters.

David switched on his laptop computer and went onto the British Airways web site. He searched for flights from LHR to Santiago departing next Tuesday. He booked three seats for one way travel. He and Hazel had agreed that they were not sure for how long they'd be in Chile. So that made sense. He found the web site for the small hotel they had used before and booked them into that for seven nights. Seven nights just in case…he also asked the hotel if they could arrange a pick up from the airport. They came back quickly and confirmed that two rooms were booked, and that a car would collect them at the airport. Senor Zarzuela would be holding a placard with their names on it at the exit to the arrivals point. All done. For now. The biggest challenge was yet to come.

For the next few days Pedro was unusually quiet. That was to be expected. He had written to Jessie and shown Hazel the letter before it was posted. It was obvious that they both felt something for each other. Jessie would be upset to hear from her mum that Pedro was going back to Chile. However, it was only to be for a short while – 'to get things sorted out'.

Hazel spoke with Maureen and gave her the address and telephone number of the hotel in Santiago. She also contacted those friends that she felt ought to be kept informed. Most wished them good luck. Keith was particularly understanding and offered to come round to say a prayer for them. Hazel agreed to this and he was due on Monday evening at six o'clock, albeit only for a few minutes he had suggested.

David had gone into the office and arranged a meeting with Trevor. His strategy was to ask Trevor for time off, but if things got awkward he would resign. He'd discussed it with Hazel and she, as usual, said it was up to David. She'd support his decision. David's meeting with Trevor got somewhat heated. Trevor couldn't understand why David wanted time off when the cardiovascular business was under threat from major competitors. He had suggested that Hazel go back with Pedro while David stayed at home. The bloody cheek of it! David brought up the matter of under-staffing. How was he supposed to grow the business with a department of amateurs? He'd lost some good, mature marketeers who had been replaced by inexpensive, young MBA graduates. All very well for giving them experience but not what a first class pharma company needed.

Trevor refused to grant David more leave and suggested they both go and see John Stephenson to discuss it further. David refused and resigned there and then. When Stephenson heard about this he'd asked David to clear his desk within thirty minutes – under supervision – and with no access to his company laptop computer. The company car keys were to be left with Human Resources who would arrange payment of one month's salary in addition to what he was owed from the current month. Jenny Bear also arranged for a taxi to take David home once his office was emptied of his personal belongings.

When David had got home he told Hazel what had happened and expected a verbal outburst at his stupidity. It was quite the reverse. She hugged and kissed him and was almost ecstatic at his brave decision. David felt that a very big weight had been lifted from his shoulders, nay from around his neck! He'd gone upstairs with briefcase and emptied bits and pieces onto the bed. He sorted through the jumble, but decided to put everything into a cardboard box and to place it in a cupboard for now. The only item he kept seperate was the photo of Pedro that had been on his desk. He placed it on his small desk in the study. He looked at the photo and kissed the glass. 'My little cowboy', he whispered.

Meanwhile Hazel was acting as strong as an Amazon warrior. She had begun sorting clothes and packing two suitcases. She'd made a list as normal and ticked off items as they were put into the luggage. David had never see her so positive. Some extra clothes were packed, just in case they stayed longer than one week. David and Hazel kept an eye on Pedro and tried to cheer him up, turning potential negative matters into 'don't worries' as often as they could. One thing that they had not shared with Pedro was that his biological mother and stepfather were planning to leave Chile. That was too much for him to take, Hazel had decided. They would deal with that in due course.

Tuesday arrived, and the weather was bright and clear. One of their neighbours from the bowls club, Jim, had offered to take them all to the aiport for the flight to Santiago. Keith had been the previous evening and had prayed for a safe journey. He blessed each one of them and gave Pedro a small wooden crucifix made from an old oak tree that had been blown down in the Surrey gales several years ago. It was attached to a thin leather cord.

Nobody knew how important that crucifix was going to be in the days ahead, maybe the man in the white suit would know?

PART NINE

Chapter 1

Fernando de Gama was a tall man with a large black moustache. He wore spectacles that clung to the tip of his long nose. He had the air of a headmaster. Next to him sat his secretary, Helena – pen in hand. The air conditioning hummed gently, keeping the room comfortable. David, Hazel and Pedro were ushered in by de Gama's assistant and invited to sit down. It was exactly two o'clock. Pedro sat between his new parents on a red leather chair.

"Thank you for coming all this way," de Gama began. "It is very important that we meet in order to clarify matters regarding the boy." de Gama looking at Pedro over his spectacles. "As you know, his biological mother wishes to have the boy re-united with her and her husband, Aurelio. In Chilean law, the birth mother has the right to make the decision as to whether she wants to bring up the child. I am sorry that Senor Velasquez made the original error regarding this fact. Senor and Senora Amaras will be joining us in ten minutes."

David and Hazel looked at each other. Hazel was trying to understand how they came to be here now? Again she thought about what had happened and everything they had been through. She held Pedro's hand and smiled at him reassuringly.

David took the opportunity to tell the lawyer how Pedro had become integrated into the family and the local community in England. His schooling, his circle of friends, even his new passport! Most of this went over the head of de Gama as he rustled papers in a large grey folder, pretending to be interested. There was a knock at the door. In came Maria and Aurelio Amaras.

They were dressed immaculately, both looking like models from a Gucci fashion show. Maria had long, black hair and wore a designer suit with a sky blue chiffon blouse. She had high cheek bones and perfect teeth. Her jewellery was expensive and the diamond ring on her right hand was the size of a golf ball – well, not far off. Aurelio bore a striking resemblance to David Beckham, Hazel thought. Slim, clean shaven and good looking.

"Welcome," said de Gama, "please sit down." Before anyone could move, Maria grabbed Pedro and held him close to her.

"Let go of me! I don't want you to touch me!" Pedro recoiled like a gun.

"Oh, Cesar, my little boy, I have missed you so much!" Pedro pulled away from her as David intervened and moved between them.

"Please sit down, everybody!" de Gama said authoritatively in a commanding voice. "This is a legal office and you must all behave appropriately!"

Tension was clearly running high and Hazel was close to tears. She couldn't imagine what was going through Pedro's mind at that instant. This strange woman who had taken hold of Pedro was his mother? How was Pedro supposed to come to terms with that? She was a complete stranger to him. Everyone sat down and de Gama opened the discussion by summarising what had occured following the visit of David and Hazel to Santiago some time ago. He was obviously well informed and had done his homework. Glances were exchanged between all four adults involved in this discussion.

de Gama mentioned the initial visit to the Refugio de Cristo, then the nunnery, and included the names of Mother Caterina and Father Rodriguez. He clarified how David and Hazel had met Pedro at the orphanage and eventually taken him to England. de Gama wanted to ensure that all of the relevant history regarding this case was completely clarified to all concerned. Maria Amaras did not seem to be interested in these details. She continued to look at Pedro and smiled at him as Hazel glared at her.

"Senora Amaras, do you and your husband still wish to take the boy into your care?"

"Of course we do! We will look after him better than this couple will do. What do they know of caring for a boy from Chile in their country where it's always cold?"

"How dare you!" Hazel looked daggers at Maria Amaras. "You gave him away, you didn't want him! You're being selfish!"

"Ladies, please, calm down – let's have some decorum." de Gama looked sternly at the two women. David held back although he was on the verge of shouting at Maria. Aurelio seemed disinterested in the whole affair.

Although de Gama had been hired by the Amaras couple to have their son returned to them, he wanted to be absolutely certain that everything was in order before he signed off on the legal document that would irreversibly transfer Pedro to his biological mother. He had asked a colleague, Senor Enzo, to run a check on both Maria and Aurelio – the equivalent of a Criminal Record Bureau assessment in the UK. Enzo had friends in high places. Enzo was completing his check in the adjacent office. de Gama called for order again amid further arguing when Enzo knocked on the door. "Come in," shouted an exasperated de Gama.

"Do you have a minute, Senor?" asked Enzo. "I need to have a quick word."

de Gama left his own office and went out with Enzo, leaving a senior colleague in charge to ensure no fighting broke out between the two couples. Poor little Pedro was scared – his body language said it all. He hung his head but kept hold of Hazel's hand.

"What is it?" enquired de Gama. "I have uncovered something that will jeopardise the case!" replied Enzo.

"What can that be? What have you found?"

Enzo continued, "Aurelio has a criminal record. It may be that his wife is unaware of this. Four years ago he was charged with interfering with a young girl. The case never came to court. He had picked up a girl of twelve years of age, and he was touching her in a most inappropriate manner in the front seat of his car. He also exposed himself to her. Later, the girl told her Roman Catholic priest that a man had put his hand up her skirt and molested her. She described him perfectly, as well as the car and the registration number. He was visited by the police and the details were placed on file. The girls' parents and the priest wanted to keep the matter private. So, it never reached the papers or the court. I got this information from a trusted friend who is high up in the police department so we must be careful how we use it."

"There is no way that we can place the boy into her care," said de Gama. "I may as well tell them straightaway. Please come with me as a witness." He signalled for Helena to leave the room with Pedro – she would get him a cold drink.

de Gama stood looking at those present – he eye-balled them one by one. "I have something important to say to you all. It is a very delicate matter but it must be stated." de Gama revealed the details from Enzo who nodded to corroborate the evidence. Aurelio looked down at the floor, clearly disgusted with himself. Maria passed out, her long hair across her face as she lay sprawled on the thick carpet. David and Hazel couldn't believe what they had just heard.

Pedro was clinging onto his wooden crucifix. Maria began to come round. Hazel thought to herself 'faith is all'. Before they departed, Hazel asked de Gama to confirm the real birth date of Pedro. de Gama checked his file.

"The 12th of November. He'll be seven years old this year."

Chapter 2

It was clear – there was no way that Maria and Aurelio could, in Chilean law, have custody of Pedro, or Cesar. 'The boy'. Aurelio's misdemeanours had scuppered that totally. It remained to be seen whether Maria would ever forgive her husband? In a way, justice had been done. Maria and Aurelio left the meeting, after some treatment for Maria for her malaise. It was obvious to de Gama and Enzo that Pedro did not belong with his biological mother. It made sense that he was being cared for and loved by his new parents. de Gama was convinced that the care of Pedro was in good hands. He had spent some time talking with 'the boy' and was certain that the future of Pedro was assured. He was only interested in getting the best outcome for Pedro.

He rewrote the conditions of adoption, citing the reasons why he, a fully qualified, experienced and competent lawyer, now believed that justice had been served and that Pedro, nee Cesar, should be in the care of David and Hazel Tate of Godalming, Surrey, England. His final report was lodged with the relevant authorities and he informed David and Hazel that they were now free to return to England with Pedro. But, did they want to go back just now? This had been a traumatic twenty four hours and maybe they needed to stay a few more days to recover? *Yes, they needed to do that!*

From the office of de Gama they strolled to a nearby park where a cafe sold hot and cold drinks as well as *helado* – ice cream. David took Pedro's hand and they walked over to an outside table. Hazel went inside and ordered two 'cafe con leche' and the double scoop knickerbocker glory with a strawberry on top for Pedro. He deserved it! Little was said for a while as all three began to come to terms with what had happened. Not for the first time did Hazel feel like it was all a dream. Here they were, herself and David both jobless, sitting in the Chilean sunshine as though on a long holiday. They had just been through a very traumatic experience and needed time to reflect.

Pedro was slowly eating his ice cream mountain and Hazel could tell he was thinking, too. The parasol over the table provided shade, and the birds sang high up in the surrounding trees. A few more visitors to the park began to fill more tables nearby.

"Hey, cowboy, are you enjoying that?" asked David.

"Yes, it's great, dad." His eyes lacked the usual sparkle and his voice was a little sombre. "Why did I have to leave the room when the two men came back in?"

"Oh, it was just that Senor de Gama and his partner wanted to tell us something about your mother and her husband. It was nothing really, and anyway Helena took you for a drink, right?"

"Had they done something wrong?"

"Well, there was an incident some time back and Senor de Gama decided that they were not the best parents for you."

Pedro put down his long spoon and jumped on David's knee. He hugged him tightly and then reached over to Hazel. He clung onto both of them as strongly as he could. "I love you both so much. I never want to leave you. Please don't let them take me away!"

Two ladies in their mid – fifties sat at the next table looked enquiringly at the threesome. *"Es todo bien?"* asked one of them. Is everything all right?

"Si, si. Esta no problema. Gracias," replied David in his pigeon Spanish. Yes, there is no problem. Thank you.

Pedro turned to the two ladies and spoke to them in Spanish. From what David and Hazel could understand he told them that he was the happiest boy in the world and everything was going to be all right. His new mum and dad were the best! The ladies weren't quite sure what to make of that, but they smiled and continued chatting. Pedro demolished the ice cream, leaving nothing but a tiny drop of caramel sauce in the bottom of the heavy glass. His smile had returned and his big eyes showed he was getting back to normal. When they had finished, they got up from the table and wandered along a wide footpath towards a small lake. Hazel had bought a bag of 'dried bread' from the cafe to feed the ducks and handed this to Pedro as they neared the edge of the water.

David and Hazel sat on a bench seat a few metres back from the pond. They watched as Pedro threw small pieces of white bread into the water. The branches of a tree offered welcome shade as David and Hazel held hands – something they hadn't done for a while.

"Penny for your thoughts, Nutty?"

Hazel didn't reply immediately. She looked pensive, gazing out over the water to the Santiago skyline. David gave her time...he wanted to let her have a chance to collect her thoughts. Several minutes went by before a long sigh brought a response.

"Do you think you could live in Chile?"

David was somewhat taken aback. "Yes, probably. Well, I think so. Yes, perhaps I could – I mean we could?"

Hazel laughed and threw her head back. "Don't you see? We're in South America where Pedro was born, right here in Santiago. This is really where he belongs, not England. What have we got in Godalming? No jobs. A few friends, the church, rubbish weather...." she trailed off. A few minutes of silence ensued. Pedro was having a great time, putting bread on the edge of the lake to entice some birds out of the water. Ducks with glorious coloured feathers in greens and reds and browns were milling around, gobbling up tiny pieces of bread that Pedro was breaking off.

"What are you saying, Nutty?" David sounded a little concerned.

"Why don't we move here? Emigrate! Sell up in Godalming and come to Chile." Hazel smiled at him. "We can all have a fresh start!"

David looked at Hazel. He was speechless. Move here? To a foreign country where we hardly speak the language? What will we do? How will we cope? What's the health service like? What about a pension? They drive on the wrong side of the road. They have different habits to the English....they probably don't play bowls?

"Well?" Hazel looked at David. His mind was working overtime.He could detect that Hazel had thought it through – to an extent – and that she wanted to emigrate.

"Let's sleep on it, Nutty. We'll both have clearer heads in the morning. Less jet lag. We've been through a lot today." Ever the logical mind, Hazel thought to herself.

When they got back to the hotel there was a envelope addressed to Pedro Tate with a British stamp on it. It had been posted three days before. Strange? Who would write to Pedro in Santiago? Who knew he was here? When they got up to their rooms Pedro opened the envelope and began to read the letter.

'My dearest Pedro,
I am missing you so much...'

It was from Jessie.

Chapter 3

Hazel recalled that she had given Maureen the hotel address before they left England. Pedro had read the letter and then shown it to Hazel.

Jessie had said that after her project on South America she was now studying 'peoples of Ecuador and Paraguay'. They had been given an opportunity to try to learn the basics of a foreign language and she had chosen Spanish over French. Her mum Maureen was doing OK, but missed Jessie's dad as he was still looking at animals in the sea in South Africa. She had made a new friend at school called Dawn and they had sleepovers at each other's house from time to time. At the end of the letter, Jessie 'sent all her love' and ended with four kisses.

Hazel couldn't help but feel that here was a close relationship that was beginning to develop between Jessie and Pedro, but where would it end? Pedro asked if he could reply to Jessie's note, and hastily went to his own room to begin writing. Hazel felt that they'd be home before the letter arrived in Durham, but Pedro seemed anxious to respond.

After they'd had their evening meal they watched some international news on Sky television and had an early night. All three of them were tired and it had been an exhausting day in more ways than one. Pedro was asleep in minutes, after both David and Hazel had kissed him good-night. His parents got ready for bed and before ten o'clock the bedside lights were switched off.

David got himself a job with a small medical company in Santiago, whilst Hazel worked for a school as an assistant to one of the English teachers. They quickly learnt the language, and listened to local news broadcasts to get a better grip of pronunciation. They began to make friends and went to the small Church of England located on the outskirts of the city. A fifteen minute bus ride took them to most places in and around Santiago. Pedro was doing really well at school and had been made a prefect. It was obvious that he would go to university one day to study some subject or other. They weren't sure what? Life seemed good for them, but David and Hazel wanted more out of their lives. They wanted some satisfying task, putting something into the community instead of taking it out. They both had a 'calling' but it was very unclear what that was to be? Voluntary work? Setting up something to help others?

"Ahhhhhh!!!" said David as he fell out of bed. Hazel was awake in an instant. "What's going on?" she asked quietly.

"I've been dreaming," he whispered. "I dreamt that we were living in Santiago and we both had jobs!"

"Shhhh, you'll waken everybody up!" David got back into bed, rubbing his left elbow to ease the slight pain. "Sorry, Nutty," he said, as he slid between the sheets. Within minutes, they were both fast asleep. No more dreams, no more thoughts, no more anything – just sleep.

And time to 'sleep on it'. Yes, 'time to sleep on it'.

Chapter 4

David had time to sleep on it. He'd had a dream that they were living in Chile. It seemed OK. Perhaps they could, or even should, do that?

"Well, what do you think?" enquired Hazel as they got ready to meet the day.

He'd gone over things in his mind as he'd laid awake since sunrise. He sensed that it was what Hazel wanted. He knew that he would analyse everything from every angle, because that's how he was made. Hazel was more impulsive – but sometimes there was nothing wrong with that.

"Let's do it!"

"Oh, David, thank you. I know it is the right decision!"

They discussed a few more aspects of it all, including how to let Pedro know. He would miss his school and friends in Godalming. And of course, Jessie? There'd be lots to organise – the sale of the house, what to do with the furniture, letting all of their friends know, cancelling direct debits and standing orders, application for citizenship of Chile, the list went on. However, David promised himself that he would adopt a positive attitude to the whole matter and support Hazel to the hilt.

They jotted down a list of 'to do' items and decided to share their new decision with Pedro over breakfast. The other issue, of course, was planning the return to the UK. They'd booked one way flights so would need three seats back to Heathrow.

The hotel rooms would need to be cancelled, although the hotel might make a charge?

Over croissants, butter, jam and fresh fruit, and lots of black coffee, they shared their news with their son. Hazel was unsure how he would take it, but within seconds Pedro's face shone like a beacon on a dark night. His eyes couldn't have been wider. They re-assured him that they would be with him and that the plan was to live as a family in the country of his birth. They would have Spanish lessons and try hard to become integrated into the way of life as quickly as they could. Pedro approved. Thank goodness!

Pedro posted his letter to Jessie in the hotel as David cancelled their rooms at reception. The hotel were very understanding, and also helped with the reservation of three seats on the next flight to London. The BA departure was leaving soon so they got packed and finalised a few matters. Hazel decided to write to Mother Caterina at the nunnery to let her know about their plans – she thought it was right that she should know. David agreed. Hazel posted the letter later that morning, having found the address in her purse where she'd written it on one of David's old business cards. 'It's useful having a batch of those cards to write things on', Hazel thought to herself.

Pedro played a game on a console in the reception area as they waited for a taxi to take them to the airport. A number of hotel guests wandered in and out of the hotel, some checking in and others going off for a look at the beautiful city. Very soon the taxi arrived and a man with a large stomach held in by a wide leather belt shouted their names. Again their surname sounded like 'Tartay' but they knew he meant Tate. The minibus soon got them to the airport, the rotund driver helped them with their luggage, and David paid him, plus a tip.

The return flight was uneventful as the Boeing made its way gracefully through southern skies towards England, the four engines powering the big jet eastwards. Food, drink and entertainment were all excellent as usual. Even the staff were overly polite, it seemed. Once fed, films or other entertainment were chosen to amuse them, and other passengers. Hazel chose to listen to Chris Dean and the Syd Lawrence Orchestra rather than watch a film. She felt as though she wanted to relax after the stresses and strains of the past few days. There'd be enough to do and worry about when they were back in Chalk Road. David watched 'The Best Exotic Marigold Hotel' while Pedro chose a Harry Potter film – he loved Harry Potter!

The flight seemed to pass quicker than ever, maybe because they had done it a few times now and knew what to expect. David had texted Ed and Dianah regarding their return trip and they'd offerred to collect them from Heathrow. They had been friends with Ed & Di for a long time and often did each other a favour. It reminded David that maybe they should arrange another visit to the Yvonne Arnaud theatre in Guildford soon. David would try to remember to offer to pay for Ed's fuel when they got home. Just to keep things right between them – so to speak.

On the way, Hazel made a mental note of a few other things that would need sorting out. It would be diplomatic to try to let certain people know about their decision in order. Family first, close friends second, the rest third. She trusted Keith Blandford and she planned to phone Keith the next day. Pedro's school would need to be made aware, and there were people like Terry Williams and Amelia Harcourt that Hazel would want to tell. Hazel began to feel free – as though a heavy yoke had been lifted from around her neck and her shoulders – somehow liberated. There was going to be so much to do yet she knew she would cope. Every hour that passed seemed to confirm that they had made the correct decision.

Ed and Di were waiting at arrivals in the terminal building as the three passed through customs and collected their luggage from carousel number 32. Pedro had his own small ruc-sack that he carried with pride. Inside it he carried the small wooden cross that Keith had given him. It was almost, like, say, a *lucky charm* and his *guardian*, too.

"Welcome home!" said Ed as they all hugged and kissed. The usual pleasantries were exchanged as they walked towards the car park and put the cases into the back of the Mondeo estate car. On the way home they chatted and Hazel explained to Dianah about their plans to move to South America. Pedro sat between the two women in the back seat, his ruc-sack on his knee.

David and Ed listened to most of the conversation coming from behind them, but talked about soccer or cricket and how badly Surrey County Cricket Club were doing lately.

They soon pulled up in Chalk Road and everyone got out. Hazel invited Ed and Di in for a cup of coffee but they declined, saying they needed to do a few things in town. More hugs and kisses followed and then Ed and Di were gone. Hazel unlocked the front door, stepping over a pile of mail as she entered the hall. David brought the luggage in and Pedro raced upstairs, saying something about checking his latest *Nintendo* game that David had bought him at the duty free shop in Santiago.

The kettle was put on and David lugged the suitcase upstairs ready for Hazel to unpack – she usually did that. Hazel flicked through the mail, putting the junk mail to one side. There were several items – bank statements, mobile phone bills and an envelope franked with the NHS logo. The last was addressed to David. When he came downstairs Hazel passed the envelope to him.

"I wonder what that is?" she asked.

"Oh, probably just routine. Maybe I need to have another blood test or something?"

David slit opened the envelope with his thumb as Hazel made the coffee. He began to read the letter and promptly sat down.

"David, are you all right?" He didn't speak, but showed Hazel the letter. She read it to herself:

'Dear Mr.Tate,

I'm afraid to inform you that a false negative was shown on your last PSA test. Although we told you that there were no cancerous cells found in the biopsy results, we now do retrospective tests.

Your last check has shown that there are distinct signs of prostate cancer and you must come to the urology department as soon as possible for further tests. Please telephone the above number to make an appointment.

Yours sincerely,
Mr. Ashley Parker F.R.C.S.
Consultant Urologist'

Hazel looked at David. He was ashen. The blood had drained from his face.

Chapter 5

The rest of the day passed in something of a blur, or even a daydream. Did this throw the biggest spanner into the works? David knew that his father had died from prostate cancer just after his fiftieth birthday. But was it genetic? David wasn't sure but maybe he'd try to find out.

What about going to Chile? What treatment or care could he expect in Santiago? So many things were going through his mind. He and Hazel sat down to talk things over. Pedro had gone round to see his friend Clarence so they had some time to themselves.

They discussed everything, including all the why's and wherefore's as well as the what if's and when. Eventually it boiled down to a simple decision – to emigrate or not? David felt that they should, after all the things that they had been through and their thinking on their last visit. Hazel was concerned that he should have further tests and see what the outcome of those were. But how long would that take? Surely it was best to see the urologist and see what was what? Until they had made a decision on this issue, they could not begin to let anyone, other than Ed and Di, know of their plans. Pedro was excited about the prospect of 'going home' but Hazel had whispered to him that it was 'their secret for the moment.' She knew he would be discreet.

Hazel suggested to David that he should telephone the hospital and see Parker as soon as possible. He agreed to do that. Three days later David went to the Royal Surrey County Hospital and waited in the Urology Department reception area. Eventually he met with the Consultant Urologist. Parker was a physician of the old school. A real gentleman with excellent manners and communication skills. He even wore a bow tie and a waistcoat! The waistcoat pocket held a gold watch on a gold chain. Parker explained to David that the PSA level was much higher than normal, but that he had some patients who had extremely high values and who appeared quite normal in every other way. Sometimes a check on blood samples did not show any abnormalities, but the re-test on David's sample had indicated a medium to high level of cancerous cells.

Parker explained the options, including surgery and other new treatments available. He had a choice to go private, but that would be expensive. David was not rushed into making a decision. He had a good memory and would be able to share all of this with Hazel when he got home.

When he got home.

He needed time to think. He took a detour on the way back to Godalming and parked up at the roadside overlooking Witley Common. He switched off the car engine as well as the radio. Silence! It gave him the chance to reflect on Parker's comments.

It came down to a choice of 'do nothing or do something'. Either way, there was no guarantee that he would be clear of cancer if he went through all the treatment. Conversely, he may not be affected by the problem if he did nothing at all. David realised he was still young, 42 going on 43. But he could live to be 90 without anything serious happening. Why go through all of the potential hospital treatment and rehabilitation and defer a departure to Chile when they had made up their minds that they were going? If he opted for treatment how long would it be before they emigrated? It could drag on and on and on.

David had to decide just what he would tell Hazel. He could either be totally honest or...

The small blue Citroen, borrowed from Julia Bosanquet, gently rolled onto the drive. David took a deep breath as he got out of the car. He locked it and went into the house.

"Hi, David. How did it go?"

"Sit down, Nutty, we need to chat." Hazel sat at the kitchen table whilst David pulled up a chair and sat next to her. David explained most of what Parker had discussed with him, and Hazel asked questions that he was able to answer or *pretend* to answer.

"I've decided what we should do. We're going to emigrate as soon as we can! Let's get things started now!" said David. Hazel hugged him tightly as they both stood up.

David caught his reflection in the glass door of the large kitchen unit and he looked at himself as they embraced.

'Have you done the right thing?' he asked himself. He was sure he had. But then again, he was fairly sure he hadn't.

Chapter 6

The decision on their future meant that they could now begin preparing for their departure from Surrey to Chile. The next few days were a flurry of activity as they ticked off people and 'things to do' from their list. Most of their friends were surprised at their choice, but began to come to terms with it when they had time to think about it. Keith Blandford had come round and been very good at listening and commenting on their plans. He offered prayers for all three of them and a blessing that Christ Jesus would be with them.

David got in touch with his three brothers via email and explained what they were going to do. Hazel spoke with Maureen in Durham. Maureen would tell Jessie, and Hazel knew what a big disappointment it would be for Jessie to learn that Pedro was going back to South America. Hazel had gone round to see Julia Bosanquet and, over coffee, had told Julia everything about Chile – from their first holiday visit up to now. Julia confessed that she would not have the courage to do what Hazel and David were planning – "how exciting!" she gasped.

Members of the church all wished them well when Keith announced their plans at the end of the Sunday service. Over tea and coffee most of Hazel's ladies group gave her a big hug and wished them well. Gertrude even suggested that Hazel should form a ladies sector at the church that they would attend in Santiago! Did they eat scones in Chile? It remained to be seen what a Sunday would offer?

The local estate agents were contacted and the house sale details were soon appearing in the local newspaper. Their bank had been informed, and various standing orders and direct debits were cancelled or amended. However, the bank manager had proposed that they keep one account in the UK open as a safeguard – 'just in case...' The bank had a branch in Santiago, anyway, so plans were made to use the same one.

Their house furniture could either be sold off, or the new owners of their property may wish to purchase it. To be advised. Hazel had been to see Pedro's headmaster and explained matters to him. Mr. Reynolds was very good about the whole affair and wished them all the best. A final date to move had yet to be made but Pedro was able to stay at school as long as was necessary.

David had taken a couple of phone calls from Smith & Johnson, including one from his secretary, Denise, as staff there heard news of their emigration. There was no contact from either Trevor or John Stephenson, but he didn't expect that anyway. He certainly wasn't going to contact them!

The members of the Bowls Club suggested a leaving party. David discussed it with Hazel and both had agreed as that would be a way to say 'good-bye' to many friends that they had made over the years. The Bowls Club had a large room for events, and their catering was first class. Having put together a chart with activities and plans for action, David had suggested a date four weeks away on a Saturday evening.

de Gama was emailed in Santiago. Both David and Hazel had thought he was a good, solid kind of lawyer who would be able to help them relocate. de Gama replied confirming that he would be pleased to assist in any way he could. David and Hazel needed to sort out rented accommodation, schooling for Pedro, banking, health care, mobile phone accounts and so forth. Another list was written!

During the coming weeks items were ticked off the lists. It was like a well carried out military plan. People had been seen, places had been visited, things had been done. A couple of injections at the local health centre were required. Pedro had been good about everything, too. He had cleared his room of playthings, and donated quite a lot to Clarence. He wrote to Jessie, telling her about the return to Chile. He hoped he would see her again, but wasn't sure when. He knew his letter would break her heart, and it was one of the hardest things he had done in his short life. He wept as he finished writing and signed it 'with all my fondest love, yours, Pedro xxx'

The house sale had gone through quicker than expected. They had accepted an offer just below the asking price and made a handsome profit on the sale of the property. The new owners had made an offer for the furniture, fixtures and fittings to David and Hazel's satisfaction. And it also saved the hassle of selling items. Things were moving rapidly now. David had written to Mr. Parker informing him that he had decided not to proceed with prostate treatment and that they were leaving the UK very shortly. He'd continue to take a saw palmetto herbal supplement and a 15 mg zinc tablet on a daily basis. Hazel hadn't totally agreed with his decision not to get treatment but David was adamant. So that was that.

David and Hazel had sorted a lot of things out in a relatively short time. In fact they couldn't believe it themselves when they took a few minutes to reflect on what they'd achieved. All the people they'd contacted, objectives achieved, future plans made. Travel insurance was checked, and they were fairly sure they had contacted everyone who needed to know of their imminent departure. Hazel opened a bottle of Chilean carmenere to celebrate and they sipped the heavenly red wine together.

It was getting late and they were all tired when the phone rang. It was Maureen from Durham. She'd suggested that she and Jessie come down to Godalming for a couple of days next weekend to see them and say their farewells. Hazel agreed. It would be good to see her. Maureen's husband had gone back to South Africa on a university exchange deal and was still studying cephalopods and other invertebrate marine life and helping the government fisheries department. Hazel knew Pedro would be pleased to see Jessie and she'd be interested to do some 'children – watching' to see how they got on.

The next day dawned bright and sunny with a few cumulus clouds scudding across the blue Surrey sky. David was in the garden shed tidying up a few bits and pieces and making a pile of unwanted items to take to the civic amenity tip. The postman was earlier than usual and placed two items of mail through the letterbox. One was the invoice from their solicitor for the house sale, and the other envelope had a Chile postmark. Hazel recognised the handwriting on the front. It was from Mother Caterina. Hazel opened it slowly.

"Dear Hazel, David and Pedro,

It was so nice to receive your letter recently with your news about your plans to move to our country.

When you get settled in you must come and visit us here at the Nunnery. We have a vision to improve and enlarge the orphanage and with God's help we pray that we shall achieve our objective.

Please telephone us first. The number is shown at the top of this letter.

We look forward to seeing you.
Love, blessings and faith to you all.
Yours in Christ,
Mother Caterina.

'That's it', thought Hazel to herself, we'll visit the orphanage as soon as we can!' She couldn't wait to tell David.

Chapter 7

Maureen and Jessie had a wonderful weekend in Godalming. David had organised things for them to do, and they had a lovely meal out on the Saturday evening in Guildford. The weather had been kind so neither coats nor hats were necessary. They had gone to the local park and Pedro and Jessie took some bread to feed the ducks – after all Pedro was now becoming an international expert in the matter! Hazel noticed how well the two youngsters got on together. They laughed and giggled and were very happy. Maureen spotted them holding hands on more than one occasion.

"It seems as though they were made for each other!", whispered Hazel to Maureen. Maureen smiled and nodded in agreement.

"Jessie is going to miss Pedro, I can tell you that," said Maureen looking at Jessie trying to 'out-throw' Pedro with lumps of bread into the middle of the water. The ducks were almost turning the water white with their flapping wings and avine arguing over their free lunch!

Pedro offered to buy Jessie an ice cream out of his pocket money so they all sat at a table near the park restaurant. A green and white parasol kept the warm sun at bay. The adults ordered coffees whilst the two 'lovers' had a large, soft ice cream cone each. They chatted amicably about the weather, South African octopi, Durham city, Chile, red wine and the big move. Jessie looked a little down as her thoughts turned to seeing the last of

Pedro over the weekend. However, she was determined to be strong and not let her feelings show. Her grandma had taught her that. Grandma Mason had been in the *Women's Land Army* and had been as tough as 'old boots'.

Sunday afternoon inevitably arrived and a taxi pulled up in Chalk Road to take Maureen and Jessie to the railway station. Hazel knew it was going to be tough, but after big hugs and kisses they all said their good-byes. David suggested that Maureen and the family visit them sometime, but his offer sounded empy as both parties knew it would not happen. Jessie and Pedro hugged in a 'childlike' sort of way, but very fondly. He clasped her hand and gave it a good shake as he kissed her on both cheeks. Spanish style.

The taxi sped off and David, Hazel and Pedro went back inside. There was still packing to be done. Clothes and personal belongings had to be sorted out. They needed to purchase a strong trunk in which to pack heavier items that would be shipped by sea. IKEA could probably help. There were some items such as old records and CD's and DVD's that they would take to the Oxfam shop in the High Street, along with books they didn't really need. To take Pedro's mind off the move, Hazel encouraged him to help begin the packing. He joined in with enthusiasm! If he wasn't sure about something, he'd ask – simple as that. There were three large suitcases to be packed, three pieces of hand luggage, and the strong trunk for shipping. If things didn't fit into any of these – too bad. They wouldn't go!

Some weeks ago David had been in touch with the Chilean Embassy in Devonshire Street in London and checked out what they had to do for them to live in their 'new country.' Forms had been downloaded from the website, printed off, completed and posted back to the embassy. They had received a phone call from the embassy to say that everything was in order and work visas and other supporting documentation would be sent to them within a few days. In order to go and live in Chile, David and Hazel needed jobs to go to. de Gama had agreed to provide them with 'temporary work' and vouch for them. When the package arrived from the embassy David showed it to Hazel and Pedro. It was concrete evidence of the fact that things were going to happen. It was no longer a dream, it was for real!

On the way home, Maureen and Jessie had a quiet journey. The railway carriage was half empty. Jessie said very little as her mum scanned the *Daily Mail* she had bought at the station. Maureen knew Jessie was deep in thought. In fact she noticed that Jessie was holding something in her hand. When Jessie noticed her mother looking at her hands she slowly opened them. On her left palm was a wooden cross on a leather cord.

It was made of oak.

It came from a tree in Surrey.

It had blown down in the gales years ago.

It was everything to her. At that moment it really was everything to her. Everything.

A tear ran down her cheek and she wiped it away gently.

Chapter 8

The party at the Bowls Club went off very well. Everyone who'd been invited actually turned up. Musical entertainment was provided by a local group known as 'The Easy Riders'. The group consisted of lead singer, Vic Yarn, and three other guys who played various instruments. The music wasn't too loud so people could actually hold conversations without the need to shout!

Mrs. Wiggins had provided the catering. Her reputation in Godalming knew no bounds. She had baked most of the quiches, sausage rolls, pies and pasties. The rustic chips, vegetables and assorted salads added to a wonderful spread fit for a king. The legs of the long table appeared to bend under the weight of Mrs. Wiggins efforts! For dessert, another table sported tropical fruit salad, individual creme brullee's, sherry trifle, Charlotte Rousse, and chocolate eclairs. Three jugs of cream were sited at each end and middle table in case anyone felt they were lacking on the calorie front! Round tables seated ten people each, and three red, white and blue balloons adorned each table. Some thought that the colours were those of the Union Flag until it was pointed out that they were the colours of the Chile national flag! Ah, well.

A good time was had by all, with food, drink and music of a first class nature. Mrs. Wiggins had made sure that Chilean wines were on tables and the bar served *Old Speckled Hen* and *Spitfire* ales to keep the beer drinkers happy. Nobody got drunk, or so it seemed, and dancing on the small, parquet floor until midnight added to the whole event. David had made a short speech, thanking everyone for everything that they had done for him, Hazel and Pedro over the time they had lived in Godalming. The Reverend Keith Blandford also stood up and gave his blessings to the family and wished them God speed and 'bon voyage' for their trip to South America. He said they would be sorely missed by the local community. A vigorous round of applause followed with a few tears shed here and there.

One or two of David and Hazel's best friends also made short speeches and dropped hints about cheap holidays in South America once they'd settled in. Taking everything into account the whole event went off very well and by half past midnight there were only a few folks left. Big hugs and cuddles had been exchanged with virtually everyone. Pedro had been squeezed so much he felt like he was going to be bruised all over! Some of the ladies from church helped to tidy up and put used dishes together as well as collecting up serviettes and knives, forks and spoons. Mrs. Wiggins told them not to do too much as she had three schoolchildren coming in on Sunday morning to wash and dry the crockery. She'd be paying them two pounds each and she wanted her money's worth, she commented!

David, Hazel and Pedro got home by one o'clock in the morning and went straight to bed. They were all tired out. It was now only a few days before the move would begin once the house keys had been handed over to the estate agent and final meter readings taken. Ninety five percent of the packing had been done and there were only a few items to be packed away. The logistics of managing their clothes needs and food requirements needed fine tuning, but they managed. Another look at their check list showed that, as far as they were aware, nothing had been left out.

The remaining days in England passed quickly. Pedro went round to see Clarence for the last time. His parents also said final farewells to their close friends. A number of phone calls were made on the last day, and they had told BT that their final bill would be paid up to midnight.

Keith Blandford had popped in and again blessed them all. He suggested that they stand and hold hands while he said a prayer for them. Pedro opened his eyes slightly and on seeing the three adults with eyes closed, did the same.

The IKEA trunk had been collected by DHL and sent to Santiago c/o the office of de Gama. The lawyer had agreed to be the 'sent to' address. Not only that, but de Gama had been working on their behalf to secure rented accommodation in a middle class suburb of Santiago. A suitable school was within walking distance and supermarket shopping in less than two kilometres. David had arranged a money transfer to the de Gama account to cover initial costs, including three months rent for their 'new home'. de Gama had emailed digital images of the house – a three bedoomed, furnished, semi-detached property with en-suite bathroom. It looked good. Air conditioning was standard, and the integral garage would be large enough for a vehicle once they'd got settled in.

From time to time, both of Pedro's parents had to pinch themselves to make certain they weren't dreaming. Seeing pictures of their new home in a leafy avenue of a city on the other side of the world just did not seem real. But it was, it was all going ahead. A new life lay ahead for them. Exactly what they weren't sure of at the moment. Jobs? Yes, they would need to do something once Pedro was organised with his school. Spanish lessons they had promised themselves so they'd need to find a school or college for that.

The fundholders of the money that Hazel had invested had been instructed to send all of it to their UK bank account. Once received, the UK bank would transfer the requested amount to their new bank account in Santiago when they got instructions from Hazel. The total was just under £1.2 million. David had suggested that they re-invest most of that sum appropriately in Chile, either in stocks and shares or some other suitable investment where it would hopefully grow. Hazel agreed. They were going to need that money for their future together as a family.

On the day of their departure with all last minute actions completed, they waited for the taxi to take them to Heathrow. Hazel had bought an inexpensive 'pay-as-you-go' mobile phone to be able to contact any friends at the last minute. Just in case. She'd entered some contact numbers into the mobile for ease of use. Her diary with contacts was somewhere at the bottom of her hand luggage. The taxi driver pulled up outside of their house, and they turned to look at it for the last time as they walked towards the taxi. He loaded the luggage into the boot of the Peugeot 407 estate car as the three passengers got in and fastened their seat belts.

"Bye, bye" said Hazel as she looked at the front of the house, almost seeing the upstairs bedroom windows like eyes, a middle landing window as a nose and the front door as a mouth. "We'll miss you." Her eyes were moist. As the taxi eased away to join the traffic Hazel's mobile phone rang. Amelia Harcourt's name came up on the phone's small screen. Hazel could not imagine why Miss Pudding would be calling her. And how did she get this mobile phone number?

She decided in an instant that she did not want to talk to her again. Whatever Miss Pudding had to say she could keep to herself!

"Who was that, Nutty? asked David.

"It was a with-held number. Someone probably misdialled."

Hazel could have taken that call. It could have proved to be important. But then, she would never know, would she?

PART TEN

Chapter 1

"Welcome to Santiago – again!" de Gama showed the three new arrivals into his office as he shook David and Hazel's hand. He also acknowledged Pedro. "Goodness, the boy has grown since I last saw him!"

de Gama ordered some refreshment for them after their long journey. Helena, his secretary, came in with tea, coffee and fruit juice. After taking their preferences, Helena poured out the drinks and stayed in the office with them, taking notes as before.

de Gama proceeded to update them on a number of issues. The semi detached villa was ready for them to move into immediately. A telephone had been installed and was available to use. The local school had been contacted with the details of Pedro Tate. David and Hazel had insisted that he keep the name on his British passport, the one they wanted for him – even when he eventually got one from Chile. de Gama made a note to this effect. His birthdate would be changed on any new documentation from 29 June to 12 November. His parents agreed to that. As a lawyer, de Gama assured them that he would help them if there were any enquiries on that point.

de Gama recommended two car dealers in the city. Both had reliable reputations and sold second hand cars as well as new ones. The better of the two was Colez and Snowdonez, the main Mitsubishi outlet. He handed David a detailed city map and a directory of local services with addresses and phone numbers.

de Gama had highlighted where their new property was located and also circled the school, local shopping facility and the two car dealerships.

David and Hazel had brought pesos with them as well as some US dollar travellers cheques, but de Gama had already obtained forms for them to complete to apply for credit cards. He stated that he was willing to act as a referee for them, if required. He had registered them at the hospital and a small health centre near their home. de Gama opened a draw and took out the keys to the property. Two sets for front and back doors, three for the garage, and one for a lockable shed in the rear garden. A few more pieces of information and David and Hazel began to feel more comfortable. It seemed that de Gama had gone the extra mile, or was it kilometre, to help them get established in Santiago. He had organised another member of staff to take them and their luggage to the villa where they'd be spending the coming months. He bade them farewell, gave them another business card, and patted Pedro on his head as they left the offices of de Gama, de Gama and Torres.

Frederico had been asked to take the three of them to the Nunoa district of Santiago, to number 37, Avenida Diagonal Oriente, Santiago 03710, Chile. Their new address, their new home! Within twenty minutes Frederico parked the car on the drive in front of the large, white, integral garage door. They slowly got out and took in their surroundings. It was wonderful! Purple flowers cascaded over the wall between them and their next door neighbour, and bright red geraniums filled two flower beds next to the garage. Two tall palm trees looked as though they were scraping the blue sky above and several brightly coloured birds flew by overhead.

David went up the three steps and opened the front door. He let Pedro go in first. It was symbolic, he thought, that as

Pedro had 'come home' he ought to be first over the threshhold. Hazel followed their son in as David helped Frederico to unload their cases and hand luggage. The IKEA trunk was still in transit but de Gama would have it delivered to them as soon as it arrived. Frederico reversed off the drive and waved as he headed back to his office.

During the next ten minutes or so they all wandered in and out of rooms, looking out of windows and simply absorbing what was before them. The furniture was more than adequate but perhaps not what Hazel would have chosen herself. Most of it was dark wood and typically Spanish. A few pictures adorned the walls but she wanted to position the painting of the nunnery above the fireplace. David would swop the picture of the Andes for the one of the nunnery when they unpacked. A 32" television set took up one corner of the lounge with a three piece suite arranged so that it could be viewed. The telephones were cordless – one in the kitchen and the other in the lounge. The kitchen was smaller than the one in Chalk Road, but an adequate dining room next to it would be where they'd eat.

The fridge had been switched on and contained a supply of milk, butter, bottled water, fruit juices and beer. 'Great!' thought David as he spotted six bottles of 'Cristal', the local beer. Two cereal boxes were in a cupboard, along with some tins of beans, tins of tuna and biscuits. There was enough to get them started. They could find the nearest supermarket, Santa Isabel, tomorrow and get more items of food. Hazel got out towels and bedding and made the beds up as David and Pedro unpacked the three suitcases. They soon found a place for most things. Pedro had chosen the largest of the two single bedrooms that contained a desk and chair. Perfect for his computer – when he got one!

Within a couple of hours they had got themselves organised. The painting of the nunnery had replaced a picture of the Andes.

It looked fine. David opened two bottles of Cristal and the large carton of mango juice. He poured the drinks and they all clinked their glasses. Pedro was missing Jessie. He had written to her twice but now wanted to send emails. After all he was computer literate, and posting letters was 'old fashioned' he thought. He'd leave it a while but find an opportunity to mention it to his mum or dad. He was sure that Maureen would have an email address. He could either use that or maybe Jessie had one? Once they were more organised in their villa he knew David would get onto the internet and obtain email addresses – hopefully for all three of them? David had already checked that yahoo.com would give him access to an email address and the internet.

The clothes they had brought with them had been hung up. Some needed ironing but Hazel was not going to bother with that today. They went out onto a small patio at the rear of the villa and sat at a round white table. A wide parasol helped keep off the warm sun. The outdoor pool looked inviting but the water was cool and none of them felt like a swim. The rear garden was simple, with further plants in borders on three sides. Another two palm trees were planted in corners of the plot and about a dozen potted plants were lined up like soldiers on sentry duty against the white wall of the villa. The three of them sat for a while to take it all in. The flight had taken its toll and tiredness began to set in. David felt himself dozing off when a voice came from over the adjoining wall.

"Buenas tardes. Welcome to Santiago!" A dark skinned man and a woman next to him were peeking over the wall. "This my wife Louisa." He looked at the woman holding onto his arm. "Can we help you with anything?"

"Hello, buenas tardes," replied David. "I'm David and this is my wife Hazel and our son Pedro. No, we are fine just now. We are a little tired. Perhaps we can see you tomorrow evening? You are welcome to come round for a glass of wine."

"That would be good. Muy bien. It depends what time I get home from the school, but is six o'clock a good time?"

David nodded and their neighbours disappeared. Little did David know he had just been talking to Pedro's new head teacher.

He hadn't given his name.

Chapter 2

Hazel had made a jug of 'pisco sour' to serve to their neighbours that evening. This was a typical Chilean drink made from pisco – a brandy distilled from muscatel grapes – mixed with sugar and lemon juice. She would add a few cubes of ice to the jug to make a delicious, tangy drink. The little booklet on 'all things South American' given to them by de Gama had come in useful for one thing! Hazel had also made some cheese straws to nibble at, thinking that their neighbours would find these unusual?

They had found the Santa Isabel supermarket and done some grocery shopping. The prices of some foods such as coffee and tea were high, but many basic items were reasonable. They had carried the plastic bags of shopping back from the supermarket, with Pedro managing – no insisting – to carry two. Soon the food and drink was packed away and they got on with organising a number of things. They had completed the forms to apply for new credit cards and made an appointment with the bank.

A language course began at the *Instituto Chileno Britanico* in a few weeks time and both had enrolled on that. They had checked on cinemas and theatres. Two good theatres were the *Sala Galpon* and the *Teatro Alcala*, both of which staged productions in English from time to time.

They might want to make some trips out and fancied another winery. Close to the city was the 'Vina Concho y Toro' founded by Don Melchor Concha y Toro in 1883. It sold excellent wines and became the first winery to appear on the New York Stock

Exchange in 1994. The brochure information indicated that you could buy your wine tasting glass for $6 US at the end of the tour. What a rip off, thought David! The previous ones from their holiday were free!

A pleasant area for a trip might be to Banos Morales, a place about 100 km out of the city towards the south west. The road headed towards San Jose de Maipo, San Alfonso and on to San Gabriel. San Jose de Maipo was the last fuel stop on the route in this valley, and the last telephone lines were just beyond San Gabriel at El Volcan. Roads became poorer as they wound up into the mountains, with Monumento Nacional el Morado being a wonderful 4,000 m high peak beyond Banos Morales. The brochure showed images of the area and they looked wonderful.

They would need to buy a car soon. Having read about some roads in Chile, David suggested a 4x4 and Hazel agreed. In winter above a few hundred metres snowfall could occur, and the poor road conditions would favour something with a good ground clearance. They visited Colez & Snowdonez and evenually decided to be frugal. They opted for a three year old Mitsubishi Pajero 2.0 with twenty thousand kilometres on the clock. It was dark red in colour with alloy wheels, parking sensors and full service history. The interior was like new. Senor Snowdonez had ensured that it came with a long tax and test certificate. David had dealt with car dealers before and was certain Snowdonez was trustworthy.

They had registered at a hospital called the *Clinica Indisa* in Avenida Santa Maria. This was only a formality but needed to be done in case of any treatment being required. A visit to Pedro's new school was planned in two days time, de Gama having given them the school address and name of the head teacher, Senor Pablo Neruda. The school was within walking distance so that made it easy for Pedro to get there. There was also a boarding facility where about one fifth of all pupils resided. The school, or college as it was preferred to be known, had a good reputation.

At just after six o'clock in the evening the front door bell rang. It was the next door neighbours. Hazel went to the door and opened it.

"Buenas tardes, Senora, we are here as invited!" he smiled.

"Come in, entrada," replied Hazel. They walked in and followed David who was standing a short distance away and who gestured for them to go out onto the patio. Hazel brought out the jug of pisco sour, clinking with ice cubes, and five glasses. Pedro was having fruit juice.

"I have not introduced myself", said the man. "I am Pablo Neruda, headmaster of the local college, and this is my wife, Louisa. We do not have any children." They all sat down at the round garden table. "Would I be correct in thinking that your son will be joining us soon?"

Of course, the penny dropped! Pedro's parents had seen the name 'Pablo Neruda' on the college information.

"I have seen his name on a list of new entrants for next term – Pedro Tatay." David diplomatically corrected Senor Neruda on the pronunciation of their surname, emphasising the name Tate with a hard letter 'a'. Neruda smiled at Pedro who was sipping his orange juice through a straw. Neruda seemed a nice man. He had a black moustache, dark eyes and his slightly receding dark hair gave him a slight look of a young David Niven. His wife, Louisa, was amply built. She was plump, but in all the wrong places. Her choice of dress didn't help either as the 'Michelin man' came to mind and David wondered what sort of tyres were fitted to the Mitsubishi Pajero?

They chatted amicably for a while, Pablo and Louisa complementing Hazel on both the pisco sour and the cheese straws. Hazel had decided not to go into too much detail about Pedro's background. It was sufficient for now to simply explain that Pedro was their adopted son and that they had decided to emigrate to Chile from England. Pablo had brought round some magazines and a large city map of Santiago. Sometimes he brought English newspapers from school and offered to pass them on to David if he was interested. They said that if David and Hazel needed any help with anything, they were pleased to help. Pablo gave them one of his personal cards with both home and school details. Louisa and Hazel talked about 'girlie' things including big store shopping, whilst Pablo shared his love of soccer with David and Pedro.

After thirty minutes or so, Pablo and Louisa got up and excused themselves. They thanked their new neighbours for their hospitality and suggested they would reciprocate next week. Both were very polite. Pablo quietly mentioned to David that he would not be able to take Pedro to school even though he lived next door. It would not be politic to be seen to be giving a lift to a pupil. David nodded in understanding. Hazel and David saw their neighbours to the front door and shouted 'adios' as they walked back down the drive.

Pedro was still sat at the garden table as David walked back through the villa. He was staring at the palm trees.

"Are you OK, cowboy?" David asked.

"Yes, great, dad. I think I'm going to like it here. I'm going to like it a lot. There's just one thing..."

"What's that?"

"I miss Jessie." Pedro was holding a small photo of her that she had sent him in her last letter. He would cherish it forever.

Chapter 3

Pedro's first week at college went off very well. He enjoyed all the lessons and took part in sports. His favourite subjects became English and English Literature, although he also excelled at geography and history. He quickly became an integral part of college life, joining the debating society and art club which met after lessons every Wednesday. David saw some of himself in Pedro as he recounted his days at school in Worcestershire.

The days went by in Santiago, as David and Hazel got to grips with life in Chile. Driving on the right hand side of the road became natural, albeit with a few near misses at times! Their bank account had been set up with cheque books and debit cards issued. They had received their new credit cards, and both had been issued with a driving licence.

A visit to a computer store resulted in two laptops being purchased, a smaller Sanyo for Pedro that he could use himself and a more expensive Toshiba for David and Hazel. Contact with yahoo.com soon enabled them to get an email address as well as internet access. Pedro's bedroom doubled as a place to sleep as well as study. Here was where he did his homework and spent much of his time. The IKEA trunk had arrived and been delivered to the villa. Pedro soon had his CD's and DVD's stacked up on a shelf!

David and Hazel discussed visits to both Valparaiso to see Father Rodriguez and to San Felipe to visit Mother Caterina. Both were within a day's drive, but they would not visit both on the same day. They chose to see Father Rodriguez first as it was there that their 'special visit' had first begun. David recalled that the *Refugio* was a charity and he suggested to Hazel that they make a donation. If they took their cheque book they could make out a cheque there and then. Their bank had confirmed the transfer of their UK funds so all financial matters were in order. However, they needed to talk to one of the banks financial advisers to discuss investments.

The days in Santiago were mild and the nights quite cold. It was just turning from winter to spring and by the time of Pedro's birthday – 12th. November – the days would be much warmer. They were planning a celebration for that although it was still early to decide on too much at the moment. Pedro was making friends at college and within a few weeks had brought home a charming boy called Philipe. He lived a couple of kilometres from Avenida Diagonal Oriente and had his own bicycle. He was very bright and spoke reasonable English. His manners were impeccable and David and Hazel agreed that Philipe was a good choice as a friend for Pedro. Pedro and his new found chum would spend time in Pedro's bedroom at the Sony laptop, checking things for homework or playing a Nintendo game. It wasn't long before Pedro asked if he could have a bicycle, too, but Hazel said 'no, maybe soon.' He didn't argue.

David and Hazel began their language course at the institute. This took place on either Monday evenings at seven o'clock, or Wednesday afternoons at two o'clock. As neither had started work yet, they opted for the Wednesday session. It lasted two hours but they were always home in time for Pedro's return from college. They had been given a CD to listen to and this helped enormously with their pronunciation. Both also tuned in to local TV channels, especially the news broadcasts. It seemed there were slightly different dialects in the country, as there are anywhere else. They both tried to get the hang of the Santiago 'twang'. Even Pablo and Louisa said how well they were speaking the language!

During a visit one evening to the home of their neighbours, Pablo mentioned that there was a vacancy at the college for a part time administrator. He asked Hazel if she might be interested? Hazel had told them that she had worked at a school in Godalming in an administrative capacity during their 'pisco sour and cheese straw' chat. He said that several of the other staff were fluent in English so that there would not be a language issue, and that it would help her to learn Spanish quicker. Pablo also assured Hazel that it was not a concern that Pedro was a pupil there.

"David, what do you think?" asked Hazel looking across the room.

"Sounds OK to me! It'll keep you busy for part of the time."

Pablo looked at Hazel and said "Well?"

"I'll do it!" Hazel exclaimed. She smiled – they all smiled. Pablo offered a small but reasonable remuneration, enough to keep them in pisco, Cristal and carmenere!

"Looks like I need to get fixed up with a job, too!" David suggested. Pablo had been told of David's background and indicated that he would be able to make some enquiries with friends. David knew about the pharmaceutical industry but little else. His skills lay in marketing, but this was transferable to other businesses. Profit and loss, promotion, sales, distribution, pricing, competitive analysis – the list went on. He would see what Pablo came up with, but he'd also look around himself. His Spanish was getting better and he felt confident that he could manage in a small business in Santiago. He'd keep his eyes open.

David and Hazel had got sorted out with email addresses for each of them and soon contacted as many of their friends in the UK as they could. Thankfully, Hazel had remembered to bring email addresses with her. The Godalming 'brigade' were contacted, as well as Maureen and a few other people they knew in England. Pedro emailed Maureen with his mum's agreement to ask if Jessie had an email address. She hadn't, but Maureen thought it was a good idea if she did have one. Within a few days, Pedro and Jessie were communicating. Hazel had decided that Pedro was mature enough, in his own way, to keep in touch with Jessie. Digital images were sent from Chile showing their villa, garden, and the surrounding area. David had bought Pedro a new camera so that he could download his own pictures to send them off to friends.

Life for Pedro and his parents passed. Days turned into weeks. Hazel began her college job and did really well. Pablo was very pleased with her performance and progress. She worked three mornings a week beginning at 0900 and getting home for noon. Much of her primary school experience came back quickly, and she improved the filing scheme at the college, as well as introducing new methods of planning and organisation. David had been given a contact by Pablo. An old school friend ran his own printing business. He employed three people, but was getting stretched and was happy to give David an opportunity to add some skills to the company. David soon became involved in marketing the business and improving profits by eliminating unecessary overheads.

They had not yet visited Father Rodriguez. They had been too busy doing other things and getting themselves sorted out. Pedro had sent two emails to Jessie but as yet he had not had a response.

One evening David suggested to Hazel that the three of them should plan to travel to Valparaiso soon. They discussed it with Pedro and all three of them looked at the calendar and picked a Saturday. Hazel had the address of the *Refugio de Cristo* but no telephone number. A map showed it was only a couple of hours drive away, maybe a little longer with a stop for coffee and an ice cream. Hazel explained to Pedro the significance of the Refugio and how they had met Father Rodriguez who put them in touch with the nunnery. Without him, Pedro would not be sitting with his mum and dad in their villa in Santiago right there and then. Pedro seemed to understand.

The Saturday arrived and after breakfast the Mitsubishi, fully fuelled up with tyres checked, was ready for off. Hazel had packed some food and drinks for the journey, including a flask of coffee. They would not be reliant on the hospitality of the Father and the other Brothers at the Refugio, and it meant they could stop off when they wanted. There were not many service stations en route. The map took them north and then west out of the sprawling Santiago suburbs. David was becoming more familiar with the street layouts, many roads running parallel north to south and east to west. In many ways it made life easier in terms of judging one's location. Hazel sat in the front and helped navigate while Pedro seemed content to sit in the back and read a book.

On the way they stopped at a small service area for a rest and David topped up the fuel tank. They decided to use the toilets and have a drink. David gave Pedro some pesos to get an ice cream. There were about a dozen other vehicles parked up. The sun was bright and the rasping sound of cicadas could be heard in the branches of nearby trees. Most of the people walking around appeared to be local, with wide brimmed hats and ponchos. Some ponchos were very bright and multi-coloured in reds and blues and yellows. This was familiar to Pedro, of course, but David and Hazel found it fascinating. Once the coffee cups were empty and the ice cream finished, they set off for their destination in Valparaiso.

The road surfaces deteriorated the further west they travelled until they got closer to the *Refugio de Cristo*, then they improved a little. The Pajero suspension was firm, but soft enough not to be uncomfortable. A drive along a small track took them along a familiar route peviously travelled in a Chilean taxi. It had not been that long ago, but Hazel felt it had been an age.

They stopped within a few meters of the building and parked the 4 x 4 under a tree. All three of them got out, Pedro rushing towards the large wooden door. David knocked hard and within seconds the door opened slowly, creaking as it did so. A Brother dressed in a long black robe looked at them. David smiled at him.

"Buenas dias, Senor. We have come to visit Father Rodriguez. We met with him some months ago and he kindly showed us around. You may remember us?"

Brother Augustus had a look on his face that made him seem depressed and very low. Americans would call it a 'hang dog look'. He did not reply, but stared at David, then Hazel, and finally Pedro. His eyes were hollow and empty.

"Are you all right, Brother?" David asked anxiously.

"It's Father Rodriguez. I'm afraid he died last month."

Chapter 4

The visitors were invited in. Brother Augustus had taken over from Father Rodriguez and they were expecting a new man to take over the running of the Refugio. David told Augustus about their first visit whilst they had been on holiday in Santiago. He also explained how they had been directed to the nunnery in San Felipe by the Father, and how they had come to see Pedro at the orphanage. Augustus managed a little smile at this news – it seemed to bring joy to his heart. He then went on to say that Father Rodriguez had passed away in his sleep after being ill for some time. Although Augustus could not say what the cause of death was, he made it clear that God had other plans for Father Rodriguez, so He'd called him away.

Father Rodriguez had left a few personal belongings in a small wooden trunk. They had not been looked at yet, but Brother Augustus would go through them sometime.

After some refreshment with Augustus and two other Brothers, David told them that it was their wish to make a donation to the work of the Refuge. He casually mentioned that they had come into some money and because of how their lives had been changed via the Refugio they wanted to 'put something back'. Augustus and the other Brothers looked pleased as David took out the cheque book. He and Hazel had agreed to make out a cheque for the equivalent of £25,000. Augustus was staggered. Being used to donations of a few pesos here and there, this was a fortune.

Before they left Augustus took his visitors to the local cemetery to show them where Father Rodriguez was laid to rest. It was within walking distance and took under ten minutes. They entered by a wrought iron gate and walked along a dusty path to the northern end of the expanse of headstones. Father Rodriguez had been buried with his feet facing west as opposed to east as was normal for other burials. Augustus explained that when he rose to meet his 'Maker', his head would rise first and see the Lord coming to meet him from the west.

He had kept in touch with Mother Caterina and had been kept informed of Pedro. He knew Pedro had gone to England and more recently, just before he passed away, Mother Caterina had told him of Pedro's impending return. His eyes lit up when she told him that.

His headstone read:

> Father Hernando Rodriguez.
> Passed away aged 61.
> He led a simple but good life.
> He achieved much in his short life on earth.
> Now at peace with the Father.
> Amen.

Tearfully, the group trudged away from the cemetery where rain laden clouds gathered overhead. Although Brother Augustus had asked them if they wished to return to the Refugio, David and Hazel decided it was time to leave. Pedro had been silent throughout the discussions, as though he had been thinking his very own thoughts. Just what had been going through his mind?

On the way home, little was said. They did stop off for a short rest and Hazel opened the plastic storage container of sandwiches that she had brought with them. They picked at one or two but none of them were hungry. David turned the radio up a little and they listened to a local music station. It soothed them as they looked out at the barren countryside between Valparaiso and the capital city.

"Hey, come on, we mustn't be sad!" Hazel said firmly. "Father Rodriguez wouldn't have wanted us to be like this, would he?" Those words seemed to lift them. Pedro smiled, weakly at first, then more broadly. David looked at both of them and realised just how lucky they all were. A family together – him and Hazel with a son! Settling down into a new life in Chile, with good prospects for Pedro Tate and jobs for him and Hazel. Learning a new language, trying new things, eating spicy foods, tasting new red wines. Life was good. It was so good.

They must plan that visit to the nunnery, and do it soon. It would be so good to see Mother Caterina again, and Sister Fatima and the other nuns. And how would Pedro feel? It would be interesting to watch him and see the look on his face as they entered the big oak gates of the nunnery.

They got back to their villa late afternoon. Pedro scooted up the stone stairs and switched on his Sanyo. Hazel unpacked the plastic container and wrapped the remaining sandwiches in cling-film. The flask was rinsed out and two cans of fizzy orange juice were put back in the fridge. David sat down in an armchair in the lounge. When Hazel came in from the kitchen he was holding his groin.

"David, are you OK. You look a bit pale?"

"Not too good, Nutty. It's a bit painful down below." His hands were clasped over his groin. He lay back.

Ashley Parker F.R.C.S. came into his head. He did not want to believe what he was beginning to think. He really didn't.

Chapter 5

Hazel insisted that David visit the Oncology Department of the Clinica Indisa. He said he was all right and that it was the travel to Valparaiso that had made him feel tired. He had taken some capsules with a long drink of water and felt all right. She pushed the matter as far as she could, and sometimes he could be stubborn, but she refrained from talking about it. At least for now.

The visit to San Felipe was planned. Hazel had a contact telephone number for Mother Caterina and would call her first as suggested. They didn't want any more surprises like the one at the refuge! The phone call was made and a date agreed. It was to be a Sunday, and they had been invited to stay for a light lunch.

In the meantime, Pedro continued to flourish at college. He did well in most subjects. David wondered what he might become when he left college? A politician, teacher, lawyer? Time would tell. Hazel enjoyed her work at the college, too, with few people realising that she was Pedro's mother. She made friends with some of the administration staff and even invited one or two back to the villa for lunch.

David was certainly thriving at the small printing business, getting to know some of the customers and making trips around the city. It was amazing how much of his marketing skills came back to him – he just exchanged pharma products for brochures and leaflets! The key difference, of course, was the language.

Every day he learnt about twenty new words. His vocabulary was growing quickly. His main struggle was making the words fit together so that they made sense. He had to master the verbs – past, present and future – but he made progress. Especially at the language school where he gained a distinction in his first exam. He was proud of himself, and Hazel knew it!

Pedro had received a reply from Jessie He was overjoyed that she had sent him a long email, telling him what she was doing, how school was, and where she'd been with her mother, Maureen. She attached two pictures – one from a school trip to Fountains Abbey near Ripon and another of herself in the back garden in Durham. Her dad was back from South Africa and had picked up a slight accent. Jessie didn't like that. Pedro did not reply straightaway but when he did he would also send his love with three kisses at the end of the email!

Soon the Sunday arrived for the trip to San Felipe. As before, a flask of coffee and two cans of juice were packed, three cups and some napkins. They allowed two and a half hours for the journey there and left Santiago at around half past nine. The road was in good condition as they headed northwards. The sun was shining again on a clear day and snow could just be seen on the higher peaks of the Andes in the distance. They had brought their cameras and stopped off at the side of the road to take some pictures. Pedro decided he would try to impress Jessie in a few days time with his 'David Bailey' compositions. He had asked David to get him a small tripod that screwed into the base of his camera to provide still shots without any hand judder. It certainly paid off as many of Pedro's pictures were really good.

With one stop for drinks on the way they arrived at the nunnery. David drove the last few hundred metres slowly to allow Pedro to get accustomed to being back at the orphanage where he'd spent his early years. Pedro strained to look at the high walls and could see the crucifix on the top of the church adjacent to the nunnery and the belltower. David parked the Mitsubishi near the big wooden doors. In a way it hadn't seemed five minutes since they were last here – and yet it seemed a lifetime ago. They all got out. Before they could knock on one of the doors it opened. Sister Fatima and Mother Caterina stood there, the latter looking as youthful as ever. She had been blessed with 'youthfullness'.

"Welcome to you all, especially you, Pedro!" said Mother Caterina. Pedro ran to them and they hugged them for all he was worth, his arms circling them like a squid holding its prey. "My, how you've grown!" Pedro was visibly moved as he looked first at the two nuns and then at his parents. There were smiles all round as the Mother beckoned them inside into the courtyard. It was as they had remembered it with pots of flowers and brightly coloured plants. Sister Fatima led them into the small room where they had first been offered iced lemonade. A large table had been set with bowls of fruit, home baked bread, olives, slices of meat, dried fish and a few cheeses. It was a banquet! After saying Grace, they helped themselves – Hazel and David were asked to go first, followed by Pedro – and then the Mother Superior and her Sister. Water, or iced lemonade, was the choice to drink, and both sat in large glass jugs on the table.

During lunch, Hazel asked how things were going at the nunnery, David enquired about the orphans, and they discussed Pedro. Hazel was proud to tell them how well Pedro had done in England and how he was progressing at his new college in Santiago. Mother Caterina couldn't get over how Pedro had developed, both physically and in his behaviour. He asked about a few of the young children who were there with Pedro. Sister Fatima went to fetch two in particular, who came into the small room to see Pedro.

"Pedro, Pedro, Pedro!" they shouted in unison. More hugs as the little trio seemed as though they were about to do a jig. They chatted in Spanish for about five minutes before Sister Fatima decided it was time to gently split the group and take the two orphans back to their rooms. They said their goodbyes with Pedro saying he'd be in touch again – *hasta luego*, he shouted. Until the next time. But he really wondered if there would be a 'next time'?

Hazel asked Mother Caterina about her plans to extend the orphanage that she had mentioned in her letter. The number of orphans had increased since Pedro had left. Costs were growing and space was decreasing. They had used a local builder to give them an estimate of an extension to the dormitory as well as adding three more classrooms for their education and a larger nursery. Hazel took the liberty of asking how much it was all going to cost? Mother Caterina hesitated, seemingly not wanting to divulge the amount. However, after Hazel maintained eye contact with an expression that said ' I'd like to help you' she relented.

"The cost will be in the region of twenty million pesos." Hazel quickly estimated this to be about £28,000.

"We want to pay for the work," replied Hazel. Her face remained calm. She looked deep into Mother Caterina's eyes.

"How can we accept that?

"Because we want you to. No, it's not just that – we insist!"

Silence followed as eyes met eyes. Even Pedro was looking at everyone else in the room.

"You are so kind. We shall never forget this." Mother Caterina gave Hazel bank account details of their bank in San Felipe.

After a few more comments, and tummies full to bursting – at least for the visitors – they all stood up. Mother Caterina led the way to the wooden doors of the nunnery. More thanks were given, and Hazel left their address in Santiago, along with their telephone number.

"You have been very kind, Hazel. We shall never forget you. Please come back and see us."

Little did Hazel know then that the next time they communicated, there would be some news that she would not believe.

She just could not have believed what was to come next.

Chapter 6

David and Hazel felt that the donation, if that's what it was, was something that they wanted to make. Hazel's good fortune with her investments really said that she had the ability to give away some of her financial growth. She wanted to do this. David and her had discussed it and they were now certain that this was what they were destined to do. How much was it worth to think that the nunnery would be able to grow, develop and be a thriving community for young children like Pedro? Priceless.

The weeks passed. David, Hazel and Pedro grew in their own ways. David became indispensible to the printing business as it grew profitably. Hazel had become an integral part of the administration department of the college.

He continued to maintain contact with Jessie and it seemed their love blossomed. Hazel started to wonder where it would lead and where it would end? After all, Maureen was Hazel's sister so that Pedro was a cousin to Jessie, wasn't he? But then, he was not a blood relation. They'd have to cross that bridge when they came to it, wouldn't they?

Emails passed between Chile and England. Hazel kept in touch with Gertrude and Rosemary as well as Keith. There was news about Godalming church but nothing too 'juicy'. Things progressed as normal – fund raising events, Sunday services with the Reverend Keith Blandford, some of the members of the Property Committee painting the railings along the front of the church wall. And so on and so on.

Hazel was able to tell them that they had found a small Church of England in the middle of Santiago. About 60 members made up the congregation, half of whom were non-Chilean. They had been attending the church for a few weeks and made some friends as a result of visiting each Sunday. David had met a man who knew about 'bowls'. It seemed that the game of bowls was little known in Chile. Was there an opportunity to start a bowls club? His name was Ken and he'd lived in Norwich almost all of his life. He said he knew Delia Smith, current chairman of Norwich City FC. How could you prove it otherwise? Maybe he would find a question to test him? For example, what was the name of her husband?

Hazel had made contact with a lady called Jeanette who had lived in Godalming as a child. She had actually gone to Godalming junior school. Hazel told her that she had worked there as an administrator so there was a common bond that formed between them very quickly. So, as time went on, life became good for the Tate family. Friendships were struck up, and David and Ken got together to discuss the feasability of forming a bowls club. What a challenge! To introduce a totally new form of game to Santiago...maybe they would need to order the bowls, set up the rules, create enthusiasm...what a challenge! David saw this as a new objective for him. A new way forward as an alternative to thinking about the printing press business?

The church in Santiago started to become a community bonding element for them. Pedro even met two new friends who went to a college three kilometres away who were boarders at their college and who liked to study geography.

Three days later Hazel got a letter in the post with a San Felipe postmark. It was from the nunnery. Mother Caterina had written to Hazel and David with a proposal. She asked them if they would like to consider moving to the nunnery to work there! What!

An invitation to go and work at the nunnery? With the extension planned, Mother Caterina had realised that she needed more staff – not necessarily qualified people with a commitment to God – but someone she knew she could trust and work with. The very fact that David and Hazel had adopted Pedro had spoken volumes to her.

"David, what do you think? Should we go? Is this a new life for us? What have we got here? Simple jobs that are OK, but are we really satisfied with what we're doing?"

David looked at Hazel for what seemed an eternity. They were only renting in Santiago. Their eyes met for a meaningful few minutes...

"Nutty, is this our destiny? This could be what we really should be doing? Where would we live?"

"Yes, I think it is... what about Pedro? Maybe he could board with the college? I'm sure Pablo would look after him?"

There was going to be more to this than David and Hazel had ever thought. There was something that maybe they didn't realise could ever happen. Did the word 'destiny' sum up what they were about to experience at the nunnery?

Only time would tell, but time could be a strange thing.

Oh, yes, time was going to bring something that would change their lives. Or, if not *both* their lives, at least one of them.

Chapter 7

They both had a lot to think about. Their key concern was Pedro. What about his schooling? He was doing well at college. David and Hazel knew they had to talk with their son and discuss the matter. They couldn't just put him in as a boarder without his agreement. They chose the right moment the next day after Pedro had come home from his studies.

"Hi, cowboy, there's something we want to chat about," said David as Pedro came through the front door. "I've poured you some juice so let's take a seat and talk." They went into the lounge of the villa- Pedro looking a little nervous.

"It's nothing to worry about," Hazel began. "We've been invited by Mother Caterina to go and work at the nunnery. That would mean living there, or very close by. We know you're doing well at college, and that you enjoy being there. If you would rather that we all stayed here, then that's fine."

Pedro was thinking this over as his dark eyes darted from the window to the door to the furniture. After what seemed an eternity Pedro replied.

"If you two want to go and work there, I'll support your decision. It's an honour to be asked. Mother Caterina is a wonderful person, dedicated to caring for others and the work of God. I think you would fit in nicely. Everybody there is so kind and thoughtful, you'd get on very well with them. I want to be successful in life, and having a good education is the key. Would you two mind if I became a boarder? I could see you at week-ends, perhaps?"

Hazel wiped a tear from her eye. Pedro sounded so grown up! He had clearly thought this out in a matter of seconds and replied in an adult manner. 'What was his destiny' Hazel asked herself again as she looked at their son, looking the ideal student.

"Are you sure, cowboy?" David looked Pedro in the eye. "We want you to be happy."

"And I want you to be happy! I think you'd both find more enjoyment at the nunnery than working here in the city. Senor Neruda will look after my studies, along with the other masters. I'll be fine. Go for it!" Hazel hugged her little boy as her eyes became damp with a few tears.

"You're an angel!", she exclaimed. David stood up and hugged both Hazel and Pedro together. He was a little choked up, too, if the truth be known.

Hazel telephoned the nunnery and spoke with Mother Caterina. She said that she and David would love to be at the nunnery but first had to sort a few things out. She asked about accommodation for her and David. A small stone *finca* that belonged to the nunnery needed refurbishing, and it was only two hundred metres away. It had two bedrooms, a kitchen and two living rooms. The roof leaked when it rained heavily, but the local builder who was to build the new extension could easily renovate the property. Mother Caterina apologised saying that David and Hazel would have to fund this work themselves. They were not concerned about that. Hazel's investment was already making a good return in the short time they'd been in Chile.

So that was that. A new chapter was about to begin in all their lives. David and Hazel met with Pablo Neruda one evening to discuss their plans. He was more than pleased to welcome Pedro as a boarding student and promised to keep an eye on him without showing favouritism. Pedro began to consider what he needed to take with him – his laptop computer, books, clothes…

David told Senor de Gama of their plans and they agreed on a moving out date at the end of the following month. Pedro would begin boarding before his parents moved out so that he could get used to it before they moved to San Felipe. David worked his notice at the printing firm. They were sorry to see him go as he had helped enormously. The manager thanked him and gave him an oil painting of Santiago showing the *Plaza de Armas* – the first public space laid out by Pedro de Valdivia when he founded the city in 1541. David would treasure it.

Bank, credit card company and others, were told of their new address. Some expressed surprise when they said 'Nunnery' in San Felipe!

Hazel continued working at the college until a week before they moved, and saw Pedro when she could. She didn't mind too much, but she realised it would be a wrench when they actually left their villa. She knew he was in good hands and within a few years he would hopefully have progressed, passing his college exams and going onto greater things. She framed a photo of Pedro that was taken in Surrey and placed it on the mantlepiece.

Hazel got in touch with the nunnery again and arranged for her and David to visit the old finca to take a look at it and make some suggestions on what they wanted the builder to do. She and David drove to San Felipe mid-week after taking a day off. It was important that the building was going to be habitable, at least. All this was achieved, and the builder, Jorge Johanns, would get his men on the job straightaway. The place was rewired, a new toilet and shower fitted, kitchen spruced up, walls plastered and emulsioned, and the roof repaired. It took ten days to complete and they did a fine job. David and Hazel paid Jorge in cash. He was delighted.

Time passed and soon the new 'volunteer workers' were settling into their new home. The finca belonged to the nunnery, so legally, the new inhabitants would never own it. However, Mother Caterina was happy for them to treat it as their own home and do whatever they wanted to the decor and any other fixtures and fittings. Hazel organised the furniture with the help of Louisa, Pablo's wife. She had been invaluable in helping with the delivery of the chairs, tables, cupboards and wardrobes from a large department store in down town Santiago.

Hazel got David to put pictures on walls, the one of the nunnery that was bought on their holiday took pride of place on an east facing wall in the lounge. The *Plaza de Armas* oil painting was put up opposite. Pedro's photo was placed in a larger frame and hung on a nail. Soon, the finca became homely. No, it was more than that – it was *their* home. Their new home together. Pedro would visit soon – David would collect him in the Mitsubishi for week-end visits. What would he make of it?

David and Hazel met with Sister Fatima to discuss their role at the nunnery and orphanage. Mother Caterina had left Fatima to spend time with the new volunteers, showing them all around the buildings, introducing them to other staff and many of the children. Within a few days, David and Hazel became an integral part of this community. They helped with the children's education, meal preparation, looking after plants and shrubs, and even cleaning! They loved it. Soon they were left to get on with things as they saw fit. At first they would ask permission to move potted plants, or do some pruning. Now they were allowed to do whatever they thought was best for the nunnery and orphanage.

Within weeks they felt completely at home and relaxed. Pedro had made a few visits and loved the *finca*. The setting was far superior to Chalk Road, with fresh open air and views to die for. Views to die for?

Hazel began to get concerned as David started to lose weight. In the next few weeks he lost seven kilograms. He was wasting away...

Chapter 8

David continued to ignore the messages that his body was telling him. He worked hard, loved the children, and enjoyed teaching them English. Hazel tried to persuade him to visit the clinic in Santiago, but he said he was OK and that it was the change of food and environment that was taking its toll. He kept taking his saw palmetto capsules and a daily zinc tablet. Hazel ensured that he ate healthily, they always had done. In fact, they ate lots of fruit and vegetables from the nunnery allotments that David kept in good order. He had planted rows of beans, carrots and potatoes. Soon the results of his efforts were plain to see. The sisters at the nunnery were impressed and actually thought David had been a professional gardener! That made him smile.

He drove to a local hardware store and purchased lengths of strong polythene sheeting to make cloches. Beneath these he grew other vegetables including lettuce, radishes and courgettes from seed. The allotment had been tidied up and Mother Caterina had never seen it so organised. David was certainly making his mark. He and Hazel had learnt the names of all the children in the orphanage. The children were polite and called them Senor and Senora, but they didn't want that. They pronounced their first names carefully and thereafter the children would use those names – heard as 'Darvid' and 'Harzel'.

Jorge the builder and his men began work on the extensions to the nunnery. He had presented plans to Mother Caterina who in turn had invited other sisters, as well as David and Hazel, to comment on them. Once agreed, Jorge had begun to dig new foundations, dismantle some existing walls, take delivery of stones, measure up for windows, bring in roof trusses and generally get on with things. It wasn't long before it was taking shape. The additional room made life easier for everyone – more room to teach, walk about, and better light from the larger, double-glazed windows. All of the staff and children were happy with the end result. It was easy to see on their faces that this was a big improvement – smiles all round for most of the time!

David and Hazel ate with the Sisters on three days of the week, and with the children at other times. This kept them in touch with all that was happening in the nunnery. In fact, this was now their life. They realised one evening when they were sat in their lounge that this was it – their new existence was what it was all about for them. They had television that they rarely watched. They read more. Hazel took up needlework and David started painting. Both began reading the Bible more. They just wanted to, not out of any obligation of their new address. After their evening meal they would take a stroll up the path that led to a small rocky area some two hundred metres above the nunnery. From there they could see down to the white buildings. There was a long, flat, slab of rock that served as a bench. This became their 'special place'. Here they would sit holding hands and gaze in awe at the vastness of the surrounding area.

"This is an unknown paradise," David said one evening as the sun began to set. "Look around you. The church down below, the nunnery, the hills and mountains, that sky."

"An unknown paradise..." Hazel's voice trailed off as she looked in awe at the vista. A small rivulet ran close to their slab of rock. It made the gentle sound of gurgling and splashing as it gently flowed down the hillside. David used to say it talked to them as it cascaded over small stones and rocks, sounding as though it had something to tell them… maybe it had a story to tell? They did not speak for several minutes as they gazed around them. It started to cool down so Hazel suggested going back down to their finca. They both stood up, still holding hands. David took a sharp intake of breath and winced, almost doubling up.

"Are you OK?", asked Hazel showing great concern.

"I'm OK, Nutty, just a bit stiff from sitting down on that cold rock. Let's go. I fancy a glass of that red stuff called wine."

They made their way slowly back down to their home. Within ten minutes the lights were switched on, along with some heating. Two glasses of carmenere were poured. They discussed Pedro's forthcoming birthday. What celebration should they plan? Pedro would still be at college.Should they have a party? There was time to decide.

David and Hazel had managed to get onto the internet and were able to contact both Pedro and friends. Hazel emailed Pedro regularly and he told her that he and Jessie were in regular contact. He missed her very much, that was clear. They had also been in contact with friends in Godalming, telling them of their new life at the nunnery. They received replies from everyone, including Keith and the ladies from the church group, as well as Ed and Dianah. This made David and Hazel feel that they were not too far from home – at least emotionally if not physically. David had told his brothers about their new life but had only heard from Geoff in Ireland who had wished them all the best. Hazel kept in touch with Maureen on a regular basis.

Over the next few weeks life was good – the weather was getting warmer and the spirit in the nunnery was excellent.

The vegetables grew, the buildings were completed, plants flourished, white walls were emulsioned, the nunnery just got so much better – thanks to David and Hazel. Pedro had passed all his exams at college and had made friends with a number of boys from good backgrounds. Life couldn't be better.

Before they retired one night, Hazel couldn't help but see how David's condition was deteriorating. He was looking more gaunt. He had lost five more kilograms in weight. She did not not want to believe that he had a real problem. But did he?

His body's defences were having trouble in coping with his problem. He ignored it. He began to put his faith in God. But was that going to be enough? He had discussed the power of prayer when he began attending Godalming church. Keith Blandford had shared some of his real life experiences with his flock. Some people with cancer who had been given six months to live had fully recovered. He had heard that Doris Day once had a serious life-threatening disease and refused surgery or treatment. She prayed, and those who knew her also prayed for her. It worked – she eventually recovered.

Hazel was clearly concerned about David but little did she know then that their 'special place' was to become so significant… oh, so significant.

Chapter 9

Pedro's birthday was a success! Hazel had arranged for his friends and a few parents to meet at a small restaurant in Santiago on the Saturday night before 12th. November. Pablo and Louisa had been invited. After the party, David and Hazel stayed with them in Avenida Diagonal Oriente. Pedro stayed, too, but returned to college on the Sunday morning. It was so good for them to have been together that evening. Hazel would remember it for a long time to come. David had made a speech, thanking everyone for coming and making it such a special occasion. They had bought Pedro a new bicycle and a video game that explored the world. Pedro managed to blow out the candles on his cake in one puff! Pedro's parents would email him on his birthday, and the presents which they'd left with Pablo Neruda would be given to him on the day.

After breakfast on the Sunday morning, Pedro's parents took him back to college and said their 'good-byes'. Again, Hazel found it difficult to give Pedro his last hug before getting into the Pajero for the two hour drive back to San Felipe. Pedro was a rock. He was strong and gave his mother the strength she needed for the return journey home. David stood by and held Hazel's hand as they got into the 4 x 4. The trip back to the nunnery seemed to last forever. Hazel kept thinking about her son. How was this affecting him? Was asking him to be a boarder the right thing to do? She prayed that it was.

Time went by and the temperatures rose. It was summer in the southern hemisphere. The number of children in the orphanage increased to 62. Additional boys and three more girls came to the 'sanctuary' that would care for them until the time came for them to leave – either to be adopted, or to leave of their own accord once they reached 'adulthood'. The children were all well behaved. Some were 'angelic' whilst others were bordering on mischievous. With the education that David and the Sisters could provide they would have a reasonably good chance in life when their time came. Both David and Hazel felt they were putting something back. It made them feel content.

David stamped his ability and friendship on the children. Many talked of his 'special' qualities. He brought three of his water colour paintings into the classroom and got a round of applause when he showed them to the children! He had them framed and the following week he had placed them on the walls of the main classroom. They were to remain there for a long time. Some of the orphans were inspired to begin painting themselves. He inspired many others to do things. In short, he was an inspiration to the children in the nunnery. He would never know that was the case – how would he?

Hazel reached a point where she felt she had to sit down and have a talk with her husband. He was feigning strength that wasn't there. He was putting on a brave face to all those he encountered. He refused to use a walking stick. However, Hazel knew all was not well. She insisted that he visit the Clinica Indisa in Santiago for a check up. After an argument that Hazel did not enjoy, David relented. He seemed to be getting stubborn?

They contacted the clinic and made an appointment for the following week.

The Oncology Department was busy and David was scared. He didn't want to be there. He had jobs to do at the nunnery.

The paving stones needed to be rid of weeds, the walls wanted another coat of white emulsion, the children were in need of more English teaching. He had so much to do there.

"This way, please, Senor Tate," a voice said from behind him. An attractive nurse with black hair and a smart figure smiled at David. He stood up and followed her. Hazel had agreed to wait in the reception area. The nurse led David into an area where he was to get undressed and don a surgical gown. From there he was shown into the suite where he was to undergo a prostate examination via his rectal passage. The urology nurse told him what was going to happen. A probe was to take eight small specimens of his prostate gland. Each needle took a very small piece of prostate tissue. It was uncomfortable rather than painful. David prepared himself for the procedure.

After about ten minutes David was having a cup of sweet tea and recovering from his experience. He hoped Hazel was all right – waiting for him next door. The urology nurse asked David to wait for an hour so that pathology could examine the prostate biopsy samples. He went back to sit with Hazel and they sat and held hands. He prayed, and prayed some more. Nothing was said. No words passed his lips.

"Senor Tate, the Urologist would like to see you now," said the young nurse, showing them the direction. David rose, took Hazel's hand, and they both followed her into a nearby office.

"Senor Tate. I'm afraid I have some bad news for you. Your PSA level is over fifteen thousand. Basically this means that you either have one month to live, or another three years. However, it appears that you have an aggressive form of prostate cancer. This type can be genetic."

There was complete silence in David's head. Nothing registered. Nothing existed anymore. He felt Hazel squeeze his hand. He began to feel faint, he swayed a little. He felt nauseous.

Almost as if he was drowning, so he had once been told, his whole life seemed to pass before him.

His schooldays, university, getting married, work, bowls, travelling to Chile – all came to him in seconds. Yet it could have been hours. His vision blurred a little as he rested his head on the wall behind his upright chair. His breathing became shallow.

What about Pedro? He had to see him grow up. And the orphanage? The children there were becoming reliant on both David and Hazel. He couldn't go anywhere now! He couldn't leave them. He had things to do – the vegetables were growing nicely, a few more jobs were on his list. Christmas was just around the corner and he was looking forward to spending it with Hazel and Pedro.

Their first Christmas together as a family. 'How marvellous, how wonderful' he thought to himself. He'd made some plans in his head. Their finca would be decorated...

But Christmas didn't arrive that year. There were no decorations. No presents. No tree. No cards.

David was soon to go on a long journey. Someone 'up there' had given him a one way ticket to another place... had other plans for him.

And he left a gap that would never be filled... never. Hazel's guardsman had finished his last tour of duty.

PART ELEVEN

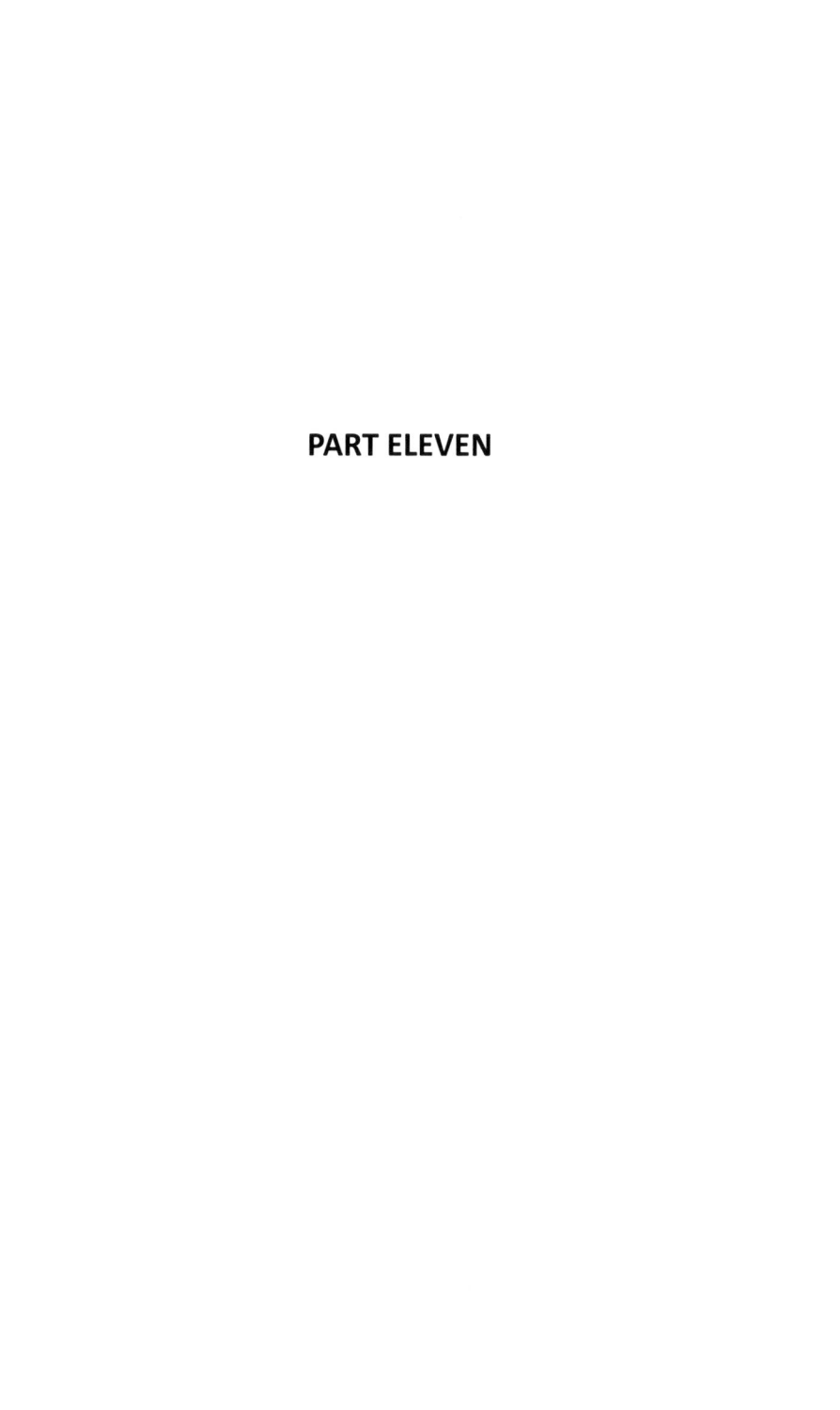

Chapter 1

After the funeral at the crematorium, many people said how sorry they were for Hazel and Pedro. But Hazel didn't want anyone to feel sorry for them. She was amazed at her own strength and that of Pedro. There would be time for grieving, but that time hadn't arrived yet. She had sought solace in her faith, and God was there to help her. Two days later the ashes were delivered to the nunnery. They were in a small wooden casket with a brass plaque on the lid. The plaque simply had his name on it – *David Charles Tate*.

Mother Caterina and the other nuns had been very supportive, offering prayers for both Hazel and Pedro. She could take as much time as she needed to get over her bereavement. But then she knew she would never get over this. Never, ever. Hazel focused on the nunnery. This was her life now. This was where they had both decided to spend their lives, working for others and especially the children.

Two weeks later Hazel walked up the path one evening to their 'special place' carrying David's ashes. She sat on the rock slab and David was beside her. This was where he would be laid to rest, she decided. He would be able to look out and see the views. Hazel would try to visit him every day, no matter what the weather was like. Perhaps if it was really wet, though, David would understand if Hazel didn't brave the elements!

Hazel built a small pile of stones, making a space in the centre where she placed the casket. One by one she placed stones upon each other to make a cairn – a rock pile looking like an ice cream cornet upside down. It was just over one metre high and totally enclosed the wooden box. She talked to David as she placed the last stone on the top.

"There you are, darling. You're home now, and safe. I'll never leave you. God bless you." Her eyes filled with tears. Pedro would approve. She knew that in her heart. She needed to be closer to her son now but took comfort in the fact that Pablo and Louisa had almost become foster parents to him. Hazel was reassured that her son was being cared for. She slowly walked down the path to her home. Walking alone with no hand to hold seemed strange. And yet there was a hand there. There always would be...

Hazel had emailed all those that she could think of to inform them of David's passing. The responses were overwhelmingly emotional.

'It's odd, isn't it', she mused to herself. 'In life very few people tell you anything positive about yourself. When you die, it all comes out.'

Many of David's ex-work colleagues at Smith & Johnson were complimentary about his work as a manager and friend. Bowls Club members had organised a charity event to raise funds for the nunnery and sent £297.45 to Hazel's bank account. She presented a cheque to the Mother Superior as soon as she could. The nuns wanted to do something with this donation in memory of David. It was decided that they would plant a tree in the centre of the garden that was now in the corner of the new extension. It had been laid with paving stones but the middle one could easily be lifted. This was done and the little tree flourished, and grew and grew.

Every evening Hazel would look up at the small cairn at the top of the path leading up the hillside. If it was pouring down she'd opt for looking from her lounge window. One evening, exactly one month to the day after David's death, she looked out of the window through the rain. The clouds were low, heavy and battleship grey in colour. She couldn't be certain, but through the rain and mist she saw someone standing next to the cairn. It looked like a man in a white suit. Hazel rushed to the door and went out onto the verandah.

There was no one there. It had been her imagination. She chastised herself for thinking she had seen somebody in this weather! The rain stopped and the sky cleared, so Hazel decided to walk up the path to that 'special place'. When she got there she looked down and saw some white stones. She counted twelve in total – David's lucky number she recalled.

The twelve stones were in the shape of a crucifix.

Chapter 2

Hazel wanted to sort through some of David's possessions. To keep the important things, and to let the less important go.

He'd painted over twenty watercolours that were neatly placed together in a large folder. His curled paintbrushes and dried paints were a reminder of his new found hobby. Hazel knew he had talent in that field but some of the paintings were incredible. She would treasure those and even get a few more framed to hang on the nunnery walls alongside the others.

Hazel had bought David a prayer book while they still lived in Godalming. It easily fitted into one hand and the small dog-eared pages indicated that he had read it several times. Hazel could not recall seeing him with it so he must have read it privately. She flicked through the pages. As she did so a piece of paper fell out. She bent to pick it up, and slowly opened it. It read:

'To my darling Nutty,
I wrote this for you – for us – a few weeks ago.

"The last time I took this ride.
We made great plans, we felt alive,
Heading south from countryside into a city of open dreams.
How our young hearts laughed and cried,
How we stood strong side by side,
Never thought we'd say goodbye to anything but youth.
I remember everything,

Fighting darkness, chasing rain.
It feels so long ago,
Whispered songs on radio,
Take me back to what I know,
It all seemed so beautiful to me.
The journey's end is here.

Faces line these old town roads.
Soft guitars, piano notes,
Linger in the air like ghosts – with nothing left to say.
Shadowed seasons brought you home,
Brighter days have come and gone,
Someone, somewhere called you on, we could not follow you.

I think I spoke the fateful lie,
That things don't leave – or break – or die.
We'll raise your body to the sky before we lay it down.
Now it seems the only path
Is the one we travel fast.
Destinations cut like glass – into our history.
The journey's end is here.

I see an unclosed door where duty used to stand.
I'm going south once more to make good on those plans.

Every station fades from view
Like the years bestowed on you
But years can be like diamonds, too, they sparkle and they shine.
So when at last we meet again
I'll shake your hand and call you friend,
Sometimes one journey has to end to let another start."

Yours always and forever,
David xxx'

She sat down. Her heart was full to overflowing. The world stopped turning. Everything just stopped…

Chapter 3

Hazel's life consisted of only two things now. Her work at the nunnery, and Pedro. Her son came to stay at the nunnery often. He enjoyed being there – his early years were spent there, of course. Mother Caterina and the other nuns loved Pedro. He tried hard to be brave but his dad had gone from his life. He was his little 'cowboy' and Pedro knew nobody could take David's place. He had never known his true father. His mother, Marie Amaras, never revealed who was Pedro's father. Did it matter? Hazel often wondered if Pedro would try to discover the identity of his biological father. Did it matter? Maybe when he grew up he would make enquiries?

Pedro kept in touch with Jessie. She was planning to read Spanish studies at Durham University when she grew up. She was growing up. She had made her mind up, that's what she wanted to do. Pedro didn't know what the future held for him – Hazel had often asked him. However, she knew in her heart that he was going to be all right. Pedro sent Jessie emails with attached digital images – the nunnery, the Andes, the orphans. She loved to receive his news, and vice versa. Hazel kept in touch with Maureen and the ladies from the church in Godalming. However, the life she led in Godalming became distant. Her life in Surrey started to fade. The intensity of her existence was now in San Felipe. She felt a vibrance – a new beginning, somehow.

On some evenings Hazel would sit looking up at David's cairn whilst playing classical music on her radio. She started to notice that a black condor would sometimes perch on the top stone of the cairn. A black condor? Where did this come from? Hazel knew that condors were birds that glided across mountains – especially the Andes. She went onto the internet and checked out 'condors'. There were South American condors with a wing span up to three metres, and a smaller species in California that had become all but extinct. Some said that these giant birds brought good luck. Other believed that they were sentinels, watching over those that needed a guardian. Needed a guardian? Did David need someone to look over him? Hazel felt that he might . . .where had his spirit gone to? Well, it was here. It was all around. Pedro felt it when he came to stay. His dad was big enough to manage on his own. Pedro wanted to plant another tree for his dad right outside the verandah. This he did. He placed a photo of his dad in a polythene wallet in the bottom of the hole before placing the tree on top. Over the years it grew, and the roots slowly pushed their way through David's photo. The tree roots, and David's image, became entwined.

His spirit grew up into the branches and leaves and beyond… they reached almost to the sky.

Chapter 4

Over the coming years Pedro progressed at college and got a scholarship to the University of Chile in the Region Metropolitana in Santiago. The university motto is 'Work is our Joy'. He studied Humanities, or 'Humanidades', as they referred to it locally. He got first class grades in geography and history at college. There were eighteen thousand undergraduates at the university and after three years of study Pedro gained a B.A. degree in Humanities. The graduation ceremony was a grand affair with almost five thousand graduates receiving their degrees in the great hall of the university.

He started work with an international humanitarian organisation with an office in Santiago and whose headquarters were in London. After only a few months his first overseas trip took him to England. He took an opportunity to see Jessie. He had emailed her giving her the details of his arrival and hotel. It was mid term so she was able to take two days off and took the train to London. Jessie arrived at the hotel in Kensington after a hectic trip on the London Underground from Kings Cross.

"I've missed you so much!" she whispered in his ear as she hugged him. "I've missed you more", replied Pedro, his face beaming at her. They had dinner at the Blue Vienna restaurant just off Oxford Street and spent one night together at the Holiday Inn in Kensington. After dinner Jessie returned to the hotel with Pedro. It was so busy in the foyer that no one noticed them take the lift to the fourth floor. Once in the bedroom they began kissing again and ended up between the sheets in a few minutes. Jessie's clothes seemed to come off easily, and Pedro got out of his in double quick time.

"That was so good!" said Jessie, gasping for breath after sitting on Pedro for a few minutes as though riding a horse. She fell over onto her side, continuing to get her breath. He smiled his smile again as he twirled her hair with his left hand. She purred like a kitten. Both were tempted to say 'I love you' but independently opted to leave it – for now. They did love each other. In fact they had loved each other since they first set eyes on each other in Durham.

Jessie graduated from Durham University with a first class honours degree in Spanish. She was bi-lingual and had a brilliant understanding of Spanish and South American issues. Her third year project was on the history of South America. She and Pedro had kept in touch but it was on and off. She had met one or two other men, but nothing serious became of it. Either they didn't have a sense of humour, or were selfish, or had some other characteristics that Jessie didn't like. Her father had left the university and had set up on his own as a freelance biologist and photographer under the name of "Lenses R'Us". Jessie thought it was corny but it attracted attention, after all, both cameras and the eyes of most animals had a lens. The business did well.

Pedro had to return to Chile and said good-bye to Jessie. She went to see him off at Heathrow airport and wondered if their kiss would be her last? She hoped not. Jessie was now a lecturer in Spanish at the University of Newcastle upon Tyne, and considered the best and most promising lecturer in the department of Foreign Languages. As she said good-bye she pressed the little wooden cross from a Surrey oak tree into Pedro's hand. She wanted him to keep it for her. "Keep in touch, Ped," she whispered, "and look after my cross". Hazel saw

Pedro disappear through the departure gates and blew him a kiss. He waved wildly, his jet black hair bobbing up and down as he strode away. They met in London on a few more occasions when Pedro had business with his company. Jessie made the time to get down to the capital. Three years later Pedro gained a Masters degree from the university that he had worked on part time. He became Head of International Business Affairs with a major global group that was involved with human rights. He was to become very successful.

He and Jessie kept in touch and Jessie spent several weeks during the next few years with Pedro in Santiago during the university vacations. They filled the time with fun – meals out, long walks, the theatre, drives into the country. They enjoyed their own company. He even took her to the nunnery that she had heard so much about. Mother Caterina was still there! She looked as radiant as ever although a few lines had developed around her eyes. They didn't stay long but it was obvious that the nuns who were there when Pedro was living at the orphanage were pleased to see him. The experience was wonderful. "One of the greatest experiences of my life", Jessie remarked as they left. Not long afterwards, Pedro emailed Jessie to tell her that he had seen an opening for a lecturer at the local university. The brief for the position seemed ideal. She applied for the job and got it!

Hazel was now virtually running the administration side of the nunnery, so allowing the nuns to focus on morning and evening prayers and caring for the orphans. David's paintings were hanging from many of the walls. There was a reminder of him everywhere she looked, the paintings, the trees...his spirit... Most evenings a black condor sat on David's cairn. On one other occasion Hazel again thought she had seen a man in a white suit standing a few metres away from the rock slab.

Was he real? Hadn't she once dreamt of someone like that? Was it all a dream again? She pinched herself. She was awake. Maybe she would ask Mother Caterina if she knew of anybody answering to the description?

Chapter 5

One morning at the *Refugio de Cristo* Brother Augustus began sorting out the few belongings of Father Rodriguez. In a box there were some items that he had collected from visits to other monasteries and refuges, letters and some certificates. Brother Augustus noticed a package addressed to Mother Caterina. Why had he left something for her? It was not for him to question this. Father Rodriguez had been faultless in his service to the refuge and to the Lord. He knew that Father Rodriguez and Mother Caterina were close – professionally as well as in the work of God. Brother Augustus took the package and arranged for the delivery of this to San Felipe. The following day it arrived and lay in an office for another two days. When Mother Caterina saw it she opened it immediately. Inside was an envelope that contained something, and a note. The short note asked for the contents to be passed to Hazel. Why would he have sent something for Hazel? What could it contain?

The next day Mother Caterina asked to see Hazel. She told Hazel about the package that had been left by Father Rodriguez after his death and that Brother Augustus had arranged to send it to her . She handed it to Hazel who decided that she would take it home and look at it later. During the day the thought of what was contained in the envelope gnawed at Hazel's patience. What on earth could it be? Should she open it now? No, she would leave it until she got back to the finca. She would put her feet up, open a bottle of wine, put some classical music on and slit the envelope.

Her walk up to the 'special place' would take priority, and she would ask for strength from David and from the Lord. As she walked up to the cairn Hazel began to sense that the package left for her may contain something significant. She gazed up to the skies and saw three condors soaring high on the warm thermals. The sun was beginning to drop behind Hazel as she climbed the path up the mountain side. She could see her shadow in front of her. Suddenly she saw two shadows, one right next to her. But did she? It was fleeting – it happened in less than the blink of an eye. Surely not? She was the only one casting a shadow. She was close to the cairn and she stopped, looking at the rock slab.

"Hello, David. I hope you are all right. I know you're with me. You're by my side right now. I miss you so much, but then you know that, don't you?" She closed her eyes and held her hands together. She prayed. She asked the Lord for strength.

She did not know how much strength she would need. Hazel had no way of knowing that the contents of the envelope would have a shattering effect on her.

Yes, a really shattering effect…

Chapter 6

Hazel slowly opened the thick envelope. Onto the floor fell a silver crucifix on a silver chain. The crucifix was about the size of a matchbox. It was heavy, and encrusted with small green stones – probably emeralds. Hazel picked it up and placed it on the table.

She unfolded the sheet of paper, put on her spectacles, and started to read.

"My dear Hazel, my Child.

By the time you read this I hope I will be in heaven, or at least on the way after I spend some time in purgatory.

There is something that has weighed very heavily on my mind for some years now. I need to share this with you.

Many years ago I was friendly with a gentleman called Antonio Amaras. He had one child, a daughter called Marie. She had been well schooled but was getting into trouble with drugs, and meeting the wrong people. Antonio asked me if she could meet with me at the refuge so that I might be able to talk with her and give her some counselling.

She came and we met in my office. Why, I do not know, and I shall never forgive myself, but we made love. I shall not try to make excuses, but it was the one and only moment of weakness in my life. The result was that she gave birth to a boy that she named Cesar. To be certain, I was able to confirm his identity with a DNA sample.

I know that she was unable to keep him and had to give him away. She chose the nunnery. Marie promised me that she would never say anything about this, and I believed her. As far as I know, this is still the case.

I felt you should know this. Please forgive me. I pray that the Lord will forgive me. I am sorry. I am so very sorry.

Yours with the blessing of the Lord Jesus Christ, the Father, Son and the Holy Spirit.

Father Hernando Rodriguez.

P.S. I want you to have my crucifix. It has been with me for over forty years. It is my most treasured possession"

Hazel held the silver crucifix tightly in her right hand and wept. She cried for a long time as if the wounds might heal. They would never heal. She had been left alone to cope as best she could. But she now knew she was capable of greater things …so much more.

Epilogue

Jessie had moved to Chile and got a position as a Lecturer, then Senior Lecturer, in Spanish at the university. She and Pedro got married in a large Santiago church and Jessie gave birth to two sons and one daughter. They were named David, Pedro and Caterina.

Pedro, David's 'little cowboy', became 'Head of Global Humanitarian Affairs' with the newly formed 'World Health Authority'. Their children grew to become fine, upstanding members of the Santiago community. David would have been proud of them. Pedro stayed in contact with Clarence Bosanquet and they remained life-long friends. Clarence followed his father and gained a law degree at Cambridge.

Hazel remained at the nunnery for a long time and set up a charitable trust called *'The Condor Foundation'* that helped orphans and other children that needed help and emotional support. It continued to thrive for many, many years. She became a wonderful grandmother to her three grandchildren, and they loved her immensely. She told them stories of their grandad, what he'd done for so many people, and what a good man he was.

Hazel's time to be with David eventually arrived. She died in her sleep. She had left her last wishes and her will in the strong box of the nunnery. They all missed her when she left them, and were sad that they didn't get to know their grandad David.

When she passed away her ashes, and the silver crucifix, were placed in a small bronze casket and put next to those of

David in the base of the cairn up on the hillside. Hazel took her 'secret' with her. She had destroyed the letter sent by Brother Augustus. Only Father Rodriguez, Hazel and her heavenly Father would ever know the contents of that note.

From the cairn, David and Hazel would always be able to see the snows of the Andes, and look down on the church and the nunnery below. This was where they had sat and held hands on many evenings. They would be here for infinity. No, it would be longer than that. Even today the locals still talk of them with fond memories. They had both made such a significant contribution to the life of the nunnery and to the local community. Hazel had left all of her assets to the nunnery in her will. It was over £2.5 million.

Sometimes, just sometimes, a man in a white suit with a white beard can be seen up near the cairn...the Sisters from the nunnery said they were certain that they had seen someone.

This was an unknown paradise. But then they knew that. They'd known it for a long time. It was their destiny...and they had faith. Oh, yes, they had faith.

Somehow, or so it seemed, all that had happened had been written in the stars, and the waters of the rivers had their stories to tell...

Until the day he died, Pedro treasured the little wooden cross from an oak tree in Surrey that once blew down in the gales.

He never questioned who his biological father was. But when it came to having a father, he knew, didn't he?

He was called David Tate... his only real dad. And Pedro was his little cowboy.

The End

------------------------oOo----------------------